Pra...
THE GOOD...

'An emotionally charged and ...
some unexpected paths. Jolting surprises and a strong ...
characters will keep you reading well into the night.'
　—*Canberra Weekly*

'A fast-paced, heart-stopping thriller full of gripping tension,
twists and turns from bestselling author Petronella McGovern.'
　—*Who Magazine*

'Intriguing . . . a lively, well-plotted tale about generosity and
betrayal.'
　—*Sydney Morning Herald*

'I loved this book . . . absolutely engaging from start to finish,
and kept me reading into the wee small hours.'
　—*Living Arts Canberra*

'Taut, tight and terrific, an addictive read.'
　—*Blue Wolf Reviews*

'McGovern has created a compelling and well-plotted second
novel . . . deserves a place at the top of your must-read list.'
　—*Pittwater Life*

'McGovern's books take us to people and places we know, the
characters ringing so true. And the books are addictive, leaving
you guessing to the very end and wanting more.'
　—*Canberra Times*

Praise for

SIX MINUTES

'Super tense from beginning to end, this is a great read that will spark plenty of book club debate.'

—*New Idea*

'Well crafted and twisty, an accomplished debut novel.'

—*Canberra Weekly*

'Ostensibly a mystery story, with a complex plot and cliffhangers aplenty, *Six Minutes* is also a beautifully drawn look at parenting and relationships. McGovern invites the reader to recognise some of the unnecessary pressures we put on ourselves as parents, as well as the terrible guilt we sometimes carry over things that are outside our control.'

—*Charming Language*

'The perfect read . . . keeps you guessing until the very end.'

—*Manly Daily*

'*Six Minutes* is a book woven from unease, threaded through with an air of creepiness that starts even before the drama of Bella's strange disappearance. As with *Broadchurch*, a TV series also set in an isolated community and involving a missing child, the central drama is really a frame from which to examine the effects of such an event on the local community, and how tragedy can draw out the best and worst in us all.'

—*Newtown Review of Books*

Petronella McGovern's books have been described as domestic noir and psychological suspense. With strong characters and gripping storylines, her novels will keep you reading—and guessing—late into the night. Petronella grew up on in a large family on a farm in the Central West of New South Wales. After travelling and working in Canberra for a number of years, she now lives on Sydney's northern beaches with her husband and their two teenagers. Petronella's bestselling debut novel, *Six Minutes*, was shortlisted for the Australian Crime Writers' Association's Ned Kelly Awards and longlisted for the Australian Independent Bookseller's Indie Book Awards. Her second novel, *The Good Teacher*, was longlisted for the Davitt Awards. *The Liars* is her third novel, coming out in September 2022.

https://www.petronellamcgovern.com.au/

THE
GOOD
TEACHER

PETRONELLA
McGOVERN

ALLEN&UNWIN
SYDNEY•MELBOURNE•AUCKLAND•LONDON

This edition published in 2022
First published in 2020

Allen & Unwin
83 Alexander Street
Crows Nest NSW 2065
Australia
Phone: (61 2) 8425 0100
Email: info@allenandunwin.com
Web: www.allenandunwin.com

A catalogue record for this book is available from the National Library of Australia

ISBN 978 1 76106 636 8

Set in Adobe Jenson Pro by Bookhouse, Sydney
Printed in Australia by McPherson's Printing Group

10 9 8 7 6 5 4 3 2 1

*The grateful heart will always find
opportunities to show its gratitude.*
Aesop, 'The Dove and the Ant'

—

*With much love and gratitude to my family,
Jamie, Jeremy & Tiu*

PART ONE

No-one is too weak to do good.
Aesop, 'The Lion and the Mouse'

1

ALLISON

Term 1, February

ALLISON GREETED EVERY CHILD BY NAME AS THEY CAME INTO THE classroom. Day three of the school year and the terrified faces were beginning to relax slightly.

'Do you want to do a puzzle or play with the blocks?' Allison asked each one.

While the children settled into their chosen activity, a transition from their parents to the school day, Allison smoothed out the name tag on the empty desk. GRACIE. A late enrolment. During the staff meeting on Monday, Allison had been hoping the girl would be placed in the other kindergarten class.

'I've put Gracie with you, Allison, because you're the most experienced,' the principal had said. 'She's going through a tough time.'

So am I.

Allison had clenched her teeth to stop the words coming out. For God's sake, how could she compare herself with this poor little girl?

'I'll do my best.'

The principal didn't know yet; he'd find out soon enough, along with the rest of the staff. And the parents.

'We need to ensure the school is accepting and welcoming,' Declan said.

'Yes, of course.' Allison tried to smile. 'After all, that's what we're known for.'

At the end of last year, Wirriga Public School had won an award for its Christmas project, 12 Days of Giving. Twelve activities to support communities in need, including a food drive for farmers in drought and a clothing collection for bush-fire victims. The children and their parents had felt they were making a small difference as the TV news streamed never-ending images of Australia's scorched landscape.

Back then, Allison hadn't known that her own life would be in ashes by New Year's Day.

'Ah, here they are,' Allison announced to the class. 'This is Gracie and her dad. Welcome to the Wirriga Wombats! A desk over here has your name on it, Gracie.'

Allison wondered how the children would react to Gracie's purple bandana. Earlier, she'd given them a brief explanation, and encouraged kindness and respect. Would they ask to see Gracie's bare scalp? The girl's face and arms were pale, unlike the other sun-kissed bodies which had spent the long summer holidays playing on the beach.

'Everyone, let's give Gracie a big welcome.'

'Hello, Gracie.' A singsong greeting from the whole class.

'Gracie has come all the way from Victoria. The biggest city is Melbourne. Has anyone been there? Ask the person next to you while I have a quick chat to Gracie's dad.'

The father was standing near Gracie's desk, a purple backpack dangling from his wrist.

'We hang the bags on these hooks just outside the door.' She led him to the corridor.

'I'm really sorry Gracie couldn't come on the first day,' he said. 'This whole move and the new hospital . . . it's been crazy.'

Luke Branson had already apologised yesterday when she'd met him at lunchtime. He'd handed over a letter from the children's hospital about Gracie's compromised immune system. Explained that they'd moved to Sydney for a doctor who was researching this rare cancer—and to get away from the memories. His voice had cracked when he'd said that.

'We'll take good care of Gracie,' she promised.

'Thank you, Mrs Walsh.'

The voice was deeper than she expected from someone in his late twenties; his hair closely cropped—shaved in solidarity with his daughter, Allison guessed. It made his eyes seem even bigger. Sad eyes full of pain.

The little girl appeared beside them in the corridor, wrapping herself around her father's legs.

'Don't go, Daddy.'

Allison noted that Gracie's socks were black instead of white. And her dress a size too big. She'd take her to the uniform shop at recess and sort her out.

'Gracie, do you want to do a puzzle with Daddy?'

As Allison led them to the puzzles corner, she breathed in deeply. *Come on, you can do this.* Over two decades at different schools, she'd never taught a child undergoing treatment for cancer. Why-oh-why did it have to be this year?

Forcing a smile, she turned to the girl and her father.

'Look at this golden lion, Gracie. Do you think you can put the pieces back together?'

'Yes! I can do it!'

Gracie sat cross-legged with the puzzle pieces out in front of her. Her father smiled his thanks and squatted down in one smooth motion. A gym type in his black Adidas shorts and t-shirt. Allison predicted it would take half an hour before he was able to leave. She brought Gracie's table buddy, Evelyn, over to join them—that should ease the separation.

'I have a book with a lion in it too.' Allison showed *Aesop's Fables* to the whole class. 'We'll sit on the mat and read it together.'

While Allison told the story of the brave lion and the timid mouse, she watched Gracie finish the puzzle and edge towards the mat. The girl was still holding on to her father's hand. He took her hand, kissed it and placed it in her lap. Then he adjusted the purple bandana and whispered in her ear. For the next few minutes, he stood by the door. When Gracie swivelled around to check on him, the father waved then stepped out into the corridor.

Would she rush after him?

'So the moral of this story is that even a teeny-weeny mouse can help save a great big lion.' Allison raised her voice to catch Gracie's attention. 'Aesop says that no-one is too little to do good. Every act of kindness, even a small one, can really matter. Now, who can make a squeaky noise like a little mouse?'

'Squeak, squeak, squeak.' The class giggled between their squeaking.

'And what about a big ROAR?'

The boys and girls opened their mouths wide to roar as loud as they could. When they'd finished, one noise continued—the sound of sobbing.

Allison put the book aside and squatted next to Gracie. She patted the girl's back and explained how everyone in the class had started new this week. Allison doubted that Gracie could hear over the crying.

'Evelyn, can you please pass Winnie the Wombat for Gracie to cuddle?'

As Allison tucked the class mascot into Gracie's lap, a head appeared around the classroom door.

'Am I being as quiet as a teeny-weeny mouse?' asked Gracie's dad.

The children burst out laughing. Gracie's laugh was the loudest.

Despite the brave smile, Allison could see the man's heart was breaking. It wasn't often that the father was the one trying to leave a child at kindy. He sat back down on the floor next to Gracie, put his arm around her, and stroked Winnie the Wombat. If Luke Branson had to stay until recess, so be it. This little girl needed extra-special care.

For the next two hours, Allison didn't think about her own problems once.

＿

At recess, Allison fitted Gracie with the right-sized uniform and popped three pairs of white socks into her bag. Her father had left just after ten o'clock and the girl seemed settled. At lunch, when the other kids ran into the playground, Allison led

7

Gracie and Evelyn into the library. With her sun sensitivity from chemotherapy, Gracie had to avoid playing outside at midday.

'Girls, this is Ms McCormack, our wonderful librarian.'

'Okay, my lovely lassies,' Shona purred in her Scottish burr, 'I've put out some colouring-in sheets for you at those corner tables, and then I'll read you a story.'

As the girls chose their pencils, Allison shared a chocolate slice with Shona. The teachers covered their mouths with their hands to hide the fact that they were eating in the library.

'Your hair looks great, Allison. You've figured out how to style it, then.'

Two weeks ago, Allison had marched into the hairdresser and asked for a makeover. She still didn't recognise the woman in the mirror with the short, choppy bob.

'Thanks. None of my clothes go with the caramel colour, though.'

'Obviously you need a whole new wardrobe!' Shona laughed.

If Allison could afford it, she would. This morning, she'd wanted to wear her favourite red top with the black spots—*my watermelon shirt*, she always joked with the class—but today it hadn't worked. Between the new hair, the comfort eating and the perimenopause, none of her clothes sat right.

She shouldn't have got the stupid haircut. It was like a neon sign flashing over her head. The only person she'd told was Shona, but this morning a year five teacher had given Allison a sideways glance. A year three teacher had frowned and said meaningfully: 'How *are* you?' And at drop-off, a group of parents Allison knew from last year had all stopped speaking the instant she'd approached.

Allison mentioned the reactions to Shona.

'Stop being paranoid. And if they know, well . . .' The younger woman shrugged. 'It doesn't matter.'

Shona had only been in Wirriga for eighteen months and the students loved her over-the-top enthusiasm and quirky expressions. She'd followed her girlfriend back to Australia and didn't seem to care what other people thought. But Shona hadn't grown up in this suburb with family and friends literally around the corner.

Wirriga still had that same village feeling as when Allison had ridden her bike to this very primary school forty years ago. When the suburb had been developed back in the 1960s, it was seen as an undesirable swamp full of mosquitoes, sandwiched between glamourous white beaches and a bushy plateau. Land had been cheap and the houses built big—two storeys, often with a pool. To Allison, Wirriga was the best-kept secret of Sydney's northern beaches. An enclave of friendly locals. Cul-de-sacs where kids could play in the street. No thoroughfares to other suburbs. No tourists—they all stayed in Manly, on the opposite side of the multi-lane freeway. A short commute to the centre of Sydney but a world away from the city's congestion. Fresh air, open space, natural bush around Manly Dam. Five minutes to the beach.

The only downside was that everyone knew everyone, and that meant gossip was rife: between the volunteers in the school canteen, on the sidelines of the kids' sports games, during the mothers' morning teas, and at the picnics in the park.

Allison had considered taking leave without pay this term, but she needed the money. Perhaps she should've asked for a transfer to another part of Sydney, but she didn't have the energy to learn new systems and build new friendships. Lack of sleep was making her brain fuzzy.

'I feel like such a middle-aged cliché,' Allison moaned to Shona. 'I'm a laughing stock.'

'No, he's the cliché,' Shona said. 'It's not your fault, hen.'

Soon, they'll all know that I'm not enough. Not interesting enough, not smart enough, not funny enough, not clever enough, not pretty enough. Not enough to keep a husband of twenty-four years.

And, evidently, not enough for her fifteen-year-old son either.

—

Shona was reading the girls a book about a female astronaut when Allison's phone buzzed. A text from Tony. *Summer soccer back on tomorrow. Will you be there? Dinner after at the Italian?*

Usually, Allison was the one telling him about their son's arrangements. She considered how to answer the message. A sarcastic response about his sudden involvement? A bitchy question about the new woman whom he wouldn't name? No, she'd wait until after school to reply.

And then another text, this time from Felix. *Can u bring my kit & boots?*

Allison sent a quick thumbs-up; safer to let the emojis say it all.

'You can be whatever you want to be.' Shona finished the last page and closed the book. 'You can fly to the moon like this amazing astronaut.'

Allison gave a tight smile. *Forget the sky-high ambitions— all Gracie wants to be is healthy. All I want is my husband and son back.*

'My mum was an astronaut,' Gracie said.

'Oh wow!' Evelyn's eyes widened. 'Have you seen a rocket?'

Should Allison pull Gracie up on the fib or just take the girls back to the classroom? When she'd asked Luke about Gracie's mother, he'd closed his eyes and put his head in his hands for a moment.

'The counsellor said to reinforce how much her mother loved her. To keep reassuring her.' He'd sighed. 'And we don't discuss the tumour in front of her. That's been our rule since Gracie was diagnosed. She knows she's sick but we don't want her to worry about the future.'

We. Our. As if his wife were still alive. Thankfully, Luke hadn't had to explain about the horrifying death. Samantha in the front office had passed on the news—a bushfire had destroyed the Bransons' farm and their lives.

'Kids can be very blunt,' Allison had said. 'Some will ask Gracie about her mum and cancer and dying.'

'Yeah, I know.' He'd sighed again. 'At least her eyelashes and eyebrows have grown back. Last year a boy at the playground called her an alien. The next round of chemo is weekly. She shouldn't be so sick this time.'

Life was cruelly unfair. Four-year-old Gracie should not be going through all this misery. And nor should forty-nine-year-old Allison.

While Shona had been reading aloud, Allison opened the note from the hospital again. It sparked a list in her head. *Don't compromise Gracie's immunity. Don't let her get breathless. Don't let her get injured. Don't let her get upset about her mother.* Allison yawned, wishing she had time for a coffee before the afternoon class. She'd have to be on high alert all day, every day, for the new girl.

—

Each time Allison walked through the front door, she expected to see her son's black sneakers kicked off in the hallway, his schoolbag dumped on the couch, a dirty cereal bowl on the kitchen benchtop. Instead, it was as tidy as when she'd last vacuumed.

And silent.

Without the ordinary background noise she used to take for granted. Felix strumming a new song on his guitar. The shouts of teenagers in the pool, splashing and somersaulting. In the evenings, Tony cheering at a soccer match on television.

Pouring herself a large gin and tonic, Allison tipped out the last few drops from the duty-free bottle Tony had bought on his way back from the funeral in England.

Should she drive down and check on him now?

He'd refused to give her his new address. *It's a legal matter,* he'd explained haughtily. *Nothing to do with you and me.* Refused to tell her anything. And so, the second time she'd dropped Felix off near Tony's new place, Allison had driven around the corner and parked. Sneaked back to see where Felix went. Now she watched the house whenever she could, desperate to catch a glimpse of the woman with no name.

The whirlwind of his departure had left her gasping for breath. And he was so fucking civilised while she ranted and raved, and bawled and blubbered. This was supposed to be *her* year—celebrating her fiftieth birthday in August with a trip to the Great Barrier Reef. Instead she was sobbing on her best friend's shoulder.

Eating dinner alone.

She'd never lived alone before.

Standing in the kitchen, Allison looked past the back deck to the pool. Still warm enough for a swim but the water was murky green. Tony had been the one to check the levels and add chemicals. As she closed the kitchen blinds to banish the accusing colour, a dark shape moved at the end of the garden. Too big to be a brush turkey jumping the fence. Allison locked the door and called Nadia.

'Stop worrying.' Her best friend's voice was a balm down the line. 'Probably just teenagers hanging out in the bush.'

The reassurance stayed with Allison until the pinky hues descended and the shadows lengthened. Even with neighbours on either side, she was conscious of the bushland behind the house. At dusk, the forest came alive, filling each room with its cacophony: kookaburras cackling, bats shrieking, frogs croaking in a deep bass line. Before, she'd loved the bush backdrop. Now, she dreaded switching off the downstairs lights every evening.

In their queen-sized bed, Allison avoided that cold empty space where Tony had slept.

Her mother had suggested audiobooks to help her fall asleep. Nadia offered sleeping pills. Shona said: 'Drink more gin.'

Instead, Allison lay awake until one in the morning, trying to ignore the numbers glowing red on the clock radio, her thoughts on a constant loop: *How did it come to this?*

At three-sixteen, she jolted awake to the sound of banging. The southerly had blown in and the house creaked with each gust. Could it be a branch whacking against the roof? None of the trees were that close.

When she'd spoken to Nadia earlier, neither of them had mentioned the break-ins around Wirriga. One at the school over the summer holidays. One at the beauty salon. And the most recent—on Allison's street, half a block away.

Where was Tony when she needed him? Or even Felix. Goddamn it, Allison called herself a feminist, and now she was wishing for the safety that came with a man. Scared of the dark in her own house. She'd fallen into another cliché.

Reach out and switch on the light, she told herself as the thudding continued.

Now that she was properly awake, Allison realised the noise was coming from above. A possum on the roof or inside the ceiling? Whatever it was, she wouldn't be sleeping for the rest of the night.

She hadn't told Nadia her real fear.

I think someone is spying on me.

Stop being paranoid, her friend would say.

But Allison was projecting her own guilty conscience—her obsession with watching Tony's new house.

Who else was living in that house? Did the new woman know—or care—that she had destroyed Allison's happy family?

2

AFTER THE SOCCER MATCH, ALLISON CONGRATULATED FELIX ON HIS goal that had won the game. Her son pushed his sweaty fringe off his forehead, smiled briefly, then tapped Tony on the shoulder.

'Dad, did you see that tackle I did on their number four?'

'Perfect, mate. And that fancy footwork got you around the number seven. You'll be a shoo-in for the top team in winter.'

Her husband flung an arm around Felix's shoulder. They were almost the same height. Had that happened in the last two weeks? Angry red pimples dotted Felix's chin. Was he using the medicated face wash she'd bought? His hair needed a cut, and she'd heard him swearing on the field. What had happened to her little boy? The one who used to sing to her while they baked cupcakes; the one who came to her first for comfort and approval.

Her aim tonight—apart from seeing Felix—was to discuss him coming home during the week. Her son had spent most of the summer holiday at Tony's place, surfing every morning and evening. He could walk to the beach from there, he'd explained.

As they entered the Italian restaurant, Allison began.

'Now that Felix is going into year ten, he needs to concentrate on his studies. He should be living at home.'

Her heart actually hurt when she said the word *home*.

'But at Dad's I can still get a surf in before school,' Felix countered. 'The waves are great.'

Tony didn't answer. Instead, he called for the waiter and ordered panzanella, rather than his usual veal parmigiana.

'It's a tomato and bread salad,' he explained, even though she hadn't asked. 'I've been eating healthier. Gotta keep the body fit.'

Allison wanted to stick her fingers in her mouth and make a gagging sound, like she had as a teenager. Was Tony keeping himself fit for the new woman? These days, Allison's emotions came fast and intense, as if she *were* a teenager again. They seemed to be on the surface of her skin, fully exposed, ready to flare in an instant. Without looking at the menu, Allison ordered veal parmigiana with extra roast potatoes. And garlic bread.

'Felix needs to come home,' she repeated. 'I don't even know the name of the woman he's living with.'

'Don't start that again, Allison. I've told you—it's for legal reasons.'

'For God's sake, I deserve a better explanation than that after twenty-four years of marriage, Tony. I can't deal with this secrecy.'

'Mum, please don't,' Felix interrupted. 'Dad's just trying to keep everyone safe.'

Tony, the bloody white knight. *Trying to keep everyone safe.* Somehow, he'd brainwashed his son as well, and Allison had become the villain by asking the questions.

'How can I know that our son is safe,' Allison snapped, 'if I don't know who he's with?'

'I can assure you that she's of good character.'

Tony and his pompous, lawyerly words. He had an answer for everything. That was what made him a good solicitor.

'Just tell me her name!' Allison had already asked so many times; she couldn't stop asking.

A pause, and then Tony finally answered, 'Call her Helena.'

Obviously a false name—one that meant Allison wouldn't be able to find the woman on social media. She thought about it for a moment.

'Helena . . . Like Helen of Troy, the most beautiful woman in the world, who men fought wars over?'

At least Tony had the decency not to respond.

Helena. A clue? Ellen was the name of his young secretary; Helen one of the soccer mums; and Heather a recently divorced friend. It had to be someone Allison knew, otherwise there'd be no need for this crazy secrecy.

While they waited for their meals to arrive, Tony switched the conversation to the English Premier League and Felix gave his opinion of which teams would win on the weekend. Allison let them talk, aware that their son should not be caught up in their arguments. In her head, she tried to recall every acquaintance whose name started with the letter H. Once she'd done that, she worked out which names rhymed with Helena: Serena, Melina, Trina, Sheena.

Tony thanked the waiter as his tomato and bread salad was placed on the table.

'Can't wait to try something different!'

And then they were all silent as they tucked into their meals—the only sounds Felix chomping on ice from his lemonade and Tony scraping his plate. Allison had to grip her knife and fork tight, fingernails biting into her palms, to prevent the fury from erupting. How dare Tony do this to their once-happy family?

Perhaps she should suggest Felix see the school counsellor. Although, unlike her, Felix seemed to be taking it all in his stride. Was it bravado? She'd phoned his best mate, Darcy, to ask how he thought Felix was doing. 'He's all good,' came the short reply.

Allison finished off her veal, noting that Tony had stolen a piece of roast potato from her plate and had taken a big hunk of garlic bread. This man she loved had two faces—the old familiar Tony and an unrecognisable stranger. She took another gulp of wine and steeled herself to raise the subject of Felix's living arrangements again. But before she could speak, Tony put a hand on her wrist.

'I was hoping we could talk about selling the house,' he said.

Snatching her arm away, she tried to remember how to breathe.

'The market's good at the moment,' he continued. 'And it's such a big place, we'll get a great price. You could buy an apartment with ocean views, like you always wanted.'

The last time Allison had mentioned an apartment with ocean views was seventeen years ago. Before Felix. When she was worrying that she'd never fall pregnant and that they should choose a different type of life.

'I . . .'

I thought this was a temporary madness.

I thought we could get through this.

I thought you were coming home.

Allison coughed. Swigged the rest of her wine down her throat to clear it. Focused on her son's face. Of course Tony had raised the subject in a public place so she wouldn't be able to scream.

'You won't have to bother about the upkeep of the pool then,' Tony said, as if by talking and talking he could make it happen. 'Have you spoken to the blond guy at the pool shop? He's really helpful.'

She kept her eyes on Felix, waiting for his reaction. Surely he'd be as upset as her; it was the only house he'd ever lived in. Until now.

Her son was staring at his lap, presumably on his phone, texting, snapping, whatsapping, whatever he did on there.

The fury from earlier doubled and threatened to overwhelm her. Swallowing hard, Allison bent down to reach under the chair for her handbag, turning her face away from her husband. She considered the bill. Were they supposed to split it now? Like a reverse first date; the first date towards divorce. She could feel Tony watching her.

Ignoring him and the bill, she dropped a kiss on her son's head. 'Well done on the goal, Felix.' She tried to make her voice normal. 'Sorry I've got to go. I have a student who's sick. I need to do some work for her tonight.'

Allison stormed out of the restaurant and drove slowly, slowly, flipping through the radio channels. When Whitney Houston's 'I Will Always Love You' trilled through the speakers, she stabbed at the button to silence it. Yet another reminder of a date with Tony in their early years. The song made her slam her hands against the steering wheel. She parked in the garage and sat there, considering the empty, silent family home.

If only her fury could keep the fear at bay each night.

3

'WE'RE GOING FOR DRINKS AT MANLY WHARF,' SHONA SAID AFTER
school on Friday. 'To celebrate surviving the first week back
and to welcome Elena. Are you coming?'

'Who's Elena?'

'The new ESL teacher. Haven't you met her?'

Allison recalled a face she didn't recognise in the staffroom
yesterday. *Elena.* A young woman wearing black glasses and
an intense expression, with thick dark hair tumbling over her
shoulders. The department had given them a new acronym
now—what was it? EAL/D: English as an additional language
or dialect.

'Where is she?'

'I think they're all in the front office, discussing who's driving.'

Allison rushed out of the library and across the courtyard
to the office. Her colleagues were standing in the entrance way,
the new teacher slightly to one side.

'Elena, where do you live?' Allison demanded.

'Sorry?' The woman turned towards her. 'You are . . . ?'

'Where's your house?' Allison was almost shouting. 'Where do you live?'

The other teachers stopped speaking and turned to her.

'Are you okay, Allison?' one of them asked. 'Have you met our new ESL teacher? She moved here from Melbourne.'

'Why did you move here, Elena? Was it because of a man?'

She knew they were watching, wondering what was going on, but Allison couldn't stop herself. Was this the reason for Tony's secrecy? Could his new girlfriend really be a teacher at her own school?

The door opened and shut behind her, and Shona was at her elbow, pulling her towards the corridor.

'Let's get a cuppa, hen. I've got some of your favourite teabags.'

Even as Shona dragged her off, Allison asked the question once more. 'Where are you living, Elena?'

The shell-shocked girl answered softly. 'Mona Vale.'

Oh dear God, what was she doing, yelling at the new teacher? Just because her name sounded like Helena. While Allison hadn't actually accused the woman of sleeping with her husband, the staff would now all be gossiping about the usually calm Mrs Walsh.

Bloody Tony, sending her mad.

'I guess you're not coming to drinks then?' Shona said, as she made the cups of tea.

'No, I've got book club anyway.'

'Do you want me to tell them what's going on? They'll all be asking now.'

Allison felt she didn't have much choice. But what if Tony's new woman *was* a teacher or parent at her school? How could she possibly turn up to work each day?

After Shona finished her cup of tea and headed off to join the others, Allison hid in her classroom. She hadn't actually lied to Shona—her book club was on that evening. The book focused on a wife murdering her unfaithful husband. Allison wasn't attending.

By five-thirty, when Allison walked into the staff car park, her silver hatchback was the only vehicle on the hot tarmac.

Unlocking the Mazda, she glanced at the car door. Rubbed at a mark underneath the handle. Was that a reflection from the wispy clouds? She rubbed again. Bloody hell—a scratch extended all the way from the bonnet to the boot. Staring around the empty car park, Allison felt the night-time fear rush through her body. Someone had keyed her car.

It couldn't be her colleagues, not even Elena—they wouldn't do that to her.

Allison dumped her folders on the passenger seat, desperate to get out of there. Switching on the ignition, she heard a soft click. What the hell? Allison tried again and again. Normally, she'd check under the bonnet but not today. With the doors locked, she rang roadside assistance for help. *We'll be with you in thirty minutes.* She couldn't sit in a hot car for that long. Should she go back into the staffroom, lock herself in there? Or ring Nadia to come and wait with her?

Be brave. Don't sit and sweat in the car.

She got out of the car, slamming the door. 'Fucking hell,' she growled to herself. 'Who did this?'

'Mrs Walsh?'

Allison turned to see Gracie and her father walking through the car park. When she'd been hiding in the classroom, she'd noticed them in the playground with a few other children.

Luke had been holding his daughter's waist as she swung her arms along the monkey bars. Despite the white socks she'd put in Gracie's schoolbag, the girl had come to school in blue socks. Allison guessed that her father hadn't unpacked her bag. This morning they'd had a quick chat about the next round of chemo. *We'll send out an email reminding children with any infectious disease to stay home,* she'd assured him. *We'll respect your privacy, of course.* Although everyone would know exactly who had cancer because of the purple bandana.

'Sorry, I'm having car trouble. I'm waiting for the NRMA.' She prayed that they hadn't heard her swearing.

From the frown on Luke's face, though, it was clear that he had.

'Are you all right?' he asked. 'You seem a bit . . . upset.'

'Thanks for your concern.' She bit her lip. 'It's been a long week.'

Oh no—now, she'd made it sound like Gracie's arrival was the cause of her exhaustion. Should she try to explain or would that make it worse?

'I'm sure it has,' Luke said, smoothing over her gaffe. 'We were hanging out with some kids in the playground. Meeting other families.'

A single dad going through a tragedy—Allison was sure that the women of Wirriga would take him into their fold. Hopefully, they wouldn't be scared off by the sick child. Allison hadn't been very attentive to Gracie today, not to any of her class; her thoughts focused on Tony wanting to sell the house.

'Where are you living?' Allison asked. 'You probably have some school families in your street.'

'Actually, we're still in a holiday flat in Manly. It's opposite the beach, which is great, but now the holidays are over, we've got backpackers upstairs. I'm trying to find somewhere to rent in Wirriga. There's not much available.'

'It's because people move in and never leave.'

Apart from Tony.

Gracie pulled at her father's hand. 'Can I go on the slide again, Daddy?'

'I guess we can stay a bit longer,' Luke said. 'Do you want to come to the playground with us, Mrs Walsh?'

She followed them over, grateful for the company. Had someone tampered with her car? Was it Tony's new woman? But why? *Helena* already had Tony; she'd won.

'Are you sure you're okay?' Luke asked as they watched Gracie clambering around the play equipment.

'I'm fine, thanks. How's Gracie coping with the move?'

'She's up and down. She misses her mum.'

'Of course she does.'

Allison still missed her dad and he'd died six years ago.

'It's good to be here, though. We came on holiday to Manly when Gracie was a baby. My wife loved this area.'

Luke ran a hand over his face and cupped it around his chin. Was he going to cry?

'I'm sorry about your wife. It must be very hard.'

'There are so many things I miss.' He shut his eyes for a second. 'And now Gracie's starting chemo again . . . we used to care for her together and discuss the treatment plan.'

'I'm not medical but I know kids. You can talk to me, if you need to.'

'I'd appreciate that. I seem to be the only single dad in the cancer clinic.' Tears glistened in his eyes. 'No-one else understands.'

'I understand a little,' she said. 'I know it's nothing like your situation, but my husband left me on New Year's Day. Completely out of the blue. Please don't mention it to anyone else at school. I'm only telling you because . . .'

. . . you share that same sense of loss. Tears were pricking her eyes now.

'I'm so sorry. That must've been such a shock.'

'We'd been married for twenty-four years. Someone told me that it's better to have loved and lost, than never to have loved at all . . . She meant well but it was horrible. Why should *we* have to be the ones who lose?'

'People think they're being helpful but they're not.' Luke shook his head. 'How are you doing now? Did you think about getting away? Going overseas? That's what I wanted to do—but I couldn't, of course, because of Gracie's treatment.'

'I thought about it.' She hesitated before admitting to her phobia. 'I'm scared of flying.'

Another thing that had probably driven Tony away. Her refusal to go on a plane, to accompany him to the funeral in England. Allison would like to disappear now; magically fly away on the weekend and not turn up to school on Monday.

'We're all scared of something,' Luke mumbled.

Her fears were pathetic—flying, being scared of the dark without her husband in the house. Luke's fear must surely be the worst one. After coming home from the restaurant last night, instead of finishing a bottle of wine, Allison had researched Gracie's disease. The girl wouldn't even be able to pronounce it: thymic carcinoma, with the complication of an autoimmune disorder, acquired pure red cell aplasia. Extremely rare in children. And with a 'poor prognosis', according to the website she'd found. No wonder Luke had moved to Sydney for a specialist.

'So, Gracie's starting chemotherapy again next Friday, is that right?'

'Yep. That means she'll have a chance to recover over the weekend—though she'll also be away this Monday for some blood tests. Still, Dr Rawson reckons she should be able to come to school most days. I know it'll be tricky, but I want her to make some friends.'

'I'm sure she will. It's a friendly school.'

'Thank you, Mrs Walsh.' He smiled properly for the first time. 'Gracie's lucky to have such a good teacher.'

Allison knew the chatter which happened in the school playground at the beginning of each year: *Which class is your child in? Did she get the good teacher?*

The good teacher.

A year ago, Allison had been 'the good teacher'. Not now.

<hr>

On Saturday morning, Allison crossed her fingers as she started the Mazda. A flat battery, the NRMA guy had said last night as he'd charged it up. Presumably not related to the scratches down the side of the car, then. Had she left a light on or a door partially open yesterday? Allison had no idea.

To her relief, it fired up normally. She'd arranged to meet Felix at Warringah Mall to go shoe-shopping. Up until now, Allison had been ignoring Tony's emails about dividing their assets, certain that he'd come to his senses. Yesterday, he'd sent a message about organising a real estate agent to look at the house. Soon they'd have to discuss the everyday logistics of paying for textbooks and soccer registration and school shoes.

Half an hour later, Felix was begging her for the most expensive shoes he'd tried on: a pair of black Nikes.

'I'll buy them if you stay with me on Monday nights,' Allison said.

Bribing her son with footwear. How had it come to this?

'Can't. I've got debating after school then Dad's set up some soccer training.'

'I didn't know you were doing debating.'

'Dad said maybe I could stay at yours on Wednesdays.'

At yours. As if Felix didn't live there anymore. Why the hell was Tony trying to keep Felix away from her? Allison placed the shoes back in the box and walked towards the entrance of the shop. Was it about childcare payments? Money? She waved impatiently for Felix to follow. Or was it something to do with the new woman? As Allison stepped through the door, the alarm went off and a security guard put his arm out in front of her. Felix sidled up next to her, keeping his eyes on the floor.

'What're you doing, Mum?' he muttered. 'You forgot to pay.'

❧

As a golden-orange sunset lit up the clouds, Allison parked behind a large van, ten houses down from the bungalow. Dog-walkers meandered along the footpath returning from the off-leash area at Curl Curl beach. Tony's cloak-and-dagger place was a weatherboard house, neither old nor new, nothing flashy, simply comfortable; the sort of bungalow where the same family might have lived happily for decades. From his street, she could hear the gentle lull of waves, the happy shouts of kids playing. She could taste salt in the air. This seaside suburb didn't have the bush backdrop of Wirriga. Everything was out in the open: old weatherboard shacks from the 1950s sat alongside brand-new mansions of brick and glass.

And yet, Allison had seen nothing.

Watching. Waiting. Four weeks now. And still the woman hadn't appeared.

A middle-aged couple stood at the bus stop, staring at their phones rather than talking to each other. In the fading light, their faces glowed blue with the reflection from the screens. Allison checked her own phone, pulling up Facebook so that she didn't look so suspicious sitting in the car. She read the article that Nadia had posted about empowering women to create their best lives. Shona had linked to a book review so she clicked through to the blog. Tried to focus on the words while peeking up at the house every few seconds. A man came out of the place next to Tony's.

This morning, she'd asked Felix outright: 'What's Dad up to this weekend?'

'Not much.'

Allison knew she shouldn't be here. She wasn't a crazy, stalking ex. But Tony's secrecy had sent her into an obsessive frenzy. After yesterday's embarrassment with Elena, she had to know. Last night, Allison had trawled through Tony's social media again. A new female friend had popped up on Facebook. This woman looked so ordinary—brown bob, white shirt, dark jacket, small smile on her ordinary face. *How dare Tony turn my life upside down for this ordinary woman?* It wasn't logical but if Tony *had* to leave her, shouldn't it be for a glamazon?

A six-foot goddess with a flat stomach and golden tresses. And then, in the midst of her anger, she'd had to laugh. As if a six-foot bronzed goddess would want Tony: fifty-one and showing every year, a slight paunch, only just six foot himself, crooked teeth, hair in his nose and his ears, balding at the temples. And smart. And funny. And kind. And caring. And hers.

She'd figured out the Facebook friend was a colleague from work.

Still no movement at the house.

The buzz of her phone was so loud in the enclosed space that she knocked her leg against the steering wheel. *Shit, don't let it be Tony.*

She checked the caller ID. 'Hi, Nadia.'

'Hi, what're you up to?'

'Nothing.' The guilt flooded through her at the lie.

'Do you want to come over for dinner?'

Sweet Nadia, a last-minute invitation, trying to keep her sane. And her poor husband, a friend of Tony's, stuck in the middle. Even he didn't know anything about the new woman.

'Thanks, that'd be nice.' Allison sighed. 'Guess what? Tony has asked an agent to look at the house.'

'You need to get some financial advice. If you want to keep the house, he'll insist you buy him out.'

'I know. I know.'

This time last year, she and Tony had been discussing restaurants for their silver wedding anniversary, talking about superannuation and long-term planning for their retirement and holidays. Now, Allison had to calculate if she could afford the mortgage on her teaching salary alone. She'd probably have to work until she was seventy-five.

'Maybe you could get some extra cash by hosting Japanese exchange students?' Nadia suggested.

'That's a better option than your joke about asking the strays to pay!'

Allison and Tony had always welcomed people to stay; Nadia had nicknamed them 'the strays'. Mostly, they were Tony's friends and family from England or their grown-up kids backpacking around Australia. Sometimes Felix's mates stayed when their parents went on overseas trips. And they'd opened their home to any others who needed it: teachers from regional areas in Sydney for professional development programs; a Japanese exchange student who'd had problems with her host family. Even a family from school with their lovely Labrador, when a tree had crushed their house and the injured dad ended up in hospital.

'Or . . .' Nadia hesitated, '. . . you could rent out the house and move into a funky apartment. Start your own new life.'

'I was happy with the old one.'

In the background, Allison heard Nadia's two girls calling out. She pictured her friend cooking dinner for her family, juggling conversations between her daughters and her husband. Wanted by everyone. Needed by everyone.

'Let's take up something new, like salsa dancing,' Nadia said. 'That club in Narrabeen is holding lessons on Thursday nights.'

'I am *not* learning to dance. And if you're trying to get me to meet men, don't!' Allison couldn't think of anything worse.

'Well, you need some kind of project to . . .'

To stop me going crazy. Oh, Nadia, if only you could see me right now.

30

4

LUKE

SITTING AT THE HOSPITAL ON MONDAY MORNING, LUKE KEPT GRACIE entertained by re-reading the dog-eared joke book.

'What do you call a blind dinosaur?'

'Do-you-think-he-saw-us.' Gracie groaned. 'That's soooo old.'

'Well, do you think Dr Rawson saw us?' Luke asked, hoping Gracie enjoyed the rhythm of the words.

'He's nice. He gave me a red frog.'

'Okay, smarty pants.' Luke patted her leg. 'What do you call a sleeping dinosaur?'

'Dino-snore!'

In addition to loving the movie *Frozen*, Gracie loved dinosaur jokes. He needed to buy some new books; she knew all these jokes off by heart. This was the only one they had from back home.

'Right, I'm going to find a joke that you've never heard before.' He searched on his phone. 'How do you ask a tyrannosaurus out to dinner?'

'How?'

31

'Tea, Rex?'

'T-rex?' she repeated, frowning.

'Some people call dinner "tea".'

The frown grew deeper.

'Don't worry about it, honey. It's silly. You can borrow a new joke book from the school library.'

The frown turned into a gigantic smile. 'Can I borrow books?'

'You sure can. Just ask Mrs Walsh.'

'I like Mrs Walsh. She's a bit like Granny.'

Mrs Walsh had been a godsend—helping with the separation anxiety, settling Gracie in gently, sitting her with a buddy. Every afternoon, when Luke picked her up, Gracie had come out of her shell a little more. Back in October, when he'd broken the news about her mother's death, Gracie had nodded solemnly and asked for hot chips as a special treat. The meltdowns had started the next day, the nightmares a week later.

'When's Mummy coming home?' She'd ask the question in the most unexpected moments.

Everyone said these were normal responses but Luke wondered if Gracie would ever go back to her old self. Giggly, cheeky, fun. Just like he'd been as a child. This move to the beaches should help. So far, the community had been welcoming. They'd already had a playdate at Evelyn's house. They'd been invited to a kindy families' picnic and he'd been put on the mailing list for morning teas and volunteering at school. The mothers in the playground had chatted to him on the second day, their eyes on Gracie's bandana as she attempted the monkey bars.

'Is she okay to do that?' one of them had whispered.

'Yes, as long as she takes it easy. No somersaults over the top!'

Mothers who'd do anything to protect their child were called 'Mama Bear'. But there was no such label for fathers. Luke had changed cities and states. Uprooted their lives for a better future.

—

Luke didn't mind the forty-minute drive between the children's hospital and Wirriga. It was a time-out between the two parts of their lives. Today, Gracie was commentating on everything they passed—a yellow Ferrari, horses near Randwick racecourse, the red and silver tram, a woman in a yellow scarf waiting to cross at the lights.

'Can we go over the sea, Daddy?'

He detoured from the entrance to the Harbour Tunnel and came out onto the bridge, the steel arches curving above them. The Jeep was handling well in the city traffic. Luke opened the windows and a strong breeze whistled in. Out towards the heads, the sun shimmered on the water like light glinting off diamonds.

'Can you spot the Opera House?' Luke asked.

'So big.' Gracie held her arms out wide.

Luke knew she wasn't talking about the Opera House itself but the whole city—high-rise towers and freeways full of cars. So different to her old life. He peered in the rear-vision mirror towards the child seat, checking her expression.

'We'll be going over the bridge every Friday, honey.'

How would she cope with the new routine and taking a day out of school each week?

'Can I have ice-cream?'

He'd bought a sugar-free sorbet but she didn't like the orange flavour.

'Do you think you'd like strawberry?'

'YUM!'

'Let's get some at home.'

He called the apartment 'home' but it didn't feel like it. Beds that had been slept in by hundreds of holiday-makers, chipped chairs and the bare necessities in the kitchen. His aim to live close to the school in Wirriga had been hampered by a lack of rentals. Mrs Walsh was right—once people moved into the suburb, they never moved out again.

In the back seat, Gracie had pulled off her bandana and tossed it on the seat. A soft fuzz covered her scalp. The baldness and the bandana made her almost unrecognisable from two years ago when she'd had dark, frizzy hair that could only be tamed with conditioner and combing. Luke remembered Gracie in the bath with her mother. The never-ending combing—adding hot water when Gracie complained it was getting cold—combing, combing until the knots were finally out. Did Gracie remember those moments too?

A year later, Gracie cried as her hair disappeared. But Luke had shaved his at the same time so they could be 'baldies' together. Rubbing her hand over his stubble, Gracie had laughed at its prickliness and hadn't said a word about her own hair since.

Adaptable. That was his Gracie.

Wirriga Wellness Centre had a light airy feel to it, although Luke wasn't sure about the name—it was basically a gym, it didn't have any of the extras that came with a 'wellness centre'. As he was peering towards the glassed studios, a voice boomed from behind him.

'Welcome! You must be Luke. Great to have you on board!'

Luke went in for a handshake but the gym owner clasped him into a half embrace. The man was a similar height to him although more muscular. The black singlet showed off his biceps inked in red and black tattoos.

'I'm Greek—we hug everyone, mate,' Nico said, slapping Luke on the shoulder. 'And when you start working here, you become family.'

Family. Luke could certainly do with a bit of that.

Over the phone, Luke had explained his situation and how he could only work school hours and not Fridays. And how sometimes he might need to stay home with Gracie. Nico hadn't been fazed. 'Thanks, Nico. I appreciate you taking me on.'

'No problem, mate. I've got an appointment, but I'll get Maz to show you around. She's between classes.' Nico pointed to a blonde girl slurping on a green smoothie in the centre's cafe. 'She's been here a few years so she knows the ropes.'

He introduced the instructor and disappeared back to his office.

'Welcome to Wirriga!' The girl had a smile that could light up the Opera House. 'You're gonna love working here. It's the best. Nico is a great boss.'

'Thanks, I'm looking forward to it.'

Maz led him down a corridor. She bounced as she walked, her high ponytail dancing from side to side, her hips swinging with every step. But it seemed unselfconscious; she wasn't sashaying on purpose. This was simply her.

She pointed out the various studios and the change rooms. The walls were emblazoned with motivational sayings.

You get out what you put in.

Failure is only a mindset.

Play your own game.

To be the best, you have to take the extra step.

Luke could imagine using these sayings as directional sign-posts. So many cancer websites had sayings about pain and battle and hope and God. These were better.

As she showed him the equipment and the storage areas, she asked, 'Have you just moved to Wirriga?'

'Ah . . . yes. I'm looking for somewhere to rent long-term.'

'My mum works at the real estate agency. Well, she's in admin, but she knows what's coming up. I can ask her if you like?'

'That'd be awesome. I haven't had much luck yet.'

'What are you after? Townhouse? Apartment? Big house?'

'I don't mind, as long as it has two bedrooms,' he said. 'I've got a four-year-old daughter.'

'Cool. I love kids. Is she at Wirriga Public?'

'Yep.'

The school was only a couple of blocks away from the gym. Gracie had been happy to go this morning after being absent yesterday. Hopefully, she'd be okay with missing Friday each week.

Maz was walking him towards the staff area now, with lockers on one side and a big cupboard on the other. This girl didn't really seem to do small talk—Luke felt she'd know everything about him in five minutes.

'Great school. I went there. I always wanted to be a teacher but I ended up here.'

'Well, you've got plenty of time for a career change.' Luke guessed that she was in her early twenties. 'You never know what the future may hold.'

'Maybe.' She smiled again. 'I've got to give you three sets of uniform.'

She pulled open the cupboard, took a black top from the shelf and held it up against him.

'Perfect,' they both said at the same time.

'Jinx,' Maz shouted and then covered her mouth. 'Sorry, my sister and I still do that. I must sound like I'm ten years old.'

'No, you sound like a ray of sunshine.' Luke laughed then put a hand over his own mouth. 'Oh shit, did I just say that out loud? It's my turn to be sorry.'

Would Maz think he was a sleaze trying to pick her up? He must have eight years on her. What he meant was that she sounded exactly like one of the nurses at the children's hospital; a nurse who delivered rays of sunshine to make life happier for the sick kids.

'That's okay.' She was blushing. 'I don't think I've ever been compared to sunshine before.'

Maz folded the three black shirts, with WIRRIGA WELLNESS printed in yellow across the top pocket, and handed them to him.

'If you have time, we could pop across to Mum at the agency,' she said. 'I've got half an hour before my next class.'

This friendliness made Wirriga feel more like a country town than a city suburb.

Hopefully, Gracie would like living here.

Hopefully, Wirriga would accept her.

5

MAZ

OH, WHY HAD SHE SAID *JINX*? SHE MUST'VE SOUNDED THE SAME AGE as his daughter.

When Nico had asked Maz to give the induction, he'd told her about Luke's wife and child. Super tragic. Maz had secretly wondered about Nico's judgement—was a broken man the right sort to be instructing at the gym? Their culture was encouragement and enthusiasm. Could Luke give that to their clients?

But now she'd met him, Maz could see why Nico had signed him on.

Yeah, he had the sad eyes—but that voice. The way he said her name was divine. Low and deep and sexy. Not that she was thinking about sex with him. Absolutely not. Too old. But the punters would follow his every instruction in class, that was for sure. Good bod, not too ripped. And with his shaved head, when he did smile, it was like his whole face was smiling.

And he'd used her favourite word: *awesome*.

Maz led him across the road to the small set of shops with the real estate agency at the far end.

'This place has the best coffee,' Maz said to Luke, pointing at Raw Espresso as they passed. 'And it does great superfood protein bowls.'

The new mothers had taken over the cafe's outdoor area for morning tea, their prams blocking the spaces between the tables. Two of them waved. They were in Maz's Mums and Bubs yoga class.

'Of course, Nico would prefer that we eat at the gym cafe, but sometimes you need a break.'

Half her clients were always at these shops so it wasn't really a break from them. If Maz had enough time, she'd zip down to Freshwater and eat her salad in the park by the beach. A salad that she made at home.

Maz had nothing to say about the newsagency, the pool shop and the post office. Presumably he knew that Coles was around the back, along with the bottle shop.

Finally, they reached the real estate agency. Maz pushed open the door and saw the empty reception desk; she should've texted first. Maz had left home early this morning, so she hadn't seen either of her parents today. But suddenly Mum was bustling down the short corridor in a red dress and black jacket. The red material puckered over her stomach and hips, the jacket pulled across her bust—had Mum put on more weight recently?

They hugged, and Maz explained that the new instructor needed somewhere to rent.

'Luke's little girl has just started at the school, so something close would be awesome.'

Mum sat them down at the desk, angling the computer screen so they could see it. Of course, Maz had already told Mum all about him last night, but if Luke wasn't going to bring up his tragic circumstances, they'd have to pretend they didn't know.

'Do you have any other transport needs?' Mum asked. 'Do you or your partner need to be close to the bus stop, for example?'

'It's just me and Gracie. My . . . er . . . my wife died.'

'Oh my gosh, I'm so terribly sorry.' Mum reached over and patted his hand; she sounded completely shocked. Maz was impressed—she'd never seen Mum in work mode like this. Shame that she hadn't got the job in sales. Maz reckoned it was because of Mum's weight. The agency's sales people were as tarted up as the houses they sold.

'We have some apartments on the edge of Manly and a reno-vated semi.' Mum clicked through the pictures on the screen. 'Nothing in Wirriga at the moment. There's a flat above an Indian restaurant on the main road in Brookvale. Lots of pol-lution from trucks, though.'

Had Mum just given herself away or did all agents talk about air pollution?

'Actually, Gracie is sick, so pollution's an issue.'

Luke looked downcast and Mum rushed to reassure him.

'Don't worry, love, we'll find a nice home for you and Gracie. It's a lovely area. Do you have any family in Sydney?'

Luke shook his head.

'What about your parents? Where are they?'

Mum was such a busybody. Maz tried to catch her eye and warn her off the interrogation but Luke didn't seem to find her questions intrusive.

'In Western Australia. We had a falling-out. They said some unforgivable things about Gracie's illness.'

What a nightmare. Maz knew her own mother would be the opposite in a medical crisis.

'Oh, love, that's so sad,' Mum said. 'Why don't you come over for lunch next Sunday? Bring little Gracie.'

—

'Five, six, seven, eight and jump. Okay, here's the swap. Make sure the other foot is out in front. Now, let's go again. Punch it, one, two, three . . .'

Maz surveyed the boxing class—a good turnout for the end of lunchtime. These days, her classes were filled almost every time. It had taken two years of hard work to get to this point. Woo-hoo. Maz gave an extra hard punch in the air and bounced her right hip up and down—her glutes rock hard, her butt tight. Man, she felt fierce. In her best shape ever. She'd be rocking it at her twenty-third birthday party in June. She just had to settle on a date and book a place. Nowhere too expensive. One of those wine bars by the beach in Manly? Or the new pub at Collaroy? She'd pay for finger food and a couple of jugs of sangria and beer to start. When she'd turned twenty-one, she hadn't been able to afford a party.

'Let's go hard, guys. You get out what you put in!'

Counting out the punches, Maz kept an eye on a man she'd never seen before. Cute bod, needed some work on his biceps and quads. Around Luke's age, or maybe older. Luke's physique was better, with just the right amount of definition. Maz couldn't imagine what Luke was going through. Her grandparents, aunts and uncles were all alive, despite their fried breakfasts, fatty chops and ready-made macaroni cheese. She'd never had a death in the family—only the one here in the gym, and that had shaken her up big-time.

After the class finished, Maz opened the storage boxes for the mats and gloves, and directed everyone to drop them in. The cute guy was hanging around. Smiling in his direction, Maz collected the last set of gloves and dragged the box back to the corner.

'Can I help you with that?' he asked, rushing over to take the other side.

'No, I'm fine, thanks.' She smiled again. 'I do it every day.'

'I was wondering if you'd like to meet for a drink one night?' He spoke with the confidence of someone who was rarely turned down. 'In the city. Maybe at one of those cool bars in Barangaroo?'

Up close, Maz realised he was older than she'd first thought. Mid-thirties maybe.

'Oh wow, that's really nice of you to ask,' Maz cooed. 'But I have a boyfriend.'

Sometimes she loved the attention, sometimes she didn't. Male punters thought they could chat up any instructor, that it was Maz's *duty* to be polite to them, date them, admire their bodies. The boyfriend tactic seemed to shut them up, as if the only reason Maz wouldn't want them was because she had a better option. At the moment, though, she was happily single. Oakley, her 'friend with benefits'—that sounded so much better than 'fuck buddy', which was what her sister liked to say—was now working as a trainer in a resort in Thailand. When Maz had commented on his awesome Insta photos, Oakley suggested she should come over. It was a stunning place to live, he'd told her, but the pay was pretty low—he was selling bodybuilding supplements to get some extra cash.

'That's a shame.' The man chuckled. 'For me, obviously, not for your boyfriend. The name's Colin, by the way. I'm already looking forward to my next class with you.'

Colin's eyes lingered on her breasts. Maz arched her back and pushed them out further. *You can gawp all you like, mate, but you're not touching these.* Em-Jay reckoned it was the best way to treat the punters who focused on her tits.

By the time Maz got home, Mum had already started dinner. A box of chicken Kiev from the supermarket freezer: battered chicken, dripping with preservatives and some kind of processed butter. Dad was mashing potato, adding more butter. Maz could see two empty bowls in the lounge room, the remnants of their barbecue chips and salty nuts. If she looked in the recycling bin, she knew there'd be three empty VB cans.

Flipping hell, Dad just needed to stop eating and drinking like this and the kilos would drop off. He was only forty-seven, but he had arthritis in both knees and his hip. Half the time, he was limping. Maz kept telling him: 'A kilo off the body is equal to four kilos of pressure off the knee.' She'd offered Dad and Mum a discounted membership at the gym but they'd said, 'It's not our kind of place.'

After what had happened last year, Maz figured they might be right. When the overweight guy on the rowing machine had collapsed, Maz assumed he was just taking a break, exhausted from a hard workout. Then one of the punters had called out, 'I think he's unconscious.'

Ten o'clock at night, Maz was on the late shift. Nico and the senior instructors had gone home. She'd trained in CPR but never actually had to perform it. The two other men in the weights room had panicked.

'Hurry up and do something,' they'd shouted at her.

He was slumped awkwardly over the rowing machine—it took all three of them to drag him clear. Maz sent one guy to get the defibrillator while the other called an ambulance. She was trying to check the man's breathing and his pulse but it was hard to find the carotid artery in his thick neck. What if she was feeling in the wrong spot? What if she started CPR when his heart was still beating?

Once Maz had turned on the AED—the automated external defibrillator—she calmed down a little as the recorded voice issued instructions. But the man's shirt was too tight and they couldn't inch it up above his chest. Someone had to find scissors but the office door was locked. Maz didn't have time to get the key. She ended up biting the material with her teeth, her face pressed against the man's sweaty groin, until she managed to make a tear. Hands shaking, she stuck the pads on his skin and delivered the shocks. Then she started compressions.

After two minutes, the machine requested another shock.

Maz stared at the man's puffy red face, the wet hair flat against his head. Somehow, she knew he wasn't going to survive.

Before the workout, he'd said, 'It's my wife's birthday tomorrow so I'm getting my exercise in tonight.'

He'd only joined the gym a week earlier; Maz had shown him how to use the machines. He'd talked about getting into shape now that he was forty, wanting to play soccer with his twin boys.

By the time the ambulance arrived, Maz's shoulders were sore from doing CPR. The adrenaline had kept her going but when the paramedics took over, she crumpled backwards against the rowing machine.

'Please save him,' she'd whispered.

They tried. They all tried.

His name was Joseph.

Two weeks later, the wife came in to thank Maz for her efforts. Four weeks later, Nico had a letter from a solicitor stating the gym had provided an inappropriate program for Joseph's weight and fitness level. The letter asked why 'inexperienced' Maz had been the only instructor on that night; whether she'd learnt first aid; and if she'd done training on an AED.

Joseph's family wanted to sue.

Nico protected Maz from the worst of it. The legal back and forth stretched on for ages but, eight months later, Nico said it'd finally been sorted. He didn't tell her how.

Every day at work, Maz glanced at the rowing machine and wondered if she'd acted quickly enough. Wondered what else she could've done to save Joseph's life.

And every time she studied her father, with the same body type as the dead man, she worried for his health.

She'd done research on turmeric and curcumin for Dad's arthritis; bought a cookbook for improving joint health; prepared nutritional dinners; coaxed him into some simple exercises. Dad had grunted through one set and refused to do any more. Before Christmas, the GP told him that he had to lose twenty kilos—and the doctor was being polite. Really, Dad needed to lose more to get to a normal BMI.

At the shampoo factory where Dad worked, the ladies baked cakes and slices for morning tea every day—it had turned into a competition. At home, Mum liked to make dessert. Everyone in their extended family thought that food meant love. No: it meant clogged arteries, sore joints and feeling exhausted all the time. By getting into the gym as teenagers, Maz and her sister had managed to see the light.

Just last week, when Maz had been looking for a pen in the kitchen drawer, she'd found Mum's terrible cholesterol test. Some of her friends complained about their parents but Maz knew she was lucky: Rick and Wendy were the very best parents a girl could have. Maz wanted them to be around for a long time yet.

Maz put the cutlery and water jug on the table for dinner. At least they were drinking more water.

'Love, can you get the carrots out of the microwave?' Mum said.

Over-cooked carrots. Not much nutrition there. Maz found some broccoli in the bottom of the fridge and zapped it. She added the vegetables to each plate as Mum served up the chicken Kiev. Dad took his to the table, along with another can of VB.

'The twenty-first is coming up soon,' Mum said. 'We'll need to get a present.'

'How about a case of beer?' Dad took a swig of his own.

Hadn't Dad taken any notice at Christmas lunch? The oldies were pissed while the younger ones glugged Coke and Red Bull. Her cousin didn't drink alcohol.

'What about a nice shirt?' Maz suggested.

'Do you know if it's a big party?'

Maz could hear the heaviness in her mother's voice.

'It's okay, Mum, I'm paying for my own birthday party.' Maz blew her a kiss.

Later, as she was clearing up after dinner, Maz heard a ding on her phone. She read the text message from her sister about drinks on Friday, then clicked onto Facebook. Luke had accepted her friend request. With one ear on Mum's conversation, Maz peeked through his profile. His most recent posts were photos of Gracie on Manly beach. *So excited to be in Wirriga and seeing the new specialist. Fingers crossed!*

Scrolling back in time, Maz came across a post by Sarah Branson—Luke's wife, she presumed—where she'd tagged Luke. A hospital in Melbourne: *Chemo day. Gracie is so brave but I'm a mess. No photos of me crying!* Then Luke with Gracie in her purple beanie: *Love my gorgeous girl.* A picture of a bunch of kale: *We're doing a superfoods diet for Gracie. Any suggestions welcome!* Maz zoomed in on the pictures of the wife. Dark curly hair. Dimples. And a thousand-watt smile. No posts in October. In November, Luke had written a tribute: *Sarah was the love of my life. The best wife and mother in the world. Our hearts are aching beyond words.* In December, a short post saying: *Thanks for your support. We really appreciate it. Gracie and I are going to the children's hospital Christmas party today.* A photo of a clown in the hospital ward. Christmas must have been horrendous.

'Maz, can you hear me?' Her mother waved a hand across the phone screen. 'What shall we do for lunch on Sunday? Sausages on the barbecue?'

'Oh no, Luke's little girl has a special diet. I'll go shopping on Saturday after class.'

Luke had mentioned Gracie's diet when she'd given him her address: sugar-free, low in red meat, high in leafy greens.

If Maz left it up to Mum, she'd kill the girl with sweet treats of kindness.

Before Luke and Gracie arrived on Sunday, Mum had gone to the garage and pulled out the old Barbie dolls and Lego. Maz couldn't believe she'd kept them.

'That was my Barbie,' her sister Kelli said.

'No, she's mine!' Maz pulled at the one in the leopard-print dress. 'I remember cutting her hair.'

'Girls, seriously,' Mum snapped, 'I didn't think you'd be arguing about dolls in your twenties. It doesn't matter whose was whose. Gracie can use them all.'

Now, Maz was sitting cross-legged on the rug in the lounge room building a Lego house big enough for Barbie to sit inside.

'Bigger! Bigger!' Gracie demanded, handing over another pile of red blocks.

When she'd first arrived, the girl clutched Luke's hand, but Maz had set up the toys and pretended to play by herself. Within minutes, Gracie sidled up next to her. As they chatted and played, Gracie draped her pale hand over Maz's knee.

'We're going to build the biggest and best Barbie house in the world,' Maz said. 'And it will have windows at just the right height for Barbie to see out.'

'Lucky Barbie.' Gracie cradled the doll against herself. 'I saw people KISSING out my window.'

When Gracie shouted the word, everyone looked up. Mum shook her head; she still hadn't been able to find a suitable rental for them.

Luke raised his eyebrows. 'Backpackers,' he mouthed.

'Oooh, kissing! I bet they were in love,' Maz said to Gracie. 'Who can Barbie fall in love with?'

Gracie scooted over to the toy box and rifled through it. She found Ken, whose arms had been eaten off by the neighbour's dog, and brought him back to Barbie.

'Mwah, mwah.' Gracie made kissing noises as she put Ken's face next to Barbie. 'Mummy and Daddy.'

The poor kid. Luke said she missed her mum so much. Without thinking, Maz bent down and dropped a quick kiss on Gracie's cheek. The girl was completely still for a moment, then she threw her arms around Maz's neck.

'She's just adorable, Luke,' her mother said, while Dad worked his way around the coffee table, refilling their drinks.

Maz caught Kelli's eye. The sisters knew exactly what each one was communicating. Kelli: *Oh shit, Mum wants grandkids.* Maz: *Your turn first. I don't even have a boyfriend.* Kelli: *Nate and I are into partying not parenting. But Luke's a bit of all right. Potential boyfriend?* Maz: *He's really nice but, you know, dead wife and sick child.* Kelli: *And don't forget old.* Maz: *But fit.*

For dessert, Maz had prepared a fruit platter with watermelon cut into star shapes for Gracie. It was still in the fridge but Mum was tipping a box of chocolates into a bowl. Where had they come from?

'Mum, we're not doing sugar,' Maz hissed. 'Put them away.'

To distract Gracie from the chocolates, Maz asked the girl to check if Barbie's arms and legs would fit into the Lego house. And then she listened in to Kelli's conversation. Her sister was asking Luke how he'd become a fitness instructor.

'I started off as a swimmer,' Luke said. 'Squads every morning at five-thirty.'

That explained his impressive shoulders and upper body.

'I made it to the Commonwealth Games. Almost got to the Olympics. Just missed out.'

Wow! She should tell Nico so he could add it to Luke's bio at the gym. Imagine being good enough to go to the Olympics— top of the top. But Maz could hear the frustration in his voice: 'almost' didn't cut it.

'Impressive!' Kelli grinned at Maz behind his back. 'Did you meet some famous people?'

Kelli shouldn't have asked that; Luke could've been one of those famous people. Another Ian Thorpe. Michael Klim. Even his name sounded right for it. Luke Branson. Maz knew that training was as much a mental game as a physical one. All those hours in the pool, following the black line. Competing with teammates for the one spot. It took a mental toughness that few possessed.

'Yeah.' Luke chuckled. 'I knew some swimmers. I met Michael Phelps once. Did you know he's won the most Olympic medals of all time? Twenty-eight. Amazing!'

'What was he like?'

'He had a few great sayings. He told me that to get to the top, you have to do things that other people aren't willing to do.'

It was similar to one of their quotes at the gym, but Luke was looking at his daughter as he said it. Maz felt he wasn't referring to swimming, but to saving Gracie.

6

ALLISON

AS NADIA SLICED THE LEMON TART FOR DESSERT, ALLISON ASKED IF SHE could stay the night. After another week where Felix had only come over once, Allison couldn't bear being home alone. On a Saturday night. A night when she and Tony were supposed to have attended his colleague's sixtieth birthday party in an Italian restaurant overlooking Sydney Harbour. Had her husband taken the new woman instead?

'We can walk you home if you're over the limit,' Nadia said. 'You can get the car tomorrow.'

'Please?' she begged. 'I'd rather stay.'

That morning, a dark green sedan had been parked opposite Allison's house. She knew all the neighbours' cars and it wasn't one of theirs. It'd been there on Thursday afternoon too. Nadia would brush it off: *Just kids going up into the bush tracks.* But this wasn't the sort of car driven by kids.

If Allison was inside her house as darkness fell, she'd check each room and close the curtains as the light faded. But if she came home in the dark, she wouldn't have a chance to prepare. When the curtains weren't closed and she turned on the lights inside, she'd see herself reflected in the window panes, terror etched across her white face.

In Nadia's guest room, listening to the sounds of the family preparing for bed, Allison prayed for sleep to come easily. Although now she was worrying about money. Unlike her, Nadia loved playing with numbers, perfect for her job as a management consultant. Tonight, they'd worked on a spreadsheet listing Allison's income and expenditure. Sixteen years ago, Allison and Tony had bought the house for a quarter of a million; Nadia estimated it would sell for six times that now. Allison needed around seven hundred thousand dollars to buy out Tony—an insane amount.

After a night when she finally slept, Sunday morning was cooler and they walked Nadia's dog along the length of Manly beach, around to the headland and back. Allison pointed out the grimy block of flats where Gracie and her father were living.

'You've got to be kidding.' Nadia made the dog sit so she could see better. 'Everyone's smoking there, and they're probably doing drugs too.'

'I've been thinking about inviting them to stay,' Allison said. 'Just until they find somewhere else to live.'

Nadia frowned. 'I know you like to take in strays, but is now the right time for you?'

'I need—' *a family to care for . . . someone in the house at night . . . a way to stop Tony . . .* '—someone else to focus on.'

'Are you sure it wouldn't be too much?'

Allison knew Nadia was choosing her words carefully. The subtext: *You're in a fragile, emotional state. You can barely look after yourself. What can you offer that poor girl?*

The front door was ajar when she arrived home mid-morning. Were the robbers brazen enough to ransack her place in full daylight? Taking a step back onto the path, Allison checked the street—two cars parked nearby; one was Tony's four-wheel drive. If he wasn't moving back home, why did he still have a key? Allison shoved the door open and voices drifted down from upstairs.

'Sorry it's a bit of a mess.' Tony apologising for her. 'Do you think we need professional styling?'

'Definitely. I can suggest a lovely woman. And you'll need to fix the pool, of course.'

'Yes, yes. That will be sparkling.'

Tony and a bloody real estate agent. She'd asked him to postpone the appointment. He'd emailed back some kind of automated meeting request which Allison hadn't even opened.

She stormed up the stairs and found them standing by her bed. The clothes she'd worn on Friday were draped over a chair. Her old beige bra had fallen onto the carpet. And, as luck would have it, she recognised the agent as a father from school.

'Ah, here's Allison,' Tony announced.

Gritting her teeth, she struggled for politeness towards the real estate agent.

'Sorry, there's been a misunderstanding. Thanks for coming but we're not quite ready to sell yet. We'll call you.'

The two men, dressed in their smart casual pants and open-necked shirts, glanced at each other. Allison knew that look: *Here's the crazy lady!* Well, stuff them. Her name was on the deeds. Tony needed her signature to sell.

'I'll have a quick squiz around the garden and meet you downstairs.' The agent hurried off into the corridor.

'This is my house, Tony,' she said. 'I'm not selling.'

'We can't afford to keep it.'

'You can't afford to keep it.' Allison tried not to shout. 'You can't afford to have two houses. This is all about what *you* want.'

'I know it's been a shock but we need to move on. It's time.'

'No. You don't get to tell me when to move on.'

He was standing against the window. Behind him, Allison could see the native forest, gum trees as tall as the house. She imagined running towards him, pushing him backwards. Watching him falling, falling. And then she imagined the opposite. Pulling him onto the bed. Their marital bed. Pulling him on top of her. The familiar outline of his body, his mouth on hers.

If only she could hold on to the house, she could hold on to the hope that one day her family would come back together.

'Allison, I haven't handled this whole thing very well. It's my fault. Please believe me when I say how sorry I am to have hurt you.'

Words, words, words. He'd said them all before. But Tony wouldn't listen to *her* words.

'I want Felix to live here with me.'

'Have you been watching my house, Allison?'

The question came from left field. Her cheeks flamed in response.

'I don't even know where you live. You won't tell me.'

'You're endangering us.'

Now it wasn't just her cheeks burning, heat flooded her whole body.

'No, I'm—'

'Perhaps you should see a psychologist?'

Tony had refused to go to marriage counselling but he wanted *her* to see a psychologist.

'Get out of my bedroom, Tony!' she shouted. Then, remembering the agent creeping around somewhere, she lowered her voice. 'Get out of this house. And give me back the fucking key.'

She held out her palm but her husband—former husband—strode past her, without handing it over.

'If I see you near our house again, I'm calling the police,' he said. 'And Felix won't be staying with you at all.'

—

After school on Tuesday, Allison and Luke stood on the hot brick steps outside the kindy classroom, watching the children play.

'She's settling in really well,' Allison told him. 'Very talented at drawing and painting. A real artist!'

He nodded distractedly. Was he even listening to her, or was he checking out Summer's mother, who'd arrived in a short pink dress and very high pink heels? She'd do herself an injury tottering around the schoolyard in those. The woman strutted in front of them and bent down to pick up a schoolbag, exposing more of her toned thighs. Allison suddenly remembered that Summer's parents had separated at the end of last year. What was the mother's name? Tony wouldn't, couldn't, have fallen in love with her . . . could he? She was the complete opposite of Allison.

Luke was talking and Allison tuned back in.

'The thing is . . . we've had some blood tests . . . some bad results . . . really bad.'

The man wasn't looking at Summer's mother. Like Allison, his mind was elsewhere.

'Bad results,' Allison repeated, giving him her full attention. 'I'm sorry to hear that. Does it mean a different kind of treatment?'

'She'll finish this round of chemo but we've run out of options in Australia.' Luke put both hands on his head and stared upwards, into the sky. 'Dr Rawson wants to get Gracie onto an immunotherapy trial in Chicago.'

Allison glanced over at the little girl, who was creating a fairy garden of sticks with Evelyn and Summer. The girl with the bandana had started to open up; she told jokes and made her classmates laugh. Although, she was still having the occasional meltdown.

'So, you're going to Chicago?'

'I don't know.' He let out a long, deep breath. 'The whole thing's so expensive. I lost so much in the fire. We were only renting the farm and we weren't properly insured. It's not just the money though—the clinic isn't keen to take a child. But Gracie's condition is so rare that Dr Rawson is hoping they'll accept her anyway.'

Allison tried to ask the next question in the most delicate way. 'And if she doesn't get accepted?'

'She needs to start the trial by May,' he whispered. 'It's her only hope.'

Oh dear God, no. With all that Luke was facing, it would've been easy for him to stop fighting. To lie down in the dirt and say: *I give up.* That was what Allison felt like doing. If she didn't have to come to school to teach the Wirriga Wombats, she wouldn't get out of bed each day.

'Maybe we can start a fundraising campaign?' Allison suggested.

'That's a kind thought.' Luke slowly shook his head. 'But I can't ask people for money.'

They both watched Gracie giggle as a pile of sticks collapsed. They couldn't lose this girl, Allison thought, they just couldn't.

━

Despite Tony's warning, Allison was again parked just up the road from his place in Curl Curl. With Felix's cap on her head and the new haircut, she barely resembled her old self. Although, of course, Tony would recognise the car. She'd driven past at four-thirty on Wednesday afternoon, ten o'clock on Thursday night, and seven on Friday morning. No sign of the mystery woman. Perhaps she would appear now, at midday on Saturday.

How could Allison win her family back when she didn't even know what she was up against? No-one could tell Allison a thing about her. It was almost as if the woman didn't exist. In all their time together, Tony had never behaved this way. Even at the beginning of their relationship, when he'd gone back to England after his student exchange, he'd written detailed letters every week, describing people and parties. Years later, when his friends and family had come over for the wedding, Allison felt she knew them all.

Watching the house would not provide any answers—Allison knew that logically. *I'm doing it for the safety of my son*, she told herself. Much like the mystery woman, her son never came out of the front door either. He'd stayed with her for one night this week and brought Darcy over to play Xbox. While they'd been eating a late afternoon tea, the boys had suddenly asked about terminations.

'We were talking about it in personal development today,' Felix had said. 'Is there, like, a time limit?'

'I think twelve weeks,' she'd answered slowly, wondering where this conversation was heading. 'But if the pregnancy is further along, they can do a different sort of procedure.'

Felix had never been interested in girls. Even when some of his friends started dating, he'd remained fanatical about soccer and surfing. Had all that changed in the last few months? He'd be so embarrassed if she brought up the subject of a girlfriend in front of Darcy.

'Is it illegal?' Darcy asked. 'Someone in class said it was.'

'No, it used to be.'

A few months ago, she would've explained how New South Wales had been the last state to decriminalise abortion; she'd have given them an overview of women's rights and men's responsibilities. But her enthusiasm for imparting knowledge to the teens had waned. Instead, she wanted to interrogate Felix about the woman in the house. *Who is she? What's she like? Take a photo. Find out her name. Do I know her? Is she one of my friends?*

Staring at the house now, Allison saw a curtain twitch. The contents of her stomach did a quick somersault. Oh God, she'd finally see her replacement; see what was so special about this woman that Tony had been willing to discard their marriage with barely a backward glance.

Come on, come on. Hurry up and show yourself.

When her mobile beeped with an incoming text, Allison realised she'd been holding her breath. If she looked down at the screen, would she miss the woman coming out of the door?

With her gaze fixed on the house, Allison felt for the phone on the passenger seat. She brought it up to the window and held it in the same frame.

The warning from Felix was written in capital letters.

GO HOME NOW B4 DAD SEES U.

—

Allison's own house seemed even quieter than when she'd left that morning. Maybe she should get a dog to welcome her home and chase the night fears—and burglars—away? There'd been another break-in last week, just a few blocks away near her mother's street.

Sitting in the car had made Allison sweat. She yearned to jump in the pool but the water was still green. A cold shower would have to do—to wash away the shame that burnt with Felix's text message. She stared into the bathroom mirror, pressing at the bags under her eyes, stretching out the lines on her forehead. 'Fifty and fabulous,' she'd toasted Nadia on her birthday last year. Allison's toast would be: 'Fifty and failed.'

Moving her fingers to her jaw, Allison flattened the skin, checking closely for the two spiky black hairs to be plucked as soon as they made their hideous appearance. *We should have tried harder for another baby.* The thought came unbidden as always. The hair on the left had grown. Allison pincered it between her thumb and index finger and yanked. Damn, it slipped out. She really should buy some tweezers. After drying her hands on the towel, she plucked at it again. This time, the offending hair lay dark and incriminating against the flesh of her thumb. She turned on the tap and washed away the evidence.

Allison had first discovered the black curling strand about six months ago. She'd shouted out to Tony in shock.

'Oh my God, I've turned into a witch.'

'You'll be growing warts on your nose next,' Tony joked.

She hadn't laughed. This was it. The Change, as her mother's generation called it. A descent from busy, fertile mother to worn-out, infertile old lady. *We should have tried harder for another baby.* The thought had almost overwhelmed her as she'd checked her body for any other signs of menopause. It'd taken years to conceive Felix, even though the medical tests showed no problems. After Felix, she was thrilled to fall pregnant again quickly, but she'd miscarried at ten weeks. Felix was three, then four, then five years old. They tried half-heartedly. Allison was edging closer to forty. The job came up at Wirriga Public and it was too good not to apply. Allison delighted in shepherding the chubby-cheeked kindy kids through their first year of big school. Allison thought she had accepted her one-child family.

When that first black hair appeared last year, she'd had no idea of the real change steamrolling towards her. The regular check for chin hairs was the least of it. But as an added insult, those two hairs grew faster than any other. And at the same time, the hair on her head began thinning. Every morning, her brush was full of loose strands.

Allison turned away from the bathroom mirror in disgust. The vanity of worrying about her own hair when little Gracie's had fallen out with the chemo. On Thursday, the girl had let Evelyn feel it when Allison was standing close by.

'It's soft,' Evelyn had said.

A silky halo growing back. Fine, dark gossamer.

Last night, over the phone, Allison had tried to explain to Nadia how Luke was clearly devoted to Gracie but also absorbed in his own grief.

'Lost—that's how I'd describe him. He's got this mournful expression.'

'But he's looking after his daughter properly?'

'Kind of. There are little things.' Allison knew they didn't amount to much on their own but they all added up. 'Gracie has a packed lunch every day—I always check. But she's still not wearing the school socks I gave them.'

She needs a mum. A sexist thing to say, but Gracie needed proper care from someone who was on top of things. A responsible adult to support her. That block of flats wasn't right for a sick child. Allison didn't want to overstep but she couldn't stand by without intervening. Little Zack was also on her watch list; he'd started school without having his four-year-old vaccinations. His mother said Zack was on a catch-up schedule but she'd also mentioned that she'd thought immunisation was harmful. If Zack caught whooping cough or measles or the flu, it could kill Gracie.

This is a home, Allison thought as she entered Nadia's kitchen that night. The aroma from the green chicken curry bubbling on the stove, half-filled glasses on the table, beach towels draped over a chair, the dog sniffing around Nadia's feet. The girls were arguing with their father about being old enough to attend a music concert. Allison tried to talk to Nadia over the noise.

'You'll be pleased to know I've decided on a project.'

'Your children's book?' Nadia guessed. 'Are you getting back to writing and painting?'

'I'm not in the right headspace for that.'

'Jewellery making? Pottery? Singing lessons? Sculpture?'

Allison wondered if her friend would understand.

'Not a hobby. More of a mission. I'm going to help little Gracie get to Chicago.'

7

MAZ

CREATE YOUR OWN DESTINY. AS MAZ FLIPPED OPEN THE FRONT OF HER blue and silver notebook, she ran a finger over the mantra embossed on the cover. If only her parents understood. Their destiny wasn't set in stone. Dad didn't have to take Panadol Osteo and rub Voltaren gel on his knees for a better sleep. If he could just lose weight, he could move properly again and live his best life yet.

Every day, Maz scrolled through the fitness gurus, the Insta influencers, the multi-millionaires who were changing people's lives. Trainers, chefs, yogis, bodybuilders, models, paleo bloggers, ex-athletes, life coaches, dancers, inspirational junkies. They all had hundreds of thousands of followers. One Brazilian bodybuilder had more than thirteen million—half of Australia's population!

Inspired, Maz was working on her own diet and fitness plan. Maz knew she could do it too. Sure, it would take hard work but she was prepared for that.

And Dad would be her first client. Her guinea pig. She needed something to give him a kick start. Certainly, Joseph's death had shocked Dad last year but it didn't linger in his mind.

Luke's roster aligned with hers today so they were meeting for a late lunch in the gym cafe. Maz planned to ask for his advice. Em-Jay had started teasing Maz about the amount of time she was spending with the new instructor.

'I'm getting jealous, Maz. I thought I was your best friend and mentor here.'

Luke knew much more than Em-Jay about muscle movement and development. And now he was teaching her. His knowledge also came in handy for Gracie's treatment. Last week, after the bad prognosis had flattened him for days, Maz got him to focus by asking how immunotherapy worked. He could understand it and explain it. But the prognosis had scared the shit out of them all. When Maz told her parents that Gracie could die within a year if she didn't get the treatment in America, Mum had burst into tears.

Maz had already eaten her homemade salad by the time Luke arrived for their late lunch. While he munched on the SuperGreen Bowl from the cafe, Maz explained her plan for her parents. She hoped it would be a helpful distraction for him.

'I've written out a program. The tricky part will be getting Dad on board.'

'He needs some kind of quick incentive,' Luke said.

'Like a reward?'

'Yep. Lose three kilos and you can . . . what does he like doing?'

'Going to musicals.'

She didn't tell everyone about her parents' passion. They sang together in a choir at Seaforth every Wednesday night. Cute but daggy.

'Okay, so look at the dates for a musical,' Luke said. 'Aim for him to lose three kilos in time to buy a ticket for the night.'

'Great idea!'

'And, of course, do the "before" photos so he can see how much he's lost.'

'I might get some proper photos taken,' she mused.

Curtis would do the photos for free, wouldn't he? She could pay him later, once the program took off.

'Do you mean professional shots?' Luke asked. 'Are you planning something else?'

'I want to set up an online program.' It was the first time she'd said it out loud properly. 'Mum and Dad are just the beginning.'

Luke listened so intently, without judgement, that she didn't feel embarrassed telling him. When she'd vaguely mentioned the idea to Em-Jay, her friend had said: 'Who do you think you are? Kayla Itsines? Michelle Bridges?' But everyone had started somewhere and worked their way up. So could Maz.

'That's awesome.' Luke smiled.

As he said her favourite word in his deep voice, Maz felt he was giving her his tick of approval. She decided to tell him more.

'I'm planning to do a nutritional course online to learn about metabolic rates and calculating macronutrients. And maybe a marketing course too.'

'I love your enthusiasm, Maz. There'll be no stopping you! I looked into online courses a couple of years ago . . .'

'We could do it together,' Maz suggested.

She could picture it. Celebrity couples doubled the potential market. And she and Luke complemented each other—her youth and vitality, his life story and life experience. What a team! They'd be the new sensation in no time.

'Happy to help, but I can't commit to anything right now.'

Flipping hell, she was an idiot. Why had she said that? Maz checked the time on her Fitbit. She needed to get ready for the next class. But she really wanted his advice on something else.

'I've got a friend over in Thailand who's selling supplements. I'm trying to get some for Dad's arthritis. But I also thought . . . maybe I could sell them here too. What do you think?'

Oakley had some contacts in the factory and suggested she give it a go. He made it sound like easy money.

'As long as they're legal, I don't see why not.' Luke shrugged. 'There's a big market. You'd have to work out which ones are harder to get here. Which would sell best.'

'Thanks, that's good advice. I've actually been setting up a website.' She took a breath. 'Do you want to see it?'

'Absolutely.'

He leant in closer to view the images on her phone. Maz had to resist the urge to run her palm over his spiky scalp. *Concentrate*, she told herself. *You do not want to be in a relationship with him. Too complicated.* But Luke was lovely and kind, and Gracie so sweet.

'The website builder is easy to use,' Maz said. 'But I'll have to make sure the site's mobile-friendly.'

She'd taught herself how to do it all online. The opening page had a photo with a big headline. *Be your best self.* One of Curtis' pictures of her from years ago, before he'd started at the newspaper. He'd been taking shots to put in his portfolio. Out on the headland at Long Reef, Maz stood tall and strong in her crop top, a hang-glider behind her right shoulder. Its blue wing matched her blue shorts. The hang-glider had been part of Curtis' plan. They were always jumping off the cliff there; Curtis just had to pick the right angle and the right moment to catch one in the background. The text below the photo said:

> Do you want to live your best life? Our supplements are medically proven to help you do just that.
>> Make you feel better. Live better. BE better.
>> BE there for your family, your partner, your kids, YOURSELF!

Last night, she'd been playing with different words. Maz's Marvellous Medicinals. Mind-blowing. Stunning Supplements. Super Supplements. Vital Vitamins. Vitality. Vim—was that retro-cool yet or still a cleaning product? Vivacious! Vibrant. Dynamic. Awesome. Maz had felt awesome at the thought of helping others.

'This is amazing, Maz. So professional.'

'Thanks. The one thing I can't decide on is a name.'

Luke read through the page again and then looked up at her. 'Antidotes for a better life,' he announced. 'That's what you should call it: Bio-Antidotes.'

'Oh my God, *yes*! Bio-Antidotes,' she repeated. 'That's perfect. I love it! Does Gracie take any supplements?'

'My wife was into all that but I haven't had time to follow up. Do you think . . .' Luke tapped his fork against the empty salad bowl. 'Could you look into supplements to boost Gracie's immune system?'

Wow—he was asking for *her* help.

'I'll do some research and get back to you tomorrow,' she promised.

'Obviously I'll check with Dr Rawson. I wouldn't give anything to Gracie without his approval.'

Among all those herbal solutions online, Maz knew she could find something to help Gracie live her best life.

Maz floated through the next class, assessing the punters not for their correct posture but for their potential as clients of her supplements business. If she started immediately, she could make some money for her birthday party. And after that, the sky was the limit. Between the online program and the supplements, Maz could create an income stream to make her rich. She'd buy a new car. So many of her friends had brand-new cars—Em-Jay even had a red Mini with white stripes. Super cool! Some of them mocked Maz's thirteen-year-old Barina but she refused to go into debt; she'd earn the money first. As much as Maz loved her parents, she would never, ever end up like them. She planned to be slim and trim, healthy and wealthy.

___

Over dinner, Maz outlined the diet and exercise program to her parents. They stared at her with tired resignation. She had to fire them up.

'Let's set some targets—twenty kilos for you, Dad, and fifteen for you, Mum.'

'Okay, love, we'll do our best,' Mum said. 'I know we need to lose it.'

'The program begins now,' Maz instructed. 'Fruit for dessert. And then we'll do a short walk.'

'You're a tyrant. Are you sure we're not being filmed for *The Biggest Loser*?' Mum laughed and held her arms out for a cuddle. Maz felt the heavy breasts and podgy tummy against her own body. Soon, that would all be gone.

After the walk, which had been at the slowest pace ever due to Dad's sore knees, Maz curled up on her bed with the laptop. Searching for 'cure for cancer' brought up three hundred million results. She refined it to 'supplements—immunity—chemotherapy' and that showed two million results.

Maz clicked on a random entry and then another. It was a bit confusing. Despite being natural, some of the supplements seemed to interact with the cancer drugs. Mushrooms could increase the risk of bleeding, while green tea could decrease the effect of some chemo. Green tea?! And she'd thought green tea had so many health benefits.

On another website, she found an article warning against echinacea, valerian root and garlic. Honestly, garlic? In the next click, there was a list of supplements you should take instead. But hadn't someone else said not to take those?

Cat's claw—that was the sort of thing Gracie needed; a wild cat scratching and fighting against the disease. Maz read some of the reviews under the product list.

—*I've been taking it for three years. All my symptoms have gone away! The doctors can't believe it.* (Sally-Anne, Washington State)

—*Be careful. I took this for four weeks and it made me sicker.* (Miguel, Taiwan)

Hmm, it seemed to work for some people but not for others.

Another page brought up mushrooms with cool names like Turkey Tail and Lion's Mane; they contained immune-boosting polysaccharopeptides. That sounded impressive. Would Luke know what that meant?

Miracle Chinese cancer cure! screamed the headline on the next website. That was fifteen years ago, so obviously it hadn't cured cancer. Another click and she discovered a traditional Chinese formula of sixteen herbs to stop the spread of cancer cells. Unlike other pages, this website had sensible subheadings and detailed diagrams. She read it over and sent the link to Luke. *I think this Detox for Cancer would be good. Do you want to show it to Gracie's doctors? I can order it if they approve.*

Maz imagined being the one to cure Gracie. Not the specialist in the Sydney hospital, nor the experimental treatment over in America, but ordinary Maz from the 'burbs, doing her research on supplements and heathy eating and beating cancer with natural goodness. Gracie would thrive, Maz's business would go viral, and Luke would become a partner in her online program.

She could save Gracie when she hadn't been able to save Joseph.

If she told Mum and Dad, they'd say it was a pipe dream. They were old school—thought that only doctors had the answers. And pharmaceutical companies. They believed everything they heard on the TV news but they didn't see the other sources—those amazing stories on Facebook and the web. Her parents didn't realise you could look outside the box, set up a new system, create your own destiny.

Maz loved the word *destiny*. Becoming what you were meant to be. Achieving your potential. That one word said it all.

That night, Maz dreamt her Bio-Antidotes saved Gracie's life.

8

ALLISON

'WHEN ARE YOU GONNA DIE?'

Allison spun around to see Zack in the reading corner, his face screwed up as he asked the question. Instead of answering, Gracie threw a puzzle piece at him. As Allison rushed over to intervene, she wondered if the story this morning had set him off. In circle time, she'd read them a book about being sick.

'Zack, that's not kind.'

She shepherded them both back to their tables and clapped her hands for the attention of the whole class.

'Okay, Wombats. We're going to do a drawing of our—'
She was about to say *house* when her gaze fell on Gracie. Her house had been burnt to the ground. And she couldn't say *family* because Gracie's family had also been wrecked.

'A drawing of our . . .'
—*our bedroom . . .*
—*our pet . . .*
—*our favourite toy . . .*
With every option, Allison saw the TV images: firefighters in helmets and visors; blackened cars; koalas drinking from

water bottles; a discarded doll, bright and colourful in the grey ashes. Gracie had been in the midst of all that. The small town of Hythorne had flashed across their television screens in late October. Farms and livestock destroyed, half the main street gone, four lives lost, dozens more injured. Unlike the bushfires in July and November, which had been ignited by lightning strikes, Hythorne's was deliberately lit. An arsonist in the forest on the edge of town. Gracie's mother had been trying to release the horses from the stables when the fire hit. She'd spent five days unconscious in hospital before succumbing. An unbearably awful death. And her heroic efforts were for nothing. Not one of the horses had survived.

'Can I draw my dog?' Zack called out.

'I don't have a dog,' whined Evelyn.

'I want a puppy called Marmalade,' Gracie announced.

Rubbing her temples, Allison blinked at the expectant little faces, all waiting for Mrs Walsh to make a decision. Gracie didn't seem distressed. The lesson plan was about location— the child's house discussed in relation to the school, the oval, the shopping centre and so on.

Allison made a decision.

'A drawing of where we live right now.'

She'd been considering the idea for two weeks. Mulled it over during the long nights while listening to the strange noises echoing through her empty house. But it was only at this moment, in the middle of the lesson, that Allison fully made up her mind.

After school, Allison collared Luke by the playground, asking Zack's mum to keep an eye on Gracie while they moved out of earshot. She didn't want an audience for this discussion; Zack or his mum would probably sell the information online. Last Friday, Zack had taken Winnie the Wombat home, along with the exercise book to detail her adventures over the weekend. The book had come back to school with a list of objects for sale—a PlayStation, an iPad, a gold necklace. Zack stood at the front of the class, asking if anyone wanted to buy them. An entrepreneurial five-year-old; she'd have to speak to his mother if it happened again.

Allison made the offer to Luke as casually as possible. 'Now that Gracie has started chemo, do you want to stay at my house? Just to get away from the holiday flats while you're looking for somewhere else to live.'

When Luke didn't say anything, she kept talking.

'I've often had people to stay in the past, including another family from school. My ex-husband will be fine with it.' She took a breath. 'My house needs a family—and you need a house. Sometimes the universe brings people together for a reason.'

She didn't believe in that destiny crap but it was useful to spout. Would Luke accept or had she made an absolute fool of herself?

'This is the best day.' A genuine smile spread across his face. 'Dr Rawson called to say Gracie has been accepted on the Chicago trial and now this . . . I'll check with Gracie but I'm sure she'll say yes. You're incredible, Mrs Walsh!'

'You'd better call me Allison.'

Allison hadn't only lied about the destiny crap. Tony would *not* be fine; he'd be furious. But for once, she was taking control. Enough of her life being dictated by him. Tony couldn't sell the house with a sick girl living inside it.

When they arrived after lunch on Sunday, the house was tidy and the pool blue. Not quite sparkling but definitely not green. Allison had to stop herself from snapping a photo and sending it to Tony.

Luke brought their suitcases up to the spare bedroom— now his room. Three suitcases. All their possessions. Staring at those bags, Allison knew she'd made the right decision, even if it had been partly for selfish reasons.

Upstairs in the smallest bedroom, which Felix had used as a music studio, Gracie darted from the toy box to the bookshelf to the wardrobe. On Thursday night, Allison and Nadia had been on a shopping spree for the four-year-old. They'd packed the toy box with dolls, dressing-up clothes and hand-me-downs from Nadia's daughters.

'Look, Daddy,' the little girl cried. 'A special room all for me!'

Her father picked her up and held her high above his head.

'Put your arms out, Ms Gracie Branson, we're coming in to land,' he instructed as she made aeroplane noises. 'Flight Seven to Wirriga Airport, are we safe to land on Gracie's new bed?'

Zooming through the air, Gracie screeched in delight. Luke flew her downwards and gently deposited her on top of the pink polka dot doona. Then he blew a raspberry on her tummy. The giggles echoed around Allison, bouncing off the walls, banishing the months of silence.

For dinner, Allison had prepared spaghetti bolognaise, hoping Gracie would like it as much as her own son did. She offered Luke a glass of red wine, desperate for one herself. It was as if the house had forgotten how to hold a man in its four walls: his deep laugh was too loud in the kitchen, his footsteps echoed in the hall, his fingers tapped up the bannister. By contrast, Gracie's sounds were soft and delightful, rising to the ceiling and hovering above them, scattering happiness like fairy dust.

But Shona had had a point when she'd called Allison 'a fecking kind-hearted bampot' for taking in a student and her father. Section twenty-one of the Department's Code of Conduct talked about a teacher's duty of care and Allison was doing her best to care for the motherless child, but section twenty-two warned against forming personal relationships. What else was she supposed to do though? The girl couldn't stay in those flats at Manly while they waited to find something more suitable. It was only for a few weeks, and she'd discussed it with the principal. Declan understood—his wife had been through surgery and chemo for breast cancer. He'd also suggested holding a school fundraiser to help Gracie pay for the treatment in Chicago, with Luke's permission, of course.

The act of cooking a family dinner made Allison feel useful again. Luke set the table and poured the wine. They toasted to Gracie being accepted onto the trial.

'Is there anything you or Gracie don't eat?' Allison asked.

'Fried food. Lollies. Sugar. Not a lot of meat.' He grinned. 'She'd say it's all the best stuff!'

The foods that Allison loved. Maybe she'd lose weight over the next few weeks.

'Is Gracie allowed ice-cream as a special treat?'

Allison crossed her fingers behind her back, hoping that she could share her favourite indulgence with this gorgeous girl.

'Just tonight. We usually have sugar-free sorbet.'

Gracie had tuned into their conversation. Now she rocked up and down on the balls of her feet. 'I *love* ice-cream.'

Tony and Felix also loved ice-cream. Felix could eat a whole tub for afternoon tea. Why the hell wasn't Felix here, sitting at the dinner table tonight? He had said he'd come and meet Luke and Gracie. Tony, the hypocrite, had demanded to know who, exactly, would be living in *his* house. He'd been forced to calm down when he discovered it was the girl with cancer. 'I'm not charging them rent,' Allison told him. 'They need their money for life-saving treatment.' Now, she cupped her hands around the ice-cream container to cool her rage.

'Sometimes I get ice-cream at the hop-i-tal,' Gracie said.

This girl was too young to go to hospital—she couldn't even say the word properly. Allison's rage changed course and crashed around Gracie's shoulders; those tiny shoulders which carried the burden of a terrible disease. Allison reached over to hug the poor girl; she'd do everything she could to help her. Gracie should know that she was loved.

⇌

They quickly settled into a routine. Allison took Gracie to school with her on Monday, Tuesday and Wednesday so Luke could teach early classes at the gym. On Friday, Luke and Gracie went to the children's hospital, and on Saturday the girl had a quiet recovery day.

Luke stuck a chart on Gracie's wardrobe. Not a star chart for good behaviour but a smiley face for each bowel movement. He put Gracie's drugs in the high cupboard above the fridge with the paracetamol and cold-and-flu tablets. Allison stared at the assortment of bottles and packets. The steroids, anti-nausea drugs, laxatives, antibiotics—all of them keeping Gracie going. For now.

At night, as Allison listened to different noises, she was so grateful to Luke for moving in. She no longer heard the squealing bats and her own heart hammering. Instead there were footsteps on the landing. The toilet flushing in the main bathroom. The soft conversations of a video playing on his laptop . . .

A piercing scream at one o'clock in the morning.

Allison was bolt upright before her consciousness had properly understood the threat. She reached out to turn on the bedside lamp, heart thudding, her forearms pricked with goosebumps. Where had she put her mobile? Shit, downstairs in her handbag. The *Northern Beaches News* had reported another break-in last week—although that robbery hadn't been successful; they'd tried to force the lock on the back door of the gym where Luke worked.

The house was heavy with silence. Perhaps she'd dreamt it, her body reacting to nightmarish thoughts.

Waiting for her heart rate to slow down, she heard another sound: a shriek from outside the window.

A bat. Definitely. She knew those noises. Shrieking and chirping and soft clicks. *Go back to sleep*, she told herself.

She hadn't seen the green sedan since Luke had moved in. Wondered if it had been an opportunistic real estate agent.

The screech came again, reverberating off the corners of her bedroom. A scream loud enough to wake her deaf neighbour.

Before she could stop to think, Allison was running down the hallway. The door to the little bedroom had been pushed open. Racing into the darkness, she was suddenly blinded as light flooded the room.

Curled up in a ball on her bed, her whole body shaking, Gracie alternated between screaming and sobbing. Luke had switched on the lamp; his arms were wrapped around his daughter.

'It was just a nightmare, honey.' He soothed. 'I'm here now. You're safe.'

Allison perched on the other side of the bed and patted Gracie's back.

'I'm here, too, Gracie. It's okay.'

As the girl quietened down, Allison started singing softly. *'Five little monkeys jumping on the bed. One fell off and hit his head.'*

It was the first song that came to mind. She'd been teaching it to them in class with hand signals to help them count backwards. By the time she got to number two, Gracie joined in the last line.

'No more monkeys jumping on the bed.'

'Silly monkeys,' Luke said.

'Can I sleep with you, Daddy?'

Luke lifted the little girl onto his waist and they disappeared into his room. Allison turned off the lamp and went back to her own bed. Gracie had slept so soundlessly for the past week that Allison had forgotten Luke's warning. He'd mentioned nightmares which had started after her mother's death. Allison wondered what terrible visions plagued the girl.

_____

The furious phone call from Tony came on a Wednesday afternoon.

'Jesus Christ, Allison. I thought you'd finally stopped now that you had the little girl living there. If you leave another note like that, I'm calling the police.'

Allison was sitting in the staffroom, writing out a lesson plan. She struggled to get her mind into gear.

'What're you talking about? I didn't leave a note.' She hadn't driven down to Curl Curl since Gracie and Luke had moved in. Occasionally, she still rang Tony's mobile, just in case the woman answered it, but uncovering her identity no longer seemed quite as urgent as it had a few weeks ago.

'Luckily I was the one who found it in the letterbox, not Felix or . . .' He stopped and sighed. 'Don't bother denying it. I can recognise your handwriting. Please don't threaten Helena like that.'

'I told you I didn't write it!' Allison snapped. 'Maybe *Helena* wrote it herself.'

'Now you're sounding truly crazy. Clearly you're not coping. You need to see a psychologist. And if it happens again, that's it—I'll involve the police.'

After hanging up on him, she glanced across at the four teachers chatting in the corner. Had they heard the heated exchange? After she'd interrogated Elena, they all knew about the marriage break-up. They'd given Allison their condolences and support—apart from Elena, who avoided her as much as possible. And now most of them knew Luke was staying with her for a few weeks. The other kindy teacher had pursed his lips and muttered: *That's a bad idea.* While Samantha from the front office winked and said: *He's a house guest who'll be easy on the eye.* But Allison wasn't into taut gym bodies; this was about helping Gracie and Luke. And having them in the house was helping with her own grief. Luke understood how life could take a sudden curve from green meadows into a dark forest of despair. As if she'd fancy him. Or any other man. More than two decades in bed with Tony, and she'd expected it to be forever.

Allison could handle the silly innuendo in the staffroom, but it would be another matter should any of the teachers discover she'd been watching Tony's house. And if the police got involved, would she lose her job? She hastily gathered up her papers, said goodbye to her colleagues and drove home.

As she entered the house, Luke had his backpack over his shoulder ready to go. Allison had forgotten that she'd promised to look after Gracie while he filled in for another instructor. Luckily, she'd made it back in time.

'Gracie's upstairs with Felix and Darcy,' Luke told her. 'They're showing her how to play the guitar.'

That was sweet of Felix. Her son didn't seem too put out by the visitors; he'd grown up having other people in the house. He talked to Luke about the gym and the best exercises to build his quads and his calves. He let Gracie play a simple game on the Xbox. The little sister he'd never had . . .

'We're going in the pool, Mum,' Felix called from upstairs.

Maybe Allison would have a swim herself later, after she'd debriefed with Nadia. Except that she couldn't. Her friend didn't know about the stalking so how could she tell her now about Tony's threat? Wandering outside, she watched Felix somersault into the pool. Gracie stood on the edge, giggling as the big splash hit her legs. Time for Allison to check the levels. The pool was like another child needing constant attention; if you neglected it for a day, it went feral.

Felix and Darcy rated each other on their somersaults then climbed out of the pool and padded towards the back door, towels hanging off their hips.

'Dry your legs,' Allison called to their receding figures. 'Don't go upstairs dripping wet.'

When she dangled the test strip in the water, Allison was pleased to see everything in balance. And the water temperature felt perfect for a swim.

After a quick dip with Gracie, she began preparing dinner. Chopping up the chicken for the stir-fry. Remembering to use the vegetable oil, not the sesame oil; Gracie's chemo drug had triggered allergies that she hadn't had before.

Darcy popped his head into the kitchen. 'Thanks for having me this arvo. I'm off now.'

'Lovely to see you, Darcy. Say hi to your mum.' Allison's farewell was automatic after all these years. Although Darcy's mother hadn't offered any support since Tony had left. Maybe that was a good thing. The boy's mother was extremely strict and judgemental—she'd have something to say about the marriage break-up. And an opinion on whose fault it was.

At the other end of the kitchen bench, Gracie hummed to herself, drawing a picture of a horse.

'Mummy's horse,' she said.

Allison glanced over and gave a quick smile. In her head, she was writing a note to Tony: *I'm going to keep the house and I can manage the pool. And I don't need you anyway. Luke's around far more than you ever were. He has domestic talents that you do not possess and he does all his own washing. And he cooks healthy food, not just barbecues.* Yes, she sounded petulant. No, she'd never send it. But just thinking the words made her feel better.

Staring out past Gracie into the backyard, Allison admired the pleasing colour of the pool. *Who needs you, Tony?* And then she noticed that the gate was partly open, caught on a pair of goggles. Allison rushed out to shut it. Even though she taught four-year-olds, having one in the house was an adjustment. She was used to teenagers at home.

When Luke returned from the gym, he poured Allison a glass of soda water and frowned at Gracie's pictures.

'Look! It's my cubbyhouse, Daddy. Remember?'

Another part of their life that had burnt to the ground.

Instead of answering, Luke began tickling Gracie's tummy. Her laughter filled the kitchen. A distraction from her dead mother.

'Two dads from school came to check out the gym this evening,' Luke told Gracie. 'Do you know Zack and Ty? Their daddies.'

'Ty's nice.'

'And Zack?'

Gracie pulled a face in reply.

'Is he mean to you?' Luke asked.

'It's okay,' Allison answered before Gracie could speak. 'He's an unusual boy but it's under control.'

When she called out for Felix to set the table, the only reply was the strumming of his guitar. Allison had to walk all the way upstairs, knock on his door, and wait for the song to finish. Just like she'd done last year, when they were a family.

'Please can you come down and lay the table?'

'All right,' Felix grumbled. 'You don't have to yell at me.'

Over dinner, though, he was chatty to Luke. He seemed to be at that age of gravitating away from women—away from his mother, at least. Presumably he didn't know about the letter. Tony wouldn't be so cruel as to tell him, would he?

Gracie was the first one to finish her dinner, hungry after the swim. Her cheeks were flushed. A healthy colour for a change. Or maybe sunburn. Shit, Allison had forgotten to put sunscreen on her this afternoon. Her skin was so sensitive.

In the kitchen, Luke was packing the dishwasher and putting everything away. (*See what I mean, Tony? Far more helpful than you.*) He picked up the soy sauce, the sweet chilli and the oil and turned to the cupboard. Stopped and stared at the label of one.

'Ally, did you put sesame oil in the stir-fry?'

'No, I used the vegetable oil.'

But the bottle in his hand was sesame. Oh God, how had that happened? She'd been too distracted by Tony's phone call and his threats. The note she'd been writing in her own head.

'I'm so sorry, Luke. I was . . . will she be all right?'

Was the redness in her face a reaction? How severe would it be?

Luke reached for his daughter, lifted her t-shirt and checked her torso. 'The hives are starting. Let's get to the hospital, honey.'

'I'll come with you.'

Luke spoke calmly to his daughter but the look he gave Allison was one of pure fear. Ignoring her offer, he took Gracie in his arms, grabbed his keys and disappeared out the front door. In seconds, Allison heard the deep throttle of the Jeep accelerating up the street.

What had she done?

9

ALLISON WAITED IN THE LOUNGE ROOM; THE TELEVISION SHOWED A wildlife documentary but she was too tense to concentrate. Felix sat with her, tapping away at his laptop. She guessed he was playing a game rather than doing his homework—she hadn't kept up with his assignments this term.

'I could've killed her.' Allison spoke aloud the words that were on repeat in her head.

'Gracie looked okay when they left,' her son tried to reassure her. 'I reckon Luke will ring soon.'

She'd taken them into her house to help them, and now she'd harmed Gracie. What sort of person was she? Vague. Irresponsible. Unreliable. Foolish. If Gracie had an anaphylactic reaction and died, she would never forgive herself.

'I was distracted because I had a horrible phone call from your father this afternoon,' she said.

'Seriously, Mum, you can't blame him for everything,' Felix said. 'You always tell me to take responsibility for my own actions.'

So much for the reassurance. A scolding from her own child. Allison probably deserved it. Why hadn't Luke rung? Forty minutes now. Gracie would have been treated straight away.

With shaking fingers, Allison pressed Luke's number. It went through to his messagebank.

'Just checking how Gracie is going,' Allison said. 'Sending her my love.'

Another twenty minutes of waiting and her phone finally rang.

'They've given her adrenaline.' Luke's voice was even deeper than usual, and gravelly. 'She's doing okay.'

Allison felt she could breathe normally for the first time since dinner. But would Luke forgive her tomorrow? Or would they move out?

—

At breakfast, Luke could barely look at her and Gracie was lethargic, dragging herself onto the stool and dribbling milk on her uniform.

'I'm so sorry about last night, sweetheart,' Allison said. 'How're you feeling?'

'Tired. But I got ice-cream at the hop-i-tal.'

'Lucky you!'

Allison turned away to pour a cup of coffee for Luke, chiding herself for her ridiculous response. She moved around Luke gingerly, apologising again, wondering if he would explode with anger.

'Can she go to school?' Allison asked. What she really meant was: *Do you still trust me?*

'The doctor said if she feels okay, she can go.'

'I'll take good care of her today. I'm so sorry. I'll do anything to make it up to you.'

Instead of the anger that Allison had expected, Luke began to cry.

'She has so much going on, and now this . . .'

Sitting on the couch last night, Allison had decided how she could make amends. She'd discussed the fundraising campaign with Luke before, but he seemed overwhelmed by the amount required—and instead he'd been focusing on getting Gracie through this last round of chemo. Meanwhile, Dr Rawson had started making arrangements for Gracie to fly to the States at the end of April. That was only six weeks away. Luke couldn't cover the costs and Gracie didn't qualify for Australia's medical overseas treatment program.

'Please let me set up a fundraising campaign for Gracie,' Allison said now. 'I'll start by donating a thousand dollars. How much do we need?'

Luke plucked a tissue from the box, blew his nose and walked over to the bin.

'Too much,' he muttered softly so that Gracie wouldn't hear. 'We don't have to pay for the trial drug but we have to pay for everything else.'

'Do you know how much exactly?'

Sighing, Luke took his laptop from his backpack and placed it on the kitchen bench. He brought up a spreadsheet that listed the cost of the flights, the doctors and the hospital time.

'Dr Rawson sent me through these figures. He reckons he can get some funding from the hospital, and I've talked to the bank about borrowing twenty thousand. So, I think we're short a hundred and forty thousand dollars.' His shoulders sagged. 'Do you really think we can do it?'

A hundred and forty thousand dollars—a huge amount but Allison was relieved Luke had finally accepted that fundraising was Gracie's best hope. Relieved, too, they weren't talking about Gracie's allergic reaction anymore.

'Yes.' Allison spoke more confidently than she felt. 'We live in such a supportive community.'

'Well, if you think it might work, we could try.' Luke glanced in Gracie's direction. 'Maz at the gym is good with online stuff. I could ask her to help too.'

When the little girl disappeared off to the bathroom, Luke opened a website showing researchers at Chicago North Hospital. He pointed to a photo of a dark-haired man wearing a purple tie.

'This is Dr Mercado—he's doing amazing work. Apparently, he has a daughter a few years older than Gracie who loves *Frozen* as much as she does. I think that's why he finally accepted her on the trial.'

Luke clicked through to another page of detailed medical information.

'The drug is called a checkpoint inhibitor and it'll stop the immune system from attacking healthy cells. There are some side effects but the worst ones are rare. It'll be a slow infusion, every third day. They've had some great results so far.'

Thank God, Luke seemed positive again and willing to let her help. Last night, she'd feared the worst—for Gracie and for herself.

─

That afternoon, Allison brought Gracie straight home after school. The girl refused to rest; she wanted a snack of Weet-Bix topped with Milo. Probably not on Luke's approved list but Gracie needed it for strength. Hopefully, the allergic reaction wouldn't stop her from having chemo tomorrow.

'Someone's here,' Gracie said as she spooned the chocolate sprinkles over her bowl.

Allison hadn't heard the knock. She darted down the hallway to the front door. She'd texted Nadia and Shona that morning about the fundraising campaign—perhaps they were coming to help. They all had to swing into action fast if they were to have any chance of achieving the goal.

Two police officers stood on the doormat, their black shoes obscuring the words *Welcome to our Home*. The man surveyed the second-floor windows, the woman stared directly at Allison. Her first thought was that Luke had reported her for child abuse.

In the lounge room, the officers perched on the edge of the couch.

'Mrs Walsh,' the policewoman began, 'your ex-husband has made a complaint about your behaviour. He claims that you've been harassing him and his family with phone calls and letters. Your car has been seen parked near their house. These incidents are considered stalking. It's a criminal offence and you could be charged under section thirteen of the Crimes Act, which covers domestic and personal violence.'

Tony. She hadn't believed he'd do it. He worked part-time at a women's shelter, he knew what dangerous people looked like, and now he was implying that *she* was dangerous. But Allison was nothing like them!

Stalking. Criminal offence. Crimes Act. She dropped her head into her hands, praying that Gracie couldn't hear from the kitchen, wishing the words—and the officers—away. She'd lose her job.

'If you do not stop harassing your ex-husband and his family,' the policeman added, 'you'll be served with an apprehended violence order.'

His family? I'm his family.

It was hardly harassment. She'd just watched their house sometimes; she'd never even seen anything. As for the phone calls and hang-ups—well, she was angry with Tony. *But I didn't write that letter.*

Was Tony doing it himself? To force her to sell the house? Surely he wouldn't stoop that low. Then again, she no longer recognised the man who had been her husband; she didn't know how low he would go.

~

On Friday afternoon, she came home to a group of five teen-agers slouched on the stools in her kitchen. Burger wrappers from McDonald's and soft-drink cups littered the benchtop. She greeted Darcy and his older sister. Felix introduced her to the two girls, friends of Darcy's sister. While Allison was pleased that Felix had come over, this was Gracie's chemo day. The little girl needed to rest.

As if her son could read her thoughts, he said, 'I told every-one about setting up the fundraising, Mum. What can we do to help?'

Allison hadn't expected assistance from the teenagers—well, not at this early stage. She'd told everyone in the staffroom today and they were supportive, especially Declan of course. And she kept remembering her promise: the first donation of one thousand dollars. The amount filled her with dread—she couldn't afford it—but it assuaged her guilt over the sesame oil.

'Maybe you could come up with a list of local shops and businesses that might want to donate products or sponsor Gracie?' Allison suggested.

Strange that they were all suddenly in her kitchen. Was Felix dating one of these older girls?

'Cool,' Darcy's sister said. 'We can do that.'

The girls picked up their phones and started tapping away. They all had the same white nail polish; Allison didn't know how they could type with those long fingernails. Teenage girls were a different breed. Would Gracie make it to this age, paint her nails and hang out with boys?

'I'll just go and say hi to Gracie and Luke. Have you seen them, Felix?'

'Nope. I haven't been upstairs.'

Gracie had set up her soft toys in groups on her bedroom floor. Luke lay on her bed, reading his laptop. When Allison walked in, Gracie jumped up for a cuddle.

'I got a red frog at the hop-i-tal today!'

Thankfully, the allergic reaction hadn't interrupted her chemo routine.

'How're you feeling, sweetheart?'

'Good! My toys are going to school and I'm the teacher. My name's Mrs Walsh.'

Playing school was one of Gracie's favourite games. The toys had to sit to attention while she pretended to read a story or write on the blackboard. This was the first time she'd called herself Mrs Walsh. Allison took it as a sign that she'd been forgiven.

When she went back down to the kitchen, the teenagers, including Felix, had disappeared. They'd left a list of Wirriga businesses with lovehearts and flowers scrawled around the edges.

Luke prepared a vegetable bake for dinner. Her determination to start the fundraiser seemed to have helped in the aftermath of the allergic reaction; they had a shared goal now.

Allison pushed the green bits around her dinner plate and forked up the potato.

'Not keen on veggies, Ally?'

He said it with a smile. Luke was the only person who called her Ally. *I haven't been called Ally since I was eleven years old,* she'd said when he first used the nickname. *I reinvented myself as Allison when I started high school.* But he insisted she looked like an Ally. She liked it. Another makeover, like her haircut.

'Mashed potato and peas are nice,' she said.

She'd managed to hide her dislike of vegetables for the past two weeks. Allison taught the food groups to her class, encouraged the kids to have their daily serve, and then avoided green veggies as much as possible.

After dinner, as she was packing the dishwasher, Luke hovered near the fridge. He'd already set Gracie up with a movie—not *Frozen*, for a change—and was about to join her in the lounge room.

'Ally, I don't know how to say this . . .'

Oh God, were they going to move out after all? He hadn't really forgiven her. Last week, he'd shown her an apartment on the edge of Wirriga and she'd told him to stop searching for a place. To stay until after the clinical trial. To save his rent money for Gracie's treatment.

Would she be rejected—and alone—again? She deserved it after what she'd done.

'What is it?'

'I think Felix is taking money from my wallet.' Luke looked directly at her and his eyes seemed sadder than ever. 'I didn't tell you on Wednesday, but it happened again tonight.'

Allison had been pleased to see Felix and his friends in the kitchen this afternoon. Just like old times. She'd thought her son wanted to be home. Had he simply come to steal?

'How much is missing?' she asked.

'Fifty dollars on Wednesday, fifty today.'

'I'm so sorry. Let me repay you and I'll speak to Felix.'

'I didn't mean to upset you, Ally. I'm only telling you in case he's in trouble.'

Allison kept her handbag in a nook by the home phone. Oh, the irony—here she was trying to raise money for Luke while her son was stealing from him. Opening her purse, she expected to see two hundred dollars that she'd taken out of the ATM yesterday. Only a hundred remained. She was sure she hadn't spent any.

Holding out the notes for Luke, she waved away his refusal.

Felix had never taken money before. But now she had to track down her son and find out what the hell was going on.

10

MAZ

IN THE GYM CAR PARK AS THE SUN WAS NUDGING WIRRIGA AWAKE ON
Friday morning, Maz handed a small blue carrier bag to a
client. Laurel was immaculate in a pin-striped skirt and jacket,
her straight hair perfectly clipped, not a single bead of sweat
on her face despite coming out of Maz's class twenty minutes
before. Dropping the paper bag into her leather briefcase, she
gave Maz eighty dollars in return. Eighty dollars! For one container of pills.

'Thanks, Maz. I'd better get going, otherwise I'll hit peak
hour on the bridge.' Laurel straightened her lapel. 'This is our
secret, right? I don't want the rest of the gym knowing.'

The woman smiled and placed the briefcase on the back seat
of her gold BMW. Revved the engine a few times, grinned at
Maz, and shot out of the car park. Laurel was slim and toned
and tanned. They'd been talking after class last week and Maz
had mentioned her Bio-Antidotes. Laurel was keen to try the
appetite suppressant: 'I'd love a little extra assistance to keep
off the weight. If I so much as look at a hamburger, I swear it
jumps onto my thighs.' Maz told her the research online had
been extremely positive.

Be brave. Live your best life. Just do it. Maz was living up to the tagline on her own website.

Seven other clients had bought supplements too; Maz had made six hundred and twenty dollars so far. Well, not exactly 'made'—that was turnover. After costs, she had a hundred and thirty dollars in profit. A good margin for simply ordering stuff online. Profit, margin, costs, turnover—she'd be an entrepreneur yet. And she was doing *good*, helping her clients to become their best selves!

And she was helping Gracie too.

After Luke had told her about the plan for Gracie's fundraising yesterday, she'd researched marketing techniques and copied ideas from a few other campaigns before setting up a website. Desperate to show him, Maz asked Luke to drop by on the way home from the hospital.

When he texted to say he was in the car park, she rushed out. Gracie, half asleep after her chemo, smiled at Maz then closed her eyes again.

'Here it is!' Maz said, passing her laptop in through the window of the Jeep. Luke balanced it against the steering wheel. He started reading out loud. An emotional plea. They'd agreed on the wording late last night by email.

Gracie Branson is fun and bubbly and four years old. She loves to tell dinosaur jokes, dress up as Princess Elsa, sing at the top of her voice, and play fairytale games.

We need to create a fairytale for Gracie.

She has a very rare cancer, thymic carcinoma. While Gracie has had wonderful treatment in Australia, she now needs a drug that is only available in America.

Please join Gracie's Gang and help us raise $140,000 to fly her to America for an immunotherapy trial in April.

By going through all the design options on the website builder, Maz had figured out how to create a countdown graphic, just like they had on the professional fundraising sites. They'd discussed whether to use a fundraising page, like GoFundMe or MyCause, or whether to set up their own website. Maz had pushed for their own website so they could add photos, blogs and videos and as much info as they wanted.

'It looks awesome,' Luke said. 'I can't believe you created it so fast.'

A warm glow enveloped her whole body. She pointed at the online calendar so he wouldn't stare at her flushed face.

'Well, we don't have long. We have to get moving.'

The calendar showed the time to target—40 DAYS!

'What did we decide about joining Gracie's Gang?' he asked.

'Everyone can be part of Gracie's Gang, but if you donate over two hundred dollars, you get a purple bracelet. I'll start making them with Gracie on the weekend.'

They'd discussed this issue for too long last night—the schoolteacher had been in the background of Luke's call and she kept disagreeing that two hundred was too much. But they needed to make a hundred and forty thousand dollars; that was a lot of donations.

'And for kids?'

'We agreed they just had to donate ten dollars.'

Luke looked from the website back to Maz. He had tears in his eyes.

'You're amazing, Maz.'

When she finished her next class, Nico was waiting at the studio door with a high school boy. They'd had a big group of teenage mates join up at the end of last year. Nico was pleased to get some new blood in the door.

'Maz, can you talk to this young fella for a minute?' he asked. 'He wants to know about courses.'

Only a few years ago, Maz had been the person asking for advice.

She explained the different paths and gushed about the college she'd attended. 'It's a fantastic career,' she told the teenager. 'And there's always work. You'll never be out of a job.'

Not like Dad. She'd seen what eighteen months of unemployment had done to him back when Maz was in year nine. Worn away his self-belief. Made him ashamed. That was when Mum had got him to join the choir—singing to keep his spirits up. They'd survived on Mum's salary for a bit and Dad had finally got a job night-stacking at Woolworths. But the cash didn't stretch very far. Maz and Kelli's tiny pay packets from Maccas only covered a few essentials. When notes were sent home for year nine camp, Mum offered to talk to the teacher but Maz wouldn't let her. 'I don't want the whole school knowing our business.' Some classmates would be kind, others would not. She made Mum write a letter saying that Maz couldn't go due to health reasons.

Then, in the months leading up to the year ten formal, her group went dress shopping, arranged hairstyles and spray tans and fake eyelashes. Maz played along, even trying on a gold dress that sparkled when she moved. None of them knew she hadn't paid for a ticket. Couldn't. On the morning of the formal, she said she had gastro—a bad prawn was making her throw up (as if they were eating prawns on their budget). That night, she lay in her bed, her eyes glued to Insta—the outfits, the limo, a boat on Sydney Harbour, the dance moves. Who kissed who in the corner. The after-party. The sneaky drinks. The fun. She hadn't told her parents—they'd have insisted she use her Maccas money on a ticket instead of tampons and toiletries. That would just create extra strain. The weekly mortgage repayments loomed over their heads like the French guillotine, which she'd been studying in history.

When Dad got a new job, their money worries eventually settled down. But they didn't emerge unscathed. Dad had stacked on the weight and drank more than ever. Mum's snapping point came much faster than before. Kelli left school and went straight into a full-time job. Maz found the gym, vowed never to eat another bite of McDonald's and never to be in that position again.

⌒

After lunch, Maz showed the fundraising site to Nico.

'What do you think?'

'It's bloody brilliant!' Nico declared. 'Gracie's a brave kid and she's part of our gym family. Let's get the gym involved.'

'Awesome. I could make some posters to stick on the walls.'

'Good idea. Get the instructors talking it up to their classes. I'll match every dollar donated.'

'Why don't we get a little gym uniform for Gracie?' Maz suggested. 'Could they print one in her size?'

'Yeah. We could take a photo of her in the outfit and put it on the poster.'

'Now that would be super cute!'

In one corner of the weights room, the teenagers were laughing, mucking around with the dumbbells, and eyeing off the woman on the lat pulldown. They'd dropped their drink bottles on the floor and draped their towels over the leg press and the rowing machine.

'Hey, guys, how're you doing?' Maz asked. 'Do you need any help with the equipment?'

'Yeah, nah. We're good.'

She wanted to tell them to tidy up, in the nicest possible way. Without sounding like a schoolteacher. When she first joined as a teenager, it had taken months for her to feel welcome with all the adults and gym junkies around.

'Can I give you a few tips on the leg press?' Maz beamed her thousand-kilowatt smile. 'It can really work your glutes, quads and hammies. And at home you can follow it up with squats.'

As Maz showed them the correct technique, she mentioned the best spot for their water bottles and towels. Each of the boys had a turn and Maz assessed their movements.

'Great. Make sure you feel comfortable at that level before taking the weights any heavier.'

'Is this the best way to bulk up our thighs?' asked the skinniest guy.

'It's a good option.'

Maz was about to leave when she noticed two boys elbowing each other.

'You ask,' one of them whispered.

'What else can I help you with?'

'We heard that there are some—' the boy looked at his friend for support '—supplements you can take to build muscle. Do you know what sort we should buy?'

'I can certainly assist you with that.'

More clients. Awesome. These guys could live their best lives too.

11

ALLISON

ALLISON CALLED FELIX, LEFT A MESSAGE, THEN TEXTED HIM. AN HOUR later he still hadn't answered. Before, she would've discussed her approach with Tony. She couldn't ask Luke for advice—he was the one from whom Felix had stolen.

Nine-thirty p.m. She left Luke watching TV and went to her bedroom to try again. If Felix didn't answer this time, Allison would call Tony and demand that her son speak to her. She listened to the ringing tone and was about to hang up when Felix's voice came down the line.

'Hi, Mum, what's up? I'm at Darcy's house, playing *FIFA*.'

He sounded happy, light-hearted. Perhaps too happy. Had he used the stolen cash for booze or weed?

'Which team are you?'

'Chelsea.' His reply was quick enough to back up his story. The cheers from the PlayStation game rumbled in the background.

'Are you winning?'

'Nah. Darcy's beating me again.'

She decided not to accuse him straight off; that would've been Tony's method. Her way was gentler.

'Listen, Felix. If you need money, you can ask me.'

He was silent for a few seconds then said, 'What're you on about?'

'There's some cash missing. A hundred dollars from Luke's wallet.'

'And he reckons I took it?'

'It happened on the nights you were here. Money has gone from my purse too.'

'So you're both blaming me?'

'I'm trying to understand . . .' She paused for a moment. 'What's going on?'

'Nothing! As if I'd steal from you. You give me money whenever I ask for it.'

He had a point. For years, she'd tried to establish a weekly pocket money routine but then she'd invariably forget. And so, she gave him cash when he needed it. He never wanted much. Since he'd been living with Tony, he hadn't asked her for anything, apart from the shoes.

And Wednesday night was when Gracie had gone to hospital. In the panic, Luke could easily have forgotten that he'd spent fifty dollars somewhere. But then, money was also taken on Friday. And from her purse as well.

'Please, Felix, talk to me. What's going on?'

'I am talking to you. Thanks for the vote of confidence, Mum.'

Allison didn't know what to think. Felix sounded hurt but that could just be an act. Despite saying all the right things, her son was communicating less and less.

'You know you can tell me anything, sweetheart.'

'Sure. Well, I'll tell you this. Helena has a seven-month-old baby.'

'What?' She felt like she'd been slapped. 'Are you joking?'

Was this why Tony had been so secretive? Because he'd fathered a child while still married to Allison? She gagged briefly as bile flooded into her mouth.

'Nope. Not a joke.' Felix gave a strange chuckle.

'I don't understand.'

'I have to go. Darcy's mum is calling us.'

The phone went dead. She stared at the screen, as if the answer were there.

When Allison came downstairs to the lounge room, Luke lay slumped on the couch, a beer in one hand. He didn't normally drink the night before an early class. She couldn't tell him about the baby, couldn't process it herself. Had Tony been cheating on her for years? The revelation had shocked her to a standstill. She couldn't text Tony, she couldn't phone Shona, she couldn't discuss it with Nadia.

She'd focus on Luke right now.

'Felix denies taking the money but I'll keep talking to him. I'm really sorry.'

When Luke didn't answer, she asked if he was okay.

'I didn't want to tell Gracie.' He stared out of the window as he spoke. 'It's her mother's birthday today. Sarah would've turned twenty-nine.'

The same week that Allison had poisoned his daughter. What a week for him.

'I'm so sorry. How did you celebrate her birthday last year?' Allison hoped it was a good memory.

'I cooked her breakfast—scrambled eggs and smoked salmon. Then Gracie and I took her outside, made her cover her eyes and we led her into the back paddock. I'd bought a new horse for her. Sarah was so surprised that she screamed like she'd been bitten by a snake. Of course, the horse bolted in fright.' A sad smile fluttered on his lips.

'What did she name it?' Allison asked.

'She let Gracie come up with a name. That was a mistake. She called him Olaf.'

The snowman from *Frozen*. Allison couldn't help but laugh.

'I really miss her.' He said it so softly that she almost didn't hear. Then he groaned and took a swig of beer. 'But enough of my memories. Grab a wine and tell me more about Tony.'

She guessed he wanted to be distracted. The most awkward timing, though, after Felix's news.

Allison poured a glass of red and began the story at the beginning of the end.

'When he was young, Tony wanted to change the world but he ended up in a big corporate firm. Then, a few years ago, he had a midlife crisis. He didn't dream of a silver convertible like most men—he wanted to do work that made a difference.'

As a teacher, Allison had understood. Her work helped to shape minds and futures; she was happy for Tony to gain that same sense of purpose in his career.

'He went part-time at the firm and started providing legal advice to women experiencing domestic violence. He works with a few different shelters and refuges across Sydney.'

'You're making him sound like a saint, Ally. So what happened?'

At the time, Allison had boasted to friends about her compassionate husband contributing in such a vital area. Now she glanced up at the wall above the dining table, the spot where their wedding photo had once hung. Replaced by a print of Monet waterlilies. The framed photo showing their radiant smiles was hidden in Tony's side of the wardrobe.

'He couldn't tell me about his work—it was all confidential, obviously. But I think something happened. He got disillusioned with the whole system. I didn't even notice. I'd finally started writing a children's book in my spare time.'

'And then?' Luke prompted her.

'Out of the blue, he said he had to leave our marriage. Change his life and make it more meaningful. He wouldn't tell me the woman's name. Or anything else.'

Like the fact that she had a baby. A boy or a girl? Did it look like Tony? Did it have his nose? His eyes?

Mere hours after singing 'Auld Lang Syne' on New Year's Eve, Tony had blurted out that he was in love with someone else. Allison had been unzipping her red dress, ready to climb into bed and make drunken love to celebrate the new year. What he said was so unexpected, she'd laughed. With the champagne fizzing around in her brain, it felt like some kind of strange foreplay. And then he'd collapsed into tears. Stupidly, Allison had comforted him.

She didn't know that he'd already signed a lease on a house near the beach. Two days later, he was gone. Her son had followed not long after. It was supposed to be for one night, but Felix only came back to collect more stuff. His soccer ball, clothes, bedding. A slow dismantling of their house, their life. The life that Tony apparently considered meaningless.

But it all made so much more sense with a baby. How had Felix kept the secret this long?

Allison blinked to see Luke sitting up straighter on the couch.

'Listen, Ally, that's shit. You're doing so much for everyone else and you're working on the fundraising for Gracie. And I know you're cut up about what happened with the sesame oil. Let me take you out tomorrow night.'

Luke organised for Maz and her mother to babysit Gracie, while they went to an African restaurant in Neutral Bay. Before dinner, he said they weren't to talk about fundraising and drug treatments. Instead, he explained the dishes on the menu and described a truck trip he and Sarah had done through eastern Africa. They'd camped near the gorillas in Uganda and climbed Mount Kilimanjaro in Tanzania. Over the lamb tagine, he brought up Tony.

'You know that Tony's a different person now,' Luke said. 'He's not the man you married.'

'Damn right. The man I married would never have left me like that.'

Nor would he have lied about a baby.

'So, in a way, the Tony you know has died.'

'Exactly.'

That was *exactly* how she felt. Her old friends were kind and comforting but all still married. Luke understood, even though his loss was a completely different set of circumstances.

'It's time for a psychological turning point. We're going to the pub and you're going to flirt with a man. Just think of it as a play with actors. Enjoy it. Take it all the way, if you want!'

Allison choked on her couscous. 'Are you kidding me? I can't do that.'

'I'll be your wingman. You're Maverick and I'm Goose.'

'Oh God, I saw *Top Gun* with my very first boyfriend.' Allison suspected it was the last time she'd flirted with a bloke other than Tony.

'Just smile and be yourself, Ally. You're gorgeous.'

She blushed and laughed. Wished she'd worn a different outfit, styled her hair properly.

They finished their dinner and walked up the road to the pub. When Luke opened the door, the sound of music and chatter wafted out; the sound of people having fun. She couldn't remember the last time she'd been here. Years ago with Tony and their friends, sitting out in the beer garden, idling away a few hours in the summer. Was Tony cheating on her then? Tonight, garlands of shamrocks hung around the walls; they were still celebrating Saint Patrick's Day from earlier in the week.

'You can have any guy you want.' Luke waved his arms, as if offering a smorgasbord.

Allison gazed around the pub. So many men. Some of them drunk and ludicrous in green hats and green sunglasses. Did they have wives at home who were putting the kids to bed? Or were they separated, like her? The discarded or the discardee?

'No, I can't.'

'You're thinking too much.' Luke propelled her towards the bar. 'It's a game. Use a different name if you like. I'm your colleague from work.'

As they drank wine, Allison made up an entire story—they worked together in a marketing company. Her name was Ruth and she'd divorced her husband ten years ago; she loved to go out to the theatre, pubs, film festivals. A party girl. Ruth was just back from a product launch for a coconut-based spirit in Byron. Cocktails all the way.

When Luke returned from getting the next round, he was accompanied by a man in his late forties.

'Ruth, this is Emmanuel.'

'Happy Saint Patrick's Day, Ruth,' the man said, raising his glass and attempting an Irish accent.

Emmanuel wore a pink-and-white-striped shirt, and no silly green hat. His jet-black hair had a slight curl, and he was taller and broader than Tony. And unlike Tony, Emmanuel was interested in everything Allison had to say. So interested that Allison started to feel guilty about the lies she was telling.

After four drinks, she confessed. 'I'm not Ruth. My name's Allison and my husband left me. My friend Luke thinks I need a shag to move on.'

Emmanuel didn't turn away. He blinked twice and then laughed so hard that beer shot out of his mouth straight onto Allison's dress. His look of horror sent Allison into a fit of giggles.

Eventually, when they'd both calmed down, he said, 'Well, you'd better come back to my place so I can clean that off.'

Giggling again, Allison was drunk enough to accept. And excited and terrified. As they walked arm in arm to his apartment, Allison argued with herself. *Go home right now. You never do anything this crazy. Apart from the stalking—that's crazy. No, this is crazy. It could be fun, though. It's okay—Luke knows where you are. But you're a married woman, you made vows. Yeah, but he's left you. And there's a baby.* The baby that Allison had always wanted.

When Emmanuel started kissing her, she decided to go with the flow. The sex was tender and sweet and strange. And somehow, she relaxed just enough to enjoy it.

On the way home in the Uber, she texted Luke: *Maverick to Goose—mission accomplished*. His reply came straight back: *Victory! Your wingman is so proud*. And then, giddy as a cherry-popped teenager, she typed out a message to Nadia: *OMG—you'll never guess what I've just done! My first-ever one-night stand!!!!!*

———

The next morning, the wine and the bravado were replaced by revulsion. She felt like she'd cheated on Tony. How absurd. How could *she* be cheating on her deceitful, disloyal, heart-breaker of a husband? How come he got to choose their new lives and she had no control? She didn't want to shag a stranger with thick springy hair on his chest; all she wanted was her family back together.

Luke gave her a hug, a different male touch again, and comforted her like a child.

'It's okay, Ally. Step by step. You'll get there—you will.'

Later, Emmanuel texted kind, funny words about 'Ruth, the party girl' and asked her out for dinner next week. She couldn't decide whether to accept or not. But she actually felt lighter. Maybe she should encourage Luke to go on a date. With Maz. The young woman was so bloody perky and optimistic all the time. And so fit. And bouncy, like Tigger in *Winnie-the-Pooh*. She clearly liked spending time with Luke, and with Gracie. The three of them had gone to the beach this morning, while Nadia grilled Allison for details of the one-night stand.

She hadn't told her friend about the baby, though—it hurt too much. As did her hangover. She was too old for this kind of behaviour. And she didn't have Tony whipping up his special hangover cure—fried eggs, bacon, baked beans and tomato juice. Along with some Berocca and Panadol.

Her body was still aching that night. Allison went to bed early, hoping she'd fall asleep quickly and wake refreshed for Monday. She had so much to organise. In a week's time, they'd be holding 'Gracie Day' at school—a fundraising fete. The timeline was ridiculously short but Declan agreed they needed to act fast to kickstart the campaign. Instead of drifting off though, Allison lay awake replaying every moment of last night. And feeling a lump each time she swallowed. Her throat was sore and scratchy.

Oh no. Allison had been the one writing emails to parents, telling them to keep their kids at home if they had an infection. She couldn't get sick. Not now. Not with Gracie in the house.

12

FELIX

FELIX COULD HEAR THEM WHISPERING IN THE FRONT ROOM. EVERY SO often, he caught the hiss of one word snaking down the corridor to his bedroom: *police*. Whispering so that Felix wouldn't hear?

He stared at the document open on his laptop. *Choose one of the main themes from Othello (jealousy, manipulation, racial prejudice, love or betrayal) and write a 600-word essay showing examples from the text*. Due tomorrow. And he hadn't written a single word. Great way to finish Sunday night. Shitty Shakespeare. Why did his class have to study an irrelevant old play? Darcy's class was doing the movie version of *Romeo and Juliet*. Frickin' lucky—they didn't even have to read, they could just watch.

On the group chat, the girls were discussing the best Iago quote about jealousy. One of them had typed out: *It is the green-eyed monster which doth mock the meat it feeds on.* Pearl sent him a DM. *If you look at another chick, I'll become a green-eyed monster!* She probably wasn't joking. Pearl wanted to spend every spare moment with him, kissing. Three months ago, Felix had never kissed a girl. The only two good things to come out of Mum and Dad's break-up—his surfing and his kissing were improving out of sight.

And he could go to parties that Mum would've banned. If she'd known about them.

When the police had arrived at the beach party last night, Felix had freaked out. Fully freaked. Darcy had got some weed and that was going around the circle. Along with a bottle of vodka. They'd teased Felix when he refused both. *You're such a fucking pussy.* When the girls stripped to their bra and undies, he'd told them not to go for a swim. Too dark, too rough. But they hadn't listened. And then, when it'd all gone down, Felix didn't even use his lifesaver skills—he'd bolted in the opposite direction. A freaking coward. So many dumb thoughts flashing through his head. *I'm not strong enough. What if they drown me?* Even though he'd been going to the gym for a few months, Felix hadn't bulked up. Mum said that he must be strong because of soccer and surfing, but his arms and legs were scrawny. Especially compared to the bodybuilders strutting around the weights room. Pearl hadn't been at the party and was annoyed with him for going; she'd probably dump him if she found out he'd run. Darcy said a policeman had rescued the girls—acted like the hero that Felix should've been. Years and years of surf lifesaving training and he'd legged it.

Scared of drowning. Scared of being caught with drugs. Scared of what Mum and Dad would say.

The others had no idea how tough it was to be the son of a teacher and a lawyer—paragons of the Wirriga community. Although their crowns might've slipped a bit with the break-up.

Felix tried to focus on the blank page. *Jealousy, manipulation, racial prejudice, love or betrayal.* If he was with Mum, she'd find a DVD of *Othello*, cook some popcorn, and watch the film with him, explaining the story as it happened on screen. Or maybe not; these days, she was all over the place.

And so bitter. He'd seen the threatening letter Mum had written to Helena. Dad had accidentally left it in the printer after he'd scanned it. Presumably piling up evidence to send to the police.

> *You are an evil, despicable woman who has stolen my husband and my son. I will do everything in my power to get them back. I will not let you be until your relationship with Tony is dissolved. I will expose you and all your lies. I will track you down. I will not stop until my family is back with me. I will be watching you. Look over your shoulder and I will be there. If you show this to Tony, you will make the situation worse. Keep it to yourself. You know what a treacherous, deceitful bitch you are. You know it in your heart. Leave this week or harm will come to you.*

He'd never heard Mum talk like that, but she'd been with Dad for so long, and the break-up was so sudden. They hadn't been arguing or anything. As far as Felix could see, they were all good on New Year's Eve and finished on New Year's Day.

Mum was in shock. And now he'd made it worse by spilling the beans about the baby. Getting back at her for accusing him of stealing the cash. Why'd she done that? Mum had always trusted him before. Maybe that was part of the reason he'd run away last night at the party—he couldn't face Mum falsely accusing him of smoking and drinking when he'd been trying his hardest to behave.

Felix thought Mum would've rung Dad about the baby straight away. But she didn't. Still hadn't.

Dad was going to be so pissed off with him.

Police. That word down the corridor again.

Groaning, Felix picked up *Othello*, then slammed the book back onto his desk. The themes listed were dumb anyway. He'd just write about murder. Was murder a theme or plot or what?

As he pushed up out of his seat, the office chair rolled against the edge of the desk, catching his fingers in between. Frickin' hell, he should've brought his own chair from home. Sucking on his fingers, Felix stalked into the lounge room. The lights were off and the two of them stood motionless at the end of the main window, peering through the blinds.

'What's going on?' Felix demanded.

'Nothing.' Dad turned around to face him. 'Have you finished your homework?'

Stepping closer to the window, Felix scanned the dark street. A couple walking a yappy little dog. The 136 at the bus stop, its internal lights glowing like a UFO in the darkness. Across the road, the schmick double-storey place was black apart from its technicolour TV screen, which took up almost an entire wall. He'd still never seen who lived there. Finally, he spotted it.

'Is that Mum's car?'

'Yes, she's here again.' Dad sighed, long and loud. 'I've warned her . . .'

'You're not really gonna call the police?'

'I already did. And still she won't stop.'

It was Felix's fault for telling her about the baby. Now, she'd be waiting here every night. Felix was at the front door, twisting the key in the deadbolt. But before he could step through, Dad jerked him back by the shoulder.

'You don't understand, Felix.'

'She's my mum. She misses me.'

Misses us. That was what he'd been planning to say but that would make Dad even angrier.

'The police have warned her—'

'Let me go out and talk to her.'

'You can call your mother on the phone,' Dad said. 'I don't want you on the street.'

No-one was supposed to know they were here; and Felix was supposed to be the smoke screen—an unknown teenager.

Shit, why had he blabbed? Dad kept complaining Mum was endangering Helena and the baby, but now he'd done exactly the same thing.

13

ALLISON

THE GUEST OF HONOUR SHIMMIED THROUGH THE PLAYGROUND IN A silver fairy tutu. For once, Gracie was not wearing her Princess Elsa costume. She stood out amid the superheroes in red and blue and black. Batman. Wonder Woman. Superman. Really, Gracie was the superhero—enduring the treatment and coping without a mother. Some of the school mums called Luke a superhero but he was just doing what all parents would—going to any lengths for their sick child. Gracie was the stoic one who had to put up with all the drugs and medical interventions.

Gracie Day, the thirtieth of March, had arrived after an insane week of organisation by the teachers, the parents and the P&C. If Luke had agreed earlier, they would've had more time. But hopefully the money would start rolling in now, despite the competition. There was so much fundraising these days for so many causes. Allison had seen a post on Facebook: a friend's twenty-year-old daughter fundraising for a spiritual trip to India. Allison had to stop herself from typing out a snarky comment: *Get a job! Pay your own way! HOW will you get through*

LIFE? And then she'd laughed at herself and wondered if she should set up a Getting Dumped & Divorced Fund with the tagline: *Please help save my house!*

The raffle was the hardest to pull together. The list from Felix and his friends had been a good starting point. From that, Zack's mum and Summer's mum had worked their way around the local shops, cobbling together some decent prizes—vouchers from the cafes, a pass for the gym, pool cleaning products, a hamper from the deli, and beauty products from the salon. The Wirriga shops had been as generous as ever.

'How much do you think we'll raise?' the principal asked as he helped lay out the raffle prizes on a table.

'Hard to say. Maybe two thousand for today and another one for the raffle,' Allison guessed. A drop in the ocean—they needed a hundred and forty. 'Hopefully, when the story hits the paper, we'll get more.'

The year Declan had started as principal at Wirriga was the same year his wife was diagnosed with breast cancer. A tough time for him. From the way he'd balanced his work and his leave, Allison knew he was a good man. Over the past week, Declan had encouraged the whole school to get on board for Gracie Day. His wife, now in remission, was helping at the canteen.

Declan had also met with Luke in his office to discuss the clinical trial and other treatment options. Offered to put him in touch with another cancer specialist and his wife's counsellor. Offered him a shoulder to cry on. That night, Luke had raved about Declan's support, said he had actually cried in his office: 'We need more men like Declan in the world.'

Sniffling, Allison searched in her pocket for a tissue. She'd been trying to keep her sore throat and runny nose away from

Gracie but it was tricky. The girl loved a cuddle each night and liked helping her in the kitchen. Allison hadn't mentioned her cold to Luke. She just couldn't after she'd caused the allergic reaction. When he was around, Allison swallowed her cough and went into the bathroom to blow her nose. She'd been dosing up on cold-and-flu tablets. Perhaps she should give Gracie some as a precaution? In the middle of the night, her thoughts spiralled around the fear that she'd harmed Gracie once without realising, and she could do it again with this cold.

But it was the worst possible timing with so much to do for Gracie Day. Allison had fired up the fundraising, she could hardly just disappear off to bed. The Wirriga Wombats had taken home raffle tickets, along with every class in the school. Parents were selling them at their work in other suburbs and in the city, spreading the financial load from the school community. Felix had even taken some for his friends and for Tony's work to sell.

Allison hadn't discussed the baby with Tony, nor with Felix. While her son had helped set up Gracie Day, he was still frosty with her. He hadn't forgiven Allison for implying that he'd stolen the money but who else could've taken it? On Tuesday, she'd finally confided in Nadia, after swearing her friend to secrecy ('You can't even tell your husband'). The shame of Tony running off with a woman and having a baby was too much. And the pain. Allison had tried for so long to fall pregnant. Tony knew how she'd feel—was that why he hadn't told her? Allison's desperation to see the new woman had evaporated completely. Now she avoided going near the house in Curl Curl. Avoided the possibility of seeing the baby. Instead, she was focused on getting Gracie to Chicago.

Tony only communicated by text, presumably so he could record it for the police. *Stop stalking us. I'll get an AVO.* Her reply: *I'm not. Busy with fundraising. I can give an alibi to the police.* Maybe she should call the police about *his* harassment. Not only the texts but a typed letter requesting they sell the house, regardless of Gracie's illness. Tony's compassion seemed to have disappeared suddenly in the wreckage of their marriage. Allison decided to ignore the request altogether. As if they could move in the middle of the fundraising campaign.

And now, here they were, at school on a Saturday afternoon. A mini school fete all for Gracie.

The supermarket had provided the food for the sausage sizzle and drinks for the lemonade stand. The fathers were on the barbecue. The mothers had baked cupcakes and slices for the cake stall. Allison had already bought a vanilla slice for her mum, and a big chocolate gateau for Felix to share with his mates—a peace offering. Evelyn's mother had created a special sugar-free marble cake for Gracie.

Allison surveyed the playground. A lucky dip, a tombola, a trash and treasure, a book table, a craft stall . . . whipped up by so many people in such a short space of time . . . would it make any proper money? Cheers echoed from the oval, where they were paying two dollars to kick a soccer ball into a goal with a smiley face. The gym instructor, Maz, had set up a weightlifting competition for the older kids. All week, Maz had been at her house, making purple bracelets with Gracie, working on the website and eyeing up Luke. Allison could see the attraction between them but when she'd mentioned it to Luke, he'd said, 'It's not the right time.'

Luke was leading a group of year four boys towards the hall for the paper aeroplane competition. As he passed by her table, he gave a thumbs-up.

'This is extraordinary! I don't know how you did it.'

'It wasn't just me,' Allison said. 'The P&C and a whole team of parents—well, mostly mothers.'

In the lead-up to Gracie Day, Allison had worried about how the little girl would cope with all the attention. She'd suggested a different name for the fundraising event. But Luke had said, 'Gracie's already had so much unwanted attention. This is good attention. It'll be fine.' As a child, Allison would've hated it; even at twenty years old, maybe even now, at forty-nine.

The little girl was at the art stall, colouring in rainbows.

'I got to be the judge,' Gracie told her. 'I chose first and second and third.'

'A real art critic! That's very grown up, Gracie.'

'I chose that one.' She pointed at a drawing of a dog. 'I wanted my rainbow to win, but they said I couldn't have a prize.'

Her bottom lip quivered. Allison automatically drew her into a cuddle. Damn, she shouldn't be getting so close to her, but how could she comfort the girl otherwise?

'The whole day is a prize for you, Gracie. For your treatment.'

'I don't want treatment.' Gracie pouted. 'I wanna go to Disneyland. Selina's going in the holidays!'

'How about I take you to Luna Park next weekend?'

'YAY!' Gracie kissed her cheek. 'You're the best, Lally.'

The nickname was perfect for their relationship—not a Mummy, not a Nanny nor a Granny but a Lally.

The journalist from the *Northern Beaches News* arrived just before the kids' disco. Tall and confident but he seemed so young. Maz had asked him to come; she'd known him at school.

Introducing himself, Curtis grabbed Allison's hand and pumped it up and down.

'I hear you're the mastermind of all this, Mrs Walsh.'

Allison's natural instinct was to tell him to speak with Luke or Declan. But today, she aimed to get the message out for Gracie, although she hoped she wouldn't have to be in a photograph.

'We're doing a triple celebration for Gracie—the fundraiser, her birthday next week and she's just finished her last round of chemotherapy.' Allison smiled. 'We're so lucky that Gracie has this chance to go to America because the drug is only in a trial stage and not available here.'

When Luke and Gracie arrived, Curtis made the questions straightforward for the little girl: What do you like about school? What fun things are you doing today? How often do you go to the hospital?

'They're nice at the hop-i-tal.' Gracie giggled. 'But I don't have to go next week.'

A chance for her body to recover before the trial.

'Dr Rawson is great,' Luke added. 'I'll give you his number and he can explain the immunotherapy. Exciting stuff. It's changing how the disease is treated.'

For the photo, Curtis wanted Gracie surrounded by her friends. Allison had assumed they'd send a photographer but Curtis doubled up in the role. With fewer and fewer pages in the local newspaper these days, Allison knew they were lucky he'd come at all. As Curtis snapped away, Gracie laughed with four other girls dressed up as fairies.

'What's the collective noun for fairies?' Curtis asked the adults. 'A flock of fairies? A charm of fairies?'

They made some guesses—a spell, a wing, a garland. They decided upon 'a flight of fairies'.

'Now, can I get a photo of Luke and Gracie together?'

'Mate, I'd rather focus on Gracie.' Luke smiled at his daughter. 'She's the star. You don't want me ruining the photo.'

Gracie giggled and wrapped her arms around Luke's waist.

'How about a shot of you giving Gracie a piggyback. I'll take it from behind and we won't see your ugly mug,' Curtis joked. 'Just Gracie looking back at the camera.'

The pose was perfect—it showed the strong bond between father and daughter.

As Curtis finished up and packed away his camera, he said, 'I'd really like to help out with this campaign. What can I do?'

The offer was so unexpected that Allison had to turn away, stare at the queue for the lucky dip. She could almost hear the accusation from Shona—*You're too judgemental with that age group, Allison. They're far more altruistic than the Boomers and Gen X.*

'We'd really appreciate that,' Luke said. 'I'd love some photos of Gracie down at Manly beach sometime. That's where she remembers going with her mum . . .'

Curtis went to shake hands but Luke pulled him into a hug. 'Thanks so much, mate. Welcome to Gracie's Gang!'

Allison prayed that Curtis' article—and his skills—could bring in some donations towards their out-of-reach goal.

—

By the time they got home at six o'clock, Gracie was exhausted. She sneezed as Luke took her up to bed. Oh shit, she'd caught it.

'Do you think she should have some cold-and-flu medicine?' Allison asked.

'Not tonight. She just needs a good sleep.'

While Luke was upstairs, Allison checked the day's takings. The canteen volunteers had put the coins through their machine and handed over bags counted into ten, twenty and fifty dollars. It was surprising that one- and two-dollar coins could add up to so much. Each stall had collected their own cash and Allison now spread it out across the dining room table.

'Wow, what a day.' Luke collapsed into the chair opposite her. 'I'm as tired as Gracie.'

'It's incredible! We've made over ten thousand dollars and that doesn't include the raffle.' Allison glanced up at Luke's face. 'The raffle should be another five. That'll be at least fifteen thousand dollars.'

'Awesome.'

He was trying to sound enthusiastic but his voice was flat, his face pale. If Allison concentrated on the money, she could put the fear about Gracie's future out of her mind. Clearly, Luke couldn't ever forget—the past or the future.

Or was he getting sick too?

'Let me look at the website. Everyone has been sharing the link on Facebook.'

She clicked it open on her phone. Studied the number. Pressed refresh in case there was some mistake.

'Oh my God, Luke. There's another eight thousand donated online. We're going to get Gracie there, I promise you.'

Luke went up to bed while Allison stared at the bundles of notes and coins. Money handed over by kids and their parents. Ten thousand, four hundred and thirty-nine dollars. Astonishing. Lifting up one bag of coins, she felt the weight of it in her hand. A bag of golden coins for a miracle. She needed another miracle to keep the house. How on earth could she afford the weekly mortgage? A thump from outside the back door made her drop the coins on the table. A possum or wallaby? Or something else? Shit, she should have left the money at school in the safe. Too many people knew where she lived.

Grabbing one of Felix's old backpacks from the hall cupboard, she swept the whole load of coins and notes inside. And then she heard a window smashing. The window by the laundry sink maybe—just low enough to crawl in or to reach a hand around to unlock the back door.

'Luke!' she screamed, taking the stairs two at a time.

When she reached the landing, he was standing in the hallway in a pair of grey boxer shorts.

'Someone's trying to break in. Call the police.'

'You phone the police. I'll go down and scare them off.'

'No, I don't think—'

He was gone before she could finish her sentence.

She threw the backpack into Felix's wardrobe, praying that a robber would never imagine the loot was hidden in a teenager's messy bedroom. Dialling 000 with shaking fingers, she begged the police to come as quickly as possible.

'You know there's been a string of robberies in Wirriga,' she screeched to the operator. 'They're here in my house—now!'

Armed with Felix's bass guitar—the only weapon she could find—Allison stationed herself outside the bedroom where Gracie was sleeping.

14

ANOTHER CRASH FROM DOWNSTAIRS. ALLISON GRIPPED THE NECK OF the guitar. Bloody hell, she needed a better weapon. If she hit someone over the head with this, it'd simply snap in two.

Were they the same robbers who had been breaking in all summer? Had they been staking out her house in a green sedan? Last month, Nadia had brushed away Allison's concerns, but maybe it hadn't been her paranoia from being alone in the house.

What if they hurt Luke? He shouldn't have gone down to the laundry. He needed to stay safe for Gracie. *Hurry up, hurry up.* The police station was in Manly, ten minutes away. Saturday night. Were they busy dealing with the drunk and disorderly on the Corso? When would they come?

Straining to hear noises from the floor below, Allison couldn't work out what was real and what she was imagining. A clicking sound. The shrieking of bats. Another thump. People moving around. Why wasn't Luke saying something?

Finally, she heard the sound she'd been waiting for: a siren echoing off the houses, coming closer and closer. As the police car parked outside her house, the walls of the corridor reflected a blue tinge from its flashing.

Doors opening and slamming.

She crept to the top of the stairs and peeked down.

Every room was flooded with light. Luke must have switched them on to startle the robbers. Two police officers strode through her lounge room in the direction of the back door.

'Ally, you can come down now. The police are here.' Luke's voice from the kitchen.

Slowly, she made her way into the laundry. A half-brick lay on the washing machine, shattered glass glittered across the sink and floor. A piece of wire had been pushed inside and was looped around the door handle. They'd been trying to open the door through the window.

'Don't come in here without shoes,' one police officer warned.

Luke had managed to scare them off. The only description he could give was two males in black beanies. They'd been outside in the dark and he couldn't see their faces. The officers went to check the entry and exit points. Nothing had been damaged out there—the men must have clambered over the back fence.

While the officers were interviewing Luke and writing up a report, Allison called a twenty-four-hour glass repair service. But, even with the window fixed, she doubted that she'd sleep tonight. Would the men come back and try again?

'They must know we have the fundraising money,' she told the police. 'It's too much of a coincidence.'

'We'll look at any connections to Wirriga school.'

Could it really be a parent from school?

—

Three hours later, the police had taken the brick as evidence, Allison had swept up the shards, and the glazier had finished putting in a new panel. She paid extra for reinforced security glass. Assessing her windows now, Allison could pinpoint the weak spots: the sliding doors that led from the kitchen onto the deck, and the window in the downstairs toilet. All accessible from the back, where an intruder could lurk without being seen. Sixteen years in the house and they'd never had anyone climb into the backyard. Not even kids.

Luke checked on Gracie again; she had slept through the whole commotion. Before going up to bed again, he made hot chocolate for Allison.

'I've hidden the money,' she said. 'I've got the keys for school so I can put it in the safe there tomorrow, then transfer it into your account on Monday.'

As long as no-one was watching her.

They left the lights blazing downstairs. The police said they'd circle back during the night to keep an eye on the place. Allison hoped it wasn't an empty promise.

She had no illusions that she'd actually fall asleep. But then she popped a night-time cold-and-flu tablet and floated away.

On Sunday morning, Gracie refused to get out of bed.

'My head hurts,' she whined. 'My throat's sore.'

'I'll get you some warm milk with honey,' Allison said. 'And you should have some cough medicine.'

'No, it doesn't work.' Luke glared at her. 'It just masks the symptoms.'

'Sorry, I'm overstepping again.'

With the little girl living in her house, Allison had automatically reverted to a mothering role. Every so often, irritation would flash across Luke's face and she'd have to pull herself back. While Allison didn't want to argue with him now, the medicine had definitely made her nose clearer and her head less woolly. She was sure it would make Gracie feel better too.

With Gracie in bed, they weren't able to go together into school and put the money in the safe. Even though daylight lessened the threat, Allison preferred not to carry the money around by herself but she didn't want it in the house again that night. She called Nadia and her husband to accompany her as bodyguards. They stood in the playground while Allison took the cash into the admin area and locked it up.

'Do you really believe it was a targeted break-in?' Nadia asked.

'It must've been.'

'What does Luke think?'

'He didn't really say. He's a bit distracted because Gracie isn't well.'

And that's my fault. Maybe even doubly my fault. Had the allergic reaction compromised the girl's immune system further? Made her more susceptible to a common cold?

—

At two o'clock, the gym rang Luke to see if he could take a weights class—the regular instructor had torn a muscle. Allison encouraged him to go.

'I'll look after Gracie,' she promised.

'But will you be okay home alone?'

'As long as you're back before dark.'

Allison and Gracie curled up under blankets and watched *Mary Poppins* together in the lounge room.

'Are you my Mary Poppins?' Gracie asked. 'Are you my nanny?'

'Sort of,' she answered. 'But you know I'm not allowed to give you any sugar to help the medicine go down!'

They both giggled and Gracie waved her empty ice-cream bowl above her head.

Now that Gracie had finished chemo, she could take regular medications—that was what the doctor had said yesterday. Although the doctor, a parent at the fundraiser, probably didn't realise Allison was acting on her advice. She'd asked the question without going into too much detail about 'the patient'. Gracie was starting the immunotherapy trial at the end of April—in exactly four weeks. Allison had to make sure that the little girl was well enough.

She'd bribed Gracie with ice-cream to take the cold-and-flu syrup.

'Don't tell Daddy,' Allison whispered. 'It's our little secret.'

15

LUKE

ANOTHER WEEK, ANOTHER TWENTY-FIVE THOUSAND DOLLARS. LUKE couldn't believe how one dedicated schoolteacher had set the ball rolling for all this fundraising. The newspaper article had been shared far and wide, and they'd run out of purple bracelets to give to the new members of Gracie's Gang. The librarian at school had started a lunchtime club for other children to help make them.

Whenever he thanked Ally, she shied away from his praise; clearly, she wasn't one for attention. Unlike his special girl Gracie, who was thriving on it.

After spending last Sunday in bed, Gracie had felt well enough for school on Monday. Even though Luke had played a prank on her first thing.

'It's the cross-country carnival today, Gracie. You need to wear your house colours—I've bought you a special blue wig as well.'

Obediently, Gracie put on her blue shorts and top, and he fitted the crazy wig onto her scalp.

'I look like Thing One from *The Cat in the Hat*!'

She wandered down to the kitchen where Ally had asked, 'Why are you wearing that outfit?'

'Daddy said it's cross-country.'

'April Fool's.' Luke clapped his hands. 'And it's only three sleeps until your birthday!'

Gracie had insisted on wearing the wig all day. She accompanied them to the bank at lunchtime to deposit the money. When the cashier learnt about Gracie's campaign, she handed over some fluffy toys and money boxes to be used as prizes. In much detail, Ally told the cashier about the break-in. It was the first of many times that week. Luke noticed she didn't share the story about the sesame oil; all her guilt was being driven into the fundraising.

By Wednesday, Gracie had stopped sneezing, and Luke thought she'd recovered from a minor cold. She'd taken cupcakes to school for her birthday on Thursday and they'd had an afternoon tea party at home. Maz brought balloons and streamers, Ally got an expensive fairy cake from the patisserie, and Curtis popped over to take more photos for a follow-up story. Gracie only mentioned her mother twice. Luke's birthday present was exactly what she'd asked for: a Barbie dream camper. She put her plastic dinosaurs inside to take them on a holiday to the beach. Presents flooded in from classmates and grown-ups; one of her favourites was an art easel from Ally.

But then, on Friday morning after all the excitement, the cold returned with a vengeance. Headache, sore throat, stuffed-up nose. Gracie stayed home from school watching *Frozen* yet again, but she didn't sing or dance along with the music. She sat still for an hour.

Gracie wanted to stay in bed on Saturday too, but Maz dropped in and urged them to come down to Manly for some fresh air. As they strolled towards the playground by the beachfront, Gracie stopped to pat an energetic black Labrador.

'When I'm all better, I'm getting a puppy,' she told the dog owner.

'Good for you,' the man said.

'I'm going to call it Marmalade.'

For two years, Gracie had been asking for a dog. An animal that needed feeding, walking and regular attention. Impossible in the midst of all this.

Before Gracie had even clambered onto the seesaw, one of the mums began speaking to her.

'Oh Gracie, it's so nice to see you out and about. I'm one of your gang!' The woman held up her wrist to show off her purple bracelet. 'Have you had a good week? How are you feeling today?'

His daughter chatted with the stranger while Luke considered her question. Would it turn into a full-blown cold? Ally had told him that at this time of year—the lead-up towards winter—coughs and snotty noses spread rapidly around the school.

'You must be Luke.' The woman beamed at him as she pushed her toddler on the swing. 'My son is starting at Wirriga next year. We'll be at the same school as you.'

'It's a good school.' Luke smiled; he'd had so many of these conversations with strangers.

'I can't imagine what it must be like for you.' She nodded down at her own child. 'Heartbreaking.'

Over the woman's shoulder, Luke watched small groups jogging down the promenade. Maz was no longer in sight—she'd set off sprinting in the direction of Shelly beach. Beyond the joggers and the power walkers, the kids on scooters and skateboards, the ocean sparkled on this bright autumn day. The surfers were out in force, black shapes in their wetsuits balancing on the waves.

'It's very difficult.' Luke sighed.

Strangers expected him to spout the right platitudes and shed a few tears on demand. Curtis wanted more and more photos, more emotions. Was that the deal Luke had made for going public? The punters paid to see the pain. As if by giving money, they were insuring their own children against the same fate. *There but for the grace of God, go I*—was that what they were thinking each time they pressed the donate button?

It wasn't something he could discuss with anyone, not even Ally. He'd sound ungrateful. But the psychology intrigued him. What made strangers give to Gracie rather than to a thirteen-year-old boy from Parramatta? When Maz had been setting up Gracie's page, they'd looked at the big fundraising sites. Clicked on various kids with cancer, including that thirteen-year-old boy. He needed five thousand for a wheelchair but he'd only received six hundred dollars.

Maz had figured that Gracie should have her own page, rather than being on the fundraising sites, to stand out from the crowd. And so far, her theory seemed to be working. When Maz checked it earlier this morning, the figure had reached $53,219.

'It's flipping awesome!' She'd bounded off the kitchen stool, picked up Gracie and spun her around. Gracie didn't complain about her sore head. Then Maz pulled Luke into the hug with them. Gracie had been giggling as Maz dropped dozens of little kisses all over her face.

'Give Daddy a kiss too,' Gracie instructed.

Her lips were hot against his cheek.

'Another!' Gracie said. 'Another!'

And so Maz had peppered his face with kisses too, the last one landing softly on his lips.

Luke had known for weeks that Maz was keen. Now Gracie seemed to be encouraging it. And Ally too. She'd already gone on a second date with Emmanuel, even though she'd said she wasn't ready.

With a new bloke on the scene, Ally had said less about her husband's new woman. When Luke first moved in, she'd tried to hide the stalking from him but Felix had brought it up over dinner. Ally was forced to explain. 'I was bit crazy and it was only once or twice. I'm done with all that now.'

Except Luke guessed she'd been there on other nights since. Had she been down there lately? Had she been seen by Tony?

How obsessed was Ally now?

As obsessed as Maz with her supplements?

Maz wasn't the only one. Some people who donated wrote long suggestions about the power of alternative therapies, natural products, herbal solutions, prayers and positive thoughts. Their messages promised magic.

—*My mother's cancer disappeared four weeks after taking these green tablets.*

—*We prayed away my daughter's tumour.*

—*This Chinese healer made my brother healthy again.*

When the comments had started coming in, Ally had gathered Luke and Curtis together on a Thursday night.

'We need to do a blog post to stop people giving advice on natural therapies,' she'd said. 'It takes away from the focus on the clinical trial.'

Luke figured he could write his own posts but Ally said he'd be too busy in Chicago and it was better to get Curtis started now. So Ally researched it and Curtis wrote it. Luke knew that Ally believed in science and nothing else. He'd met her mother, Barbara, a former physics teacher. Her father had been a civil engineer. Her family had no time for solutions that weren't backed up by medical science.

'Won't a post like that put some people offside?' Luke had asked.

'You don't want those people on your side,' Ally snapped.

So Luke had posted their efforts on the website:

Thank you to everyone who has contacted me with suggestions and therapies for Gracie. I appreciate your kindness and passion. But everyone's cancer is different. The smart thing is to work with your own medical team. Gracie's medical specialists are the experts in her care.

We need to be wary of those promising an expensive 'miracle cure'. We're in a vulnerable place and, of course, we're hoping for a wonder drug. But if it sounds too good to be true, it probably is. And it's not just on the internet. A hundred years ago, back in 1916, Clark Stanley was fined $20 for selling his Snake Oil Liniment which contained no actual oil from snakes but lots of false advertising. He claimed his snake oil was the best liniment for pain, lameness, rheumatism, neuralgia, bad back, lumbago, contracted cords, toothache, sprains, swellings, frost bite, chilblains, bruises, sore throat, bites of animals, insects and reptiles. One cure for everything, right?!

> Nope. These days, scientists know the best way to treat an individual's cancer is by individualising the treatment, through things like cell therapy, personalised vaccines, gene editing and immunotherapy. We're so lucky that Gracie has been accepted for a new immunotherapy drug. It's at the forefront of research and will change how the Big C is treated.

Ally had gone on and on about Clark Stanley, the snake oil guy. And then, she'd compared Stanley to a cure-all centre just outside Los Angeles.

'It says it can cure everything from asthma to cancer to diabetes by using light and music therapy. Have you ever heard anything so stupid?'

The website pictured a teenage girl who was now proclaimed cancer-free.

'But what if it works?' Luke had asked, knowing he was entering a minefield.

'Don't fall for it. There's no scientific proof.' Ally stabbed a finger at the girl's face. 'They're just tricking desperate patients to pay thousands of dollars.'

'What about the power of belief?'

'Belief doesn't cure cancer. Belief can't do anything.'

Ally was wrong. Belief could do *everything*.

Luke stared at his daughter as she twirled a red plastic ball along the rope at the bottom of the climbing frame. The other mother in the playground was still talking to him but he'd lost track of the conversation. Perhaps he'd email that cure-all centre tomorrow.

16

MAZ

MAZ SQUEEZED PAST THE CROWDS CHATTING NEAR THE SURF LIFE-saving club. A Saturday run at Manly was an obstacle course in avoiding dawdling tourists and the weekend workout types. But today, Maz didn't care.

Since the little girl had finished her last round of chemo, Gracie's hair was starting to sprout and her skin had a healthy pink glow. Maz thought her immune-boosting supplements must have something to do with it. When she'd heard Gracie sniffling that morning, she'd wondered if the dose should be doubled.

Donations were climbing steadily. And the other offers. Gracie had received tickets to Luna Park, the zoo, a kids' show at the Opera House, a Wiggles concert and heaps more.

Mum and Dad were scraping together as much as they could for Gracie; they'd cut right back—no movies, no fancy steak, no takeaways. Dad had told Maz that she could save more money if she stopped buying 'those bloody vitamin pills'. Biting her lip to hide her smirk, she hadn't replied. More new orders today! Those teenage boys couldn't get enough. Maz was waiting until she grew the business; only then would she show off her success to her parents. She'd promised ten per cent of all profits from her Bio-Antidotes to Gracie and she'd given up her one daily treat—the green smoothie from the gym cafe. It wouldn't bring in a huge amount but every donation was one dollar closer to the goal.

Sidestepping her way through the crowd, Maz smiled at the kids, swung her ponytail and accelerated past the prams. $53,219. Amazingly awesome in two weeks. They would definitely hit the target in time. And, on top of that, she'd kissed Luke on the lips.

He hadn't pulled away but she'd felt his nervousness. Of course, it must be difficult to be with another woman after his wife's death, but the electricity had been sparking between them since they'd first met. Over the past few months, Maz had been on dates with other guys but none of them had Luke's intensity. And the love he had for Gracie shone from within. Luke was the perfect father. The perfect business partner and workout partner. And, if she played her cards right, the perfect lover.

Back at the playground, Maz had a drink and a quick stretch.

'One of the mums said there's a seal on the headland near Curl Curl.' Luke jiggled his keys in his pocket. 'Gracie's keen to see it. Shall we go?'

'Absolutely!'

They drove in the Jeep with its top down, Maz loving the cool wind against her sweaty body. In the back seat, Gracie had to hold on to her cap. Together, they'd slathered the girl in sunscreen before the outing. Even though the weather was cooler now, Luke still took every precaution.

Only a few others were standing on the rocky headland. While they were waiting to catch sight of the seal, a seaplane chugged overhead. Low and loud. One day, it would be Maz peering down from those tiny windows, marvelling at the coastline from above, whizzing up to Palm Beach for a fancy lunch.

When the seal lumbered up onto the rocks, Gracie cheered.

'And look, there's another one!' Maz pointed into the waves.

'And another!' Gracie yelled. A third seal was poking its head out of the water.

The seals rolled and twisted in the swell.

'I think those are two boys trying to impress the girl on the rock.' Luke laughed. 'Which boyfriend is trying to impress you this week, Gracie?'

'Silly, Daddy.' Gracie poked him in the side. 'Kids don't have boyfriends.'

Over the top of her head, Luke smiled slowly at Maz. Wow, this was it. She wanted to throw herself right at him, right now. Maz wished that Gracie wasn't standing between them. Wished they could sneak behind the rocks, into the bushes.

Walking back to the Jeep, Luke took her hand. Stroked the back of it. Maz's body tingled in anticipation. And then, Gracie sneezed. Two long rivers of snot cascaded from her nose. Letting go of his hand, Maz searched in her backpack for tissues. But Luke beat her to it, producing some from his pocket.

'Have a good blow,' he told Gracie.

'She must've caught it from Allison,' Maz whispered. The teacher had been sick for two weeks. Instead of staying in bed, Allison had gone to school and to meetings about Gracie Day, spreading her germs further. And Gracie was there with her, living in a sick house, going off to a sick school.

'Has Gracie seen the doctor lately?' Maz asked.

'Yep. On Thursday. It's a normal cold, apparently.'

'I think you should move out for a few days to stop her getting worse.' Maz was thinking aloud. If only she could say, *Come and stay with me.* But there wasn't enough room at her place.

Luke pulled up next to the kerb in front of Maz's house. He'd never mentioned the size of her home but the whole thing could fit into the same space as Allison's two living areas. 'Emmanuel has a holiday house up the coast at Avoca—I could ask him,' Luke said. 'It'd be good for Gracie to have a break. Maybe you could come with us?'

—

A trip to Avoca was exactly the break they needed. And a chance for Maz to have Luke to herself. Since they'd set up the fundraiser, everyone had developed a crush on Luke. Clients were choosing his class over every other; instructors were flirting with him; punters were asking Maz if he had a girlfriend. *Hands off! He's mine!* She wanted to scream it out at the gym.

Early April meant they had the beach to themselves. The cafes and the shops had a totally relaxed vibe. Even Luke seemed to slow down and open up.

They were walking a few steps behind Gracie as she collected shells in a bucket, when Luke began speaking about his wife.

'Sarah was dedicated to Gracie. After the surgery and before the first chemo, she booked a place at Apollo Bay. One afternoon, we climbed the lighthouse at Cape Otway. I carried Gracie all the way to the top. It was magical.'

Maz felt him take her hand, entwine his fingers around hers. She looked up to see happiness in his eyes.

'Sarah would be relieved to see Gracie smiling again,' he said. 'And that's because of you, Maz.'

—

The sex, when it finally happened that night, was even more awesome than she'd imagined. Tender but frenzied. As if Luke couldn't get enough of her. With Gracie asleep in the next room, Maz pressed her mouth against Luke's shoulder to silence her moans. Afterwards, they lay panting, their breaths an echo of the waves pounding Avoca beach.

Beforehand, he'd said, 'This will be my first time since . . .'

In the heat of the moment, Maz had forgotten but now, in the afterglow, she remembered. Running her fingers over his chest, she asked if he was okay.

'More than okay. That was awesome.'

Maz giggled and rolled on top of him, pinning down his arms, kissing his eyes, nose, mouth.

'You're awesome!'

They'd be doing it once more tonight, Maz was certain.

—

The next day, Maz wondered if Gracie would be aware of the change. But the little girl behaved the same as usual. She didn't comment when Maz and Luke walked into the old-time movie theatre holding hands. Or when Maz sprawled against Luke on the picnic blanket by the rockpool.

'Come and see this crab,' Gracie called to her.

'Don't step in the water,' Luke warned his daughter. 'We don't want that cold to get any worse.'

Maz forced herself off the blanket, her thigh still tingling from where Luke's fingers had been tracing a line upwards.

'Gee, that crab is crawling super fast.' Maz tried to sound interested but she was counting the number of hours until Gracie went to sleep. They should have left the little girl with the schoolteacher. *No, the reason we came was to get away from the sick teacher.*

Over dinner of salmon and Asian greens, Gracie couldn't stop coughing.

'We should double the dose of her supplements,' Maz said. 'She has to be as healthy as possible for Chicago.'

'I don't want to change anything without asking Dr Rawson.'

'Can you text him now?'

'He wouldn't appreciate a call at seven o'clock at night. Gracie isn't his only patient.'

Luke gave a little laugh to soften his words but Maz blushed anyway. Luke worshipped Dr Rawson—his word was law. After Curtis had done a phone interview with the doctor, he'd reported back: *That man has the biggest brain. He explained about those new drugs but I didn't really understand. It's so complicated.* Of course Luke had a man crush on the specialist who was opening doors to save Gracie's life.

Dr Rawson had approved the supplements. Surely it would be beneficial for Gracie to double the dose.

Maz would get the containers out after dinner, while Luke was in the shower.

17

ALLISON

ALLISON COULDN'T STOP THINKING ABOUT HOW SHE'D JEOPARDISED Gracie's health twice. Before Luke went to Avoca, she made a decision.

'I'll sell the house, then I can loan you the rest of the money straight up,' she told Luke. 'Once the fundraiser gets to that amount, you can pay me back.'

Instead of being grateful as she'd expected, Luke shook his head.

'You can't do that, Ally. It's your house and your money. I thought you never wanted to sell.'

'I could sell for the right reason. For Gracie. Not because of Tony.'

Tony wouldn't stop texting her about the house. Her last response to him had said: *I will consider selling after Gracie is back from Chicago in June.* Although Allison could do it right now, if she wanted. But she'd suddenly realised the sale would take too long to deliver the money for Gracie's treatment.

'You need to look after your money,' Luke said. 'I saw it when my aunt got divorced. She lost everything. When you sell the house, invest the cash.'

If Allison invested the money, maybe she could make more for Gracie. Not in time for this treatment but the next one. If this round worked well, Dr Rawson said they'd do another in four months. Emmanuel was into investments—she'd talk to him. He was a nice guy but life was complicated at the moment. Would Emmanuel be another complication? They'd had sex on that first night but not since then; Allison insisted on taking it very, very slowly. Emmanuel joked that it was a bit late for that. But he didn't pressure her. They'd been out for dinner twice. He'd supported the fundraising by sending the link to his wealthy financial colleagues and encouraging them to join Gracie's Gang. And he'd lent Luke his holiday house for a few days.

When Luke returned from Avoca, he was upbeat, and upfront.

'Maz and I are kind of . . . dating now.' He ran a hand through his spiky hair. 'She's got so much energy and she's great with Gracie. It might sound weird to say this, but I know Sarah would approve. She'd like Maz's zest for life.'

That zest for life was certainly impressive. And also irritating. How could Maz be so happy *all* the time? Was it possible for the bouncy instructor to be even happier now that she'd snagged her prize? While Allison had suggested the match, she found it infuriating to see young love in her house—the two of them radiated some kind of sexual glow.

Allison had been hoping to take Gracie to the Royal Easter Show as a belated birthday present. She especially wanted to take her into the petting zoo and to see the horses—a link to her mother. But Gracie wasn't interested. Allison wondered if part of her sickness and lethargy was psychological, the sadness of her fifth birthday without her mum.

The fundraising campaign had started as Allison's project but it expanded without her input. A bunch of mums from school had organised a family fun run around Narrabeen Lake. Some of the kids raised hundreds of dollars in sponsorship from their relatives. An instructor who worked with Luke set up a wine fundraiser. The stories in the *Northern Beaches News* inspired two of the local pubs to donate the takings from their weekly trivia nights. Maz's grandmother called bingo at the retirement village and asked residents to hand over coins for every bingo counter they used. Allison's mother hosted a very successful fundraising lunch at her golf club.

'Everyone was very generous,' Barbara reported back. 'Especially Sally. You remember her grandson died last year.'

Allison pictured the sixteen-year-old. A healthy happy teenager one month, gone the next. Some kind of infection.

'How's the family?'

'Getting through it day by day. I thought Sally would be too upset to come but she insisted. She donated eight hundred dollars at the beginning of lunch, and then another eight hundred at the end.'

'That's extremely generous.' Allison considered what she knew of Sally. 'Can she afford it, though?'

'She wants to help.'

So many people wanted to help. Schoolchildren were giving up their pocket money. Teenagers handed over precious dollars from their weekend jobs. Little by little, it was adding up. One of the clubs in Dee Why held a karaoke fundraising night. An anonymous donor transferred five thousand. Shona contacted three radio stations and told Gracie's story on air in her lovely, lilting accent; the donations skyrocketed.

They celebrated when the total hit eighty thousand, then a hundred, then a hundred and twenty. When they'd set up the campaign, Allison had imagined the target as a pot of gold at the end of the rainbow—the end of that rainbow was now in sight.

After recess on Friday morning, as Allison was handing out a worksheet on matching pictures and words, Shona appeared in the doorway.

'You're wanted in the office,' she said. 'I'll mind your class.'

Then Shona leant in close and whispered: 'Two police officers are waiting to see you.'

Oh God, Tony. Had he followed through with his threat of an AVO? But she hadn't been near his place for weeks. And surely the police wouldn't serve her with an AVO at school. Not here, in front of staff and students. It was bullshit anyway. Tony was making it up to force her to sell the house. She'd call him out for domestic abuse—Tony, the solicitor who had helped so many other women. It would ruin his career. Was that what he wanted?

The police officers were waiting in the staffroom for her, their caps in their hands. Not the same couple as last time. Younger, both male.

'Mrs Walsh, we're sorry to disturb you during class time.'

Even though they were standing, Allison decided to sit; she needed the support underneath her body.

'We've made some arrests on the robberies,' said the one with the crew cut. 'The attempt at your house was the breakthrough for the case.'

The robberies. Not an AVO. Double relief. She'd been reading the crime section of the paper each week, waiting for the next report. There hadn't been one since her house. And the fact that the robbers hadn't moved on concerned Allison. She wondered if they were following her and Luke as they collected fundraising money.

'Thank God. Maybe I'll be able to sleep now.'

She wasn't joking.

'One of the perpetrators was from your school community, as you suggested, Mrs Walsh. His son, Zack, is in your class.'

Bloody hell. She should've realised when Zack was trying to sell stuff—Allison had assumed it was his family's belongings, not stolen goods. Allison had only seen Zack's dad once. Dressed in trendy sports clothes, he looked like a rapper: designer tracksuit pants, gleaming white sneakers, a black cap on his head. Along with bloodshot eyes and the most charming smile.

'Does Zack know his father has been arrested?'

'Yes, he was in the home when the arrest was made last night.'

Closing her eyes, Allison imagined Zack's fear and confusion. Most kids thought the police only arrested 'the bad guys'; it'd be hard for Zack to reconcile that concept with his own dad going to jail. How would he cope? He wasn't in today. The family must be in a state of shock.

Another child to discuss with the school counsellor.

The Easter Hat Parade was on Wednesday, just before the school holidays. The Wombats had made cardboard hats with bunny ears sticking out the top. After last-minute tears from Evelyn, who accidentally ripped hers as she was adjusting it, the class strode out onto the basketball court smiling proudly. During the parade, they collected gold coin donations for Gracie, the last fundraiser before Chicago. Zack's mum pulled Allison to one side and apologised on behalf of her husband. She passed over an envelope with five hundred dollars cash for Gracie's fund. Should Allison take it to the police or bank it? She'd let Luke decide.

When Allison had checked the total this morning, it was hovering around one hundred and thirty-seven thousand dollars. So close. A few days of school holidays and then Gracie would be in America. Unbelievable. This *annus horribilis* might possibly turn into a good year.

Gracie knelt on the kitchen stool, sprinkling hundreds and thousands across her buttered bread. Tiny balls of colour dotted the benchtop. Allison would have to make sure she wiped up every last one, leaving no trace of the sugary afternoon tea by the time Luke got home at six-thirty. They'd also shared Easter eggs at school—oops, definitely too much sugar today.

In the five days since Gracie had come back from Avoca, her cough had improved. Allison blamed herself for the illness. She should've put herself into quarantine when she'd first felt ill to avoid any risk of Gracie catching it. But she'd had to organise

Gracie Day. Bizarrely, Allison had endangered Gracie's life in order to save it.

Still wearing her Easter hat over the top of her pink beanie, Gracie concentrated on the fairy bread. She used a knife to smooth out the sprinkles so they weren't clumped together.

'Do you want milk with your fairy bread?' Allison asked.

'Yes, please.'

'Lovely manners, sweetheart.'

Sometimes, with all the attention, Gracie was not so lovely. One recess, Allison had caught the girl standing by the canteen, telling the children at the back of the queue that they should donate their money to her. A few of them had already handed over their coins; two of them were arguing, and another had begun shoving Gracie out of the way.

Allison was pouring the milk into a plastic cup when she heard her mobile ding. A message from the president of Wirriga soccer club. *We've just donated the BBQ money. $3800. All the best to Gracie.*

The club had pledged its takings from the summer soccer barbecues on Monday, Wednesday and Friday nights, along with some gala days and registration events. Allison opened the laptop and added the donation to the tally on the website, as Maz had shown her.

'Oh my God, Gracie. We've done it!'

'What?' The little girl was licking sprinkles from her fingers. Green and blue balls stuck to her nose.

Allison turned the laptop around to show her the tally line, now fully orange all the way along with no grey section waiting to be filled. A brand-new tagline shouted: *GOAL ACHIEVED:*

$140,702 of $140,000 goal. It had been a crazy four weeks of fundraising but Wirriga had made magic happen.

'We can get you to the special clinic in America!'

Allison pulled Gracie off the stool and twirled her around the kitchen.

'Are we dancing, Lally?'

'Yes, we're dancing! We have enough money for the plane and the hospital and the doctor.'

'Yay! Can you come with me and Daddy?'

Allison desperately wanted to go. To be Gracie's stand-in mother. But Luke might not want her there after she'd jeopardised his daughter's health. And, of course, there was Allison's fear of flying. And the question of money. She couldn't afford it. How would it look if the 'fundraising manager' used the funds for her own ticket?

'You'll only be away for one month.' Allison cuddled the girl. 'And when you come back, you'll feel so much better!'

'One month.' Gracie grinned. 'One month is thirty days.'

Allison had been teaching them about time in class.

'I can't believe we've done it!' Allison danced Gracie around the kitchen again.

—

On Friday evening, balloons and streamers dotted Allison's lounge room. Thirty of Gracie's Gang held their glasses high and toasted the little girl. Allison, Nadia and Shona had champagne while Maz and the gym crowd were drinking cranberry mocktails. Felix had poured lemonade for his mates, and apple juice for the children. Maz's parents were cuddling Gracie on the couch; the girl was trying to escape and join the other kids.

'Speech! Speech!' Maz clapped her hands and stared adoringly at Luke.

'Thank you everyone for creating Gracie's Gang and making this happen.' He sniffed back a tear. 'When Dr Rawson first mentioned immunotherapy, I was over the moon. But then he told me the cost and I didn't know how I'd ever come up with that kind of money—especially after everything we've been through. But you guys have done it. Thank you especially to Allison and Maz.'

Allison stood up before Maz had a chance to respond.

'Our small suburb has conjured up a miracle for little Gracie.' Allison held out her arms to encompass them all. 'And we've done it without a major sponsor in sight. I couldn't be prouder of this community and Wirriga Public School.'

'It just shows that every single dollar counts,' Maz interrupted. 'And I feel that we're following my favourite motto, which is to create your own destiny. We're doing that for Gracie. Creating a destiny for her.'

Maz's motto made no sense in this context; no-one wanted cancer in their destiny.

'This will be our front-page news.' Curtis raised his voice to be heard over the excitement. 'The power of the people to make dreams come true.'

'What was Dr Rawson's reaction?' Shona asked.

'He said, "I never doubted you'd do it."' Luke chuckled. 'And he was also relieved because everything is planned and ready to go. Here's to Chicago!'

Everyone raised their glasses again and shouted, 'Good luck in Chicago, Gracie!'

PART
TWO

Avoid a remedy that is worse than the disease.
Aesop, 'The Hawk, the Kite and the Pigeons'

18

ALLISON

Term 2, May

'WELCOME BACK, MY WONDERFUL WOMBATS.'

Allison smiled at her class of twenty-three children; only one missing. Some had damp fringes, their hair plastered in straight lines across their foreheads. Rain dripped down the window-panes and beat a steady drum on the roof. A cold wetness had settled in the small gap between Allison's trouser leg and her left shoe. No-one was ever prepared for rain on the first day of term. At least inside the classroom shimmered with colour—the silver starfish mobiles hanging from the ceiling, the coral reef collages stuck to the walls. The heavy coastal rain made it feel like they were actually living in their under-the-sea theme.

'Did everyone have a lovely holiday?'

'Yes, Mrs Walsh.' A chorus of voices.

'My granny took me to Sea World,' Zack called out. 'I saw dolphins jump in the air. They can talk!'

Allison had read his father was in jail, awaiting trial—he hadn't been granted bail.

'Yes, Zack, dolphins are very intelligent. Thank you for sharing. Let's remember to put our hands up before speaking.'

Instantly, Evelyn's arm shot into the air. 'Mrs Walsh, I think I forgot my lunch.'

Anxious Evelyn. Her sandwich would've been carefully wrapped by her mother and put inside her lunchbox into her bag. But if Evelyn didn't look now, she'd be edging towards the door, asking over and over, distracting the class.

'I'm sure it's there, Evelyn.' Allison smiled at her. 'But why don't you have a quick check?'

The girl's next worry would be the empty chair beside her. Having a classmate with cancer had increased her anxiety a thousandfold.

'Wonderful Wombats, come onto the mat and we'll take it in turns to talk about our holidays.' Allison beckoned them over to the sky-blue rug. 'When you're all sitting nicely, I'm going to start with some great news about Gracie.'

At six-fifteen this morning, when the radio alarm blared into the darkness, Allison had at first confused the pitter-patter of the rain with the sound of Luke showering. Lying there, cocooned in her doona, she'd ached for that first weekend of the school holidays. Gracie creeping into her bedroom and pretending to whisper: *Are you awake, Lally?* One morning, dancing around the bed, singing 'Let It Go', high-pitched and sweet and awfully off-key.

Instead of Gracie's giggles this morning, it was the radio news. *In the continuing fallout from the banking royal commission, another CEO has had his contract terminated with an alleged payout of one and a half million dollars.* Allison had jabbed at the button to silence it. Over a million dollars for an unscrupulous banker to spend on sports cars and houses when it could be used on research and medicine to save countless lives.

'Listen up, everyone.' Allison waited for the children to settle on the mat before continuing. 'Remember how Gracie was going on the plane to America in the school holidays?'

At the end of last term, the solar-powered school sign had flashed out a message: GOOD LUCK IN CHICAGO, GRACIE!!!!! Curtis had taken a photo of Gracie underneath the sign for the *Northern Beaches News*.

'She's at the hospital over there and she's had three infusions now. An infusion is a medicine put inside her body. It's all going really, really well and Gracie feels great.'

Three infusions down, nine to go. Depending on the blood counts and scans, another round in four months. Thank God, they hadn't closed the website after they'd achieved the goal; donations were still coming in and the extra money could go towards the second round.

'Can we send her a photo?'

'Good idea, Ty. Let's squish together on the rug so you all fit in the frame. We'll do a smiling photo and then one with crazy faces. Ready?'

After Allison had taken the photos, she showed them a picture of Gracie smiling on the Navy Pier Ferris wheel, with the Chicago skyscrapers behind her shimmering in the sun. Gracie would've loved being up so high. In her arms, she held Winnie the Wombat—the class had sent the mascot along with her to America for good luck.

Anxious Evelyn piped up: 'Is she all better now?'

'Almost. She needs a few more infusions. Let's send her the crazy picture and she might reply before the end of the day.'

Underneath the photo, Allison typed: *Good luck, Gracie! Love from the Wirriga Wombats.*

Late last night, Luke had called with praise for the clinical team: 'They're so sweet with Gracie. They make it into a game.' He was focusing on the positives, trying to keep Gracie's fear at bay. 'She's blowing you a kiss down the phone, Ally, and said she'll see you in two weeks, which is—hold on, Gracie's working it out . . . nope, she doesn't have enough fingers.' Luke had laughed before repeating her words: 'Half a whole month.' Gracie's funny words and Luke's deep chortle had made them feel present in the house. But at two in the morning, Allison was awake, hot with a night sweat and the shame of her thoughts. *If the infusions work and Gracie gets better, they'll move out. I'll sell the house. What will become of me then?*

She wouldn't be surprised if Tony marched in the real estate agents while Gracie was in America. In one of his texts, he'd accused her of stalking again, parking her car outside his house on the day Gracie had flown out. *I wasn't even on the Northern Beaches for most of Monday,* she replied. After the emotional farewell at the airport, Emmanuel had driven to her house, picked her up and taken her out to dinner. Like an old-fashioned gentleman. She'd stayed the night at his place in Neutral Bay and, this time, she'd studied his apartment, wondering what it would be like to create a new home, a new life.

———

When her phone rang at recess, Allison was surprised to see Tony's number flash up. He'd only call if something had happened to Felix. His complaints were all by text. She slipped out of the fire exit at the back of the staffroom and leant against the brick wall, out of sight of both staff and students.

'Is Felix all right?' she asked before he could speak.

'What?' One word of irritation. 'Yes, he's fine.'

'Good.'

'Allison, I've called the police again. You're insane.'

'I told you I wasn't even in the area that day.'

Should Allison admit that she'd stayed overnight with another man? Would that shock Tony into silence?

'I can't believe you sent that letter,' Tony went on. 'It's awful. Why would you scare us like that? All of us.'

'What are you talking about?'

'The threats you made in that letter.'

'I didn't write any letter,' she hissed, her hand shielding her mouth from any busybodies around the playground. 'Not this one, not the last one. Stop trying to manipulate me to sell the house.'

'It's in your handwriting. You've gone crazy.'

'I know about the baby, Tony.'

That stopped him for a moment. She heard a deep intake of breath.

'How do you know? Who've you told?'

Not: *I'm sorry for having an affair. For having a baby with another woman when we couldn't have one. You must be devastated.*

'Are you using Felix for free babysitting? Is that why you won't let him come home?' She responded to his questions with her own, unable to ask the one she really wanted—*How could you do this to me?*

'Who've you told?' Tony repeated. 'It's important, Allison.'

Because he was ashamed?

'Nadia.'

'Please, don't tell anyone else. I'm sorry I've been so secretive. It's a DV situation. Change of name, change of address and so on.'

He made it sound so professional. Not like it really was. Unethical. Inappropriate. Completely wrong.

'What? You ran off with a client? You had a baby with her!' She couldn't keep her voice down now. 'Oh my God, you should be struck off.'

'No, no, it's not like that. I never took advantage of her. I helped her out. Her husband went ballistic after the baby arrived.'

Had her principled, honourable husband slept with his client while he was still married to Allison?

'Your baby?'

'NO!' She could hear him striding around his office. 'Is that why you sent the letter? Because you thought the baby was mine?'

'I didn't write any bloody letter!'

Above Allison's head, the school bell clanged. She ended the call without saying goodbye. Took five slow breaths before re-entering the staffroom. Now it all made sense. The suddenness of his leaving, the secrecy, his furious reaction about her so-called stalking. Protecting the woman and her baby, protecting his reputation. Presumably the staff at the women's shelter didn't know; it would be against all the rules. But how could Tony have trusted his son with this information and not his wife of twenty-four years? Bastard. Did he think that, in her state of abandonment, she'd leak it, ruin his career?

And what about Helena's ex-husband? Was he controlling? Or physically violent?

Tony had put their son at risk.

If Allison hadn't been the one writing the letters and hadn't been the one sitting outside their house recently, then who was the person watching them?

—

During the next period, Allison found it hard to focus on teaching as she tried to figure out the situation. Was Tony worried about Helena's ex-husband or sure that he wouldn't find her? Tony had stayed away from Wirriga, from all their old friends. Was the man someone they knew? While she asked the class to think of words beginning with the letter H, her thoughts looped around and around. H for House. H for Home. H for Happy. Husband. Heinous. Hazardous. Hateful. Hostile.

By the time the bell rang at lunch, Allison couldn't see the other side of the oval for the torrents of rain. The hollow next to the toilet block had turned into a pond. Puddles dotted the playground, the basketball court was a slick of dark green. An announcement over the loudspeaker informed everyone they'd be staying inside today.

'Please get your lunchboxes from your bags,' Allison said, 'and come down onto the rug.'

Lunch in the classroom would send them all mad, particularly on the first day of term. The hyperactive ones were tumbling puppies who needed their daily exercise to stay calm inside.

Within ten minutes, the noise was bouncing off the ceiling.

'Zack took my apple.'

'Where's the red Lego?'

'Can I have a fairy picture?'

Searching through her folder of colouring-in sheets, Allison realised she'd given all the fairies to Gracie to keep her occupied on the plane. She found a hot-air balloon and handed it to Selina. This morning, when a group of kindy parents had asked about Gracie, Selina's mother wanted to know more about the infusions.

'It's a new drug,' Allison had explained. 'They give a small dose every few days.'

'Immunotherapy didn't help my brother.' Selina's mother shook her head sadly. 'It's meant to be a wonder drug but it doesn't work for everyone.'

Allison had nodded her understanding while silently imploring: *Please don't tell me your negative cancer story.*

'Well, there are all kinds of immunotherapy drugs,' Allison had said. 'This is a different type.'

The type to bring hope.

Selina gathered a handful of crayons for her hot-air balloon and began colouring. After Allison had divided the pile of Lego between four children, she opened her bag to take out her sandwich. And for a quick peek at her mobile. Had Tony called back or set a lawyer on to her? Had Gracie replied to their photo?

The screen was busy but not with text messages.

Eleven missed calls from Luke.

162

Whatever Luke had to tell her could not be said in a recorded message. Five times Allison called him back. No answer. By then, she was home, on to her umpteenth cup of tea, prowling the empty rooms of the house. Each time she went to add milk to her mug, Allison stood staring at the sparkly heart frame stuck to the fridge: her and Gracie at Luna Park. The sky blue above them, the Harbour Bridge in the background, their faces glowing. That day, she'd had Gracie to herself; they'd gone on the merry-go-round, bumbled through the maze of mirrors in Coney Island and whizzed down the big slides on sacks. Then Gracie had asked about the Ferris wheel.

'I don't think our ticket covers that ride,' Allison had said.

'Oh.' A sigh of disappointment. 'Daddy says it's a bird's-eye view.'

Gracie had been on a high all day and, just like that, Allison had punctured her joy with a lie. A pin popping a balloon.

'The truth is, sweetheart—' the Ferris wheel seemed to sway above her '—I'm scared of heights.'

'What do you call a bird that's scared of heights?' Gracie rushed out the joke that she'd told many times before.

'I don't know.'

'A chicken!' Gracie had laughed. 'Birds can't be scared of heights. And not you, Lally. Grown-ups aren't scared.'

'Well, grown-ups *can* be scared.' Allison took a deep breath. 'I'm scared to go on that Ferris wheel.'

'Don't be silly, Lally. I'll look after you.'

Allison's legs had trembled as she stepped from the platform into the carriage. Gracie's hand snaked into hers and held it tight. Up in the sky, heart hammering, stomach queasy,

163

Allison had to keep her eyes fixed straight ahead on the horizon. Afterwards, they'd bought a bucket of hot chips and chocolate gelato. Not on Luke's approved list but she needed them to settle her tummy. Slurping on her gelato, Gracie had echoed one of Luke's gym phrases: 'You did good!'

The mobile rang while Allison was staring out of the sliding doors, watching the rain in the gum trees. The leaves glossy green with the wetness, the trunks orange-red.

'Ally . . .' Luke said. His words dissolved into soft sobs.

Allison leant backwards against the kitchen bench, pressing the phone hard to her ear.

'What's happened?'

'She had a reaction. Her body went into shock.' Another sob. 'They don't understand why.'

'How is she now? Are they taking her off the trial?'

A silence. Was Gracie's last hope gone after all their efforts to get her there?

'She didn't recover.'

The edge of the kitchen bench wasn't holding her up. Pulling out the stool, Allison collapsed onto it.

'They tried everything . . . they couldn't save her.' He was sobbing loudly down the line, his breath coming in great gasps every few seconds.

Allison gritted her teeth to prevent the pain in her chest from erupting as a deep moan. 'She was supposed to stay the same or get better,' she muttered. 'They said the drugs couldn't harm her.'

'You know they told us about the risks.'

But Allison had refused to hear.

If they raised enough money, if they flew Gracie across the world to the right hospital, if they saw the right doctors who provided the right infusion of drugs, if the whole community treasured her enough . . .

All of that medical support and the power of love from a whole community should have been able to protect their little girl.

19

UPSTAIRS IN GRACIE'S BEDROOM, ALLISON OPENED THE WARDROBE and touched the school dress. Imagined the little girl inside it, running through the playground, swinging on the monkey bars—even when she wasn't supposed to. Circled by friends.

'Gracie, let's build a fort under the tree.'

'Gracie, come play our game!'

'Gracie, when are you gonna die?'

Cradling the green uniform, Allison slumped onto the bed. A bare bed without the usual collection of animals; Gracie had taken her stuffed toys on the plane with her, along with Winnie the Wombat. Allison hoped she'd been holding one of her favourite toys, that she hadn't been frightened. *She asked me to come. I should've been there.*

Tears dripped down Allison's face and onto the school uniform, creating dark splotches. Overhead, the rain continued its drumbeat on the roof. From Gracie's window, usually she could see the bush leading towards Manly Dam but the trees had disappeared into a mist of cloud and drizzle. Like Gracie. Was she somewhere white, in heaven? With her mother? Allison mouthed a prayer into the whiteness: *Dear God, take Gracie into your care and protection. Please look after our special girl.*

―

It seemed that Allison's mother arrived as soon as she'd hung up the phone but time must have passed. When she opened the front door, the sky was dark and streetlights had flickered on.

Mum hugged her so tightly that Allison felt faint.

'Such terrible news, darling.'

Nodding, she disentangled herself from her mother's grasp and walked into the lounge room. In here, there were no photos of Gracie. When Allison sank onto the couch, Barbara sat next to her and patted her thigh.

'I was positive it would work,' Barbara said.

'The infusions were meant to boost her immune system.' Allison shut her eyes. 'She wasn't supposed to . . . die.'

The word echoed off the walls. What if Gracie's cold—the cold that Allison had passed on to her—had made her more susceptible to the rare side effects? What if the allergic reaction caused by Allison had harmed her immune system?

Barbara sniffled and searched for a handkerchief in her bag.

'Luke's not coping,' Allison said.

'Of course, he's not.'

'No, I mean, his body's not coping. He's gone into shock. Not shock.' Allison had been the one in shock; too shocked to listen properly. 'He's had some kind of heart episode.'

'That happened to one of our golf ladies when her husband died.' Barbara clutched her hands against her own heart. 'The symptoms of a heart attack but no permanent damage. They had to postpone her husband's funeral until she was out of hospital.'

A funeral. Luke's approach to Gracie's illness had been smiles and sunshine. They'd never discussed her death. His wife's funeral had been organised by her parents; he'd said he was too numb. *I'll always regret not doing the eulogy for her. I didn't even choose our favourite song.* Sarah's death had blindsided him. At the time, they'd been focusing on getting Gracie through chemo.

A funeral. A coffin. Or would he have to choose a cheaper option—cremation—to get Gracie home? Oh God, now Luke was a patient in an American hospital, he'd have to pay for his own care.

'They're doing tests on his heart,' Allison explained. 'He doesn't know how long he'll have to stay in there.'

'It's probably Takotsubo cardiomyopathy. They call it broken heart syndrome.'

Allison could feel her own pulse throbbing in her neck.

Broken heart syndrome.

All of Wirriga would be suffering from it.

—

Allison followed her mother into the kitchen and watched as she poured tomato soup from a tin into a saucepan. At the sight of the oozing blood red mixture, her stomach cramped. The green smoothies, the restricted diet, Luke's approved list, no sugar, no junk food—all for nothing. Gracie should have been allowed to eat ice-cream every day of her short life. Allison reached down to the cupboard where the bullet blender was kept. Yanked it out and, with the power cord trailing on the floor, carried it across to the kitchen bin. When she went to close the cupboard, the door caught on a small plastic container. As she kicked at it, Allison realised there were more of them; they'd been hidden behind the blender. Four different containers of pills and a glass bottle with liquid inside. *Super Strong for Super Bones*, read one label. *Great Greens, Great Health. Detox for Cancer.*

She'd never seen them before. Had Luke been blending these in with the green smoothies? Allison shook the containers—less than half full. No list of ingredients. The labels said: *Detox for Life! Bounce Back the Natural Way. Imported by the Bio-Antidotes Company.*

How had these containers ended up in her kitchen cupboard? They'd talked about the evils of alternative remedies; Curtis had even written that blog post. She thought Luke agreed. Some of those so-called remedies made patients sicker. Just like Aesop's fable about the pigeons inviting in a hawk to protect them from the kite; the hawk had slaughtered the defenceless birds. She'd read it to the children last term and explained the moral: *Avoid a remedy that is worse than the disease.*

'Are you okay, darling?'

Her mother must have overheard her muttered swearing.

What if this herbal shit had killed Gracie? Allison closed her fist around the plastic container. She'd taken the lead in encouraging Wirriga to donate for Gracie's exciting new treatment—thousands and thousands of dollars from mums and dads, grandparents, sports clubs and local businesses. Oh dear God, what if all of that had been undone by something that had happened in her house?

'Allison?'

The note of alarm in Mum's voice made the decision for her. Allison put the pills back on the shelf, shut the cupboard doors, and stood up. For once, she was going to make a fast decision and overcome her fear. She had to find out the reason for Gracie's unexpected death.

'I'm going to America tomorrow.'

—

After her mum had left, Allison scrolled through a list of flights on her laptop. Twenty hours to Chicago via Los Angeles—nearly a whole day up in the air; she wouldn't think about that part. Gracie had been brave, and she'd follow her example. Last year, they'd planned to go to Hawaii for Nadia's fiftieth birthday. She'd found an online course which was supposed to cure the fear of flying, plus her GP had given her a prescription for Valium. Allison had got her passport and the electronic travel authorisation to enter America. But she'd never made that flight. A week before, Tony's best friend in England died from a stroke. So unexpected. Tony had begged Allison to come to the funeral but she couldn't do it; the sudden death had made Allison even more afraid to fly.

Slouching over the desk, Allison wondered if she should take the rest of the year off, get a one-way ticket, stay in America, hide out as far away from Wirriga as possible. Sell the bloody house. Get away from Tony and his new woman and baby. Walk away from everything. But that would mean leaving Felix. She groaned at the thought of having to tell her son the news. Her poor boy was having such a rough year and now this.

With a heavy heart she dialled his number, but there was no answer. She'd only seen him twice in the school holidays: at the party when they'd celebrated achieving the goal and the night he'd come over to say goodbye to Gracie. He'd given her a small electronic game to play on the plane. Allison had no idea where he'd got the money. Felix still hadn't forgiven her for accusing him of stealing. *You took Luke's side over mine without even checking!* She'd offered to help him with homework, drive him to holiday activities, but each time, he'd say, 'No, thanks'. Perhaps he was avoiding her so she couldn't ask about the baby.

When Felix rang back an hour later, she found it hard to break the news.

'What're you saying, Allison?' he asked.

Three weeks ago, he'd stopped calling her Mum. That tone, every time he used her name, was a slap in the face.

'I'm so, so sorry to tell you that Gracie died at the hospital.'

'What? Fucking hell!'

Allison let the swear word pass by; it was warranted in these circumstances. More hurt and confusion for him. And this time, she'd brought it into Felix's life. She explained that she was flying to Chicago tomorrow to sort out the logistics. Presumably there would have to be an autopsy. What would they find?

'You're going on a plane?' Felix made a choking sound. 'By yourself? No way. Dad won't believe it.'

Tony would be happy to have her out of the country, on the other side of the planet.

'Please let him know.' She wished Felix was at home with her now, so she could enfold him in her arms like she used to. 'I love you, sweetheart. I'll text you from Chicago.'

'Don't text. Use WhatsApp. It's free. Remember? I set it up for you.'

'Okay, thanks.'

'Good luck, Mum.'

A glass of wine in one hand, Allison unzipped her bright red carry-on suitcase and wondered what to pack. It wouldn't be cold in Chicago; despite being spring there, the weather was similar to Sydney's autumn. She'd take the pills to show Dr Mercado. Sitting on the bed next to the empty suitcase, Allison made two more difficult phone calls, to Nadia and Shona.

Ten p.m.—still too early to phone Luke again. She had no idea how he'd cope with Gracie's death. This broken heart syndrome—she'd googled Takotsubo cardiomyopathy—would take weeks to recover from. He wouldn't be able to tackle his despair by training in the gym, pressing weights, jogging for endless miles.

Her mobile rang, and Allison grabbed for it, nearly knocking over the wineglass.

'Hey, Ally.' His voice so quiet she could barely hear him. He should be resting.

'How're you feeling? I mean, how's your heart?'

'My whole body hurts. I keep thinking of my brave little girl being stuck in a hospital bed just like this. She never complained.'

'I'm coming over,' she told him. 'I'll be with you soon.'

'But you're scared of flying, Ally. Don't worry about me. Brian is coming from Boston.'

The kindness of strangers. Brian's brother had died from thymic carcinoma last year and now Brian was campaigning for more research into this rare disease. That was how he'd come across Gracie. He'd emailed Luke all sorts of information about new treatment options in America.

'I've already booked the flight,' Allison said.

'Won't the children need you there?'

Luke sounded exhausted—physically and emotionally. And in the midst of his own grief, he was thinking of others. But for once, Allison was thinking of herself. She couldn't go to school tomorrow, hide her own broken heart, and help the children through their sadness.

'Shona and Declan will look after them. I'll be there for you.'

'You've already done so much, Ally. I can't ask you to do more.'

He hadn't asked her to do any of it. In fact, it was Gracie and Luke who had kept *her* going this year.

When they'd said good-bye, the house was silent again apart from the drip-drip-drip of rain in the gutters. It reminded her of Gracie's footsteps tapping up the stairs. Dancing around the room. Jumping up and down for her rabbit joke. *How do rabbits like to dance? Hip-hop style!*

On the laptop, Allison clicked to the blog post from two weeks ago, when Gracie had been starting the immunotherapy trial and they'd all been full of hope. Luke had explained the treatment, and underneath were dozens of comments wishing Gracie good luck. The last one stood out—Allison hadn't seen it before.

TN from Georgetown: *Why has this child been accepted onto this clinical trial? Please get a second opinion.*

Allison stared at the words: *second opinion.* Luke had moved to Sydney for Dr Rawson; he'd always trusted the specialist's advice. Never questioned the treatment. Followed the recommendation for the trial, despite the enormous cost and the upheaval in Gracie's life.

Why didn't Luke get a second opinion? What if Dr Rawson made a mistake in sending Gracie to that clinic in Chicago?

20

MAZ

MAZ PLACED THE PLATE OF CHICKEN BREAST AND GREEN VEGETABLES in front of Dad, and sat down opposite Mum. She'd rushed to get home, have a shower and cook a healthy dinner for them.

'Thanks, love,' Dad said. 'Don't we normally have mash with this?'

'Remember, we're carb-free this week, Dad. How much have you lost now?'

Dad picked up his knife and fork. 'Dunno. Maybe twelve.' He polished off the chicken breast in three mouthfuls.

'That's awesome! Don't give up after all your effort.'

'I'm tired, love. Long day at work.'

When Maz studied him properly, she could see a tinge of grey around his eyes. Despite that, he was almost a different person from three months ago. The extra layer of flab under his chin had shrunk right back and he had some definition around his cheekbones. These days, he looked nothing like Joseph, the man who'd collapsed at the gym.

'Have you heard from Luke?' Mum asked.

'He texted early this morning. Gracie's doing well.'

She'd sent him a selfie taken at the gym: in her Lycra, chest out, ponytail over one shoulder, holding up a boxing glove. Her lips in a kiss for him. Her reflection replicated over and over in the mirror behind. *I'm gunning for you & Gracie*, she'd typed under the photo.

Luke had texted straight back. *Too hot to handle! Miss you lots. Love you, babe. xx*

Neither of them had said the L word before. Oh my God, did he actually mean it? They made such a good team. Maz had spent ages working out her reply. She typed back slowly: *Miss you too. Hope it's going well. Love you + hugs + kisses.* She'd added two smiley face emojis, a love heart and a balloon.

Maz watched as Dad left the dinner table and helped himself to a VB from the fridge. So much for no alcohol during the week. But she wouldn't say anything; he seemed shattered.

~

In her bedroom, Maz checked the time in Chicago. Two a.m. Luke would be asleep. As she clicked through the phone, she realised she'd missed a WhatsApp call from him. Wait, it showed that he was online now. Maz typed out a quick message: *Are you awake?*

He rang instantly. As Luke told her the news, she started shaking. She could still see Gracie waving goodbye from the back seat of Allison's car as they set off for the airport. Grinning with excitement about America.

'Oh, babe,' she whispered. 'Gracie seemed so much better when she left. I thought the pills were helping . . .'

Maz suddenly felt very young; she didn't know the right words to say, didn't know how to comfort him. Could she help him through this into their future together?

After they hung up, Maz lay on her bed, staring at the ceiling. Oh God, Gracie had *died*. DIED. She rubbed at the purple bracelet on her wrist. And Luke was all the way over in America by himself, sick in a hospital bed. He'd asked her to tell everyone—her parents, her sister, Nico at the gym, all the instructors, his clients. They'd all donated. When Nico had given nine thousand dollars, she'd overheard another instructor complain it was an insane amount that would affect their wages and equipment. All of that money to save Gracie's life and now . . . Unable to be saved, just like Joseph.

First, Maz rang her sister, asked her to come over so they could tell the parents together.

'You've gotta be kidding me,' Kelli shouted down the phone. 'Gracie was s'posed to get better. Not fuckin' die.'

'Calm down before you get here. Mum and Dad are going to be so upset.'

Mum had taken Gracie under her wing. Played games with her, babysat, watched kids' TV shows. Even when Maz was at work, Mum would invite the little girl over.

'It's just plain wrong,' Kelli said. 'It should be old Mrs Grainger down the street. She's ninety-five. She's already had ninety more years than Gracie.'

Maz couldn't wrap her head around that.

'Just hurry up,' Maz said. 'I can't leave my bedroom until you're here.'

'Okay, I'm coming. By the way, you might want to think about your website. Is Gracie still the poster girl?'

Normally, Maz loved early mornings best: a time for those who wanted to make the most of their lives. The magical dawn of a great day, with endless possibilities. Not today. Mum and Dad had been as upset as she expected last night. And now she had to tell Nico before anyone else.

The gym was already buzzing at five-thirty. Maz got through her two early classes, a fake smile on her face, her body heavy with every step. By eight, Nico was in his office. When he heard the news, he leapt from behind his desk and wrapped his arms around Maz. It wasn't a comforting hug; with his huge biceps, Nico could probably squeeze her to death like one of those pythons with their prey.

'How's Luke?'

'Not good,' Maz admitted. 'And he's in hospital over there. He's got this heart thing.'

'We all think we're so strong, but we're soft. In here.' Nico held his hand over his chest. 'You too, Maz. You shouldn't have come in this morning. Take the rest of the day off. And tomorrow too.'

'It's okay. I can do tomorrow's classes.'

If she didn't instruct, she didn't get paid.

She parked at the headland north of Freshwater beach and climbed down the wet, slippery rocks. Positioned herself so she could see the long curving sands of Manly to the south and the jutting rocks of Long Reef to the north. Clouds hung low in the sky, staining the sea dark grey. This was where the seals had been playing last month. They'd planned a whale-watching cruise in winter; Gracie had been excited by the idea of even bigger sea creatures.

Luke hadn't talked about his fears with Maz. One motto on the gym wall declared: *There's no such thing as failure, it's all about your viewpoint.* But how could there possibly be a different viewpoint here?

Gracie was dead.

Ting. Ting. Ting. The texts and messages rolled in to Maz's phone.

—*Devastating.*

—*I'm heartbroken. You must be too.*

—*How's Luke holding up? Give him my condolences.*

—*OMFG! What a shock!!!!!!!!*

—*Wasn't this the cure? How could it happen?*

Jiggling her legs, Maz didn't know what to do with these twisting, twirling sensations radiating from her tummy. Like one of those old lava lamps with heavy blobs bouncing around inside her. Apart from Joseph's death, which had crushed her self-confidence at work, her only other loss had been Smokey. Maz and Kelli used to fight over whose bed Smokey would sleep on each night, although the cat mostly decided herself. And then, when Maz was sixteen, Smokey kept getting tick after tick. They'd given her the tick treatment but it wasn't working. Old and exhausted, Smokey's body gave out. For months after, whenever Maz came home from school, she was heartbroken anew that Smokey didn't thread her sinewy body through Maz's legs as she unlocked the door.

Losing Gracie did not feel like that.

The little girl had been so alive when Maz hugged her goodbye. Maz had given her a *Frozen* colouring-in book, along with some protein balls for strength. When Gracie saw the cover of the book, she screeched, 'ELSA!' Briefly Maz had wished she were going to America too—she'd never been overseas—but a trip to a hospital in Chicago would not be her first choice.

Moving would help. Running, dancing, jumping. Any activity to shift the uncomfortable sensations inside her body. Maz clambered back up to the car park and jogged along the clifftop path to Curl Curl beach. She sprinted down to the sand, yanked off her shoes and leggings, and ran into the waves in her g-string and crop top. The shock of the cold water against her skin overrode the other sensations. Afterwards, to dry off without a towel, she spun around in circles, staring up at the grey sky, until the world was one big giant blur. It was something that Gracie used to do.

Em-Jay popped in to see her at home after lunch. Kelli called from work on her three o'clock break. Other friends posted condolences on Maz's Insta page. When she was alone again, Maz pulled out the bag of purple bracelets from her top drawer. With the help of the school lunchtime club, she and Gracie had finally caught up with demand. Instead of planning tonight's healthy dinner, Maz sat on her bed and counted the bracelets. Fifty-seven. She'd never imagined that she would be giving them out at Gracie's funeral.

Curtis came by on his way home from the office.

'I'm so sorry,' he said, handing her a bouquet of purple flowers.

Following her into the kitchen, he dumped his backpack on a chair and slumped at the round table. His lanky legs stretched out across the lino.

'Is it up online already?' Maz asked.

She hadn't checked yet, but once Curtis decided to publish, everyone would know.

'Just a short piece. I'm doing an article for tomorrow but I wanted to talk to Luke first. Have you got any vodka?'

'Vodka?'

'Yeah. I think a fucking tragedy like this calls for vodka.'

The parentals' drinks cupboard had a range of spirits but no vodka.

'Brandy?' she called over her shoulder.

'Sure. Anything.'

Maz poured a large glass for Curtis and a tiny one for herself. She rarely drank. Some of her friends popped tabs for a high time without the hangover. But not Maz—she'd seen enough pictures of beautiful teenagers dying at music festivals.

Curtis took a large slug of the brandy and coughed.

'That's pretty rough.' He coughed again. Took another mouthful. 'How's Luke? I just can't imagine . . .'

'Devastated.' Maz pretended to take a sip. The brandy fumes wafted upwards and tickled her nose.

'We'll do a full spread in the Saturday paper. Gracie touched so many people.'

Maz couldn't stomach the brandy. She went to get the jug of cold water from the fridge. When she sat down again, Curtis had his camera out on the kitchen table.

'What're you doing?'

'I thought we could take a photo and you can give me a quote about Gracie.' He shrugged and held out his hands, palms open, long skinny fingers reaching out towards her. 'I'm going to interview the school principal and Nico and Dr Rawson. I've left a message with Allison but she hasn't called back.'

'I don't know.' Maz twisted her ponytail and squirmed in her seat. 'Can't you write something for me?'

Steepling his fingers against his nose, Curtis frowned at her. He looked like a granddad when he did that. The boys at school had teased him for it—'Fag Old Man'—they'd yell when he was considering a problem in maths class. Maz hadn't really known him back then; it was only after the bullying that they'd become friends, when he'd arrived at the gym to bulk up.

When Curtis didn't answer immediately, Maz asked him a different question.

'I haven't seen you at the gym lately. Where've you been?'

'I was there a few weeks ago. Went to Luke's class.'

Duh, of course. All the gay blokes preferred Luke's class to any other. She'd seen how Curtis looked at Luke and wondered if others recognised the same desire in her own eyes. Luke was so tactile, touching Curtis on the shoulder, throwing his arms around Nico, holding a client's hips to show her how to move properly. It made him a great trainer. Maz tried not to feel jealous.

'You could just say that Gracie was a gorgeous girl and the whole gym was supporting her and her dad,' Curtis suggested.

She suspected that Luke would rather she said nothing. Oh God, she still hadn't edited her website—she needed to remove Gracie's smiling face from the homepage and disable the donate button and the links to Curtis' articles.

'Can we take the photo now?' Curtis asked, standing up to tower over her. 'We could do it in the front garden next to that bush with the red leaves. Or you could hold up the purple bouquet?'

The bouquet lay in its plastic wrapping on the counter next to the sink. She should find a vase and stick it in water. Pushing herself out of her chair, Maz fought an overwhelming tiredness.

'Quick, let's take it in the front garden before Mum and Dad get home. They're pretty upset.'

Having her photo taken by Curtis was usually a good experience—he brought the best out of her. She'd grin, slightly raise an eyebrow, tilt her head down and flick her ponytail over her shoulder. But today was sombre. She sat on the brick wall, the red bush behind her, another tree in the background, bare of leaves. The dampness of yesterday's rain seeped through her leggings, chilling her bum and the backs of her thighs. Curtis asked her to put one hand under her chin and stare off down the street.

'As if waiting for Luke and Gracie to come home.'

At that point, Maz burst into tears.

'Perfect.' Curtis kept clicking.

When they finished, Maz expected Curtis to leave but he collected the mail from their letterbox and followed her inside again. He studied one of the letters before handing it over.

'Why is the Australian Border Force writing to you?' he asked. 'You've never been out of the country.'

The envelope was addressed to her personally. She took it from him and opened it.

Notice of Seizure
Your package has been seized by Australian Border Force and will be destroyed.

It contains a prohibited substance and its supply in Australia is illegal. These capsules do not meet the quality and safety standards to be included on the Australian Register of Therapeutic Goods. They pose a risk to your health. They show an increased risk of liver damage, hepatitis and acute liver failure causing death. If you have any capsules in your possession, stop taking them immediately. Consult your doctor if you have any concerns about your health.

It is an offence against Australian customs law to import prohibited goods. For some goods, the penalty may be up to ten years' imprisonment. Australian Border Force can, and does, prosecute offenders.

Maz put a hand on the back of the chair to steady herself. Australian Border Force—all she knew about them was from the TV show, where they took suspicious airline passengers off to a small room and arrested them for importing drugs.

'We urge Australians to use extreme caution when considering buying medicines online . . .' Curtis was reading aloud over her shoulder. 'What the fuck?'

Dropping the letter onto the kitchen table, Maz covered her face with her hands.

'What's the prohibited substance?' Curtis asked.

Maz wished Curtis would disappear. The words ricocheted in her head. *Acute liver failure causing death.* Why exactly had Gracie died? Luke mentioned a reaction. Was it liver failure?

'We could do an exposé in the paper.' Curtis rested his hands on her shoulders, as some kind of comfort. 'Without naming you, of course. The dangers of buying medicines online—a cautionary tale to others.'

'Shut up, Curtis.'

'Sorry, but you know I'm only on a short-term contract. I need some good stories if I'm going to be made permanent. Maybe I could take some photos of the pills before you throw them away. How much did they cost?'

'Just go!'

He put his camera in his backpack, and let himself out the front door. Maz stared at the letter again, focusing on the last line—*up to ten years' imprisonment*. Australian Border Force had taken her package, they had her name and address; they could turn up at her house at any moment. The letter listed a chemical but Maz didn't know which product it was in. She'd been importing fourteen different products—supplements for her gym clients and herbal medicines for Gracie. The labels didn't list all the ingredients. How could she work it out?

Maz checked her Fitbit—5.45 p.m. Mum and Dad should've been home by now. She folded the letter into a small square and hid it underneath an old jewellery box, in her bedside drawer. All she wanted to do was talk to Luke, but he was the one person Maz couldn't tell. Maybe she could start by googling each product to see if the ingredients were listed online.

On the bedside table, her mobile buzzed. A text from Mum.

We're at the hospital. Dad's not well but don't panic. Can you meet us in Emergency?

21

LUKE

Luke finished typing and pressed share. The news would send shockwaves through Wirriga and the surrounding suburbs. There were people he should ring but he didn't have the energy. Ally and Maz would tell everyone. In his experience, bad news spread faster than good.

All the hospital visits, the diet, the supplements, the online research, the queries to overseas doctors, the reading-up on drugs and alternative remedies, raising more than one hundred and forty thousand dollars . . . all of it had led to this moment.

The most devastating news. Our amazing Gracie has lost the battle. She had a very rare reaction to the treatment.

I can't thank you enough for your love and support to give her the best possible chance.

If you wish to donate in Gracie's memory, the funds will go to the Sydney Children's Hospital.

The shock has resulted in a minor heart issue for me and I'm in hospital in Chicago. That means funeral arrangements

will be delayed. Thank you to everyone who joined Gracie's
Gang to help a beautiful, happy, one-of-a-kind little girl.

Gracie will be in our hearts forever.

The last time he'd kissed Gracie's forehead, he'd noticed that
her hair was growing again. Wispy strands, dark against her pale
scalp. Luke had tucked the white sheet around his daughter's body
and gazed at the blank walls of the room. Anonymous, sterile.

Had he done all that he could?

Or had he made one little mistake that affected everything?

22

ALLISON

ALLISON GUESSED SHE'D HAD LESS THAN TWO HOURS SLEEP—HER thoughts flicking from memories of Gracie, to worry about Luke, to plans for her class, to speculation about the identity of Helena's ex-husband. But the same question was running through all of it: *Why did Gracie die?*

At three in the morning, she called Dr Mercado's clinic in Chicago.

'We cannot give out information about a patient.'

Whatever Allison said, the woman on the other end repeated the same line. It was like talking to a robot. Luke had described the team as 'caring', but clearly that didn't include the receptionist. When Allison tried to make an appointment, it was a three-month wait.

Three months to hide whatever had happened to Gracie.

Then she attempted to track down TN, the person on the blog page who had questioned the clinical trial. But there was no contact information. She sent a message to Brian in Boston asking if he could help. She didn't want to bother Luke with her concerns, didn't want to put any more stress on his heart.

At five a.m., she typed a list detailing lessons for the Wirriga Wombats for the next week and a half.

At five-thirty, she texted Luke a copy of her flight arrival time.

At six, she showered and finished packing.

The bright red suitcase sat in the front hall ready to go. Now, a quick breakfast, a call to Declan and then off to the airport. She'd been planning to catch public transport; after splurging on the ticket, Allison needed to watch her cash flow again. *Take care of the pennies and the pounds will look after themselves.* Her father's motto. But when she spoke to Nadia last night, her friend had offered to pick her up.

Was it too early to call the principal? She'd worked with Declan Considine for five years but she didn't know his morning routine. His wife answered his mobile.

'How's Gracie? We've been thinking of her. Declan's just coming out of the shower.'

An image of Declan nude shot into her head. Knobbly knees, wrinkly skin, white concave stomach, elbows jutting out from his skinny arms.

'I . . . um . . . thanks, Kathleen. I can ring back later.'

'Wait a sec. He's here now.'

Could Allison tell the principal the awful news while he stood there in a towel? He needed more protection, some body armour against the blow.

'I'm so sorry, Declan,' Allison said, apologising for being the bearer of bad news, even though her own heart was hurting.

He sighed heavily. 'So she's lost the battle.'

Battle. Allison hated that word. It was mentioned in almost every newspaper article, every online story. Gracie was a little girl, not a soldier; she shouldn't have had to go into battle. Ironic that she'd started the treatment on ANZAC Day—Curtis had made it the focus of one article. Oh no, the *Northern Beaches News* would run a story. Allison had imagined Gracie coming back as a medical marvel. Not this. She'd been so busy whipping up media for the fundraising, it'd never occurred to her that, one day, she might not want Curtis to report on Gracie.

Quickly, she explained to Declan about going to Chicago.

'I understand. We'll sort out a substitute. Thank you for organising your lessons.'

'Shall we do a special assembly when I'm back?' she asked. 'So Luke can be there also?'

'Of course. And we'll bring in another school counsellor. It'll hit them all so hard.'

In the background, she heard Kathleen start to sob.

The staff, the students, everyone who had become a part of Gracie's Gang . . . they'd all expected Gracie to get better. So many families had donated time and money, and invested their hope in one special little girl. Had all their efforts been compromised somehow by the actions of Allison or Luke or Dr Rawson?

The traffic in the Harbour Tunnel slowed. Nadia changed lanes, although the other one seemed to be going at a snail's pace too.

'Have you told Tony you're going?' Nadia asked.

'No, I asked Felix to do it.' She flinched as the truck next to them blasted its horn. 'Tony will take it as a sign that he can sell the house.'

'Oh, come on, Allison. Give him a bit of credit.'

When Allison had first invited Luke and Gracie to stay, she'd presented it as purely altruistic. *That poor girl with cancer can't live in those horrible holiday flats.* Even to Nadia, she hadn't admitted her ulterior motive: *I'm stopping Tony from selling.* How fast would he act now? At least he wouldn't be able to accuse her of stalking while she was out of the country; the police couldn't take it to the next level.

At the airport, Nadia wanted to come inside the terminal, but Allison felt that would increase her anxiety. Without a friend to lean on, she had to be strong. She hadn't been so strong when she'd driven Luke and Gracie to the airport. As they were about to check in, Allison had failed to hold back the tears.

'Maybe you should go now,' Luke had whispered.

He'd seen her distress and wanted to protect Gracie. So Allison had taken a quick photo of them for Facebook and the blog: Gracie pointing excitedly up at the departures board. She'd hugged the little girl tight, pleased that Gracie was excited, not terrified.

Now, as she handed over her passport at the check-in counter, Allison's heart was thumping. Oh dear God, this was a mistake. How could she possibly board this flight without Tony or Nadia next to her? The minute she was finished with the check-in, she'd take the Valium.

And then she'd be going through security with her carry-on bag.

Security. All at once it occurred to her: Allison had packed the herbal pills but she had no idea what they were. Would she be arrested before she even boarded the plane?

23

FELIX

FELIX FLINCHED AT THE COOL WATER SEEPING THROUGH HIS WETSUIT and paddled into the break. Only a small crew this morning. Yesterday's rain and the foamy backwash had put some off. But it'd be worth it for the clean little sets.

The water reflected the grey skies. Grey below, grey above. Even the long beach was washed of colour—a dark beige instead of its usual sparkling gold. He used to see Luke and Maz jogging along the sand early on Sunday mornings. They blended in with all the other fit bods working out. Before Mum and Dad had split up, he mostly surfed at Queenscliff—easier to get to, but so many tourists and wannabes. Here at Curl Curl, he just had to watch out for the strong rip.

A chopper buzzed overhead. Autumn, so it couldn't be beach safety and shark monitoring patrols. Maybe a rescue helicopter heading for the hospital. Paddling hard for a left shoulder, Felix felt the power of the ocean surging around him. Then he was popping up. Balanced on the surfboard, the curve of the water, the swish of his speed. Three seconds of perfection. Soaring, gliding, riding the sea.

In and out, up and down, Felix could do this all day.

Dad had left at seven-fifteen this morning, as usual. Felix had told Helena that sport was first period and he had surfing; she didn't know his timetable.

School. Who needed that shit today? He'd set up a fake Google account and sent an email. *Felix Walsh is sick today and will not be attending. He should be better by tomorrow. Kind regards, Allison Walsh*. They couldn't check with Mum; she'd be in the air on the way to Chicago.

Sitting on his board, he turned back towards the beach, counting the number of surfers. Ten and one just coming into the sea now. No-one hanging around the sand, apart from one woman spinning in a circle. Felix frowned and watched her. That was Maz. She'd ordered some more protein powder for him, along with a new performance enhancer, creatine. It was working—his quads and biceps were bulking up. Even Pearl had noticed. Next time Felix needed to do any kind of surf rescue, he'd be straight in, not freaking out about his lack of strength.

Maz had made a promise not to tell his mum about the protein powder, nor Luke, who might accidentally mention it. Felix and Darcy took it in turns to pay for it. Dumb move by Darcy to steal from Luke's wallet and Mum's purse. Freaking obvious. But Felix forgave him.

Darcy had been pretty stressed about his sister's pregnancy. If his strict-as parents found out, they would've gone ballistic. Together, Darcy and his sister had got enough money in time for her to do the medical termination—two tablets. Otherwise it was going to be more money and full-on surgery. His sister didn't bother telling the dope-head boyfriend; he had no cash to spare.

Felix looked back at the sand. Maz was still there, spinning. Why was she dancing on the beach after Gracie had died?

Cute little Gracie. Luke with a heart attack. Fuuuucckkkk. It happened to other people—on the news, whatever—but not to people living in his own house. At first, he'd hated that they were there, but then Luke was pretty chill. Gave Felix tips on training at the gym. Talked to him as one adult to another. Not like Mum and Dad, who treated him like he was still ten years old. And Gracie was funny. She loved telling him jokes. *Why is Cinderella so bad at soccer? Because she always runs away from the ball.* Sometimes Gracie laughed before she even got to the punchline.

Felix did a duck dive, let the water wash over him.

When Dad heard the news, he'd been sad for precisely ninety seconds.

'Oh, how terrible. That drug was supposed to be the miracle cure.'

Then he'd gone back to watching a climate debate on *Four Corners.* As if it was no big deal that a kid—a five-year-old—had just died. Helena had cracked open the door of the little bedroom and stood in the dark staring at her sleeping baby.

Sleep didn't happen for him last night; Felix had too much shit going through his head. Mum wouldn't cope with this, not after everything else. She'd be devo. He should go and stay with her for a bit when she got back.

Dad had blasted him yesterday, before they'd found out about Gracie. *Why did you tell your mother about the baby?* Felix couldn't believe that it had taken Mum more than a month to bring it up. Couldn't believe that she hadn't been interrogating him every second day.

And now, Dad was checking the doors more often. Peeking out at the street. He'd told them the letterbox was off limits; that didn't matter because no-one was getting mail here anyway.

Last night, Felix had caught the end of a conversation between Dad and Helena.

'She keeps denying it. I'm starting to believe her.'

Mum didn't seem to get that her actions had been scaring them all.

'But if it's not Allison, does that mean *he* knows where we're living?'

Who was *he*? Should Felix be looking over his shoulder too?

Felix just wanted life to go back to some kind of normal—a new normal, where Mum and Dad lived together by the beach and he could surf every day. That'd never happen though.

Another set was coming in, hopefully he'd get a good one here. He nodded across at Jed, the plumber who seemed to spend more time on the waves than working. Felix understood: life was better out here. These guys were older than his school mates, they'd done stuff, been places. Maybe he and Jed could grab a bacon-and-egg roll from the cafe later. Analyse the waves, the tides, the sandbanks, the clouds, the rip, the forecast for tomorrow. Anything but what was rushing through Felix's head.

If a five-year-old girl could die, it could happen to anyone.

24

MAZ

MAZ STEERED HER BARINA UP AND AROUND EACH RAMP OF THE MULTI-
storey car park. Finally, on level seven, an empty spot appeared
and she manoeuvred into it. Clients at the gym said the car
park of the new hospital had an amazing view from the top.
Glancing out, Maz noticed the orange sunset was bathing everything in a golden light—the ocean stretching from Manly to
Palm Beach, the jagged skylines of Bondi Junction and the
city. But Maz didn't have time for an Insta post; she had to
get inside to see Dad.

The lobby's atrium had coloured glass panels, like a hip
office building, not a hospital. All shiny and new. Maz hadn't
taken much notice of the years of controversy—the destruc-
tion of natural forest, the closing down of the old hospital, the
lack of supplies on opening. But now Dad was here, they'd
better have sorted out the teething problems.

As she followed the signs to Emergency, Maz slowed with
each step. What state would Dad be in? She took a deep
breath as the nurse pulled open the curtain surrounding her
father's bed.

'Ah, here's my girl.' Dad smiled and held out his arms towards Maz. The action made him wince.

Tubes snaked into his nose, and stickers and wires were poking out of the white hospital gown. They were linked to a machine that beeped every second or so. The colour of Dad's face matched the grey of the nurse's hair; she fussed around checking the monitor. Mum was sitting on the chair next to him, a magazine balanced on her lap. MEGHAN AND HARRY SPLIT UP shouted the front cover.

Maz hugged Dad carefully, avoiding the tubes.

'How're you feeling?'

'They've told me I've got the heart of an Olympic athlete,' her dad boasted.

Biting her lip, Maz said nothing.

'An Olympic athlete who's been put out to pasture.' Dad laughed at his own joke, then winced again.

Mum explained to Maz that he had chest pain and also nausea, which were symptoms of a heart attack, though the doctors were investigating a range of potential causes.

'So you might have had a heart attack?' Maz asked.

Just like Joseph. But Dad was here, conscious, talking.

Dad nodded and avoided Maz's eyes. Flipping hell, she'd said it to him so many times: *Dad, you're a heart attack waiting to happen.* But he'd lost all that weight, he was getting healthy. Why would it happen now?

Mum beckoned Maz closer and turned away from the bed slightly, the nurse a barrier between them and Dad.

'Dad told the doctors that he's been really stressed lately,' Mum whispered.

Now that Maz thought about it, her father had been grumpy in the last few weeks.

'Apparently, they're doing lay-offs at his work.'

Oh shit, none of them wanted to go back to those days. At least she and Kelli were both working. And maybe Kelli would get a bonus tonight—she was at a fancy restaurant in Darling Harbour for the Fashionista sales awards and hoping to win top sales assistant.

The nurse finished and disappeared out through the curtain. That woman was a saint for working here. Maz hated hospitals. Poor Gracie having to go every Friday. Maz wanted to inspire people so they didn't end up in hospital. Empower them to look after their bodies. Sadly, so many people were self-sabotaging: *I deserve a piece of cake* instead of *I deserve a healthy active body*. And that was why Luke was so special: he wanted to make the world better, just like she did.

Would he be too devastated to come onboard with her program?

Dad was supposed to be their first success story.

The curtain opened again and three people in green outfits appeared as if they were performing on stage.

'We're taking you up to Imaging, Rick.' The nurse announced this like Dad had won some kind of prize. 'They're going to scan your heart.'

Two of them unhooked the wires and tubes from the machine while the third bent down to unlock the wheels on the bed.

Mum managed to blow a kiss to Dad as the curtain swished closed behind them.

Two hours later, they'd admitted Dad into a ward; he was staying overnight. Maz thought that would make him feel worse but he was treating it like the best option.

'One of the nurses called it an *episode*,' Dad said.

'Like an episode of *Game of Thrones*? Cool. You can be king of the Dothraki!'

Oops, didn't that character die in an early season? She shouldn't have mentioned him, but there was a hint of a smile on Dad's lips.

'Luckily medicine has come a long way since then,' Dad said. 'You should've seen the CAT scan machine. Very sophisticated.'

Eight o'clock. Maz was desperate to get home, delete her website and collapse into her own bed. She pictured Luke in hospital, just like Dad—lying flat under a white sheet, nurses popping by, but no visitors to cheer him up. Since she'd been at the hospital, dozens more messages had flooded in. Friends, colleagues, clients. She forwarded some to Luke, to make sure he understood how much everyone cared.

As she was about to say goodnight to Dad, a man came into the room. Attractive, well-built, mid-thirties, wearing a sports jacket and dark trousers—the guy was familiar. He headed straight for Dad's bed.

'Hi there—Rick, isn't it?' He held out his hand to shake Dad's. 'I'm the cardiologist who'll be reporting on your scans tomorrow. My name's Colin Simmons.'

Colin. From the gym. Em-Jay would *not* believe this.

'Thanks for coming in so late to see me.' Dad beamed at the specialist, suddenly brighter than he'd been for the past hour.

'We want you to be comfortable and get some sleep. Let the nurse know if you're in any pain. I'll be in at eight o'clock tomorrow morning and I'll see you then.'

Dad nodded like a puppy dog wagging its tail. 'Thank you so much, Dr Simmons.'

Colin patted Dad on the shoulder, then smiled at Maz.

'Nice to see you.' He turned to Dad and explained. 'I go to Wirriga gym. Your daughter looks sweet but she's brutal in class. She pushes us hard!'

Wasn't it wrong to crack on to your patient's daughter? She'd let him down gently before but she had to be even nicer to him now.

'What a coincidence.' Maz blushed. 'I didn't know you worked here.'

'Ah well, if we'd had that drink . . .' He grinned.

'I'm sorry,' Maz mumbled. 'As I said, I have a boyfriend.'

'Don't worry, I'm teasing you.' He smiled again. In his work clothes, Colin appeared so professional, so knowledgeable. He'd been coming to her early classes most Saturday mornings for months now and he'd never been sleazy again. Hopefully, Colin could make Dad healthy.

—

By the time she was home in bed, Maz felt it had been the longest day of her life. Those twirling sensations had morphed into one big mass stretching from under her ribs to her abdomen. Curling up in the fetal position helped a bit. She rubbed her belly then googled the time in Chicago. Five in the morning. She hadn't spoken to Luke today, only texted. In case he was awake, all alone with his grief in a sleeping ward, Maz tapped out a message.

Sending lots of hugs and kisses. At the hospital with Dad tonight, I was thinking of all your hospital visits with Gracie. You're an amazing father. You did so much for her xxxxxxxxxxxx

Maz didn't know how to comfort Luke nor help Dad.

A message popped up. As she'd guessed, he was awake. She opened the message. Two short sentences.

It's all my fault. I don't know how to get through this.

Luke could *not* give up, it wasn't in his DNA. That was what had attracted Maz to him. Sure, Luke's body was ripped and he had a great smile, but his attitude was ten out of ten. He gave everyone—particularly his daughter—a hundred and ten percent every time.

And why was it his fault anyway?

She pressed his number and held her breath. When the call was answered, Maz suddenly didn't know what to say.

'Luke, it's me.'

'Hey, babe.' His voice—defeated, flat.

'I know you're hurting something bad. What can I do to help?'

'I don't think anyone can help.' He sniffled. 'This is too big.'

'You've been through so much.' Maz hesitated. 'Do you want me to fly over?'

She didn't have a passport, couldn't afford the time off work, wouldn't be able to finance her birthday party if she spent her savings on a flight to Chicago, but she'd do it for him.

'It's okay, babe. Ally will be here soon.'

Maz pushed the twinge of jealousy aside. Well, the school-teacher could do all the grown-up organising stuff and then, when Luke was home, Maz would do all the physical comforting.

'I'm here for you too.' She tried to think of a motivational saying. 'Remember that quote on the studio wall? When you decide not to surrender, that is strength.'

'I'm so tired of the battle.' He groaned. 'What's this about your dad being sick?'

As Maz explained, Luke started consoling her; it made her feel guilty.

'Don't worry about Dad, that's my job.' She traced the seam of her doona cover. 'Luke, it's not your fault. You did everything you could for Gracie.'

'Those pills . . .'

Maz couldn't breathe.

'I didn't tell the doctors,' Luke muttered, 'but I think they interacted—'

'You said you spoke to Dr Rawson.'

All Maz's research had been online; Luke had promised to check with the specialists.

'I thought they wouldn't take her on the clinical trial if they knew.' Luke hesitated. 'I didn't tell Dr Mercado.'

25

ALLISON

AT LAST, ALLISON WAS OUT OF THE CRAMPED AEROPLANE AND ONTO American soil—the Valium had done its job. A number of flights must have landed around the same time; she was swept along in a mass of humanity towards LAX Passport Control. At the edge of her vision, Allison spotted the police in their dark uniforms, their guns strapped to their bodies. So many of them, watching everything. Instead of making her feel safer, they made her more nervous. Avoiding eye contact, Allison queued up behind a Korean family for the passport scanner machine. Snippets of different languages floated in the air. Eventually, it was her turn to scan her passport and her fingerprints. Like a criminal. When the machine spat out the piece of paper, she looked like a drug mule in her photo. Oh God, would they let her into the country? These days, they used any excuse to turn foreigners away. That Australian children's author had been detained for having the wrong visa even though it was the right one.

Allison moved on to the next queue. It snaked around and around with tired travellers rocking on the spot. Tension hung above them like an invisible mist. Off to her left, Allison heard shouting. A tight circle of officers, their shirts emblazoned with DEPARTMENT OF HOMELAND SECURITY, were dragging off a scruffy young guy. Allison staggered forward to the counter with her passport and print-out.

'What's the purpose of your visit?' The officer demanded.

'Holiday.' Allison tried to smile through her lie. 'Vacation.'

'Are you travelling alone?'

Why can't a woman of forty-nine holiday alone . . . is there a law against that?

'My friend is already in Chicago. I'm meeting him tonight.'

Not at a wine bar. In the hospital. Later at the morgue.

'How long are you intending to stay?'

'Ten days.'

'Are you here for work?'

'No, not work.' Was he trying to trick her? She repeated what she'd said before. 'A holiday.'

Finally she was through. But the next checkpoint was Customs with her suitcase, where she must declare all food and drugs.

She stood still as the throng ebbed and flowed around her. Think logically, she told herself. Despite her worry, the pills had passed through Australian security without question. Presumably they would have taken them if they were illegal. But as a schoolteacher, she couldn't afford to get arrested. If she lost her job, she'd lose the house. Then she would've lost everything.

Would they find the pills and drag her off, like that man earlier?

Allison had to make a fast decision or risk missing her flight to Chicago.

The police paced back and forth across the baggage area. A few had dogs on leads clambering and sniffing around the bags. One was coming towards Allison's bag.

Backing away from the dog, she turned and hurried towards the toilets. Once she was locked inside a cubicle, Allison pulled out the containers. She tried to unstick the labels but they came off in bits. Crappy glue. No, she couldn't go through Customs carrying these. With her phone, Allison took photos of the remaining parts of the labels. No ingredients listed. Just a tagline—*Better Antidotes for a Better Life*. Allison found a blue plastic bag in her suitcase, emptied it out and put the containers inside. She opened the door of the cubicle. While no-one was watching, Allison pushed the plastic bag deep into the rubbish bin, washed her hands carefully, and hurried out of the bathrooms.

Deep breaths in the queue for Customs.

'Do you have anything to declare?'

'No,' she whispered.

'This way, then.' The officer pointed her towards the exit.

Thank God, she was through.

—

On the approach to O'Hare Airport, Allison gripped the seat and closed her eyes. The Valium had worn off completely. Swallowing hard, she tasted her last meal, scrambled eggs and hash browns. *Keep it down.* Where was her chewing gum? She couldn't open her eyes or move her hands to find it now. The throb of the plane's engines hummed through every nerve in her body. A baby began wailing and Allison wanted to join in. *Please, God, don't let me die.* Tony should be here, holding her hand, talking her down.

'Breathe,' instructed a voice next to her.

The American boy with dreadlocks and a t-shirt dotted with holes. He'd been on a gap year, backpacking around Asia. All of nineteen years old. Coming home wiser, stronger. Allison would've been terrified at his age.

'Breathe,' he said again. 'We're nearly there. Soon we'll be on the ground.'

She focused on his voice. He was listing off the city sights: Millennium Park, the Navy Pier, the Tribune Tower, Skydeck in the old Sears Tower ('Now it's called the Willis Tower and you can see as far as four states!'), the Art Institute, the Magnificent Mile, the John Hancock Centre, the Crown Fountain, the Riverwalk.

He patted her hand, which was still gripped tight around the armrest.

'It's okay now. You're all good. We've landed.'

If Gracie hadn't died, Allison would be marvelling at herself: booking a ticket yesterday and flying halfway across the world on her own. With instructions from the dreadlocked teenager, Allison managed to catch the train—the Blue Line—to Downtown, then the Red Line to her hotel near the hospital on the North Side. When they'd flown in, she'd spotted the ultra-modern skyscrapers and the vast lake. Now, she walked past homeless people sitting on the footpath with cardboard signs asking for help. 'God bless you, darling,' an old, bearded black man called out to her. But she didn't have any small change yet. The sight of so many beggars shocked her. Too many to help.

The hotel was business-like, apart from the couches in the lobby. Patterned with bright purple flowers. Gracie's favourite colour. Had Gracie jumped on these couches while Luke checked in? Had she copied the design into her sketch book?

Allison glanced at her watch. With changing countries and crossing the international date line, she had no sense of time. Four-thirty in the afternoon. The same afternoon she'd left Sydney. Flying around the world, gaining a day in the process. The jet lag made her head ache.

The man at the desk stood up straighter as she approached and snapped out a quick greeting. She asked for a room near Luke's.

After a few clicks on the computer, the man leant forward and spoke quietly.

'I'm sorry, ma'am, there's no guest by that name.'

Allison stared at his mouth, the teeth white against his dark face, trying to interpret his words. Yawning, she calculated how many hours it had been since she'd left home: nineteen or twenty-one? Maybe Luke had checked out when he'd gone into hospital. He'd definitely listed this hotel on his schedule. Oh God, Gracie's suitcase—where was it? In the hospital with him or here in the hotel luggage room? Presumably, they'd have to choose a coffin, contact the airline, the Australian embassy, the hospital, a funeral home in Sydney . . . the logistics made her head spin. Allison needed to lie down, just for a moment.

'Can I please book a room?'

In the shower, she washed away the day and night of travelling. Her eyes were red and closing of their own accord.

An hour's rest and then she'd go to the hospital. Just as she crawled into bed, a WhatsApp message popped up from Luke.

There's a flu outbreak in the ward. Concerns about an infection in my heart & lungs. They've put me in quarantine.

26

DRAGGING OPEN HER EYES, ALLISON STARED AROUND THE DARK ROOM. Why had the door to her ensuite changed positions? She closed her eyes for a brief moment, hoping the world would right itself, then switched on the bedside lamp. Beige walls, brown carpet, a pine desk and a flowery armchair. Heavy bronze curtains, closed. For a few moments, Allison remained untethered in this strange no-man's-land. And then her brain caught up.

Chicago.

Red numerals on the clock radio: 8.55. Had Luke been staring at his phone for the past four hours, waiting for her to call? She remembered his last message said he was in quarantine. Her thoughts were in slow motion tonight—the effect of the Valium and alcohol, jet lag and grief. In the bathroom, light was streaming through the little window. Sunshine? Good God, it was eight fifty-five in the morning. She'd slept for sixteen hours, not four.

A hard ball of guilt lodged in her chest. She'd flown all this way to comfort Luke and on the very first night, she'd let him down.

Picking up her phone, she checked the text messages.

A missed call from Maz. She listened to the message of the young woman crying and wanting to talk about Luke. Allison clicked on WhatsApp.

—*Congrats on flying through your fear! Love Nadia*

—*Hiya. How was the plane? How's Luke? Ring me when you can. We've told the bairns—they're right wobbly with much crying. Tomorrow'll be better, I'm sure. Sending lots of love, Shona xxxxxxxx*

Closing her eyes, Allison pictured the school. The teachers hurting inside and trying to be strong for the students. The younger children only half understanding, missing Gracie, crying one moment, laughing the next. The older kids seeing mortality up close for the first time; this moment would rock their world. For them, it wouldn't just be about Gracie but about their pets, their grandparents, their parents, themselves. Some of them would go home and ask: 'Mum, what date will I die?'

Allison scrolled through all the options for a message— email, Messenger, Facebook, Gracie's fundraising page. Plenty of condolence messages from friends and people who had become part of Gracie's Gang. Nothing from Luke. She called his number, but he didn't pick up.

⟍

Allison stood on the opposite side of the road from Chicago North. 'You can't miss it,' the concierge had told her. Each time she had to cross a street, she was shocked that the cars were coming at her from the wrong direction. The hospital seemed to be spread over blocks and blocks and blocks. The main part reminded her of the Empire State Building—that Art Deco style, the same-coloured bricks. Behind were new skyscrapers of glass and steel. Gracie would have loved the turret of the old section. Especially the flag on top. 'A fairy castle,' she'd have said.

Patients, doctors and staff scurried by—half of them were wearing face masks. A precaution against the flu outbreak that Luke had mentioned, no doubt. Allison would make sure to wash her hands and stay away from coughing people so she didn't catch it and pass it on to Luke. She stared at the map; she'd downloaded it at home but hadn't envisaged the scale of the place. Around her, she heard conversations; she had to concentrate to decipher the strong American accents, but at the same time, it all seemed so familiar from TV and the movies— as if she'd materialised on the set of an American sitcom.

She'd finally figured out in which direction to head when Luke rang.

'I'm being sent off for chest X-rays now.' He coughed. 'They think I've got a pulmonary oedema.'

'What's that?'

'Fluid in the lungs from the stress on my heart.'

One thing after another. With Gracie's death, the whole world had fallen apart at the seams.

'Can I see you this afternoon?' She asked. 'Which building are you in?'

'I'm on the fifth floor of block D, but I'll probably still be quarantined. I'll text you after the X-ray.'

'Did Brian come over from Boston?'

She prayed that someone had been here, looking after him.

'He cancelled the flight when he heard about the quarantine. But he's contacted a doctor for me. They might move me to a different clinic, away from the flu outbreak.'

Brian understood the American medical system; he'd be useful.

'Do you need me to get you anything? Toiletries?'

Allison didn't know how to ask about his suitcase or Gracie's belongings. Or her body.

Luke coughed again before he spoke. His voice came out croaky. 'It's my fault, Ally. I shouldn't have pushed for her to go on this new treatment.'

'You were doing everything you could. It was the only chance.'

'I let Gracie down. And you. I was giving her supplements from Maz and I didn't tell the doctors.'

What? No, no, no. Why did he jeopardise her treatment when all those specialists were trying to help?

'The ones near the blender?' she asked, trying to keep her voice steady. 'The Bio-Antidotes?'

'Yep. Maz got them from overseas. Thailand.'

Half an hour later, on the seventh floor, Allison found Dr Mercado's clinic. The receptionist was dealing with a patient—a guy whose eyes appeared too big for his face. Allison scanned the small waiting area, almost expecting to see Luke sitting there, dishevelled, in the same clothes as when they'd said goodbye at Sydney airport. *Tell Dr Mercado*, Allison would have said. *He has to know about the pills.*

A middle-aged Indian couple sat in one corner and an older white man in the other. Allison lingered by the desk. The receptionist stopped talking to the patient and eyeballed Allison.

'Please take a seat,' she said.

While she waited, Allison googled Bio-Antidotes. An image popped up on her screen. Gracie's face. Allison clicked on the company information. *Director Maz Humphrey believes we should all be living our best life. Fully trained as a fitness instructor, Maz cares for her clients' wellbeing. We only have one body and one life, so we should be making the most of it. Bio-Antidotes will help you do just that.*

Dear God, Maz was the director. Did she decide to set up her own company and import pills? With no knowledge. No medical experience. No fucking idea. She could kill people!

Had she killed Gracie?

Why would Luke have accepted Maz's pills?

Allison rubbed her temples and listened to snatches of the discussion between the receptionist and the patient. Treatment regime. Costs. Luke had already paid the bulk of the doctor's fee. The patient was collected by a nurse and taken down the corridor. Allison sent a prayer along with him.

The receptionist dealt with the other patients and finally asked Allison to step up to the desk.

'Thanks for waiting. How can I help you?'

'Actually, I've just flown in from Australia. I rang yesterday.'

Allison hoped the receptionist might make the link without her having to spell it out. But the woman's face remained expressionless. Was this the same woman who'd been so unhelpful over the phone?

'I've come about a patient,' Allison continued. 'I was hoping to speak to Dr Mercado.'

'What's the patient's name and how are you related?'

How was Allison supposed to describe her relationship with the little girl who'd been living in her house? Once she said the patient's name, the relationship shouldn't matter.

'Gracie Branson.'

Allison waited for the flash of recognition. But the receptionist merely frowned and tapped her long fingers against the computer keys.

'Gracie,' the woman repeated as she stared at the screen. 'Branson.'

The answers would come now, and this strange fog would lift. Seeing Gracie in the morgue might break her heart but Allison had to do it. To apologise for letting her down. To say goodbye. She could hear Gracie talking to her: 'Silly Lally, don't be scared about seeing me.'

The receptionist had been impassive, but Allison imagined her standing up to hug the traveller who'd come halfway across the world to see a dead girl.

'We don't have a patient called Gracie Branson.'

They weren't the words of condolence that she'd been expecting.

'She came from Australia. A five-year-old girl. Gorgeous little girl.' Allison rushed on. 'Were you working here last week? Last Wednesday. Or was it Thursday with the time difference? Chicago is a day behind us. She started infusions on the twenty-fifth of April.'

When Allison took a breath, the receptionist managed to answer.

'I work here every day.'

'Right then, you would've met her. She's had three infusions for thymic carcinoma. Dr Mercado agreed to take her on his new immunotherapy trial. Her dad, Luke, was with her. You'd remember him. A gym instructor. When she . . . his heart . . .'

The woman led Allison back to the waiting area, sat her down and gave her a glass of water.

Sipping it slowly, Allison ignored the two new people who had arrived.

'You know what happened to Gracie then?' Allison asked the receptionist.

'Dr Mercado didn't see your friend.' The woman shook her head. 'He doesn't treat children.'

But she'd read the emails from this clinic. Luke had shown her the stories online about Dr Mercado's successful treatments.

'I know he doesn't normally, and at first he refused. But Luke—her dad—sent a photo of Gracie in her Elsa costume. Dr Mercado said his daughter loved *Frozen* too. He made an exception for Gracie.'

The woman frowned and changed her tone.

'Listen, hon, this is a big teaching and research hospital. There are so many physicians here. The main reception can help you find out which one she's seeing.'

'Gracie died.'

Around the waiting room, the patients' heads snapped up to stare at Allison.

The receptionist patted her shoulder. 'I'm so sorry for your loss.'

Not just my loss, Allison wanted to shout. *A loss for everyone*. The miracle of a child with so much potential. Who knew if Gracie could have been the next Frida Kahlo or Marie Curie?

'The main reception will definitely be able to help you.' The woman smiled gently. 'I have to admit the next patients, but my colleague Violetta can take you down to the lovely ladies in the main building.'

The lovely ladies in the main building were sympathetic and they tried to help. But like Dr Mercado's receptionist, they had no records of Gracie Branson. Allison steeled herself to ask the next question.

'Can you please check the hospital morgue?'

But Gracie wasn't listed there either. Would she have been taken to another morgue? A city morgue? Allison sighed and pushed away the confusion that threatened to overwhelm her. She'd texted Luke but he hadn't answered. Still in the X-ray area presumably.

'We have a number of research hospitals in Chicago,' one of the ladies said.

The thought of traipsing across this unknown city exhausted her; facing each labyrinth of buildings, trying to understand where to go, who to ask, and then deciphering their accents.

The young woman, Violetta, had been standing next to Allison, listening to the outcome.

'I've got to grab some food from the cafeteria,' she said. 'Do you want to come and I can make some phone calls for you?'

'That's so kind . . . I'd really appreciate it.'

Allison was always the one assisting others. Strange to be on the opposite side. Violetta smiled, showing her slightly crooked teeth. Round-faced, dark hair in a bun, purple blouse and black pants. The bright purple was exactly the shade Gracie loved. Somehow Gracie must be watching down from above, working her magic on people.

Inside the cafeteria, with its smell of reheated food and rows of coloured plastic chairs, Allison could have been back in any big hospital in Australia. Apart from the food itself.

'That counter has fried chicken, that one has subs—they've got Italian beef—and you can get salads or sushi over there.' Violetta pointed to another section. 'And there's the grill if you want a burger.'

Too many choices. Allison stood stock-still between the many counters while Violetta ordered a plate of fried chicken. A large man in scrubs, wearing a mask, brushed past her as he headed for the sushi fridge. He selected a container and Allison copied his movements. At the till, she struggled to figure out her American dollars, crammed in behind the orange and blue Aussie ones. All the denominations were the same colour. Finally, she handed over the right note.

Violetta waved from a table near the window.

'The hospital's hectic at the moment—a flu outbreak in the wrong season,' Violetta said. 'I'm glad I'm not on the wards.'

The smell of Violetta's fried chicken made her salivate; it looked like KFC except for the side of baked beans. Allison couldn't remember when she'd last eaten.

'Thanks again for helping,' Allison said. 'I wish Luke would call back. I'm sure he'll explain everything.'

Or would he? He'd lied about the pills.

'I probably shouldn't be telling you this but I overheard your conversation earlier ...' Violetta paused for a moment. 'Dr Mercado doesn't have kids.'

'Is there another doctor with a similar name?'

'I guess your girl could've gone to the university hospital or the children's one,' Violetta said. 'I'll phone them for you.'

Had Dr Mercado sent Gracie to a different clinic, one that specialised in children, after all? To a specialist with a daughter who loved *Frozen*?

But listening to Violetta's side of the conversation as she called one clinic then the other, Allison could work out what they were telling her.

No-one had heard of Gracie Branson.

27

MAZ

SEVEN FIFTY-FIVE IN THE MORNING. MAZ HAD RUNG NICO AND SWAPPED shifts so she could be at the hospital with Mum for the discussion with Dad's specialist.

'How're you doing, Rick?' Dr Simmons checked the chart at the end of Dad's bed as he spoke, his attention solely focused on his patient. 'Good, your heart has settled down. Did you manage to sleep?'

'Yes, thanks.'

'Great. So, I've had a look at your scans this morning and I'd like to do an angiogram.'

Dad gripped at the bedsheets. 'What does that mean?'

'We inject a dye so we can see the blood vessels. It'll give us a good picture of any blockages or heart disease.'

The doctor sounded so calm and rational, taking it step by step. But Maz couldn't wait for the steps.

'Will Dad die?' she blurted out.

Colin turned to her. Intelligent, caring face, a brain full of the knowledge and skills that would help her father.

'He's going to be okay, Maz. We'll work out the cause of this attack so we can make him healthier for the future.'

'Sorry, our friend's daughter just died. Of cancer.' *And Joseph. I couldn't save either of them.* 'We're all upset.'

'Gracie?' he asked.

Maz nodded.

'She had a rare cancer with an unusual set of complications,' Colin said. 'We were all wishing for the best outcome for her.'

When Maz had rung Nico about changing shifts, he'd asked when the funeral would be. Apparently clients wanted to know. The thought of the whole community crying together over Gracie made her legs shake. Maybe Luke couldn't face it either. Maybe he'd stay in America.

'Did you know Gracie?' Mum was asking the doctor.

'Not the young girl herself but I met Luke at the gym and helped him out with a few medical things. Very sad.'

Of course he knew Luke. Everyone in Wirriga knew Luke and his sick daughter.

'Gracie was very special to us,' Mum said.

Mum told the doctor a long story about them taking Gracie on the Manly ferry into the city. They'd walked around the Opera House and had lunch at an outdoor cafe, with the seagulls swooping their plates. Maz remembered another moment—Luke racing her to the top of the steps. He'd won, as he did with every race. They'd kissed in the shadow of the Opera House sails. Somewhere on her phone was a selfie of them leaning up against the white tiles, arms entwined. That night, she'd heard him say to Allison, 'I promised to take Sarah to the Opera House. But I never did.'

Since their trip to Avoca, he'd opened up more about Sarah, but Maz didn't ask much, not wanting to cause him further pain. She knew his wife had died trying to save her horses. Without telling Luke, she'd googled and found Sarah's memorial page. Tragic.

When Mum finally finished her story, Colin turned to Maz. 'Your father's very proud of you,' he said. 'He told the doctor in ER that his super-healthy, super-fit daughter had chosen some supplements for him.'

Maz wanted to run. Away from the ward. Down the long corridor. Out through the shiny lobby. Along the main road still full of diggers and witches hats and workmen in high-vis. Run, run, run. Far from here.

She managed to nod.

'Do you know off the top of your head what he's been taking?'

'I'll have to check at home.'

'Okay. Can you give me the names later today?' Colin glanced down at his pager, ready to move on to the next patient. 'I assume you bought the supplements locally. The ones from overseas don't always list the ingredients.'

—

Last night, she'd read the letter again. *Prosecute offenders. Ten years' imprisonment.*

But she was only trying to help the people she loved. And Dad had lost twelve kilos on her eating and exercise plan. Maz had bought him a funky new shirt for his birthday that he could wear for the 'after' photo shoot. They'd done the 'before' shots at the park. For once, Maz had asked Curtis to take an unflattering picture. 'When you photograph Dad,' she'd whispered, 'do it from a really bad angle and make him look as fat as possible.' Curtis had burst out laughing, but he'd done a great job of capturing every one of Rick's many kilograms.

In those early days, Maz had given him a few capsules to kickstart the weight loss. She knew that *success breeds success*. If Dad got off to a flying start, he'd see the difference immediately and want to keep going. Mum didn't like taking any tablets, not even paracetamol, so Maz hadn't offered any to her.

For Mum's 'after' shot, Maz was hoping that her sister could borrow a dress from the boutique.

And then Maz needed someone younger, a woman who'd gone from wearing an enormous ugly blouse to a slinky red dress. Those were the transformations that inspired others.

Could any of it still happen?

When Mum disappeared off to the visitors' toilet down the corridor, Maz finally had a moment alone with her father.

'Dad, were you still taking the pink pills?'

'I dunno, love, I just swallowed what you said. You're the boss.'

Dad was staring at the tiny television. Onscreen, a politician chatted with factory workers at a barbecue. He held up a burnt sausage in a roll, slathered with tomato sauce.

'Bet he doesn't eat that once the cameras are off,' Dad said. Then he turned his focus on Maz. 'What's the problem with the pink tablets? Are they the ones that stop you feeling hungry?'

Maz thought her father hadn't listened to her explanation for each pill; it seemed like he had.

'No problem.' She smiled. 'Just trying to work out what you were taking.'

'I wanted to make you proud, love. Be a success for your program.'

'You've been awesome, Dad!'

But still, he'd ended up here.

'Don't tell your mother about the pills.' Dad was fussing with the small cup of water on his tray table. 'She thinks it was all my own hard work.'

'So were you still taking the pink ones?'

'Yep, pretty regularly.'

Too often?

'Okay, I'll write a list for the doctor and bring it in.'

Dad reached out and patted Maz's arm. 'Don't worry, love. It's nothing to do with your pills. It's those layoffs at work. They've put stress on my heart. Maybe I should sue the bastards?'

—

With her ancient laptop on the kitchen table, Maz cranked up Rita Ora's song, 'Let You Love Me'. Sang along to every word. Maz wished that she was with Luke. Wished Gracie was alive. Wished Dad was happy and healthy at home. Wished that Smokey was curled up beside her now, a soft fluffy ball of comfort.

On her website, Maz had two photos of Gracie—a kind of before and after. In the first, she was bald and not smiling, wearing a hospital gown; it was an old picture from Luke. In the second, Gracie floated through the air on the swings at Manly beach, the sea sparkling behind her. Dressed in a bright purple t-shirt and shorts. Her head covered by a pink beanie with shiny hearts.

Bio-Antidotes have been helping Gracie to live a Better Life.
Gracie has a rare cancer which has spread through her
lymph nodes. Together with the medicines from the hospital,

our awesome antidotes are giving Gracie's body the strength
to fight this disease. The antidotes are boosting her immune
system so that all parts of her body are stronger.

Gracie is seeking further treatment in America and needs our
help to get there. Bio-Antidotes will donate 10% of every sale to
Gracie's campaign. You can also donate by clicking on this link.

Note: If you are having chemotherapy or any other
treatment, please seek medical advice before taking
Bio-Antidotes.

She'd added that last line to cover herself. Luke said he'd
spoken to Dr Rawson about the supplements and she was
sure he must have; he was so protective of Gracie's health. But
then he hadn't told Dr Mercado.

According to Colin, overseas supplements didn't always
list every ingredient. Was that why she'd got the letter from
Australian Border Force? A quick online search brought up an
article on a Chinese medicine that included a poisonous herb
banned by the USA. The poisonous herb wasn't listed as an
ingredient, and it had been linked to cancer! The article ended
with this message: *There is a common misconception that because
these remedies are 'natural', they are healthy. This is not so. They
need to be treated like medicines, with testing, medical trials, regu-
lations and labelling laws. Consumers need to know that the drugs
they are taking are legal and safe.*

Why hadn't she seen all this when she'd been researching
which supplements to import?

With shaking fingers, Maz clicked on to the site manager
menu of her Bio-Antidotes website and pressed the button—
Unpublish Site Now. After tapping to confirm, she went back
online. Refreshed the page.

Thank God, the website was gone.

Now she had to ring her clients.

—

The *Northern Beaches News* arrived in her letterbox after lunch with Curtis' story on page three. Maz scrutinised the photo of herself, sitting on the front wall staring down the street. She had a funny expression on her face, a half-smile, turned down at the sides, with sadness in her eyes. She'd had to fight that automatic urge to smile.

Maz found her quote in the midst of a section about Nico's gym. It included the picture of Gracie in her tiny gym outfit.

Luke's workplace, the Wirriga Wellness Club, has also been instrumental in raising funds. One of the gym instructors, Marilyn Humphrey, expressed her shock about Gracie's death.

'We were so sure this treatment would work,' she said.
'I can't believe that Gracie's not coming back. If only love and support could make a sick person better, then Gracie would be here with us today. She had the love of a whole community.'

Geez, why had Curtis called her Marilyn? No-one knew her by that name. The quote he'd come up with was okay but she wouldn't have said it herself. Luke always believed: 'You need more than love and luck; you have to work hard to make your own luck.' But as hard as he'd tried, Luke hadn't managed to do it. Twice, with his wife and his daughter, luck had gone against him.

What time was it in Chicago now? Four p.m. Maz rang Luke's mobile. It went straight to voicemail and she left a brief message. 'Thinking of you, babe. Hope you're doing okay. Love you lots.' He seemed so far away and her words so meaningless.

Maz read the article again, slowly this time. The main photo was from Gracie Day, the event they'd held at school. At the end, Curtis had mentioned another type of Gracie Day—one that the little girl wouldn't be attending.

A number of community groups are discussing a Wirriga picnic to celebrate Gracie's life. Once the details of Gracie's memorial service and the picnic have been finalised, we will announce them in the paper and online.

How could Maz have been so reckless? An unqualified twenty-two-year-old like her should not be importing and selling pills. Why had Luke encouraged her? He was smart—much smarter than her.

Had he been too desperate for a cure, too desperate to try anything and everything?

28

LUKE

LUKE LAY ON HIS BACK, THE GRASS SCRATCHY AGAINST HIS SHIRT, staring up at the clouds. They resembled the shoreline of a beach, scalloped, wispy, as though the waves were lapping against it. Just like Curl Curl. That beach had everything—a long stretch of sand to sprint along with Maz, a pool for laps, and waves for surfing. Even a short clifftop walk for people like Ally who didn't enjoy exercise. And ice-cream for Gracie. Forbidden ice-cream, which Ally thought was a secret, but his daughter told him everything.

Being on that beach was certainly better than the hours spent at the hospital.

But no more hospitals.

And no more Curl Curl beach.

Luke clutched his phone to his chest, his fingers curling around the sleek screen. What could he say to all the caring followers? Wirriga had been good to his gorgeous girl. And Ally had cared. Properly cared. She'd given them a roof over their heads, nourishing food and love for Gracie. Overcome her fear of flying to get to Chicago. That shocked him. She had no idea of her own strength. Above and beyond what he ever could have imagined—an incredible force driving the fundraising, galvanising a whole community. His little girl had been so special to them all. Brought the community together in one common goal.

But last week, Gracie confessed that Ally had given her medicine when she'd been sick.

'Why didn't you tell me at the time?' he'd demanded.

'I didn't want to get Lally in trouble. She was helping me.'

Despite everything she'd done, Allison had no right to give Gracie any medicine; she hadn't even asked his permission. What was that word she used? *Overstepping.* Yes, that was definitely overstepping. The good teacher had crossed the line. Luke had seen that look in her eyes: she'd wanted Gracie as her own.

Would Ally blame herself? Or Maz? Or turn it back onto him?

Maz—well, she *would* be blaming herself about the supplements. She should've done more research.

They all should have.

He'd been considering a farewell note for the blog. Should he just say a personal goodbye?

Luke brought his phone up, squinting at the screen against the whiteness of the sky behind. The wind must be strong up there, the wispy clouds had been painted over in grey. Dark, heavy clouds that would bring the rain. Further north, they'd had storm warnings.

How would Ally and Maz—and all of Wirriga—weather the coming storm? Sadly, Luke wouldn't be there to find out.

29

MAZ

MAZ COULD ONLY TALK TO ONE PERSON ABOUT BOTH LUKE AND THE supplements. Nico pulled her into his office and hugged her tight. The message on his singlet read: *No pain, no gain.*

What were they gaining from the pain of Gracie's death?

'I'm scared for Luke,' Maz said. 'He's giving up on life.'

'Not Luke. He's not the type to throw in the towel,' Nico said. 'He'll come through this. And when he gets back from Chicago, we'll have a picnic in Gracie's memory.' The gym owner sniffed and rubbed the back of his hand against his eyes. Behind him on the wall were two framed photos of his stepchildren. When they were old enough, Maz expected that Nico would start training them in the gym, just like he'd done with her.

'Nico, I was wondering . . .' She pushed the hand weights on his desk, rolling them back and forth. 'Those supplements that come in from Asia . . . do you know anyone who's got sick from them?'

'Sick? Nah. They make you healthier. Stronger.'

'But apparently some can affect the liver. There's some kind of . . . toxicity.'

'Oh yeah, I heard about a guy in Queensland. Nearly died from a natural green tea extract. It wasn't listed on the protein powder packet. He needed an emergency liver transplant.' Nico shrugged his thick shoulders. 'But that hardly ever happens. It's, like, one in a million.'

—

The text from Curtis asked her to come for lunch at the nursing home up on the plateau, where he was doing a series on the residents. As Maz stepped inside the entrance, the smell hit her. Disinfectant, food and a flowery air freshener to mask it all. In the front lounge area, a woman in a wheelchair waved and said hello. Maybe Maz could offer some gentle exercise classes, help the old people live out their best lives in here? She pushed the thought away. No more grand plans. That lump of fear inside her stomach was putting a hold on everything.

Curtis sat at a table with a red plastic flower in a crystal vase atop a white doily. He had a pot of tea and a plate of muffins.

'I'm here all day,' he said. 'There are so many amazing stories. One woman owned an outback pub, another helped with early malaria research. That guy over there circumnavigated the world in a freighter.'

'Interesting.'

All Maz wanted to talk about was Gracie.

'They've lived incredible lives and we treat them as a burden on society. My series is going to change that.' Curtis sighed. 'And bring in advertising revenue from retirement villages. And calm people down about the royal commission.'

'I thought the royal commission was on banks.'

'That's finished. They're moving on to aged care now.'

If there was a royal commission, shouldn't Curtis be writing about the bad aspects? Anyway, none of this was relevant to Maz.

'You said you wanted to talk about Gracie,' she prompted.

'Have you heard from Luke?' Curtis asked.

'Not today. I'm really worried about him.'

Curtis leaned forward and did his steeple pose.

'Allison rang me.' He frowned. 'She hasn't been able to see Luke.'

'That's because he's in quarantine. There's some terrible flu going around and they're worried about an infection in his lungs.'

'Yeah, I heard that from Allison. When she couldn't see Luke, she went to Dr Mercado's clinic. They have no record of Gracie.'

'What? I don't understand.'

That doctor had been Gracie's best hope. He'd worked out a low dose of the drug which meant treatment every third day. Luke would've done anything, raised any amount of money, given up his kidney, his blood, his bone marrow—whatever it took to make Gracie better.

'The clinic has never heard of Gracie,' Curtis repeated, then paused. 'Allison also told me she found some strange herbal pills. She says they came from you. Are these the same pills you got the letter about?'

Maz reached down to her bag for her water bottle. Took a long gulp before answering. 'No, they're not the same ones.'

Well, she didn't think so. Would Curtis be obliged to haul her to the police? Thank God she'd taken the website down.

'What are they then?'

'The pills were to boost Gracie's immune system. I only gave them to Luke on the condition that he get Dr Rawson's approval. He promised me he had.' She knew she sounded like a child, passing the blame, but it was true.

'And then?'

'Luke didn't tell Dr Mercado about them. He thought they wouldn't take Gracie on the drug trial because of it. And now he's worried the combination led to . . . her death.'

Would Gracie be alive now if Maz hadn't ordered those pills online?

'But according to Allison, Dr Mercado never saw Gracie.'

The schoolteacher was super kind and super caring but also bitter and distracted about her marriage break-up. Had Allison somehow gone to the wrong hospital or the wrong location? Luke had been so excited about Dr Mercado's clinic.

Allison had sent one message the other day saying she was flying to Chicago but nothing since. Maz wanted to commiserate with her—they had both loved Gracie—but the teacher hadn't returned her call. Perhaps she'd already known about the pills then. Although, she'd always been a bit prickly with Maz. Was it because her husband had run off with another woman? Maz had tried to help her out, offering discount classes at the gym. Even though Allison wasn't particularly overweight, she could do with more exercise, toning her arms and legs, getting some endorphins. And the camaraderie. 'Come and join the gym family,' Maz had said, but the teacher had stared daggers and muttered something under her breath.

Or perhaps Allison knew Maz was selling supplements to her son. Oh shit, another client to contact.

Curtis helped himself to an orange poppyseed muffin, and offered some to Maz as an afterthought. Normally she didn't eat cake, but today she needed all the sustenance she could get.

'Did you hear about that Chinese healer in Darwin?' Curtis asked. 'He's been charged with manslaughter after he put a kid on a diet of herbs to cure a bad rash. The poor thing died from starvation.'

Maz shook her head; the less she thought about alternative remedies, the better.

'I'm just wondering . . .' Curtis said. 'Do you think Luke could have taken Gracie somewhere else?'

'Why would he do that?'

'A different kind of healing place. A wellness retreat that not everyone would approve of.'

Gracie had been doing chemo for months and months, so Luke clearly believed in mainstream medicine—although the chemo had stopped working. Did he turn to something else then? Allison wouldn't have agreed; she'd have labelled it wacky. Lots of people wouldn't have donated.

'Did he ever talk about anywhere like that?' Curtis asked.

Luke had talked about everything: health, food, exercise, marathons, medicine, the power of positive thinking. Had he ever discussed some other kind of therapy?

'I can't remember,' she said. 'But he was on the laptop all the time, researching things.'

Curtis picked up his mobile. Maz could see that he had Luke's name in his favourites list. When he dialled the number, it went through to voice message.

'Can you give him a try?' Curtis asked. 'It's still early evening over there.'

But the same thing happened with Maz's call. She left a message: *Luke, it's me, please ring. We're worried about you. Love you lots, babe. Hang in there.* They'd only been saying the L word for a few days and yet it felt so natural already.

'I'm scared for him,' Maz whispered. 'He told me that, after his wife died, he only kept going for Gracie.'

Nodding, Curtis tapped some more numbers into his mobile.

'I rang Dr Rawson yesterday to get a quote about Gracie's death. He didn't ring back. I'll try again now. Surely he must know what's going on.'

Maz remembered how Luke's face had glowed whenever he'd mentioned the specialist, but his idol hadn't managed to save his little girl. She listened to Curtis leave another message for Dr Rawson.

'Maybe the doctor's feeling guilty because Gracie died?' Maz said. 'After all his efforts to get Gracie to America, it didn't work.'

If Maz could blame Dr Rawson, then she and Luke were off the hook. She texted him: *It's not your fault. Dr Rawson pushed for the wrong treatment.* Maz had seen a comment on the blog questioning if it was the right drug and recommending a second opinion.

'I'm sure Dr Rawson suggested what he thought was right. He sounded very competent and knowledgeable when I interviewed him. But it's really weird that the clinic in Chicago has no record of Gracie. Hopefully, Luke will call. Or Allison.'

Maz's phone pinged and they both glanced down to check it. A text from Mum.

Dad's having the angiogram shortly. Come in at 3 p.m. Bring blue pyjamas and undies. xxxxx

Would they have a diagnosis by the end of the day? As a distraction, Maz googled Dr Colin Simmons. He had his own private practice in St Leonards and worked at two different hospitals. Once a month, Colin travelled out west to consult in Dubbo. Oh God, clever and kind. Suddenly, Maz could see why Luke admired Dr Rawson so much.

Blue pyjamas. Maz guessed she'd find them in Dad's second drawer. She'd started texting Mum back when she remembered the night up in Avoca. Luke had been online looking at photos of a healing centre. Maz thought it was beautiful and spiritual. Serene, like her favourite beauty salon. He'd grinned when he saw the mantra on the wall—one of their sayings from the gym. *Believe you deserve it and the universe will serve it.*

'Maybe that's what Gracie needs,' Luke had said, pointing at the screen. 'A relaxation retreat. All this driving to and from the hospital—it's exhausting her.'

But then he hadn't talked about the healing centre again. He'd been focused on the immunotherapy and Dr Mercado.

What if Maz's pills had made Gracie too sick for the trial?

What if he'd taken her to a place of serenity to die?

Maz's mobile pinged again. She picked it up to read the message. Luke at last.

Life's impossible without Gracie. I'm so sorry but I can't keep going. Thank you for your support & encouragement. You're an awesome woman, Maz, & you have a great future. I'm sorry I won't be here to see it. Love you forever, babe. xx

30

ALLISON

AFTER LUNCH, ALLISON WENT TO THE CHILDREN'S HOSPITAL AROUND the corner, then the university research centre two blocks further north. Even though Violetta had called them, she decided to double-check. But neither had any record of Gracie. Luke hadn't responded to her question: *Where was Gracie treated?*

Now, Allison was lying on her hotel bed, wondering what the hell was going on and when she'd be allowed to see him. Presumably not this evening. On the small desk, her phone vibrated. Allison lunged sideways to answer it. Luke. Now he'd clear up this crazy confusion.

Not a phone call but a text.

Thank you for your love for Gracie and your support. I keep blaming myself. I'm sorry. I can't go on.

Bloody hell. NO! He couldn't give up. That was why she'd come over—to help him get through this. With trembling fingers, she pushed the buttons to call him back. Luke didn't answer. Leaving a long message, Allison promised him there was hope for the future. Next, she sent him a series of texts.

Please don't give up. It seems impossible now but the pain will lessen. We'll never forget Gracie and she'll always be a part of us. You need to survive for her memory.

You have so much support from the Wirriga community. Friends who love you. We'll help guide you into the future.

Your fundraising has done so much to publicise the need for research and treatment. Your donation to the children's hospital will save lives. Gracie's fight has made a difference to others.

And then, finally, a text about herself.

My life was broken when you and Gracie walked into it. You saved me. Now let me save you.

Still no answer.

Grabbing her handbag, Allison raced out of the hotel room and down to the street. Straight back to Chicago North, where she'd been that morning. But this time, she went to block D, fifth floor.

The security guard refused to let her out of the lift.

'You can't come up here. It's not visiting hours and it's a restricted area.'

'My friend is . . . dying.'

'Sorry but you need to go back downstairs and ask them to call.'

On the ground floor, the operator put her through to the ward but no-one could locate Luke Branson.

'Please help him,' Allison begged.

'He's in safe care,' the man on the other end of the line replied calmly.

'But how would you know if you can't find him? I'm not leaving here until I talk to Luke.'

As Allison stood next to the reception desk waiting, she recognised a woman behind the counter—one of the 'lovely ladies' from the main building who'd made calls for her that morning. Allison waved and the woman beckoned her over.

'Have you found where Gracie was treated?' the woman asked.

Allison shook her head.

'You're having a terrible time.'

This receptionist was kind; she'd understand the need to see Luke immediately.

'He's lost his wife and his child. He can't cope anymore. He's giving up.'

'Let me try,' she said. 'Luke Branson, is that the name? I'll find out which room he's in.'

The receptionist looked it up on the computer then said, 'I've got a Luke Branson, but he's in the rehab ward after a hip replacement.'

'No, Luke's in isolation. He's got a heart problem.'

'Sixty-eight years old. Male. From Noble Square.'

'What's Noble Square?'

'It's a neighbourhood not too far from here.'

'Well, that's not him.' Allison massaged her forehead. 'He's Australian. And he's thirty, not sixty-eight.'

'She was here this morning about a little girl,' the receptionist explained to the other women at the desk. 'We had no record of her either.'

'I've come all the way from Australia.' Allison could hear the shrillness in her own voice. 'Gracie's dead and now Luke's going to die too. Just let me talk to him.'

The woman looked sideways, then down. Anywhere apart from Allison's face. She started typing something into the computer.

'I'm sorry, I don't think we can help you.'

'Yes, you can. He's in isolation on level five.'

'He's not here.'

Could Luke have been transferred to a different hospital already? He'd said Brian was contacting another doctor, to move him away from the flu outbreak. They should have a record of his transfer. Was that what she should ask for? Allison was trying to figure it out when a security guard approached her.

'This way, please, ma'am.'

She stepped around his bulk and kept talking to the receptionist.

'Luke's going to hurt himself. Please help me find him. Could he have been transferred?'

None of the women replied. The security guard steered her away from the counter. Allison shouted back at the receptionists as she was herded out of the automatic doors.

'Is this hospital going to have another death on its hands?'

In her hotel room, using the free wi-fi, Allison went through all the hospitals in Chicago. Phone call after phone call. Not one had a patient called Gracie Branson or Luke Branson. She googled 'Chicago specialists' along with 'thymic carcinoma'. Could they have gone to a different type of medical clinic, rather than a hospital? Clicking open a page at random, Allison read about survival rates for this rare type of cancer. She scrolled down to another subheading: *Your survivorship care plan*. The medical world had a different language. Survivorship. She'd never heard it before. But it was what she needed now.

Survivorship. For Luke. And for herself.

After an hour, she boiled the kettle, dangled the teabag into a tiny cup. Spilt the milk as she poured it in. Tried to understand what was happening. She messaged Brian, introduced herself as Luke's friend who had arrived in Chicago to help him. *I can't find the doctor who treated Gracie. I can't find Luke. He says he can't go on. Please help!*

Brian answered almost immediately. *He sounded unhinged last time I spoke to him. Thanked me for my help but basically told me to get out of his life. I was angry after my brother died. But I got through with my wife's help. I can't imagine how he feels.*

She felt bad for dragging Brian into this but he was her only contact in America. *Luke said you were phoning a doctor, trying to get him moved to another hospital. Did they transfer him?*

While she waited for Brian's answer, she checked her WhatsApp and Messenger. Nothing from Luke. Was he dead already?

I don't know. I didn't make any calls for him. But I've done some quick research for you. Try these two specialists—they work with patients with thymic carcinoma.

Allison rang their numbers but, like everyone else, they'd never heard of Gracie or Luke Branson.

Why would he make up a lie about Brian? To delay her? So he could die in peace?

Ten minutes later, Brian sent another message. *I got in touch with TN from Gracie's website—the guy who questioned the clinical trial. Turns out he wanted to apply for that trial. He was kinda hoping Gracie would give up her place for him.*

Oh God, the desperation. Everyone desperate to find a magic pill.

Allison lay back on the hotel bed and closed her eyes. Forced herself to sit up, have another cup of tea. Avoided spilling the milk this time. Then she rang Cook County Morgue. They suggested she ring the police.

'Have you registered a missing persons report?'

Maybe she *should* involve the police; Luke and Gracie were definitely missing.

This bewilderment was similar to how she'd felt when Tony had left—off balance, staggering along an uneven path with the facts she thought she knew crumbling underfoot. Opening Luke's blog, Allison wondered if he'd left a clue on there. She scrolled through the old posts from months ago. When she'd finished reading, she called Curtis.

Initially, she'd felt disloyal telling Curtis about Dr Mercado. But given the latest text, they needed to find Luke as quickly as possible.

'You know how we wrote that blog post about alternative remedies—did Luke get you to research any specific healing places?'

'There was one centre. Maz remembers him mentioning it,' he said. 'Maz said it was serene and had beautiful gardens.'

Over the phone, she could hear Curtis tapping away.

'I'm looking at the map—it's a few suburbs north of the hospital there. An all-natural healing centre called The Happy Place.'

'Do you think he could've taken Gracie there?'

'Maybe. They said a thirteen-year-old boy had been healed and was now cancer-free. Luke thought it sounded amazing. I'll text you the contact details.'

Whenever Allison had ranted about non-conventional treatments, Luke had been quick to agree with her. Too quick. While he'd been saying yes to Allison, he'd also been saying yes to Maz with her herbal products and pseudo-science.

'You shouldn't be so down on the herbs,' Maz had argued with her during their fundraising campaign. 'Some of our medicines started out that way. Aspirin came from willow bark and sweet wormwood is used to treat malaria.'

'Two success stories don't justify all the other hocus-pocus crap. And those ones were properly tested. You're not to give Gracie any herbal stuff,' Allison had instructed, as if Gracie were her own daughter.

Had Luke skipped conventional medicine all together in America?

Allison called the number that Curtis had sent through. The recorded message said The Happy Place was closed for the day and would open again at nine in the morning. The website showed a vast array of so-called treatments—green enemas, raw food, mud spas, urine therapy, meditation, oxygen, light, music and electromagnetic waves. Urine therapy: what the hell was that? She texted Luke: *Are you at the healing centre? I understand. Stay strong and I'll see you tomorrow.*

Curtis was right—the Wirriga community would not have donated for mud spas and urine therapy. And Allison certainly wouldn't have led a fundraising drive.

When she put the name of The Happy Place into a web search, an article popped up from the *Chicago Tribune*.

FRENCH FAMILY SUES HEALING CENTRE AFTER SON'S DEATH.

An image of the centre's entrance gates accompanied the article, along with a photo of a young boy.

The Happy Place is facing legal action after the death of a ten-year-old boy. His family from Marseilles, France, paid $15,000 for three weeks of controversial therapies to cure his leukaemia. They believed it was a last-ditch effort to save their son's life. In their correspondence, the centre had encouraged the family to cease conventional treatment. The boy's haematologist said he would have survived with chemotherapy.

'I'm heartbroken by the preventable loss of this beautiful boy,' his doctor said. 'We are happy to combine medicine with alternative therapies, but these therapies must be scientifically proven.'

If Gracie had died at this centre, Luke would definitely be unable to live with himself.

31

ON THE CAB RIDE FROM HER HOTEL, ALLISON WONDERED IF THE HAPPY Place might be in lockdown after the newspaper article, but as they pulled up at the entrance, the big white gates automatically opened, and the car drove Allison along the driveway, right to the front door. She counted out the fare quickly, too muddled to be able to convert it into Australian dollars.

The reception area had a lovely feel to it. Lounges, cushions, colourful paintings, a bubbling fountain and a waft of scented candles. Comforting. On the wall, an inspirational motto inside a heart: *Believe you deserve it and the universe will serve it.*

A woman in black jeans and a lime-green shirt approached her.

'Hi, you must be Jordan.' She took Allison's hands, clasped them in her own, squeezed them softly. 'Welcome to our place of healing. My name is Tamara. I'll help you check in.'

When Allison explained that she was looking for a patient from Australia, she waited for the concern to flood across the woman's face. Instead Tamara smiled gently.

'I'm sorry but you must have the wrong centre.' Her long silver earrings jangled as she shook her head. 'We have no patients from Australia.'

The truth or a cover-up?

'Please, could you check their names in the system?'

'We're a small, personalised centre,' Tamara said. 'I know the names of all of our clients.'

Clients, not patients.

'Gracie died.' Allison stared at the stupid quote on the wall. 'She died. Just like that French boy.'

Tamara reached for Allison's hands again. 'Oh, honey, my heart goes out to you. A little girl gone too. We were so sad to lose Ruben. Such a charming boy.'

She'd expected the centre staff to be defensive and yet this woman was holding Allison's hands. Over her shoulder, out in the garden, Allison could see three people chatting. Two women and a man with his back to her. A man with closely cropped dark hair.

Allison pulled her hands free from Tamara's clasp and rushed out into the beautiful, peaceful garden with its cascading fountains and blue glass statues. In the distance, small studios were dotted between the bushes. Studios for accommodation or treatment? Had Gracie been staying in one of them?

The group was sitting on benches either side of a wooden table with folders and checklists laid out for signing.

'Luke, thank God, you're here.' She placed her hands on the man's shoulders. 'I've found you.'

But when Luke lifted his face to her, the features were all wrong. The same hair, the same physique, a different person.

'I . . . uh . . . a mistake,' she muttered.

She stumbled back into the reception area and sank onto the couch, a fog of confusion clouding her thoughts.

'What's going on?' Tamara asked. 'Are you a reporter?'

'I'm a schoolteacher from Australia and I think Gracie was here.'

'It's time for you to leave.'

Would Allison be ejected by security yet again, without discovering anything?

'We lost a five-year-old girl. We all believed she should live, the universe needed her, so why did she die? What does your quote even mean? Of course she deserved to live.' The words burst out unbidden. 'Did Gracie die here? Are you hiding her death?'

Tamara bundled Allison off the couch, towards the door. Sweetly but firmly. She didn't seem shocked by Allison's ranting.

'Honey, I understand you're upset. You're mourning a terrible loss. But you're wrong about our centre. We believe in what we do. And it works for many people. We give them hope and life.'

'No, you sell fake hope and snake oil. Trick people and take their money as a last resort. You're quacks who kill people.'

Hot anger raced through Allison, along with the confusion. Why had Luke come to Chicago? Where the hell was he? The only clue she had was Navy Pier. That last Facebook post: Gracie smiling on the big Ferris wheel, her favourite purple beanie covering her head. The caption full of hope and happiness: *We're here in Chicago, ready to start treatment tomorrow.*

What treatment?

Tamara had moved Allison through the door to the top of the small set of steps. She must have been expecting resistance as she gave Allison a slight nudge. Unbalanced, Allison's feet slipped on the step and she started falling. Tamara caught her around the waist in a hug and steadied her.

'I'm so sorry. Are you okay?'

The shock snatched Allison's anger away; she gave a half-sob.

'I'm jetlagged and I can't find Luke. I've been all over Chicago, but he's not here. I can't find where Gracie went. Where she died.'

'There are lots of cancer centres in the States,' Tamara said. 'And some clinics in Mexico.'

'He must be at some alternative place.' Allison sighed. 'It's the only explanation.'

'We definitely didn't treat Gracie.' Tamara hesitated and Allison was suddenly alert to the familiar way she'd said the girl's name. 'Her father sent us an enquiry but they never came.'

Finally, someone in Chicago had heard of Gracie.

'Did he say why?'

'He gave us the dates and Gracie's medical information . . .'

'Why didn't you tell me this straight away?'

'I thought you were a reporter at first, but then I could see that you were truly upset about Gracie.'

Tamara was doing something with her phone. The big gate at the end of the driveway opened up for a cab.

'The thing is . . . I'm sorry, but I thought her father was a reporter too. Some of the questions he asked . . . I turned them away.'

—

It was still too early to ring Australia so Allison couldn't share the news with Curtis: *Someone has heard of Gracie.* In her hotel room, she began researching treatment centres in Mexico and how to repatriate a body from America to Australia. Gracie's body. Oh dear God, what if she was too late and she had to take home Luke's body as well?

Sniffing back her tears, Allison read through the logistics of repatriation. One website listed the repatriation companies and the official requirements. *The death of an Australian overseas must be reported to the Australian Embassy.* Had Luke done that already? *Contact the travel insurance provider.* He must have had travel insurance in case of any medical issue. Allison scanned through the pages. *Human remains can pose a biosecurity risk.* What sort of drugs had been in Gracie's system? What was the official cause of death?

When she could finally phone Curtis, he had no answers either. No-one had heard from Luke. Dr Rawson hadn't returned the journalist's phone calls and Maz was worried about her father in hospital.

'Please, can you hold off telling people that I can't find Luke?' she asked Curtis. 'There must be a sensible explanation. I don't want the children and the community upset for no reason.'

Protecting Luke. Possibly protecting Maz. But also protecting herself. The fundraiser had been Allison's responsibility.

Curtis agreed and vowed to keep trying to locate them from his end.

She texted Nadia: *I don't understand this place and the accents. It's like being on another planet. I want to come home but I can't find them. I'm scared Luke has gone too.* She added the same entreaty as she had to Curtis. *Please don't tell anyone yet.*

Meanwhile, Felix had sent her a message over WhatsApp about his soccer game. He added a line at the end: *I saw Maz dancing on the beach the day after Gracie died. Weird!*

Had Maz and Luke done something to Gracie? With the pills? Allison's brain whirled with possibilities.

The next message was from Shona—an email describing how the kids were creating artworks in memory of Gracie. It was supposed to be life-affirming but some of the year three children had drawn gravestones and crosses. Two year six kids had written poems about death coming to take them in their sleep. The counsellor had been called in for extra days at the school. They were planning the school memorial assembly. It was important for Luke to be there—did Allison have any idea of when they'd arrive back?

How could she possibly explain to the whole school—to all of Wirriga—that Luke was missing, possibly dead? And she couldn't find Gracie's body to bring home.

—

Allison dragged herself down to the hotel restaurant for dinner. With her body clock still on Australian time, she'd barely eaten during the day and had then been starving at midnight. A slightly nauseous feeling had been hanging over her ever since she'd arrived. She ordered the local special: pizza. Deep-dish with a thick buttery crust—almost like a pie. Better than almost any pizza she'd eaten in Sydney. But after three bites, she was full. And sick with worry.

Curtis' number flashed on her mobile.

'Have you heard from Dr Rawson?' she asked. 'Does he know where Gracie was being treated?'

'No, but I've found something else.' Curtis sounded breathless. 'It's not what you'd expect.'

At this point, Allison didn't know what to expect.

'I've got a contact in Immigration. Apparently, Luke and Gracie never went through Customs.'

'What're you talking about? I took them to the airport.'

Allison remembered hugging Gracie, taking the photo, watching them wheel their bags off towards the check-in counter. And then, when she was tearing up, waving and rushing back to the car.

'My contact was definite,' Curtis said. 'Luke and Gracie Branson are still in Australia.'

PART THREE

Things are not always as they seem.
Aesop, 'The Bee-Keeper and the Thief'

32

ALLISON

THE CUSTOMER SERVICE OFFICER AT THE AMERICAN AIRLINES DESK listened to Allison's request, nodded and clicked at her screen.

'The earliest flight might not be the most direct,' she warned.

'That's fine,' Allison said. 'I just need to get home.'

And figure out what the hell Luke had done. To her. To them all. In one instant, her exhaustion and confusion had snapped into fury—the same rage that had consumed her after Tony had decimated their family. Shoving clothes into her bag, she'd checked out of the hotel and caught the train straight to O'Hare.

As the woman tapped on her keyboard, Allison wondered if her credit card had enough to cover the fee for changing the flight. A few days in Chicago—three thousand dollars, four, five? She couldn't bear to add up the cost of this bizarre trip.

After a few minutes' silence, the woman raised her inscrutable face from the computer.

'Mrs Walsh, this flight goes from Chicago to LA.' She twisted the monitor so Allison could see the list of times and connections. 'Then via Melbourne to Sydney.'

She pronounced Melbourne with a strange inflection, emphasising the second syllable.

'That will be fine. Thanks so much.'

With a four-hour wait, Allison knew her fear of flying would start spiking soon. She went to the bathrooms and tipped the last Valium into the palm of her hand. Staring at it, she could feel the anxiety knotting through her body, beating a fast drum in her chest. It swirled in and out of her fury about Luke. All the time she'd been in Chicago, her brain had been fuzzy. Now, she needed clarity. Turning on the tap, she let the yellow tablet wash down the plughole. Her heart beat even faster as it disappeared into the darkness below. *Ground yourself, Allison: focus on the water pooling and circling in the sink. Think about the water: does it really go the opposite way in the northern hemisphere?* Like with everything else in Chicago, she didn't have an answer.

In the departures area, Allison stared at the Jamba Juice bar. Luke would have loved its Amazing Greens smoothies and acai bowls. But he'd never been through this airport. Why had he posted a picture of Gracie in Chicago and let Allison follow them here?

When a call from Curtis came through, she hoped for more news.

'I did a credit check on Luke, but nothing came up,' Curtis said. 'I tried to get his tax file number from Nico at the gym, but he was being paid in cash, on a casual arrangement, so he could save as much as possible for Gracie's treatment.'

'I think there are three possibilities,' Allison said. 'Gracie is having some unusual treatment in Australia. Or he's decided against any more treatment and they've gone somewhere to die. Or he's taken the money and run. What do you think?'

Curtis answered slowly. 'I'm keeping an open mind.'

'Are you going to publish something or can you delay it until I'm back?' Allison guessed it would go against his journalistic tendencies to wait. 'I'd rather find out the truth before I tell the school. They're all so sad about Gracie.'

'Yep, I'd prefer to publish when I know what's going on. A lot of people are going to be pissed off that Gracie isn't on a clinical trial in Chicago.'

'I know. Do you think she's dead?'

'Yes.'

Allison's heart kept flip-flopping between the two options: dead or alive. Or had something unexpected happened—like a fatal allergic reaction at the airport before they flew out? But why would Luke lie to her?

'My flight's going via Melbourne, so I'll stop off there and drive up to Hythorne. I have a feeling that he's taken her home.'

A calm, quiet place in the countryside with special memories. As well as Sarah Branson's horrendous death. Had he gone there with Gracie to end it all?

The next caller was Tony.

Her husband didn't say how impressed he was at Allison getting on a plane by herself. Although that brave behaviour was paling in comparison to the search for Luke. Every moment in Chicago had been way out of her comfort zone.

'Let me start by apologising,' Tony said. 'I know that sometimes you were watching the house but now I realise it wasn't every time. We've received another threatening letter, which clearly you didn't write because you're in Chicago.'

She sat down heavily on the nearest seat and took a deep breath—was her son in danger?

'Is Felix okay? Why didn't you believe me earlier?' she snapped. 'The police would be onto it by now. Who *is* stalking you?'

'Well, actually, that's why I'm calling—to ask a favour for Felix.' He cleared his throat. 'I'm sorry to disturb you right now, with Gracie and everything . . .'

He didn't know the half of it.

'What's the favour?'

'I'm wondering if we could . . . if you'd possibly allow us to . . .' A formal voice, as though they'd never been married. 'I wondered if we might stay in the house for a week. While you're away.'

'Are you kidding me?'

She was ready to hang up immediately.

'I'd be happy to go to an apartment but Felix wants to come home. He says he'll feel safer in Wirriga.'

The bastard for dragging her son into his disaster.

'Felix can stay with my mum, and you and your woman and the baby can go to an apartment.'

'Please, Allison, I'm begging you. It'd be better if I'm with him. Just for a few days while we organise safer accommodation.'

Did Tony have any idea of what he'd put her through? And he'd made her own son accuse her of stalking as well. For God's sake, she didn't have the energy to think about all his crap. Not right now.

In the silence, he began speaking again.

'I wish I'd told you everything from the start.' He groaned. 'I was just trying to protect Helena and her baby. Keep them safe.'

And to cover up his unethical behaviour. Whatever Tony said, it was wrong to fall in love with your client.

'The system wasn't working for her. We couldn't find a safe place for her to stay.'

'So you left our marriage and set one up?'

Her husband—a fucking knight in shining armour.

'But it's not safe here anymore. Please.' He was pleading now. 'Felix will be so much happier.'

He'd made Felix lie about the woman and that poor defence-less baby. Had Tony used their son as some kind of bodyguard against an abusive, jealous ex-partner? Bloody hell.

'I'll be back in two days,' she said. 'You can stay for the weekend. Please be out by Monday morning.'

Hopefully, she'd know by then where Luke and Gracie had gone.

'That would be a great help.' She could hear the relief in his voice. 'Thank you so much. I really appreciate it. There'll be absolutely no sign of us on Monday.'

She couldn't have said no; couldn't have told her son that he wasn't allowed to come home while she wasn't there.

'Don't go into my room.' She enunciated the words clearly to make sure he got the message. 'Look after our son.'

Waiting for her flight, with the noise of planes taking off around her, Allison kept her eyes on the phone. She hadn't told Curtis her other theory. Prayed that it couldn't be true. Not while Luke was living in her own home.

Allison had seen Gracie's scans and blood tests, the tablets and the steroids. But what if Luke had somehow caused it all? Munchausen syndrome by proxy. The thought of Luke slowly poisoning his daughter made her stomach cramp.

Allison read about the syndrome on her phone. Some of the red flags sounded just like Luke.

Appears devoted to his or her child.

May suddenly change doctors.

The child has a repeated or unusual illness.

The other parent is not involved in the child's care.

But then others weren't like him at all.

The caregiver is usually the mother.

The caregiver often has low self-esteem or feels their life is out of their control.

The caregiver has medical skills or experience.

The next section talked about the attention that the person received from medical staff and the local community: *Neighbours may bring in meals and do chores.* But Luke was the one cooking and doing his own washing at her house.

The last line read: *The attention may encourage the caregiver to continue their behaviour.* Allison, Declan, Maz and Curtis—they'd all been showering Gracie and Luke with love, care and money, organising fundraising events and activities.

What if they'd actually been encouraging Luke to make Gracie sick?

33

FELIX

DARCY HAD SAID 'SLEEP OVER AT MINE' BUT FELIX WANTED TO BE IN HIS own bed in his own house. Close to Dad. He really wanted Mum but she was still up in the air, flying back from Chicago. She'd rung before she got on the plane but Felix was at soccer training and only heard the message later. *I'm coming home early. See you on Monday. I love you, sweetheart.* Mum hadn't called him 'sweetheart' in ages.

Being back in the house made him relax a little. Most of the neighbours had lived here for ages. And the brick walls felt stronger than the flimsy weatherboard house near the beach. His bedroom upstairs was further away from the front door—a door which had a security screen, as well as a deadlock.

He'd never seen Dad like that before. Shaky, pale, testing all the locks on the windows and the doors. Dad had tried to hide it from them but he couldn't. It'd freaked Felix out. If Dad was worried . . .

In all the whispered conversations at the house in Curl Curl, Felix hadn't heard what the ex-husband had actually done to Helena, but he'd picked up bits and pieces.

He thinks he owns me.

So jealous of every person I speak to.

Tracking my phone.

Every time the baby cried, he'd snap.

Blamed the baby for making him tired for work.

Mum was so angry about Helena but she didn't get that the woman was terrified. Felix had learnt to be calm and quiet, no sudden movements, no shouting. Since they'd been living together in Curl Curl, Helena had barely left the house. The drive-bys, the phone calls—Mum's dumb behaviour had made everything worse. And it meant that Dad had asked Felix to stay home as much as possible too.

Dad set himself and Helena up in the guest bedroom— Luke's room—and put the baby in Gracie's room. It was weird to see them all here. Dad back home but in the wrong bedroom. Dad hadn't said anything about Luke, only that Mum was coming home early. Even though Gracie was in kindergarten, her death had been all over the socials. Some kids at Felix's high school still had siblings at Wirriga Public, so they'd posted love hearts and crying emojis. When he'd gone back to school the day after, all the girls were wearing their purple bracelets. Pearl had written him a card with a poem and Darcy gave him a block of dark chocolate.

'It's not like Gracie's his sister,' one jerk had said.

'But she was living in his house,' Pearl argued. 'And she was only five years old.'

That was the thing that scared the shit out of him.

Felix hadn't been back in the house since Gracie had died. When he went to get the ice-cream out of the freezer, he stopped with the door half open. He'd forgotten about the photos of Gracie on the fridge. Gracie with Mum, with Luke, by herself and one with Felix. Standing on the beach, Felix with his surfboard, Gracie with a bucket. She'd been making mini sandcastles that day. At one point, she'd asked Felix to collect shells for her so she could decorate them. Felix had rolled his eyes and pretended not to hear. Walked away. Embarrassed that some of the other surfers might see him with a kid on the beach. And then Luke had jogged down to the shore with him. Felix knew that all the sun-baking girls were watching, comparing the two of them. Felix's arms and legs would appear even skinnier next to Luke's toned muscles. The gym instructor could've stepped out of a magazine with his bronzed thighs in short trunks.

'You must have strong abs to pull yourself up on the board,' Luke had said. 'I've always swum but I've never been into surfing. Can you show me a few moves?'

Felix gave him a lesson on how to kneel, stand up and balance. Luke fell off a few times; he really didn't know how to surf. Mum had taken some photos of them—another embarrassment. But at least the girls on the beach would've seen Felix instructing the guy with the pecs.

Later, Luke had been spooning sand into a bucket for Gracie to build another castle.

'Can you find us a few shells, mate?' he'd asked Felix.

'Sure—big or small?'

≁

The sound of the doorbell made Helena rush towards Dad.

'Stay in the kitchen with Felix,' Dad said, shutting the doors between them as he went towards the front of the house.

They could hear a young female voice, and then Dad called out for Felix to join them.

'Felix, do you know this woman?' Dad asked.

'Yeah, it's Maz. She's Luke's friend.'

Maz was in leggings and a red Nike hoodie, like she'd just come from the gym.

'I was telling your dad that I'd lent Luke some supplements and I've run out myself so I just wanted to get them. And I know exactly where they are in the kitchen.' Maz spoke without taking a breath.

'You can follow Felix into the kitchen.' Dad nodded in that direction. 'I'll lock the door.'

Funny how Dad was telling Maz where to go, as if she hadn't been here heaps of times. But of course, he wouldn't know; Dad hadn't been in the house for months. Helena said a quick hello, then disappeared upstairs to the baby.

Maz went straight to a cupboard below the microwave. She squatted down in one smooth motion. Felix could see the outline of her quads through her tight black leggings; the sides had a band of netting down them, showing the skin underneath.

'How's Luke?' he asked.

'Well, you know, it's hit him pretty hard.' Maz shook her head and the blonde ponytail swung from side to side.

'I guess now's probably the wrong time to ask about the protein powder? I'm running out.'

'Sorry, I'll sort that out next week. Just keep on training.'

Felix already had the money for her. When Dad had asked Felix to stay home more with Helena and the baby, he'd started handing over cash regularly. An unofficial babysitting job.

A bodyguard against Helena's husband. But what if the man arrived and Felix ran, just like he'd done at the beach?

Maz was still fumbling around in the cupboard.

'Luke kept the supplements here,' she said. 'Have you seen them?'

'Nup.'

'Where's the blender? Wasn't it down here?' Maz opened the cupboard doors on either side. Did the same thing all the way around the kitchen.

'Have you seen any pill containers?' she asked. 'White ones called Bio-Antidotes. Not the same as your creatine.'

'Nup, sorry.'

The other kids at school bought protein powder from the discount chemist but Maz said hers was better—more powerful, because it came from overseas. Was it the same with these supplements?

'Did your mum mention any herbal pills to you?'

Shaking his head, Felix didn't like to admit that he'd barely been here lately.

Maz started opening drawers.

'We keep our medicines up the top, above the fridge,' Felix said. 'You know—out of reach of . . . children.'

He'd been about to say 'out of reach of Gracie'.

'I don't think they'll be there,' she said but looked anyway.

After another frantic search, Maz stopped and stood still in the middle of the kitchen, her hands on her hips, her usual smile replaced by closed lips in a long thin line.

'Maybe Luke took them with him,' Felix said with a shrug.

Was it really that big a deal?

34

ALLISON

ENCLOSED IN AN ALTERNATE UNIVERSE INSIDE A METAL BOX IN THE SKY, Allison's flight seemed to take days and days. She dozed on and off, tried to watch a movie, but her thoughts kept circling. Had Luke killed his own daughter? He didn't seem to fit the profile of Munchausen by proxy; didn't appear to be deliberately seeking attention. But everyone wanted to help the widower with those sad eyes and sick child. Working through hypothesis after hypothesis distracted Allison from her fear of the plane crashing.

When they touched down in Melbourne and Allison opened her eyes to see the safety of the ground, she wished she were in Sydney. Where she could go home, have a shower, collapse, hug her son. While she'd been in the air, her phone had filled with messages. None from Luke. One with No Caller ID. Luke on a different phone? A doctor? The police? She dragged her suitcase to an empty seat away from the luggage carousel and dialled the number for her messages. Would the police leave a message? With the loudspeaker announcements and noise of the travellers around her, she had to push the phone hard against her ear to hear anything.

'Hi, Allison. How are you?' A deep voice, vaguely like Luke's but not quite. Tired by the long flight, muddled by the time difference, Allison struggled to recognise it. '*I left a message last week with my condolences. I'm so sorry to hear about Gracie. I'm guessing you're busy with . . . everything, but if you need a hand or a shoulder to cry on, I'm here. Can you give me a call, please? I wanted to ask you something.*'

Emmanuel. He must be ringing from a work phone. She didn't have the headspace for him right now. Whenever Allison gazed into the future, the picture was too cloudy—she couldn't imagine Tony coming home but then she couldn't imagine being with Emmanuel.

Crowded into a bathroom at the airport with other exhausted passengers, she splashed water on her face and sprayed deodorant under her arms. Watched the water go down the plughole. She couldn't remember if it had swirled the opposite way in the sink at O'Hare airport. Allison stopped for a moment to study her reflection: bloodshot eyes and slightly greasy hair. She'd done it—flown halfway across the world by herself, without Tony or Nadia or Valium. That feeling of empowerment should keep her going for the next few hours. She grabbed a flat white, a ham-and-cheese croissant, a packet of chips and a bottle of Coke. Rushed out to the rental car place. If Tony were with her, he'd tell her this was 'unwise'—driving out into the country-side after a day and a half in the air.

Plugging the destination into her phone, a robotic voice told her the journey time: two hours and twenty minutes. She could stay awake for that long.

The bungalows of the flat Melbourne suburbs gave way to paddocks, then hills lined with gum trees. Allison had only been in America for a few days but she'd been wobbly the whole time, struggling to orientate herself in the city, connect with the people. Driving along this country highway, a place she'd never been before, felt like coming home.

The lower part of the hills hadn't been impacted by the fires; the blaze must have come from the north—the remote mountains of the national park. On an unusually hot, windy day last October, before summer had even officially begun, a young man lit a series of small fires which had rapidly combined. With so little rain over the previous six months, the forest went up like fireworks. No-one had been prepared. Allison remembered reading about the heroics at the school: in minutes, two teachers had crammed the children into a minibus and driven them down the hill, away from the flames and smoke. The fire had burnt half of the classrooms.

Along the road winding up to Hythorne, the grass was growing again in patches, green here, brown there. Before, the dense undergrowth would have hidden the lay of the land. Today, Allison could see each dip and curve of the mountain range, its underbelly exposed. A single dark shape circled beneath the grey clouds, wings wide—a wedge-tailed eagle, searching for prey.

As Allison drove into the small town, the scarred reality stood out: twisted metal sheeting, a brick wall in a blank space between the houses that had been spared. The church had no roof, its stone walls standing by themselves, as if the BFG,

Gracie's favourite giant, had plucked off the top to peer in at the tiny people.

Outside the general store, Allison was opening her car door when a huge truck groaned by, blasting its horn. She pulled the door closed again and leant back against the seat. Shut her eyes for a moment. When she looked again, the truck was half a block in front of her, trundling down the main road, its tray heavy with bricks.

Compared to the devastation out on the streets, inside the general store resembled a fairytale land. Shelves of brightly coloured tins and packets, a freezer offering a rainbow of ice-blocks. Everything new and modern and clean.

The woman behind the counter was flipping through a postage folder, organising pages of stamps. 'Hello, love. Come on in. The baskets are over there.'

In her blue faded apron, the middle-aged shop assistant seemed friendly enough. Above her top pocket, a name had been embroidered in red thread—*Kayleigh*.

'Actually, I was hoping you could help me find a friend.'

The woman stopped flipping through the stamps and glared at her.

'Are you a journalist?'

Allison had seen the newspapers at Melbourne airport that morning. Seven months after the fire, the headlines were still on the town: an investigation and a court case against the arsonist.

'No, I'm a schoolteacher from Sydney.'

As Allison repeated the words she'd spoken at the healing centre in Chicago, jetlag made her head spin. Two very different people in different hemispheres distrustful of the media.

'Sydney, huh?' Kayleigh shrugged as if Sydneysiders were as bad as journalists. 'Listen, love, would you mind buying something? A lot of people come up here, ask questions, take photos and buy nothing. We're just trying to survive.'

Her cousins in Tathra had echoed a similar sentiment after a fire which had destroyed more than a hundred buildings in their small town. Journalists and politicians had been and gone while everyday people found ways to help. Donations of furniture and food, bedding and books. A community had come together then, just like Wirriga had for Gracie.

But with two hundred serious fires burning in Queensland last November, had Hythorne been overlooked? The top half of Australia had seen hundreds of thousands of hectares burnt; farms, houses, livestock and wildlife obliterated. Further south, Hythorne, with its arsonist and its anger, hadn't captured the nation's sympathy in quite the same way.

Allison grabbed a small shopping basket and began filling it with snacks. She threw in a bottle of red wine for good measure.

As the shopkeeper scanned the items through the cash register, she examined Allison from head to toe. Flushing, Allison moved the bottle of wine and the nuts to one side and slid them across the counter.

'These are for you,' she said.

Kayleigh laughed and her face lit up. Allison guessed that, before the fires, this had been her typical expression.

'You've only been here five minutes and you know my reputation. Thanks, love, I'll enjoy that wine tonight. So, who's this friend you're trying to find?'

'Luke Branson and his daughter Gracie.' Allison steeled herself to say the next sentence. For all she knew, Kayleigh could have been his wife's best friend. 'Gracie's five years old. Gorgeous girl. She has cancer.'

The woman massaged her left temple with two fingers and said nothing. Allison didn't know whether to push on; she didn't want to cause anyone in this town more pain. Finally, Kayleigh raised her eyebrows in a question, so Allison continued.

'Their house was lost in the fire. And Gracie's mother . . . passed away afterwards. Luke and Gracie moved to Sydney.'

'Sorry, love. Never heard of any Bransons. Well, only that rich fella—Richard Branson—but I reckon he never lived here.' She barked out a bitter laugh.

'They kept horses,' Allison added. 'They lived out of town, so maybe you didn't know them.'

'I've been working here for twenty years. I know everyone.'

Sighing, Kayleigh reached under the counter and pulled out a box. She sifted through bits of paper. Produced a double-page spread from the Melbourne newspaper, with four large portraits.

'This is a list of—' Kayleigh cleared her throat '—the people who . . .'

The fire hadn't discriminated: male and female, two young, two old. Sarah Branson had died from injuries after the fire, perhaps that was why she didn't appear on the list. Or maybe she went by her maiden name. Turning the page over, Allison found another list: twenty-one people who had sustained injuries.

The bell above the door jangled and an old farmer in King Gees and an Akubra entered the shop. Kayleigh called out a cheerful hello and moved the box of newspaper clippings under the counter, out of his sight. She picked up a green shopping basket and carried it over to him.

Allison read every name on the list of injured. No Sarah.

The farmer acknowledged Allison with a nod. 'Up from the city?' he asked.

'She's from Sydney,' Kayleigh answered for her. 'Looking for a family called Branson. Know them?'

'Nope.' The old man's watery eyes, a startling light blue, fixed on her. 'Not like the Harveys, are they? Those bastards didn't lose anything and put in the biggest insurance claim. Made it harder for the rest of us.'

'I'm sorry to hear that.' Allison had to turn away from his piercing gaze. 'This isn't to do with insurance.'

After he'd left the shop, Allison tried once more with Kayleigh. On her phone, she clicked onto Sarah's online memorial site and showed the photo.

'Never seen her before in my life,' Kayleigh said. 'Does it actually mention Hythorne? Are you sure it's not another town?'

'Luke said they lived in Hythorne but it's not written here.' Allison only noticed that as she was re-reading the webpage now. 'Sarah was a dental nurse who kept horses.'

'No dentist in Hythorne.' Kayleigh ran her fingers through her unruly fringe, then patted it back in line. 'The only family with lots of horses are the Luxfords. Terrible tragedy. Rose died in the fire trying to release them.'

The same heartbreaking ending as Sarah Branson. But the picture in the paper of Rose Luxford showed an older woman, around sixty-five, short blonde hair, glasses, outdoorsy type. Nothing like Sarah Branson.

'Thanks for your help anyway. I appreciate it.'

Taking a step towards the door, Allison stumbled as the whole world tilted in front of her eyes. Kayleigh was beside her in an instant, holding her up.

'All right, love?'

'Jetlag,' Allison mumbled.

And fear.

'Oh-la-la. Fancy shmancy,' Kayleigh muttered loudly enough for Allison to hear.

'Would I be able to . . . can I just sit down for a minute?'

'Sure, come out the back and I'll get you a cuppa. You're in no state to drive.'

━

Twenty minutes later, revived by Kayleigh's tea and kindness, Allison walked along the main street of Hythorne. The cool air bit into her and she wished she had a thicker jumper or a coat. In the petrol station and the hardware store, she approached the shop assistants and presented the photos to them: Sarah on the memorial page, Gracie on the blog, Luke on Facebook.

'Obviously Gracie would've looked different with hair,' she explained.

'Sorry, don't know them,' came the replies.

Allison asked at the vet and the bakery. Knocked on the door of the boutique winery with its For Sale sign. Finally, she reached the old pub on the corner, a relic from bushranger days. Its wooden balconies had survived the fire and the white wrought-iron railings were freshly painted. Inside, a log fire warmed the six drinkers scattered at tables. Allison spoke to the barman and each of the customers.

Not one of them had heard of the Bransons.

With no idea of where to go next, Allison slumped onto a bar stool and ordered a lemonade. She imagined resting her head on the wooden countertop, letting her mind go blank, falling asleep right here. And waking up with all the answers. Her phone buzzed, jolting her thoughts. Luke? She grabbed the mobile from her bag, flipped it over and saw a message from Felix.

I don't feel safe. Please come home. Love you.

35

ALLISON CALLED FELIX IMMEDIATELY. 'ARE YOU OKAY, SWEETHEART? What's happened?'

'There were some kids in the bush last night. Behind the house. Helena completely freaked out. Dad called the police. They're here again now, downstairs.' He paused for breath. 'The police, I mean.'

'I'm sure it was just teenagers drinking. Nothing to worry about.'

The same reassurance that Nadia had given her at the beginning of the year. With Zack's father behind bars, the robberies had stopped but the prospect of Helena's husband could be far worse.

'The police wanted a statement from me but I didn't see anything. What am I supposed to tell them?'

'It's all right, Felix. Just tell them the truth.'

Her poor boy, flipping between terrified and tough.

'Maz came over the other night, looking for some pills,' he said. 'Did you know that?'

'No. Thanks for telling me.'

Did Luke still have a key to the house? Had he given one to Maz? Why had Maz been dancing on the beach the day after Gracie died? Were they in it together?

Oh God, Allison would have to tell Tony, the police, everyone . . . Sweet little Gracie. What had happened to her?

'When are you coming home, Mum? Where are you?'

'I had to do a stopover in Melbourne. I'm jetlagged and I was going to stay down here tonight, but I can fly back earlier if you need me to?'

The longer she could avoid facing Gracie's Gang, the better. She had no answers and no explanations. But of course she'd come back if Felix asked. Although she didn't want to spend the night at the house with Tony and Helena and the baby. She hadn't wanted Tony to come home like that. The replacement of Allison Walsh was now complete.

'It's okay. Darcy and I are going to a Manly United game this arvo. Will you be here when I get home from school tomorrow?'

'Yes, I'll be there.'

After ending the call, Allison noticed that Curtis had sent a text: *I've got nothing to report and Dr Rawson still hasn't rung back.* Was the doctor helping to cover Luke's tracks? Or Curtis himself? The journalist was the only one who'd ever spoken to Dr Rawson.

Allison went back to the general store for some supplies to keep her awake on the drive to Melbourne. She couldn't stop yawning. This trip had been another bloody wild-goose chase. As she was paying for the Coke and chips, Kayleigh asked about her next movements.

'I'll stay the night at a hotel on the outskirts of Melbourne.' Allison yawned again. 'Fly back to Sydney tomorrow lunchtime.'

'You're exhausted, darl, and we don't need another tragedy.' Kayleigh grimaced then rearranged her face into a smile. 'Why don't you stay in my guesthouse tonight? My husband's away so you can help me drink that bottle of wine.'

The Currawong Guesthouse perched on the edge of town: an old two-storey cottage, painted blue and pink. The views should have been stunning. Instead, the verandah overlooked a desolate moonscape studded with singed trunks.

'No tourists these days,' Kayleigh grunted. 'One insurance guy came but he left pretty quick. No government people, not even bloody journalists. They all stay at the bottom of the mountain, where they can escape the sight of it.'

They could hear the currawongs chattering to each other; their long, double call ended in a wolf whistle that echoed around the valley.

'It's good they're back,' Kayleigh said. 'For months after, we didn't hear a single bird. I'll do dinner at seven.'

'Great, thanks.'

If Allison could stay awake that long.

Sinking into an old-fashioned armchair, she traced her fingers over the fabric—wrens perched atop golden leaves. *Love you*, Felix had typed. Over the past five months, she'd kept saying it to him but he'd stopped saying it back.

Noise outside the window startled her. She must have fallen asleep. A huge currawong was swooping downwards onto a smaller, squawking bird. Attacking the bird or protecting its own? Allison checked her phone: messages from Shona and Mum.

Nothing from Luke.

He'd lied to her about Chicago. About Hythorne. Why? Her instinct to see the best in people, to allow the benefit of the doubt, was being pushed beyond logic. Where the hell was he? She decided to try Facebook Messenger—if he was using another phone, he should still be able to see that. But what to say? He'd never answer if he knew Allison was here in Hythorne.

I'm worried for you. I know you're not in Chicago. I'm back now and I can help you. I loved Gracie too. Just let me know where you are and if you're okay?

On Luke's Facebook page, hundreds of people had written their condolences underneath the photo of Gracie on the Ferris wheel in Chicago.

—*My daughter will miss Gracie so much.*

—*When's the funeral? We want to be there for you and to farewell Gracie.*

—*She's with her mum in Heaven. xx*

—*Please let us know what we can do to help.*

Allison read each name and checked for any responses from Luke. Love hearts and sad face emojis had been added next to the comments, but none by Luke. Staring at the Facebook page, Allison wondered about his six hundred and eighty-three friends. One of them must know where Luke had gone.

She began typing: *After the tragic loss of Gracie, Luke has stopped answering his calls. We're all worried about him. Does anyone know where he is?*

Re-reading the words, she glanced at the Facebook friends again. Some of them were mums and dads from school. They knew Luke had been staying with her—what would they think of this message? That she and Luke had argued? That she was incompetent at looking after both Gracie and Luke? But bloody hell, she had to do something. She hit 'post' on the dialogue button and waited for it to appear on his timeline.

Nothing happened.

Allison tried again. Still nothing. There must be some privacy settings in place. The only other option was to put her message in a comment at the bottom of the post. Hopefully, some of his friends would see it there. After adding her words, she clicked onto the 'friends' box and examined them. So many people he'd never mentioned. Friends from high school, swimming, gym, uni? People who'd known his family?

Luke was an only child whose elderly parents had disappointed him and vice versa. They'd pushed him with the swimming, but when he'd failed to get into the Olympic team, they'd lost interest. He'd been backpacking in Peru when his father was in a bad car accident. Apparently his mum had said he shouldn't cut his trip short—he'd worked hard to earn the money for travelling and he should stay there and enjoy it. That was them, he said. Unsentimental. Even with their only son.

'Did you come back?' Allison had asked. No way could she 'stay on and enjoy a trip' while her father was in a critical condition in hospital. 'We were in a remote town. The bus to Trujillo only came every second day. And then I had to get another bus to Lima. Another day to get a flight out. By the time I got home, Dad was still in hospital but unlikely to die. My mother wasn't particularly pleased to see me—said I shouldn't have bothered.'

When Luke had spoken about his uncaring family, Allison was impressed that he'd managed to break the mould with his own parenting. Could she track down his mum and dad?

As she scrolled through the list of friends, Allison noticed Sarah Branson's name. She clicked on the image and Sarah's profile came up. Gracie hadn't gone to the funeral, Luke said. It was too much for her during chemo.

Was it mawkish to keep Facebook pages of the dead? Or comforting—as if they were still here, just in a different room with a locked door. Even from the photo, Allison could see that Sarah had a vitality, an aura of happiness. Her last post had been of horses running in a paddock. *Trying to decide which one Gracie should ride . . . Silver is too feisty, Topaz is too big and Amber loves to gallop! Time to buy a pony for my little girl?*

Enlarging the picture on Facebook, Allison focused on the paddocks. If the Bransons never lived in Hythorne, where and how had Sarah died?

At first light, the currawongs called Allison out of her dream in which she'd been madly trying to bake a cake for Gracie and catch a plane. She checked Facebook straight away. Nothing from Luke but some responses from his friends.

—*Have you tried their old town in Victoria?*

—*His mum's from Perth. I'll see if I can find her number.*

—*Have you talked to Maz?*

All useful suggestions but then the tone turned:

—*Maybe he needs some time out and you should leave him alone.*

—*Yeah, give the guy a break, he's been through some tough shit.*

—*Luke knows how much we all love him. He'll be back when he's ready.*

—*You've had your five minutes of fame, Ms Teacher, get out of the limelight.*

—*Stop being a jerk. Mrs Walsh has done so much for Gracie. She's a legend.*

—*Umm, hello. A little girl just died. Some decorum here, please.*

She'd never heard of the friend who was telling her to get out of the limelight. A personal trainer from Ballarat. As if Allison had ever wanted fame; she hated the limelight. Allison was fine standing up and talking to the kids, but replace them with adults and her hands started shaking. She recognised the people defending her—parents from school. *She's a legend.* Huh. So much of a legend that she had no idea if Gracie was dead or alive, Luke had disappeared, Felix was terrified, and her husband had brought his new girlfriend and baby into their house. An absolute legend.

After breakfast, when Allison thanked Kayleigh for her hospitality, the woman wished her luck.

'I hope you find out where they've gone,' Kayleigh said, before repeating her line from last night. 'I don't understand why Luke would say his wife died in Hythorne. Why did he choose *our* town?'

Kayleigh had lost a friend and an acquaintance. Her whole community had been affected. Allison could feel her simmering rage. Hard enough to go through the tragedy, the clean-up, the rebuilding—but then to have someone 'steal' their horrific experiences . . .

'Luke really did seem traumatised by his wife's death,' Allison answered. 'Maybe it hurt too much to say the name of their own town?'

His wife's death was what had connected them; Luke had understood Allison's own loss. It couldn't be a lie.

—

At the airport, waiting to board the plane, Allison sent a text to Curtis and Maz.

Hi—can you meet at my house at 6 tonight? Anyone heard from Luke?

Was his last message three days ago? With the time difference between America and Australia, Allison wasn't sure. Back then, when she'd got his message, she'd assumed he was in Chicago. That she'd find him—save him—and they'd come home together.

Maz replied immediately. *He won't answer. I'm scared for him. I can be at yours tonight.*

With everything else going on, Allison hadn't had a chance to look into Maz's supplements. The gym instructor had been sleeping with Luke; she must know something.

36

MAZ

OVER THE WEEKEND, MAZ HAD CALLED EACH OF HER CLIENTS. ASKED them how they were feeling. Any signs of illness? All of them said they were fine.

'I'm sorry, but I can't sell the supplements anymore,' she'd explained. 'You should go into the stores at Manly or Chatswood. Discuss your needs with them. Don't buy them online.'

Trying to warn her clients while covering her arse. Only one asked why she was stopping.

'I've got too many other things on.'

A missing—presumed dead—boyfriend. A dad in hospital. An online program in ashes. And a child's death.

For all of which Maz might be to blame.

I was only trying to help.

She couldn't get on to her last client, Laurel, so Maz tracked her down after a class. Maz thought the woman would be angry and worried, but Laurel seemed to be expecting another delivery.

'You have to stop taking them,' Maz said. 'They could make you sick.'

'That's unfortunate.' Laurel didn't sound particularly concerned. 'They were definitely working. Look at my flat stomach.'

Should Maz tell her that the pills might contain a substance that was banned in Australia?

'I'll refund all your money.'

Breaking into the safety net she'd just started accruing. There'd be no twenty-third birthday party now. No new car in a few years' time.

'Thanks for letting me know. Can you recommend any other appetite suppressants?'

'No, you should talk to your doctor.'

A strange conversation. Maz wondered if Laurel didn't believe her or if the desire to be thin was stronger than any other health considerations. Hopefully, Laurel wouldn't start buying them online herself.

Of course, she told Oakley about the letter from Australian Border Force. She didn't want to get him, or the factory in Thailand, into trouble.

'Freakin' hell, your package was confiscated—that's heavy, man,' he said.

'I'm shutting up shop.'

'But it's all good stuff. Australia shouldn't be banning it.'

'Only one lot has a banned substance but I can't work out which one it is.'

'Well, you know the protein powder's okay,' Oakley reasoned. 'Keep selling that. Make some money and meet up with me.'

Hook up with me, he meant. An overseas trip would be a distraction from all the shit going on here. And then she remembered that Border Force had her name on file. What if they arrested her leaving Australia?

'I can't keep selling,' she mumbled. 'I think I'm s'posed to have a licence or something.'

—

Text. WhatsApp. Messenger. She'd called Luke again and again. Saturday and Sunday. Morning and night. No response to any of it. His WhatsApp remained offline. The sick feeling about Gracie had taken over her whole body. Curtis said their passports hadn't left the country but Maz didn't believe it. Fake news. Either his source was wrong or their passports were in a different name. And the whole thing with Dr Mercado—Allison had stuffed up somehow. Or the clinic refused to tell her because she wasn't family. There were any number of reasons why the teacher hadn't found them. Luke was in Chicago, she knew it.

But that didn't stop Maz's fear. Had Luke gone ahead and checked out?

—

Mid-morning on Monday, Maz entered the hospital ward swinging a bag with more clothes for Dad. He wanted to be ready to go whenever they let him. Hopefully soon. Maz plastered a smile on her face.

'Here she is.' Mum jumped up to give her a hug.

The hug was tight and long.

'What about a cuddle for your old man?' Dad asked from his hospital bed. 'I'm missing out.'

She sat on the edge of the bed and bent awkwardly to wrap her arms around him. The hospital antiseptic had overpowered Dad's usual scent—a combination of his deodorant, the shampoo he got free from the factory and Mum's washing powder.

'How's Luke doing?' Mum asked.

Avoiding Wendy's enquiring eyes, Maz stared past her, through the big window to where the sea shimmered in the far distance. The horizon made a neat divide between the green-blue water and the pale blue sky. Higher up, clouds stretched in long, thin shapes, wispy at each end. She imagined them as kayaks gliding across the water.

'Ummm, Luke is . . .'

Mum grabbed at her arm. 'Is he back from America? He can stay at our house if he needs to.'

While Dad had been in hospital, Mum hadn't slept properly. Her face was puffy and she had dark half-circles under her eyes. Maz couldn't remember the last time her parents had spent a night apart.

'Luke is . . .' She searched for a way to reassure Mum—and herself. 'He's devastated. But he'll be okay eventually. You know how positive he is.'

'Any funeral plans yet?'

What if they had to organise a double funeral? Maz walked over to the window so Mum wouldn't see her tears.

＊

Maz had written out the list of supplements but she didn't know which, if any, had caused the episode. As she was about to leave Dad's bedside, Dr Simmons appeared.

'The angiogram has given us some unexpected results,' he said. 'You seem to have no indications of heart disease, Rick.'

'Well, that's great news.' Mum smiled brightly and patted Dad on the shoulder.

'We were expecting to see some sign of arteriosclerosis or atherosclerosis—that's a thickening of the arteries and a build-up of plaque.'

'So I've got a healthy heart!' Dad was grinning as if he'd won a medal.

'Yes, but we're still trying to work out *why* you had the chest pains.' Dr Simmons raised his eyebrows. 'Have you been taking cocaine or any other illicit drugs?'

'Cocaine?' Dad gave a full belly laugh, making the bed move slightly. 'Do I look like someone who takes cocaine? A raver, is that what you call them, Maz?'

Maz couldn't smile. She forced herself to say the next words.

'Dad, you did give Dr Simmons the list of supplements, didn't you?'

'Yes, and he said they wouldn't have affected my heart.'

Dr Simmons nodded.

'What about the appetite suppressant?' Maz whispered to Dad, avoiding eye contact with the doctor.

Before Dad could answer, Dr Simmons spoke. 'That wasn't on your list. Which brand?'

'Not really a brand exactly. I wrote it down but perhaps the name didn't mean anything.' Maz didn't know how to make it clear without incriminating herself. 'They, uh, they came from Thailand too.'

'How long has Rick been taking them?'

Maz had only given him a few tablets to start him off. Then he'd secretly taken more. She looked towards Dad, waiting for his answer. But he stayed silent.

'Maybe four months.'

'That might explain it. Some of those diet pills speed up the metabolism to dangerously high levels. Can you bring them in?'

Gripping the bed rails, Maz wished she'd told the doctor straight away. Even if meant going to jail, she should've fessed up.

'I got a letter from Australian Border Force.' Her words were barely audible. 'It said something about increased risk of liver failure causing death.'

'Your father hasn't suffered liver failure,' Dr Simmons said. 'But I'll organise a blood test, and see if there are any chemicals still in his system. We can determine if it has caused the coronary artery vasospasm. Let's keep you in another day, Rick, so we can sort this all out. And, Maz, please bring in the pills. We can get them analysed in the lab.'

Without saying goodbye, Dr Simmons spun around and left the ward. Mum stared at the space where the doctor had been and burst into tears.

'It's all right, Mum.'

When Maz tried to give her a gentle squeeze, Mum shrugged her off.

'No, it's not all right. Why would you take pills like that, Rick?'

'It helped me lose weight.' Dad's chin wobbled. 'I just wanted to be a success for our Maz. For her exercise program.'

Mum stood at the end of his bed, her arms crossed over her chest.

'You could've killed yourself.'

When Maz arrived at Allison's house that evening, the ex-husband and his new lover had gone. The other night, she'd been too busy searching for the pills to notice how empty the place seemed without Luke and Gracie. The last time she'd been in the lounge room with Luke, they were sitting on the couch, his arm around her shoulder, her head against his chest. Maz had been wondering about the future after Chicago—would they stay together and set up the online program? Would Gracie get better with her pills? Would they become a celebrity couple?

And that same night, after Gracie was in bed, Maz had offered to help Luke pack. Instead, they'd shut the door to his room and hadn't made it as far as the bed. Frantic, noisy, desperate sex on the carpet. Maz was sure the teacher must have heard. Later, after they had packed Luke's bag, she'd kissed him and they'd fallen into bed. Slower, quieter lovemaking the second time.

As Maz sat in the lounge room with Allison and Curtis, that farewell seemed months ago, not weeks. Before, Allison had always been buzzing around, in and out of the kitchen, organising things—dinner or an outing for Gracie. Now, she was on the couch with her legs curled up underneath her, not moving at all. She'd prepared a platter of humus and crackers, which sat untouched in the middle of the coffee table.

Allison told them about visiting a number of hospitals and clinics in Chicago. Maz had to admit that it sounded like she'd made a big effort to find where Gracie had been treated.

'Maybe they were using a different name?' Maz suggested. 'With both the hospital and the passports.'

She saw a look of disbelief pass between Allison and Curtis.

'Even if they were using a different name, they'd remember a young Australian girl with thymic carcinoma,' Curtis said. 'It's pretty unusual.'

'I never saw their passports,' Allison added, 'but I can double-check Gracie's name with the school tomorrow. They'll have a copy of Gracie's birth certificate for enrolment.'

'I still think they're in Chicago,' Maz insisted.

'Maz, he lied about Dr Mercado's clinic.' Curtis hit the cushion as he spoke. 'He lied about Hythorne. Why wouldn't he lie about Chicago too?'

'I don't know. I just feel that's where he is.'

Oh shit. Had Curtis told Allison about the Border Force letter?

'Dr Rawson won't get back to me,' Curtis said. 'And the main reception desk wasn't helpful. I'll drive out to the hospital tomorrow and try in person.'

Felix wandered in from the kitchen. More clients. Maz had forgotten about the teenage boys. She'd have to tell them to stop taking their supplements and that she wasn't supplying any more.

'Does anyone want a cup of tea?' Felix's voice went high then deep, on the verge of breaking.

They shook their heads.

Allison explained that she'd asked everyone on Luke's Facebook page to help locate him. Not one of the six hundred and eighty-three friends had seen him.

'I can go online now and see if there's been any update, Mum,' Felix offered.

'I'll check the blog, too,' Curtis said. 'Maybe he's staying with someone who donated?'

Curtis tapped on his mobile and then scowled at Maz. 'I can't find the page.'

Instantly, she searched on her phone. It wasn't there.

'He's taken it down.' Maz gave a tiny woo-hoo. 'That means he's still alive.'

Luke and Allison were the only ones with access to the website apart from Maz. He had to be alive. Pressing his number on her phone, Maz ached for him to answer. But he didn't.

Hey, Luke here. Sorry I can't make it to the phone. Leave a message and I'll catch you later. Maz had been so sure he'd pick up that she didn't have a message prepared. His deep voice so strong, so sexy. *Please be alive.* She rushed out some words. 'We're so worried about you. Where are you? Please call me. Love you, babe.'

The others were watching her; they sighed when she hung up.

'Maz, you know him best,' Allison said. 'Where do you think he is?'

The teacher always spoke to her as if she were a child. Did Allison think she'd hidden him away somewhere?

'He talked about friends in Melbourne and a mate from college in Queensland,' Maz said. 'I don't know their names or numbers. His wife's family lived somewhere in South Australia.'

'We need to find out where Sarah died.' The teacher was rubbing her forehead. 'I feel that's where he is. Curtis, can you retrieve death records?'

'I'll see what I can find out.'

'Maz, can you go to the police station and report him missing?'

'Oh no, you'd be much better at that, Allison,' she argued, terrified at the thought of meeting with the police. 'You can explain about Chicago.'

Curtis poured more red wine into the almost-empty glasses. Maz accepted the refill and guzzled it. She shouldn't be drinking. She didn't drink.

The evening sky was completely black; no moon shone through the windows. With the curtains still open and the lights on, Maz felt that the three of them were on show. Anyone could be peeking in through the front window or watching them from the back garden. Shivering, she lifted her wineglass again.

'I've got a few theories.' As Allison started to speak, she eyeballed Maz. 'One is that Gracie got sick, maybe died, from the herbal pills—'

Felix shouted from the kitchen: 'Mum, I think you should come and look at this.'

They followed Allison into the next room and crowded around the kitchen bench. Felix had the laptop open; one tab showed Luke's Facebook page and another had a picture of an attractive woman with dark curly hair.

'That's Sarah Branson,' Allison said. 'You've found her. Did you figure out where she died?'

'I did a reverse image search on Sarah's photo.' The teenager gnawed on his bottom lip. 'It matches a woman called Florencia Concepción Fernández de León. She's a marketing manager who lives in Mexico City.'

37

ALLISON

ALLISON EDGED FELIX OUT OF HIS STOOL AND TOOK HIS SEAT. MEXICO City? The woman at The Happy Place had mentioned Mexico. Sick Americans went to clinics there for procedures not approved by the FDA, and a famous ice hockey player once had stem-cell treatment there—had she heard all that from Luke?

'Are you sure it's Sarah?' Maz asked. 'Could it be like when Facebook tags someone else with similar features?'

'It's not a hundred per cent, but no matching photo came up in Australia.'

Curtis pushed in closer, next to Allison's left elbow.

'Has this woman died?'

'I don't know.' Allison stared at the screen as if the photo could tell her. 'I can't read Spanish.'

She copied a slab of text and put it into Google Translate.

'It sounds like she just went to some kind of product launch so I guess she's alive.'

If Florencia were Gracie's mum, why was she in Mexico City, rather than here in Sydney looking after her sick little girl? Allison could see a slight resemblance but it was hard to be sure with Gracie's bandana and bald head. Was Florencia a good-time mum—she left when Gracie got sick? But Luke could have told them that. Unless he was protecting Gracie. Or unless he'd taken her to Mexico?

'It's a mistake,' Maz said, repeating her line from earlier.

Allison heard Felix take a deep breath.

'Mum, I think it's all a scam.'

Since Allison had discovered that Luke wasn't in Chicago, she'd kept coming back to this idea. Her mind chipping away at it, like an axe into hard wood. But each time she found a single fact and made some progress, another thought would sneak out and glance the axe off in a different direction. She couldn't get a firm grip on what might be true and what might not. Gracie's tiny body, lying on the couch after a hospital visit, snuggled under a blanket, watching *Play School* on TV—she'd definitely seen that.

Allison imagined somehow sewing together all the tiny bits of data scattered around online to create a full picture.

'Do that reverse image search on Luke,' she said to Felix.

As her son uploaded a photo, Allison noticed that Luke was standing sideways, not showing his whole face. The search came up with no result.

'Try a different photo, where he's looking at the camera,' she suggested.

Felix scrolled through Facebook but Luke was side-on in all of them.

Allison flicked through the photo albums on her phone. She remembered having more of Luke on the beach and at the celebration party. He must've been through her phone and deleted any images that clearly showed his likeness. The bastard. This tiny invasion of privacy was nothing compared to all the lies but it was one small thing that she knew for sure.

'We have to go to the police,' Allison said.

In furious denial, Maz stormed to the other side of the kitchen and leant against the doorframe, lifted her mobile to her ear. And then she started sobbing.

'His number's been disconnected. He must be dead.'

'He's not dead,' Curtis bellowed. 'He's fucking duped us.'

—

The others left with specific plans for tomorrow—Curtis would contact the Victorian regional papers to find any evidence of Sarah Branson, and he'd visit Dr Rawson at the children's hospital. Maz, when she eventually stopped crying, agreed to go to the police station on the way home and register Luke and Gracie as missing persons. Allison planned to get a copy of Gracie's birth certificate from the school office, and take it to the police tomorrow morning.

Luke had been playing them all—their sympathy for his dead wife, their empathy for his sick daughter. And could she trust Curtis and Maz, or was one of them in on it too?

Allison ordered Indian takeaway and tried to enjoy a homecoming feast with her son. The two of them at this dining table, a simple act she'd taken for granted last year. Tony and his girlfriend had moved into a short-stay apartment; Allison didn't know where.

Accompanying them to dinner, though, was an unwelcome guest—her shame. While her first reaction had been anger at Luke, it'd quickly turned inwards. Now the shame burnt inside her, rendering each mouthful of rogan josh tasteless.

Felix scooped mango chutney onto a pappadum and demolished the whole thing in one bite. When she'd hugged him earlier, she'd had to reach up around his shoulders, higher than before. His voice was deeper, flecks of dark hair sprouted above his upper lip. He'd need to start shaving soon.

'I know you're embarrassed, Mum,' Felix said, shovelling down another pappadum.

She'd forgotten that—his ability to perceive how she was feeling at certain moments.

'I'm jetlagged, honey, and I don't understand what's going on. How could he have tricked us like that?'

Not only had she been deceived, but Luke had used her to dupe others. Mrs Allison Walsh—well-known, well-liked, well-respected schoolteacher—had inadvertently deceived an entire community.

'Mum, there are heaps of scams,' Felix said. 'We did it in class. Relationship scams, business scams.' He paused to make a point. 'In the tax office scam, people were ordered to pay extra tax, so they just paid it. They weren't stupid. It all looked legit.'

Allison didn't need her teenage son telling her about scams; she knew enough. Last year, she'd read the story of a fifty-two-year-old divorcee from Sydney who'd fallen in love with a handsome American soldier. She transferred cash to him because he was in Afghanistan and couldn't access his accounts. They declared their love for each other. Talked on the phone. Sent flowers and love tokens. Planned to meet in Paris. So romantic. Except that the American soldier was a seventeen-year-old Ghanaian boy sweet-talking women from an internet cafe in Accra. A boy barely older than Felix.

But Luke wasn't a stranger over the internet. He'd lived here in her home. She'd seen his sick daughter with her own eyes. Cared for them both.

'I never thought I'd fall for a scam.' She put her hands over her cheeks; they were hot to touch. Ashamed in front of her own son. 'I thought I'd spot it a mile off.'

'Except that you and Dad want to *help* people. You at school, Dad with the women's refuges.'

The way Felix said *help* made it sound like a dirty word.

—

In the morning, Allison was woken by Felix placing a cup of tea on her bedside table. Tea with just the right amount of milk in her favourite blue dotty mug. Delivered to her in bed. The only time he'd done that before was on Mother's Day, with Tony directing him. Did Tony make Helena a cup of tea in bed every morning? The thought flashed past and she pushed it away. Felix was here, at home, dressed in his grey school uniform. Allison reached up and stroked his hair, longer than usual. He'd always hated having a cut; she'd been the one to insist upon it.

'You slept in, Mum. I'll be back about five this arvo after the soccer trials.'

'Good luck, sweetheart.'

When Felix leant down to kiss her goodbye, she pulled him into a tight hug.

—

The blender still sat in the kitchen bin, now covered by the remains of their Indian takeaway. Allison tied up the bag and padded outside to dump it in the wheelie bin. Piled atop the other rubbish were nappies. Dear God, a baby. For one millisecond, she felt sorry for Tony. And then the outrage was back. How dare he put Felix in that position?

When Tony heard about Luke, would he be saying the same to her?

But Luke wasn't dangerous. Whatever the situation, Gracie had needed her. And Gracie had blossomed in Wirriga. Over the last three months, she'd made friends, she'd been loved.

Before doing anything else, Allison poured another cup of tea and phoned Nadia. Talked her through the strange set of events. Cried about her own gullibility. Nadia was shocked into silence and then tried to comfort her.

'It's not your fault, Al. You've got a good heart. Wirriga won't blame you.'

Allison didn't believe the reassurances.

Her friend offered to look into Luke's financials. Allison gave her the bank account details and the name of the cashier who'd helped them with the deposit from Gracie Day.

Unpacking her suitcase, Allison wished she hadn't thrown away the plastic containers of supplements in Los Angeles. She had photos of the labels on her phone: *Super Strong for Super Bones. Great Greens, Great Health. Detox for Cancer.* Did they matter now or not? Either way, she'd show them at the police station after she picked up the birth certificate from school.

Samantha wouldn't be in the office for another half hour so Allison went into the spare room. When Luke had arrived in her house in February, he'd brought so little with him. Now, he'd taken most of that to Chicago. Not Chicago. Allison had to rejig her thoughts. One winter jacket hung in the wardrobe, a set of weights lay at the bottom along with a pair of old running shoes. She opened the drawers—brochures from three different real estate agents. Had he ever actually looked for a place to rent? An empty can of deodorant, Lynx. It smelt just like him.

In a frenzy, she felt through the pockets of his winter coat, shoved her fingers inside the shoes, yanked out the drawers in the bedside table, searched through the bookcase.

Threw his shoes across the room.

'Lying, cheating, deceiving bastard!'

Allison shoved the mattress from its base and tipped it up. No secrets hidden underneath there. The dust made her sneeze.

Her watch said eight ten. She could ring Samantha in the front office now.

As soon as Samantha sniffed her condolences down the phone, Allison realised she had to make a decision. Should she protect Luke—and her own reputation—until she figured out where he was? Or should she ask everyone to help her find him?

She'd make that decision after she spoke to the police.

'When's the funeral?' Samantha asked. 'We've been planning the memorial assembly. The kids are coming up with suggestions to remember Gracie. One wants to build a theme park on the oval in her name.'

Allison gave a short chuckle.

'Luke has . . .' Allison stared at his shoes—one had landed near the bookcase, the other by the door. 'Luke is . . . still away but he needs a copy of Gracie's birth certificate for the . . . arrangements. I can't find it here. Could you pull it out of the files for me, please?'

'Just give me a sec.'

She could hear Samantha clicking on the computer then bustling about with the filing cabinet. The birth certificate had to say the mother's name. Sarah Branson? Florencia Concepción Fernández de León? Someone else altogether? Allison was sure that she—or the police—would be one step closer to locating Luke with that information.

Samantha's voice came down the line again.

'That's right, I remember now. We don't have any identification documents for Gracie on file. No birth certificate, no Medicare. No vaccinations. Luke was applying for new ones. They were all lost in the fire.'

38

MAZ

AS INSTRUCTED, MAZ WENT INTO MANLY POLICE STATION STRAIGHT from Allison's house. An old drunk guy was lying at the end of a row of seats. The smell of urine surrounded him like a cloud.

Maz cleared her throat and spoke to the young policeman behind the counter.

'I want to report my boyfriend missing.'

When she gave her name, would there be some reference to the letter from Border Force? Was there some kind of alert?

The officer helped her fill out a missing persons form. Maz stumbled over every answer.

Last seen: Sydney airport with his daughter.

Likely destination: Chicago—but they never arrived.

The last time she'd been in his bedroom, she'd spotted the itinerary printed out. She remembered now: the names on it were Luke Branson and Grace Branson. If they'd used passports, they'd have to be in those names. Curtis must be right.

The officer asked about friends or family that Luke might contact, and Maz became tongue-tied. She started to say 'friends and family in Hythorne', changed it to Perth, stumbled over Melbourne. She finally came out with a sentence.

'He's not in touch with his family.'

'Are you the child's mother?' the policeman asked. 'Is this a custody issue?'

'No. Her mother passed away.'

'Is he on any medications?'

'He's not but the little girl has cancer. She died last week.'

The officer hadn't heard of Gracie's fundraising campaign. Maz wasn't doing a good job of explaining; Allison should've come instead, but she'd said she was too exhausted from the overseas flight and wanted to stay home with her son.

'My friend is bringing some ID in tomorrow for them.'

'Okay, we'll start looking into it tonight and your friend can add her information to the file tomorrow.'

Maz didn't know how to answer his last question.

'Do you have concerns for Luke's welfare?'

I think he's suicidal with grief. My friends think he made it all up.

—

When she got home, Maz logged on to Facebook and scrolled through Luke's page. People were still responding to Allison's question about trying to find him. She typed slowly into Messenger: *Where are you, Luke? I'm so scared for you. Please, please, please get in touch. Love you, babe xxxxxxx*

His Insta account was still up there. Most of the posts were about training and fitness. A few featured him and Maz together, lifting weights, running on the beach, doing star jumps in the park. He even had a video discussing how to 'live your best life'. Clicking on it, Maz listened to his deep voice, watched him grinning, imagined herself in his arms. This was their future together—the fitness program. How could he give up on her?

Scrolling through his photos, Maz came across one that she'd never noticed before. Luke on a beach in his swimmers completing a triathlon. Bright sunshine, a long strip of sand and skyscrapers in the background. That wasn't Sydney. Where had he been? Not Melbourne.

She sent a quick text to Curtis. *Check out this photo on Luke's Insta page. I think it's the Gold Coast.*

⚊

'Okay, now we're running on the spot for three minutes.' Maz surveyed the class. 'Let's get those knees up high!'

The eight o'clock class was better than the six a.m. It'd taken Maz twenty minutes to fire up her positivity. Beforehand, clients had rushed over to commiserate about Gracie and ask after Luke. She didn't know how to respond. Simply said: 'I'll let him know you're thinking of him.'

This second class wasn't so bad—she could lose herself in the music and counting out the rotations. Nico had said to take as much time off as she needed, but with Dad in hospital and Mum only popping into work part-time, Maz had to bring in an income. Who knew what the future would hold for Dad's earning capacity? They could always do a fundraising campaign, like Gracie. Dad wouldn't get the same support though; he was old and chubby, not young and cute.

After the class, Maz helped Em-Jay sort out the yoga mats. She swore her friend to secrecy then told her Luke was missing.

Em-Jay grabbed her mobile. 'I'll google-stalk the shit out of him,' she announced. 'I'm great at tracking my exes.'

Em-Jay started on his Facebook page, clicking away with her eyes glued to her new iPhone. She had a fab phone cover: an athlete in blue fitness gear doing a headstand against a blue sky. When Maz commented on it, Em-Jay seemed pleased.

'It's a photo of me,' she said. 'Curtis did a shoot by the beach. You can see the surfers in the background. Cool, hey?'

Curtis hadn't told her that he was doing photos for other instructors. He'd given her the impression that Maz and Luke were his only clients from the gym.

She checked her own phone. Curtis had finally answered her text from last night.

Yes, it's the Gold Coast. That triathlon was before he came to Wirriga. I'm on my way to the children's hospital.

Sydney had two children's hospitals—one in the eastern suburbs and one out west. Both were a long drive from Wirriga. Gracie had been going to the one in the east. Sometimes, Luke complained about the traffic. But he'd taken Gracie out there every Friday to the dedicated Dr Rawson. Maz had considered going along with them to show her support—and also because Luke had talked about a lovely young nurse called April a few times. He said April had a smile 'like a ray of sunshine': the same words he'd used with Maz the first day they'd met. But visiting the hospital meant missing five classes for which she wouldn't be paid. Hating herself for her jealousy, Maz had asked Gracie what April looked like.

Gracie had screwed her face up in the effort of remembering. Eventually she shrugged and said, 'Like a nurse.'

Did April exist? But even if Luke had scammed them all for money, their lovemaking was definitely real—he couldn't fake that intensity. Luke loved her; Maz was sure of that. He wouldn't betray her.

'Shit, I'm normally good at this,' Em-Jay said, her eyes still fixed on the phone. 'I can't find any other links about him.'

'What about a reverse image search? That's what the teacher's son did last night.'

Em-Jay tapped her fingernail against the phone. 'Nothing,' she said. 'Perhaps he got everything wiped after his wife died? Maybe there were photos of her and it was all too painful?'

If he had a wife.

The thought popped into Maz's head unexpectedly. Flipping hell, she didn't know whether to be worried for Luke or pissed off.

If it was a scam, Luke must have a really good reason.

He loved her. They were great together. A perfect match.

And if it was a scam, then what about Gracie? He was a devoted dad, everyone could see that. Dedicated to saving Gracie's life. There was no faking the love he had for his daughter.

He's gone crazy with grief, that's it.

But his dead wife didn't seem to exist.

—

The entire time Maz was running the ten o'clock Mums and Bubs class, her mind was on Curtis out at the children's hospital.

'Maz, should we be lifting the babies in this exercise?' one of the mums was asking.

'Yes, of course. Backs up straight, hold in the core. Let's go.'

They were sitting in a circle, their precious bundles on their laps. Each time the mums lifted their babies, they would smile and make goo-goo noises.

Nico had started this class because the gym wasn't big enough to have a creche but he was keen to get the new mummies in somehow. Apparently they spent up big in the cafe afterwards.

Luke, of course, had been a favourite instructor for this class. Now, because they were sitting in a circle, they had plenty of chances to ask about him. What was she supposed to say? Freaking hell, they'd all find out soon enough.

'He's still in Chicago, sorting things out,' Maz said.

After one more class, Body Pump, Maz went straight to her locker and her phone. A text from Mum: *Dr Simmons coming in at 1 p.m. xx*. Dad's health was in his hands—those same hands that had been lifting weights in the gym. Not that she'd seen him since they'd met at the hospital; he must be busy at work or on a different schedule. Would he tell the police about the pills?

Four missed calls and a text from Curtis.

Why aren't you picking up? Are you teaching? Dr Rawson doesn't exist.

39

ALLISON

THE SCHOOL HAD NO BIRTH CERTIFICATE, NO IDENTIFICATION FOR Gracie. This morning, Curtis had found no evidence of Sarah Branson's death.

And now the children's hospital did not have a cancer specialist called Dr Rawson.

'I can't believe it,' Curtis shouted down the phone. 'There's no-one on the medical staff by that name. I showed Dr Rawson's webpage to the hospital administrator. She looked up his registration on the medical board. He doesn't exist.'

'A fake website.' Allison sighed. 'Just like Sarah Branson's memorial page.'

Until this moment, she'd held onto a tiny skerrick of hope that, amid all the lies, there was one truth. That they'd been fundraising for a reason. The relief she felt that Gracie didn't have life-threatening cancer was tempered by her fear—where was the girl right now? Dead or alive?

'You know how I interviewed Dr Rawson by phone,' Curtis fumed. 'It must've been Luke disguising his voice. I'm going to lose my job for this.'

'No, you won't. Luke tricked us all.'

She recognised the waves of shame engulfing him. Both of them had been duped, personally and professionally.

'My reputation will be ruined. How can I have a future in journalism? Word will get around that I'm a chump.'

As Curtis ranted, Allison pictured herself back in Chicago, trying to get answers. Except here in Sydney, she'd watched Luke and Gracie go off to the hospital each week. She'd seen the bandaids on Gracie's arms from the needles. She'd listened to their stories about Dr Rawson and his red frogs. She'd heard how hard Dr Rawson had tried to get Gracie onto the clinical trial. She'd felt guilty for passing on her cold to Gracie, compromising her immunity. Guilty for not putting on sunscreen every minute for her chemo sensitivity. Guilty for causing an allergic reaction with the sesame oil. Had Luke faked the allergy and the trip to Emergency? To make her beholden to him?

'I'm going to call the children's hospital in Melbourne,' Curtis said. 'See if they have any record of Gracie.'

'They won't.'

The girl wasn't sick.

Unless Luke had harmed her.

━

Allison stormed into Gracie's room and began pulling it apart. Luke's bedroom had been clean. Did Gracie leave any clues in hers?

Upending the drawers, she watched the shorts and t-shirts tumbling onto the carpet. Nothing else in there. Only clothes. She felt through the pockets. Empty.

She attacked the bookcase. Books they'd curled up with each night. The *Treehouse* series, *How to Train Your Dragon*, *Charlie and the Chocolate Factory*, *The BFG*, *Winnie-the-Pooh* and *Mary Poppins*. Dozens more. Flicking through each page, looking inside the covers.

Nothing.

Gracie's drawings were on the wall above the bookcase. In one, she'd tried to draw their old farm—fence posts and hills and badly shaped horses. They must've lived on a farm. They must've had horses. Even Luke couldn't have made a child lie for so long.

But if there were clues in those drawings, Allison couldn't work them out. When she'd asked about Sarah's family, Luke said they didn't deserve to hear from Gracie. The family refused to believe that Luke hadn't received a big insurance payout from the fire and they demanded he repay a loan they'd given Sarah years before.

The farm, the horses, the fire, the horrible in-laws—all carefully constructed to present Luke and Gracie as alone in the world.

Had Luke seen Allison's state of bewilderment at the beginning of the year and targeted her? She was the one who'd invited him to stay; he'd never asked for anything. If he'd pushed, she would've suspected something.

He'd simply presented problems to her, and she'd tried to help.

All of Wirriga had tried to help.

With Gracie's room in disarray, Allison suddenly remembered Luke's Jeep. He always parked around the corner in a quiet cul-de-sac. She rushed outside and down the street.

Coming into the cul-de-sac, Allison could see a builder's truck that took over half the road. It hid any cars parked behind.

She ran the last few metres to peer past it. No dark green Jeep. In its place, a green sedan with an Uber sign stuck to the back window.

Somehow, after she'd dropped him at the airport, Luke had come back to Wirriga undetected to collect his car. The risk of his actions astounded her. Although risk was involved in all of his actions. He must've been thrilled every day that he got away with it.

But actually, she realised, he could have moved the Jeep before he went. Hardly anyone came up here. If Allison had asked where it was, no doubt he would have whipped out a plausible answer. *It's at the mechanic's* or *I lent it to one of the gym instructors.*

And, like everything else, Allison would have believed it.

—

At Manly police station, the sergeant opened the missing persons report that Maz had lodged last night. It listed her concern for Luke's mental health after the loss of his daughter.

'Do you believe this man is at risk of self-harm?'

Allison should've come down herself but she'd been so tired and now Maz had made a complete mess of it.

'No, I think he's defrauded us all. And God knows what he's done with Gracie.'

'Gracie with the purple bandana?' The sergeant leant towards her. 'We did a fun run from the Spit Bridge to Manly and had three morning teas for her. Raised five thousand dollars. I heard she died.'

'She never went to Chicago,' Allison explained. 'She never went on a clinical trial.'

'What? Everyone had a stake in that fundraising money.'

While Allison waited for the sergeant to do some checks on the database, Nadia rang.

'I've found something,' she said. 'The same bank account was used for twelve other websites.'

'More fundraising for Gracie?'

Luke had never mentioned any other sites.

'No, not for Gracie. These were other sick people from all around the world. I'll email you the list.'

When the sergeant returned, his announcement came as no surprise.

'We can't find a person matching your description of Luke Branson. He must have set up a fake identity.'

'But he managed to open a bank account.'

'Yes, but the address on it is yours. Either he's stolen identification documents or bought them illegally. We'll request information from the account and try to find a money trail. I'm guessing the money has been moved already. Can you stay a bit longer and speak to a detective?'

Allison showed him the list from Nadia on her phone: the names of twelve strangers connected to Luke through one bank account number. The sergeant opened up each one on the computer.

Jessica Moore from South Africa with breast cancer. Tiny Lily Ng in Hong Kong with head injuries after a car accident.

'Do you know any of these people?' the sergeant asked.

Phillip Saunders in England with leukaemia.

'No. And Luke never mentioned them. He only talked about travelling overseas with his wife.'

Hannah Bennett in Canada with ovarian cancer.

When she saw the photo, Allison gasped.

Hannah Bennett. Young, blonde, gorgeous. A ponytail flipped over her shoulder, a smile to light up a room. Yep, people would definitely donate to save the life of this attractive young woman.

Only the photo was of someone Allison recognised. Someone in the absolute bloom of health.

—

In the months Luke had been living with her, Allison had managed to avoid entering the gym. These places made her break out into a sweat—and not from the exercise. She felt like an alien: old, frumpy, overdressed, a different species. Everyone around here had super six-packs and pumped-up biceps.

The first person she bumped into was her mum.

'I've just done Yoga for Seniors.' Barbara seemed to be walking taller. 'It's improving my flexibility.'

Allison found Maz on a break, sitting in a corner of the cafe, eating a salad with another young instructor. The salad was in an old Tupperware container; she'd obviously brought it from home. Maz dropped her fork and rushed to greet her.

'Have you heard something?'

The girl always reminded her of a Labrador pup, bouncy and excitable, desperate for a pat and a rub. Had Luke been the one giving her attention, giving her orders, and now he'd let her off the leash to fend for herself?

'I haven't heard from Luke but we found out ...' Allison looked around at all the customers in the cafe. 'Can we talk somewhere quieter?'

Maz led her to the little patio—the tables were empty; too cold to eat outside today. Without explanation, Allison took out her phone and opened it up to the fundraising page for Hannah Bennett.

'The poor woman. Ovarian cancer,' Maz tutted. 'Wait, that's me!'

'Did you know about this? Did you set it up with Luke?'

'NO!'

'Was he paying you part of the profits?'

'No . . . but he did give me some money.'

'What for?'

'The herbal pills. I offered them for free but he insisted on paying.'

'How much?'

'I tried not to take it. Honestly. We were all saving for Gracie.'

Allison believed the girl. Her face seemed incapable of telling a lie.

'How much?' Allison repeated.

'A hundred dollars.'

Oh God, this poor girl. Allison had thought she was going to say twenty thousand dollars. Leaning across the cold metal table, she took Maz's hands in her own. They were warm, much warmer than she'd expected.

'He had twelve other fundraising pages. All fake.' Allison gazed at the innocent girl. 'I think he was setting you up to take the fall for him.'

Maz wrenched her hands out of Allison's grasp. Glared at her. Then her face collapsed.

'I thought he loved me,' she whimpered. 'He just used me.'

'He used all of us.'

Maz's body and passion. Allison's kindness and reputation. Curtis' job. The school principal's standing in the community.

And Gracie herself, of course. Gracie was a cash cow, a sympathy grabber, an enabler for his lifestyle. He needed his daughter to open doors to mothers and families. But perhaps all the publicity generated by Allison had been too much.

In reaching out to the community to raise funds, had Allison put Gracie's life in danger?

—

At home, alone in her big house, Allison didn't know what to do with the anger coursing through her body. It made concentrating on one thought or one task impossible. Perth or the Gold Coast—those were the two places that Maz felt Luke might be. Opposite sides of the country. From her bedroom window, Allison could see the pool. Dead brown leaves dotted the base. The creepy crawler wasn't working again. *I'll ask Luke to fix it.* The thought came before she could censor it.

At some point soon, she'd have to go into school and tell the principal. With Gracie Day, Declan had bent the rules. And Allison had run with it—taking the fundraising to another level. Getting the *Northern Beaches News* involved. Would they both be sacked for misconduct when they'd only been trying to help?

She'd given Luke and Gracie everything.

Her house.

Her money.

Her love.

Shona had warned against taking them in, called her 'a fecking bampot' for being too kind-hearted.

'But if we don't look after them,' Allison had said, 'then what sort of people does that make us?'

It had seemed that Luke and Gracie were alone in the world without a safety net of family.

Or was there a mother waiting in another town? Forcing her child to go out and do three months' work, whipping up cash? The cruelty of it made Allison's eyes sting.

The shame of it drove her into the shower, to wash herself clean.

Detective Sergeant Rejman had asked for everything she could remember. Allison started writing in an exercise book, filling fourteen pages with notes. She took the photos of Gracie off the fridge and laid them out on the dining table next to the book. Worked through her memories; a quicksand of stories which couldn't be trusted.

His parents in Perth. Training for the Olympics. Backpacking in Peru. Trekking in Nepal. Living in London for a few years. Meeting Sarah in Melbourne. Moving to Hythorne. Horses and a country lifestyle. His grief after his wife's death. The hurt caused by Sarah's family.

How could they separate the lies from any grain of truth?

She wrote down the definite fabrications: Dr Rawson, the chemotherapy, Dr Mercado, the clinical trial.

Other children were really going through it—cancer and chemo, surgery and radiation. The pain, the heartbreak and the cost of last-option treatments. They needed the community's love and support and money.

Not Luke.

He'd faked it and taken all that from Wirriga.

Their cash, their kindness, their trust.

Detective Sergeant Rejman had printed out a list and asked Allison to look through it.

'These are the characteristics of con artists. Can you tick which ones apply to Luke Branson?'

Confident.

Builds rapport quickly with their mark.

Puts the victim at ease by revealing his own failings.

Plays on the emotions.

Inspires trust.

Dresses the part.

Reads people and responds to their needs.

As she read down the list, Allison had ticked them all.

'A lot of con men—and women—get away with it,' the detective had said, 'Because their victims are so embarrassed about being taken in. They don't report it.'

He'd then asked Allison about her own personal situation.

'Is that relevant?' she snapped.

'Con men often target people going through a life change. When they're at their most vulnerable.'

'Yes, well . . .' She was hesitant about sharing the details of her marriage break-up. 'I've always helped people. It's what I do.'

'Perhaps you didn't get quite so involved before?'

The detective was right. She'd refused to lend money to the Japanese exchange student; she'd given the school family four weeks to find another place to live while their house was being fixed. She'd set boundaries.

But for Gracie, she'd been all in.

Curtis sent through an email with an article attached. One paragraph stood out to Allison: *If the con artist does his job properly, you'll be the one doing most of the persuading yourself. He manipulates you to the point where you are deceiving yourself.*

At the bottom of the article, it said: *Ironically, con men are sometimes the easiest to scam because their confidence makes them believe they are impenetrable.*

Curtis had typed a query before signing off: *Should we go for a vigilante approach—splash his face across the internet? Or should we try to scam the scammer?*

40

MAZ

DAD WAS FINALLY HOME FROM HOSPITAL, WITH A HEART MONITOR strapped to his chest for the next twenty-four hours and instructions to take it easy. His toxicology report showed nothing unusual but the doctor had sent the pills off for analysis and expected a result next week.

Over the past two days, Maz had cleaned the house, been shopping, prepared some dinners and changed the sheets on her parents' bed.

'Thanks, love, that bed looks much comfier than the hospital one.' Dad gave her a hug.

Mum had told Kelli about the possible link between the diet pills and Dad's episode; now, Kelli wasn't speaking to Maz. Mum was barely speaking to anyone. Her cheeks were almost as grey as Dad's had been; they'd be admitting her to hospital next. Maz couldn't bear to see her mother like this. And it was all her fault.

No wonder Luke had gone crazy after his wife had died so tragically last year. If Dad died, their family would never be the same again. Out of kilter. All wrong.

Flipping hell, Luke's wife hadn't died in the Hythorne fire. Every time she thought about Luke, she had to untangle the lies.

Maz had washed her own sheets, drowned the last remaining hint of Luke's aftershave in hot water and detergent. Had he loved her at all? Her first grown-up relationship, one that she'd expected to go on for years and years. They'd had chemistry, sexually and mentally.

Or so she'd thought.

While Maz had shut down her Bio-Antidotes website, she hadn't done anything with the rest of the stock. Supplements she'd ordered for existing clients were still hidden in the top of her wardrobe. Reaching up, she found the containers. Took the whole box and dumped it in the bin outside. Farewell to that crap.

Allison had called and instructed her not to tell anyone yet about Luke's deception.

'Curtis and I are working on a plan with the police,' the teacher said. 'Come over tonight.'

Now she had to lie while everyone was asking about Luke. *When will he be back? When's the picnic? When's the funeral?*

Everyone cared.

At Allison's house, Maz took the proffered glass of wine. All of this shit was turning her into a drinker. Curtis had arrived before her. They were talking about how a detective had been assigned to the case.

'The police are assessing when they'll do a public appeal,' Allison said. 'So we've only got a short window for this to work.'

After Allison had explained the idea, Maz didn't know what to think.

'I'm not sure,' she said. 'Luke's really smart.'

'It'll appeal to his ego. That huge ego of his.' Curtis held out his arms in the shape of a giant beach ball. 'That's exactly why he'll fall for it.'

They'd roped in another journalist, an older guy who had inspired Curtis in his choice of career. While he knew Curtis' dad, there were no connections between him and Curtis online.

'That's important,' Allison said. 'You know he'll check it inside and out. The story has to be watertight.'

'So what do you want me to do?' Maz asked.

'Can you put some more posts on Facebook? Pretend you still believe him. Something loving. Make it sound like I haven't told anyone about Chicago.'

Maz did it straight away. At the bottom of the last post, she composed a comment. *Babe, I'm so worried about you. Please call. I know you're hurting something bad. Love you always xx*

Copying and pasting, she put the same post on Messenger.

'Great.' Curtis gave her a thumbs-up. 'Now we can get Fletcher to do his stuff.'

After Curtis had made his phone call, Allison produced the book in which she was writing down Luke's stories. Maz flipped through the pages.

'He must've said something that was true,' Curtis said. 'It can't all be made up.'

Maz had believed that his love for her was true. And his love for Gracie.

'Maybe we should try and work out *why* he did it.' Maz refilled her glass of wine. 'Has he gone bankrupt? Does he need money?'

'I don't think he's that type of fraudster,' Curtis said. 'This wasn't just about money. He wanted the attention. And he wanted to trick people, right in their own houses. He's morally bankrupt.'

While Curtis was reading through Allison's book, Maz went to the kitchen on the pretext of making tea. She put the kettle on, got out the mugs and opened the Messenger app.

Babe, it's absolute hell here. I think I'm going to jail—the appetite suppressants put Dad in hospital. I know you lied about some stuff but I still love you. Now I'm on the wrong side of the law, I can't stay here. Please can I come with you? We're so good together. You're an inspiration to me, stepping outside the box, creating your own destiny. You're so clever, you can teach me things. Love you xx

Maz glanced through the door to the lounge room, double-checking that the others were still engrossed in the exercise book. She pressed send, then made three cups of tea.

'How long do we have for Luke to take the bait?' Allison asked Curtis. 'I have to tell the school principal soon.'

'The detective is giving us forty-eight hours. Fletcher is saying he's on a publishing deadline so he needs a fast answer.'

'A deadline.' Allison snorted. 'That's what all the best scammers do. It's what Luke did to us—a deadline to get the money for Chicago.'

The front door banged and Felix appeared from the hallway, a backpack slung over his shoulder, airpods in. He sank into the chair opposite his mother and dropped his bag on the floor.

'How was your day?' His mother reached out to pat his leg.

'You'll never believe it.' Felix's words came out in a rush. 'Helena has left Dad.'

41

LUKE

ALLY HAD MADE IT SO EASY AND COMFORTABLE FOR LUKE TO STAY IN Wirriga. She'd opened her house to him. Encouraged people to donate. Made his bank account grow bigger day by day. And then he'd seen another opportunity—the marriage break-up. If she sold the house, Allison would suddenly have a spare five hundred thousand in the bank. Lots of cash for someone like him to help 'invest'.

He simply took Allison's stalking one step further. The campaign was supposed to put a rocket up Tony and make him move fast. The letters in her handwriting, driving her car by Tony's place, phone calls and hang-ups from her home phone.

Tony had been too fucking nice about it all. 'I know you're having a hard time, Allison. You should see a psychologist.'

Seriously? Man, grow a pair. If your ex is stalking you, retaliate as fast as possible.

Luke kept waiting but then Tony had agreed not to sell while Gracie was living in the house. That didn't help anyone. The whole point was to access the cash from the asset.

Tony deserved that last letter to keep him looking over his shoulder. If only Tony had followed through on his original threat to offload the house, then none of the stalking would've been necessary. It would've saved Luke a whole lot of time and effort. Later, when he checked Ally's phone, he'd seen some messages about Tony wanting to sell. The stalking *had* been effective but then Ally had created a catch-22 for them all—wanting to keep the house as a safe place for Gracie to live and needing the money for the treatment. When she'd finally made the offer to sell and loan him the money, it was too late. Luke's escape plans were in place.

The journalist, though, was far easier to manipulate. Luke had seen the lust in his eyes—and used it. Curtis' articles had helped bring in the cash; his blog posts made Luke's research more readable and legit. All along, Luke had been wondering if Curtis would take his research deeper and come up against an inconsistency. But Dr Rawson's online presence had stood up to scrutiny. Would the journalist respond furiously, like a lover scorned? Or remain quiet, like Ally, worried for his career? The hoodwinked reporter—the most damaging story in town.

If the school principal found out, he'd be straight down to the coppers. That was part of the reason they had to leave: Declan was relentless with the medical questions. All those heart-to-heart chats in his office; Luke had to break down in tears to avoid answering. The research was getting harder and harder, and Luke was losing track of his explanations. He'd considered giving Gracie a miraculous cure so he could enjoy the lifestyle a little longer, but the principal would have cottoned on.

If Ally hadn't followed him to America, it all would've held. He'd laid enough groundwork. She was the reason he'd decided on Chicago—Luke could 'die' there along with Gracie and no-one would follow up. But Ally was too bloody kind for her own good; overcame her fear of a long-haul flight to be with him. He reckoned she'd be crying alone in her big house now; another humiliation from another man. Too ashamed to talk to the police.

He'd conned them all: the solicitor, the journalist, the teacher, the principal. The entire school community—doctors, accountants, designers, architects, stockbrokers. All those people who thought they were smarter than him, a mere gym instructor. The way they treated him, as if he didn't have a brain. They deserved to be parted with their money.

Waiting to see if it would come out, he'd set up a google news alert for 'Luke Branson'. At night, he imagined the headlines. CON MAN SCAMS COMMUNITY. Luke Branson—a cool name to immortalise. Strong and powerful.

If the police got involved, would they try and track his movements from the airport? At that bland airport hotel, he'd checked in with a different name and dressed Gracie as a boy in black jeans and a red baseball cap. It was in the hotel that he'd noticed how fast her hair was growing since he'd stopped shaving it.

He'd enjoyed the comfortable house in Wirriga and the gym and the childcare and the sex. But it was time to wrap up the loose ends. He'd closed down the website but the Facebook page was still online, bringing in a few donations. He clicked on the page—a sweet comment from Maz. That girl really adored him.

And a message from a stranger. He'd had plenty of those, wishing them well, giving advice for Gracie's treatments, offering support. Two women had suggested he come over for some 'time out' and to 'relax his body'; unfortunately, they both lived in distant towns. Thanks to Curtis' news stories and Ally's connections, his fundraising had reached far and wide. This new message was nothing like that, though.

Dear Luke,

My name is Fletcher Moncur and I'm a financial journalist. I've worked with all the major Australian newspapers and a few in the UK. You may have seen my segment on Channel 7. I've also written a number of books. I've been following the story of your little girl, Gracie. It's difficult to write this message delicately so please let me apologise in advance if I cause you upset. There are some things about your story that felt a little odd. Nothing factual, more to do with 'a feeling', the journalist's nose, so to speak. If I'm off track here, please accept my deepest sympathies.

However, if my old nose is serving me correctly, then I would be interested in interviewing you for my next book. It's a compilation of the top ten financial cons in Australia. I'm focusing on 'the ones that got away'—the unknown, undiscovered scams. Obviously, I will ensure anonymity, as I have done with the other individuals. I can offer you $10,000 for your story.

In all honesty, I have finished the manuscript and it has been sent to the publisher. But I feel your story deserves to be in there. If you're keen to talk, and, depending upon what you say, then I can delete the current number 10 story and replace it with yours. Due to the publishing schedule, I'll need

*an answer within 12 hours. I've already had some enquiries
about film rights for the book. The public are certainly interested in Australia's own tales of* Catch Me If You Can.

*Hoping to hear from you by tomorrow. Again, many apol-
ogies and condolences if I have misinterpreted the situation.*

Kind regards, Fletcher Moncur

What the fuck? How had this journalist seen through
his online stories? They were perfectly researched. But wait,
Fletcher didn't say he'd found any mistakes, just that he had 'a
feeling' about it. A feeling—was that how journalists worked?

Fletcher Moncur. His profile picture online looked exactly
like he sounded—mid-fifties, grey hair, glasses, a sports jacket.
Penetrating eyes and a slight smile. Possibly clever. Luke opened
a YouTube clip from the TV show.

The guy was a natural for television; he made the financial
news entertaining. Luke searched again—Fletcher had written
five books on a range of business topics, one on the psychology
of business. On his website, there was a page about this new
book—COMING SOON: *Australia's Top Ten Secret Cons:
The masters who've never been caught.*

Top ten masters—Luke liked that.

Perhaps he should be number one, not number ten. How
much would he have to reveal for that to happen?

A movie. A buff actor would have to play Luke. Someone
with the body and the charm to attract the ladies.

Had Fletcher Moncur really interviewed ten other con artists,
or was it a ruse for Luke to incriminate himself? He would do
some more digging later. In the meantime, a fast answer. He'd
leave the Facebook page open for another twelve hours.

Hey, Fletch—you really know how to kick a man when he's down. I'm donating the remainder of Gracie's fund to the children's hospital. If you have a spare $10K to speak to criminals, then put it towards saving sick children. The bank account details are on my FB page. It might go some way to paying for your disgusting innuendo.

42

FELIX

MUM WAS FUMING ABOUT HELENA BREAKING UP THEIR MARRIAGE, USING and abusing Dad, and then disappearing. But to Felix, Helena wasn't 'abusing' anyone—she was terrified and trying to protect her baby. Dad had been so gentle with her. And Mum was so kind to Gracie and Luke. Felix had seen the best of them both. How crazy, though, that they were looking after strangers and not each other.

Luke didn't deserve any kindness—the psycho. Who did that stuff? Made up a whole life. Used his kid to get cash. Felix was desperate to talk to Pearl and Darcy, and get the tech heads at school on the case, but Mum had said to keep it quiet for now.

Felix decided to do some tracking himself.

Sitting at his old desk, with its view of the bush towards Manly Dam, he shoved his English books to one side. Another shitty exercise on *Othello*: *Write a contemporary adaptation using Shakespeare's characters, on the theme of betrayal.* He'd do it later, ask Mum for help.

Opening Facebook on his laptop, he brought up the list of Luke's six hundred and eighty-three friends. Boxes and boxes of faces. After ruling out the ones with Wirriga connections, Felix was down to half. Clicking on one woman at random, he checked the profile. A nurse from the children's hospital in Melbourne with one hundred and fifty-two friends. Another click, a buff personal trainer from Ballarat with one hundred and fifty-seven friends. Another click, a female nutritionist with one hundred and fifty-four friends. They all had around a hundred and fifty friends. But each one seemed real. The personal trainer with exercise techniques for his clients, the nutritionist posting about supplements, the nurse complaining about a night shift. Choosing the personal trainer, Felix did a reverse image search. The photo matched an actor represented by a Los Angeles agency. When he did the same for the 'nurse', there was a link to a dating site in Russia. The 'nutritionist' was a long-distance runner from South Africa. Had Luke created Facebook profiles for these people and linked them all to his? Fake profiles, fake friends, fake posts. Woah, what a lot of work. Luke could've written *Othello* with all those characters.

Could Felix find someone on this page who knew Luke's real identity? Or were they all fake?

On Friday afternoon, Felix answered a knock on the front door, expecting it to be Darcy dropping in after tennis. When he saw the older guy with a bunch of flowers, he wondered how fast he could slam it closed.

'You must be Felix. Is your Mum in?'

'No-one's here.' Felix edged his body back behind the door.

'I'm sorry to miss her. I need to contact her urgently but she won't return my calls.'

'She's been overseas.'

If Felix shouted for help, would the neighbours come running? Dad had assured him that Helena left of her own accord, but it was all too weird. She'd lived in fear of her ex-husband for five months, she'd barely left the house—how could she suddenly pack up and leave? Didn't the crazy ex know that Helena had gone?

'What time will your mother be back? Can I wait for her?'

'She's at the police station.'

Would that scare him off?

'Can I ask you to pass on a message then?'

'What did you say your name was?'

'Emmanuel. The flowers were just . . .' He waved the bouquet slightly. 'I really need to talk to her. It's about her friend Luke.'

43

ALLISON

AT THE POLICE STATION, DETECTIVE SERGEANT REJMAN HAD LITTLE TO report. They were investigating the twelve other fundraising sites, which had brought in over ten thousand dollars each. Apart from Maz's image, the photos had been stolen from various places on the internet and given new names. These 'sick patients' weren't who Luke had said they were.

Much like Luke himself. Like Gracie.

'We've got no identification on either of them,' the detective said. 'We've checked all the custody cases. No mother has reported a missing father and daughter with their description. And Gracie's birthday date hasn't matched up with any leads.'

Allison had worked hard to make that celebration extra special. 'It probably wasn't even her birthday.'

'Probably not,' he agreed.

'Do you think Luke shaved their heads so they couldn't be recognised?'

'Perhaps. It was brazen to be photographed for the fundraising site and the newspaper.'

Allison suddenly remembered the photographs on Gracie Day. Luke saying: *You don't want me ruining the photo.*

'The journalist has contacted him through Facebook Messenger,' Allison said. 'Did Curtis forward you the message?'

The detective nodded. 'Yes, Luke's shown himself after his apparent suicide. But he's sticking to the line that Gracie died in Chicago.'

The detective had organised photofit images of Luke and Gracie with hair. In one of them, Luke had thick brown locks, a fringe sweeping across his forehead. He could've been a swarthy millionaire relaxing on his yacht. They'd given Gracie a bob, just like her friend Evelyn.

'This is a very sophisticated scam. The level of detail he's created online, the medical information, the fake sites for his wife and the doctor . . .' Detective Sergeant Rejman took off his glasses and tapped them against his palm. 'Along with the overseas fundraising sites. It can't be the first time he's done this. We're cross-referencing the photofits to see if we can link it to past fraud.'

'Do you have any leads yet?'

'No, but I'm guessing he has some kind of medical background.'

When Luke had discussed drugs and treatment, Allison assumed his knowledge had come from living through Gracie's illness as a caring father.

'Can I get an electronic copy of the photos? I'd like to send them to Hythorne.'

While the detective hadn't found any connection to Hythorne yet, Allison was sure there must be something. Luke had stolen the name of their town and the story of Rose Luxford trying desperately to save her horses from the fire. Someone might recognise new photos.

'Sure. I'll forward them to you,' the detective said. 'We'll give Luke the chance to respond to the journalist over the weekend, and then we're going public on Monday. We need to determine if Gracie is alive and in danger.'

⟿

As soon as Allison received the message from Felix, she phoned Emmanuel. She accepted his condolences about Gracie, not yet ready to reveal Luke's deception.

'Felix said you wanted to tell me something about Luke?'

'I'm sorry to bring it up, especially now, with Gracie. But I just wondered if you—or he—had kept a key to the beach house.'

'What's happened?' Had Luke dragged Emmanuel into this?

'The other day my neighbour emailed me quotes for the new fence,' Emmanuel explained. 'And she sent her best wishes to my niece—the one having chemo who'd been staying there. I wouldn't have minded if Luke had asked. I'm just worried about security.'

'When exactly was this?'

'They stayed there about three weeks ago.'

'We need to check it out right now. Can you pick me up? I have to ring the police. I'll explain on the way.'

Three weeks ago. Around the time Gracie had supposedly started the clinical trial in Chicago. Three weeks ago, Gracie had definitely been alive.

⟿

When Emmanuel heard the story, he understood why Allison had been too busy to return his calls.

'I've been trying to call Luke too,' he said. 'And now I know why the number's disconnected. He must have copied the key. Do you think he's ransacked the place?'

Emmanuel had furnished his beach house with expensive items—a fancy coffee machine, flat screen TV, artworks. If Luke was setting up a new home, he'd certainly want it all.

As they drove north on the Pacific Highway and across the bridge over the Hawkesbury River, Allison prayed that Gracie was still alive. She feared for the girl's future. And her own. Soon, she'd have to go back to work. Reassure her class and anxious Evelyn. Parents would want explanations that she couldn't give. People would want their money back.

And bad luck to the next person looking for donations, the one who really needed money for life-saving medicine—Wirriga had been burnt. They'd all be wary next time.

'In America, there are so many online scams,' Allison said to break the silence inside the car. 'People pretend they have cancer but they want the money for a motorbike or a holiday. One woman got a boob job.'

'They have no conscience.'

'Yep! And some of the scammers are teenagers.' Allison shook her head in disbelief. 'One girl had the name of a fake baby tattooed to her wrist.'

'So strange.'

But Luke hadn't seemed strange.

—

By the time they arrived at the beachside town, the local police were waiting for them, their uniforms incongruous against the backdrop of golden sand and crashing waves. Emmanuel unlocked the house and the officers went in first. Allison tagged along, scanning each room as she entered. The artworks adorned the walls, the TV was in place and the stainless-steel coffee machine gleamed on the kitchen bench.

'Can you see anything missing?' the female officer asked.

'Nothing that's immediately apparent,' Emmanuel said. 'I'll have a look through the cupboards.'

In the bedroom with the bunks, Allison stripped back the doonas, lifted up the pillows, searched between the wall and the mattress. No trace of Gracie. She made the beds again, fluffing out the covers—a surfboard pattern on the bottom bunk for Emmanuel's twelve-year-old daughter and a Tardis on the top for his fourteen-year-old son. He'd talked about them fondly on their second date—his tomboy girl and his nerdy boy who were always trying to teach each other a thing or two. They lived with Emmanuel for half of the week. Four years after their divorce, Emmanuel and his ex-wife seemed to have an amicable relationship.

Allison lay down on the bottom bunk and closed her eyes. Would she and Tony ever have an amicable relationship? In three years, their son would be an adult—he'd have finished school and would be making his own decisions about his life. When Allison opened her eyes, she spotted a piece of fur poking out from the top of the wardrobe. Clambering off the bed, she reached for it. Winnie the Wombat. Their class mascot. She hugged the soft toy, its fur tickled her nose.

Winnie the Wombat, last seen on a Ferris wheel in Chicago. Luke had been meticulous. Doctoring photos, medical reports, emails. Maybe Maz was right; they couldn't scam the scammer. He was too clever.

Through the open front door, Allison could hear the neighbour speaking to the police officers.

'He parked the Jeep in the driveway and told us he was Emmanuel's ex-wife's cousin. When the man was taking the bags out of the car, I asked the girl if this was a special holiday. She said they were driving up to Movie World.'

Movie World. She texted Maz straight away: *I think you were right about the Gold Coast.*

But how would the police find them?

—

Back in Sydney, Emmanuel stayed for a cup of coffee in her kitchen. The flowers he'd given her were too big for one vase— she'd divided them into bouquets for the kitchen and the dining room table.

'I'm sorry my coffee plunger isn't quite up to the standard of your super-duper coffee machine.'

For the first time that day, they both laughed.

'I'm pleased the machine is still there—it's top of the range. Luke could've sold it for a thousand at least.'

Allison dreaded to think how much Emmanuel had bought it for. He had the same expensive machine in his apartment in Neutral Bay.

'I told the police that Luke was targeting me for more money,' Emmanuel said. 'I'd donated a thousand dollars to Gracie's fund but he kept asking me about investments.'

A thousand dollars for a child he didn't even know. Luke had worked his magic on Emmanuel as well.

'What investments?'

'Luke said he wanted to help me after all I'd done. You know, the donation and the holiday house. He was giving me tips about stocks, offering to invest large sums for me.'

'Oh God, you didn't give him any money to invest, did you?'

'No, it seemed bizarre that a gym instructor was giving me financial advice. He knows I'm a financial adviser. I think he was trying to impress me. I looked up the stocks though. They're all legitimate and doing well.'

Allison gave him the detective's phone number. If they could bring enough strands together, maybe they could catch this bastard.

After the coffee, Allison walked him out. Emmanuel kissed her cheek and said goodbye, but hesitated before getting into his car.

'Let's go out to dinner soon. I mean, when things are back to normal.'

Allison didn't know what normal was anymore.

'I'll have to do a police check on you,' she said. 'Or at least meet your boss, your ex-wife and ten friends who'll vouch for you.'

Tipping back his head, exposing a tanned neck, Emmanuel laughed long and hard. He gave her a jaunty wave and tooted as he drove off.

She wasn't really joking.

~

Late on Friday night, Tony came over to cry about Helena. The irony wasn't lost on Allison. She'd listen but she wasn't going to comfort him.

335

'Helena said I'd helped make her strong enough to be alone. She's gone to her sister in New Zealand.' Tony slumped forward, his head in his hands. 'She couldn't stay around here.'

'Because of the ex-husband?'

'Yes, her ex had a solid alibi for every stalking incident. Helena thinks he got his brother to harass her. Keep her scared.'

'Perhaps she was too traumatised to be in a relationship. You moved too fast.'

'You're right. It was a whirlwind,' he said. 'From when we met to when we moved in together.'

Bloody hell, he'd just agreed with her. Tony *was* in a bad way.

'But she was so scared he'd hurt the baby,' Tony continued. 'Scared she wouldn't find anywhere safe to live. She kept asking me for help. Told me she felt a connection with me. And I felt it too. She told me I was a good, honourable man who'd do the right thing by her.'

'Honourable, huh!'

'It's coming out all wrong.'

'You mean she flattered you. Made you feel useful while I took you for granted.'

'Turning fifty was hard for me,' Tony mumbled. 'After Bryce's death and Melody's murder . . . life was meaningless.'

His best friend had died two months before Tony's birthday. And then his dad got sick, but he'd recovered now. Tony had avoided talking about the murder—on her way home from work, Melody Knox had been killed by her estranged husband. A man with no record of violence. At the time, Tony had said he'd never met the woman, that she hadn't come through one of his shelters.

'Shit, Tony, why didn't you tell me that you knew her?'

It must have broken him.

'I felt so useless. But responsible, too. Unable to help, unable to change anything. Between all the support systems and the police and the law, we should've been able to protect Melody. And we didn't. Then, when Helena came along with her tiny baby, I couldn't . . . I couldn't let that happen to them.'

Would their marriage have been saved if he'd confided his fears? Allison never foresaw the earth-shattering fissure that would cleave them apart.

'Did you tell anyone at work that Helena was living with you?'

'I . . . ummm.' His guilty flush answered the question. 'Professional standards. Inappropriate conduct and all that . . . But part of the reason was her husband. He's a judge.'

Dear God. A judge. Now she understood the need for secrecy. And why they'd assumed Allison was doing the stalking rather than him. Walking over to the sideboard for more red wine, Allison wondered if they'd both lose their jobs. In the fallout, could they patch up their relationship? The thought was quickly replaced by another: *Do I still want to after he discarded our marriage so quickly?*

'Sorry, I'm going on and on.' Tony looked up from the floor to her face. 'I haven't even asked about Chicago. Will there be a funeral for Gracie? How's Luke doing?'

'Oh, Tony. Settle yourself in. I've got so much to tell you.'

‑

Up late, talking to Tony over yet another glass of wine, trying to unravel Luke's life, Allison realised how much she'd missed their discussions. For some reason, Tony thought he should've suspected Luke, but he'd only met the man once. The first threatening letter, though, had been on blue paper from her study, in her handwriting. Tony had recognised the paper and the handwriting. No wonder he'd assumed it was her; now, he was convinced that Luke had been responsible.

Her family was back together in the house: Tony staying the night in the spare room, Felix in his own bedroom. It gave her a moment of peace.

As Allison switched out the lights downstairs, a late-night text came through from Curtis. Short and to the point. *Fletcher is still trying. No answer yet.*

The police had one lead—Movie World. Allison had a feeling that it would take years to track him down. Luke was too good at covering his tracks. In three months of living together, Gracie hadn't dropped a single clue. Even when she'd talked about her mother. They probably weren't going to Movie World; Luke would have primed Gracie to say that.

After responding to Curtis' text, she opened up Facebook. Perhaps Luke had replied to Maz's message. Allison clicked on his name but nothing came up.

Luke Branson's Facebook page had disappeared.

That was it—their last chance at contacting him. Gone.

44

LUKE

RATHER THAN PUTTING TEN THOUSAND DOLLARS IN HIS FUNDRAISING account as Luke had requested, Fletcher Moncur wrote another message.

Perhaps it would be better to meet in person so I can offer my donation in cash. You may contact me on the following number. As I mentioned, the publishing schedule is tight. I'm hoping to have you as one of Australia's top ten masters.

'I'm already a master, thanks very much, Fletch,' Luke said aloud.

No-one would be able to track the money—he'd moved the donations from the banking system entirely. The bank account set up with a false ID. Amazing what counterfeiters in China offered. A Medicare card, a Victorian driver's licence. Neither particularly expensive. And now he was using a new set. Evan Wood. It would take a bit of getting used to but he practised saying it in front of the mirror. Evan. Maybe he'd shorten it to Van.

Luke remained undecided about Fletcher Moncur. If this wasn't a set-up, then Fletch was a greedy bastard, profiting off people like him. Not a bad idea, though, this book. Maybe Luke should write his own—cut out the middle man. Get the income directly. Or sell his life story to a filmmaker. More money there.

Luke hadn't found anything to link Fletcher to Wirriga. The journalist lived in the eastern suburbs on the other side of Sydney. Could he be working for a private investigator? Or the police?

On Fletcher's website, Luke checked the name of his book publisher. Dialling the number for publicity, Luke recalled what he knew of the financial journalist.

'Good morning, my name's Gordon Johns.' Luke put on a posh English accent. 'I'm a journalist visiting from London. I believe you publish my old colleague, Fletcher Moncur. We used to work on the *Financial Times* together.'

'Fletcher? Oh yes, the business books.' The female voice on the other end sounded very young. And keen to help, like Maz.

'Dear old Fletcher told me he has a new book coming out soon. Sounds fascinating. I'm hoping to do a piece on it. I didn't want to tell Fletch yet, just in case my rather erratic editor doesn't agree.'

'Okay.'

'But I'm trying to schedule the story for our best chance. Can you tell me the title and the publication date, please?'

'His business psychology book was released last year. Is that the one you mean?'

'Ah, no. I thought he had another one coming out soon. He's so prolific, old Fletch. Something to do with financial scams.'

Luke could hear her flicking through some pages.

'I've got the schedule for the next twelve months and we don't have anything listed from Fletcher. I can check with his editor and get back to you?'

'No problem. I'll talk to him myself. I'm catching up with him next week. My mistake. I must've have misunderstood.' A pause for effect. 'Fletcher wouldn't be publishing with another company, would he?'

'No, we've published all his books.'

Ha. Gotcha, Fletcher.

—

Luke had read Maz's message again and again. The words were definitely hers. She was always talking about inspiration and stepping outside the box. *Create your own destiny*, that was one of her favourites. She knew about his lies and she still loved him. He could be himself with her, just like with Gracie.

Maz's supplements. Luke couldn't stop thinking about them. They were the future. All that medical knowledge he'd gained could be put to good use. A huge online business selling cures for everything. The modern-day snake oil, like that blog Curtis had written.

He and Maz could lie low for a bit, enjoy the beach life, then market the shit out of their supplements.

His supplements would offer to cure everything—Maz's dad with his arthritis, Allison with her menopausal symptoms. The testimonials would almost write themselves. He'd reuse some of the scans and photos from the children's hospital. Copy stuff from online—so many blogs and pictures detailing individual journeys through cancer and depression, heart problems, asthma and allergies. The cardiologist, Dr Colin Simmons, would come in handy. He'd been very obliging, giving Luke a letter of introduction to a colleague in Chicago. Luke could use that letterhead to falsify a medical recommendation about the efficiency—no, the *efficacy*, that was the word they used—of the supplements from a respected cardiologist.

He'd need a web designer and an untraceable set-up. Possibly all in Colin's name—*Renowned cardiologist Dr Simmons founded the company when he saw the positive results of these supplements on his patients. Blood pressure, cholesterol and heart disease all saw improvements after a six-month trial. Dr Simmons has worked with other specialists to determine the best supplements for a range of conditions.*

Cool, this could be a thing. He'd change the spelling slightly—Dr Col Simons—so the website didn't come up when real patients googled their doctor. Give it a year using Col Simon's name then swap it to another doctor. And maybe combine supplements *and* diet and exercise. The plan he'd talked about with Maz.

He could see Maz here with him, in the black bikini that showed off her taut figure. She loved the beach.

Wait. A clean break, no trail of relationships—that was his rule. Was it too risky to hook up with her?

But Maz was always so willing to please, in every possible way. She wanted to learn from him, the master. He'd be careful, as usual, but he knew Maz. She wasn't smart enough to double-cross him. Her open face, her sweet innocence, would serve him well. Just like Gracie had.

Hey babe, love to see you. Here's my new number.

45

MAZ

ON SATURDAY MORNING, MAZ LED THE SCHOOLTEACHER INTO HER SMALL lounge room, embarrassed by what Allison would make of her tiny house.

'Have a seat.' Maz pointed at the floral couch that they'd had since forever.

The sound of Dad's snoring drifted from the bedroom. Mum had popped out to Nanna's place. Dad was recovering well and Mum had started talking to Maz again. They were both hoping to get back to choir next Wednesday.

'Luke's taken down the Facebook page,' Allison said. 'What are we going to do now?'

Maz hadn't explained the plan over the phone—she wanted to discuss it in person. Curtis and Allison hadn't been able to do it. The esteemed business journalist had failed. But Maz had succeeded.

'I sent him a message and he answered,' Maz announced. Still standing, with one hand on her hip, she looked down on the older woman. 'I'm going to run away with him.'

'Are you kidding me?' Allison was suddenly back on her feet, eye-to-eye with Maz. 'After everything he's done?'

The teacher was supposed to be impressed, not treat her like an idiot.

'I'm scamming the scammer,' Maz said, slowly enough for her to understand. 'Like you were trying to do.'

As Maz talked her through the messages with Luke, the teacher eventually sat down again and smiled.

'Well done.' Allison clapped her hands together. 'You appealed to his sense of superiority. He wants you to be his protégé.'

Maz had considered going to see Luke by herself and then calling the cops when she knew where he was staying, but Luke wasn't making that easy.

'He wants to meet at a kids' playground in Tweed Heads,' Maz explained. 'Somewhere out in the open.'

'I guess he's being cautious,' Allison said, reaching for her large handbag and pulling out her mobile phone.

'What're you doing?'

'I'm calling the detective.'

'No, no, no,' Maz protested. 'I told him I'm running away. If he sees anyone who looks like an officer, he'll disappear into thin air again.'

'I'm sure they'll wear plain clothes.'

This was supposed to be Maz's plan—she'd set it all up. But Allison was taking over and telling her what to do.

'Luke's smart. He'll spot a copper at a hundred metres.'

Turning the phone over in her hands, Allison seemed to be thinking it through.

'So when do we call them in?'

'When I've won his trust and I'm back in his hotel room.'

'Really? Do you want to risk being alone with him?' The teacher was studying her face. 'Do you think you can carry it off?'

'Of course.'

If she was honest with herself, Maz wasn't entirely sure. Hate and shame bubbled behind her quick smile, festered inside her toned bod. Would Luke see that instantly?

'I'm coming with you,' Allison said. 'I need to know if Gracie's alive.'

'But if Luke recognises you, he'll be off in a shot.'

'Don't worry. We'll work out a plan.'

Maz thought she'd already done that. And it didn't include the schoolteacher tagging along. Although, deep down, Maz was terrified. Perhaps Allison could be useful. She'd said the police thought this wasn't his first scam. They had no idea what else Luke was running from.

⁓

Out of the tiny aeroplane window, Maz could see why the Gold Coast was called Surfers Paradise. Long white beaches stretching for miles, and empty of crowds at this time of year. Next to the sand, high-rise buildings soared, glass and metal reflecting the blue of the sea up into the sky. Unlike her classmates, Maz hadn't been to the Gold Coast for schoolies, another trip she couldn't afford. She'd been here once when she was little. Maz couldn't remember the holiday but there were photos in the family album of her watching the dolphin show, being splashed by one of the tails. A little girl the same age as Gracie, with two happy, loving parents.

In his last message, Luke promised to explain everything.

I guess you're wondering why I did this—things have been tough the past few years. Don't think this is a glamorous life. You have to be prepared to work hard.

He was already starting the lessons.

The plane's undercarriage made a groaning noise as the wheels came down for landing. Next to her, Allison seemed to be praying. The teacher reached for Maz's wrist on the shared armrest and tightened her hands around it—almost like the Chinese burns that she and Kelli used to give each other.

'It's all good,' Maz reassured the older woman.

Maz hadn't known about Allison's fear of flying until they walked into Sydney airport. Then the teacher had become flustered, dropped her ticket on the floor and refused to go near any windows. Apparently, smaller planes were worse. Maz was stunned she'd made it to Chicago and back. For a moment, it stopped her from thinking about Luke.

⌁

They were staying in an apartment hotel just south of the Gold Coast. Allison had booked it, said it was 'mid-range' but Maz was pretty impressed. From their room, she could look down to the blue pool straight below and out to a sparkling ocean. The view didn't help settle the butterflies in her tummy, though. Now that they were here, Maz worried that Allison would wreck her plan. The teacher had a disguise, but was it good enough?

'What do you think Luke is capable of?' Maz asked.

Even though another man had been charged with arson for the Hythorne bushfire, Maz couldn't help but wonder if Luke was somehow involved. There must be a reason why he'd chosen that town. But if his wife hadn't died in the fire, then what the hell had he done with her?

'When Luke first moved in,' Allison said, 'Nadia joked that he didn't look like an axe murderer. Now, I'm not so sure.'

Her answer wasn't very reassuring. How would Luke react if he discovered Maz was double-crossing him?

Allison left the apartment to pick up some essentials for her disguise, and Maz flopped on the bed. She should've agreed to let Allison get the police involved.

'I'll see you at the playground,' Allison had said as a parting comment. 'Don't get in a car with him.'

They didn't know if he had a car. The green Jeep—*The only other thing I have in the world apart from Gracie*—had been found in Newcastle, just north of Avoca. When the police checked the records, it was still registered to the guy who'd sold it to Luke back in January. He'd bought it in south Sydney, just before arriving in Wirriga. The Jeep had never been in the Victorian countryside.

Last night, he'd texted Maz about the new supplements business. *Got some great ideas. We'll be marketing all over Oz. Can't wait to get planning with you. It'll be awesome!*

Reading the message, she'd realised that it wasn't just about the money for him—Luke needed an adoring audience cheering him on. As the single father of a 'sick' child, he'd been hero-worshipped. He needed that attention.

Where was the sick child now?

Taking a deep breath, Maz stood up and stretched her body tall. Before heading out the door, she texted him a breezy message. *Just arrived. So much hotter than Sydney. My kind of weather. This is the place to be! Can't wait to see you, babe xxxx*

She walked the five blocks to the park. Luke wouldn't expect her to arrive in a taxi; he knew she was saving her cash— what little she had left after donating to Gracie and repaying her clients. And the cost of the flight up here. Maz tried to banish the bitterness from her face by thinking about Dad. Dr Simmons said he was going to be okay. The doctor thought Maz might be fined for importing a prohibited substance— more money—but that was way better than jail. Did Luke have any idea what it was like to actually sit by the bedside of a loved one, terrified that they might die? Did he understand the fear of death? Trying to resuscitate an overweight man on the floor of the gym and failing? He'd cruelly created the dread of Gracie dying. Manipulated their emotions. Fuck him.

Together with Allison, she'd studied the map and photos of the park and the playground. The amount of information on the internet was incredible. That must've been how Luke got images from Chicago: copied everything from the web and photoshopped in Gracie. When Maz walked along the edge of the park, she almost felt like she'd been here before—everything just as it was in the photos online. The expanse of grass going down to the river, the playground in the middle, a boat ramp at the end of the car park, trees and a wooden bridge up the end. She could hear the buzz of the four-lane Pacific Highway. Plenty of escape routes for Luke.

No-one knew she was here, apart from Allison.

Mum and Dad thought she was staying overnight with Em-Jay. She'd asked Nico for a few days off work and he'd agreed immediately. The gym owner had been trying to contact Luke to offer his support and set a date for the picnic.

'He's shut his website, Facebook, phone—everything,' Maz told him. 'He's in a really bad way but I'll tell him that you're thinking of him. He'll appreciate it.'

People at the gym were still asking about Luke but they'd been distracted by the rugby league. The Manly Sea Eagles had a big game at Brookvale Oval tonight—the team needed a win.

But regardless of whether Maz succeeded, everyone would learn of Luke's deception tomorrow, Monday, when the police launched a public appeal.

Maz set off along one of the winding footpaths towards the playground, legs shaking with each step. If she were instructing her Power Hard class, what would she tell them? *You can do this, you've got it. Go hard or go home.* And what would Luke say, if he knew? *Believe you deserve it and the universe will serve it.* To Maz, that motto always sounded too demanding, too expectant. She preferred *Create your own destiny.* That was what she was doing.

Her destiny. His destiny. She stopped and scanned the park, straining to catch sight of him.

What if he'd seen through her ruse and hadn't come?

Or what if he was watching her?

With a deliberate toss of her ponytail, Maz started walking again, more slowly this time.

And then she saw him.

Casually perched on the back of a bench, his body balanced on the top, feet on the seat. Legs wide apart. Wearing a white cap with the words *Gold Coast Marathon.* Not hiding or skulking or keeping a low profile. Cool as a cucumber, he stood up on the bench and waved both arms.

Act natural, she told herself. Break into a grin. Run towards him. Flipping hell, she'd never been a good liar.

In her mind, he was tainted, black and monstrous. But Luke looked exactly the same as before, in a pair of Nike shorts and a bright blue t-shirt. The same hot bod, the same charming grin.

'I've missed you, babe,' she breathed, throwing herself into his arms, forcing herself to kiss him, properly.

When they broke away, Luke was grinning, as if he knew she couldn't live without him. Had he always been so smug?

'Me too.' He caressed her cheek, ran his fingers through her ponytail. 'So what's happening in Wirriga?'

'It's crazy. Dad was in hospital with chest pains. I got this letter from Border Force about the supplements. I'm freaking out that they're gonna send me to jail.'

When she sat down next to him on the bench, his hand splayed out over her thigh, his thumb rubbed a groove down her skin. Just as he'd done on the beach in Avoca. How could he pretend to love someone like this? Maz had to separate herself from her body so that she didn't recoil. He'd pretended day in, day out—in Allison's house, at the gym, in Maz's bedroom. Even naked, Luke had been concealing so much.

'Mmmm. Sounds pretty shit,' he said. 'And what about Gracie? Is everyone still upset?'

Maz understood what he really meant—*What about me? What does everyone know about ME?*

'They were devastated. But Allison was pretty mad she couldn't find you in Chicago. She doesn't believe you're dead. And she thinks I'm in on it.'

'Ha, doesn't think I could pull it off by myself?'

'Well, if you did, you're awesome!'

She choked on the word—their special word that had bonded them all those months ago.

"Course I did.' He squeezed the back of her neck; he couldn't seem to stop touching her. 'So what's Ally been doing? Has she told everyone?'

'No, she's so embarrassed. She doesn't want anyone to know. But she's still trying to figure out if Gracie ever had cancer.' Maz paused. 'She's worried that you made Gracie sick.'

Maz glanced towards the small playground dotted with kids. Where the hell *was* Gracie?

46

ALLISON

ALLISON CAME OVER THE WOODEN BRIDGE AT THE BACK, ALONGSIDE the river. The playground boasted a big slide, a climbing frame, swings. Not elaborate equipment like the pirate ship further up on the Gold Coast, but every one of her Wirriga Wombats would have loved playing here, Gracie included.

What had he done with Gracie?

After leaving the apartment hotel, Allison had picked up the special package from the shop. On the taxi ride to the park, she'd cradled it on her lap.

'It's a surprise for my granddaughter's birthday,' she told the driver. 'We're celebrating with a party at the park.'

With every white lie, she wondered if she were becoming more like Luke. On the plane, Maz told her the package would complicate the 'meet', as she was calling it. But Maz didn't know kids like she did. It was her one weapon against Luke.

At the thought of seeing him, bile rose in her throat.

How could he use his own child like that? Make Gracie afraid for her future? Luke had always insisted Gracie was 'special'. Now Allison could see that Luke had been striving to make her extra-special to everyone. Extra-special meant more money, more attention.

The river curved along one side of the park, with a strip of white beach. Even though winter had almost arrived, up here the sun was still hot and a group of toddlers dipped in and out, splashing each other. Normal families and their kids having normal fun.

With her back bent slightly, Allison adjusted her glasses and touched her springy white hair to make sure it was in place. Would Luke see through her disguise?

Maz was supposed to be meeting Luke on the other side of the playground. At first, Allison worried that Maz couldn't be trusted. She'd listened to her ridiculous plan, poking holes in it. But finally she'd seen the young woman's anger.

'It's his fault that Dad's sick. I believed his advice. Most of those pills I was selling were his suggestions. He encouraged me.'

Except that Maz had gone gung-ho for it. So young, so brash—thought she knew better than the doctors and the health professionals. Buying strange remedies from overseas. But that confidence had been dented. Allison disagreed with her about the police, though. A streak of confidence was still shining through there. Maz believed she could take Luke down single-handedly. Or perhaps it was less of a belief, more of a vendetta. He'd been intimate with her—taken advantage of her youth, her enthusiasm, her body.

Sunday lunchtime, the playground was filled with children clambering and swinging, while families picnicked on the grass. Good, it gave them more cover. The detective had promised that Maz—and Luke—wouldn't be able to spot them. He was right. None of the happy families looked like police officers. They'd better be here, though.

Allison examined the faces of the children nearby, checking their features quickly to see if she recognised one in particular. In class and in the playground, it was a skill—identifying one child among the many others. But here, none of the faces were familiar.

'Awww, so cute!'

A curly-haired boy had come running over to her and was now kneeling on the ground, patting the special package—a cavoodle.

The most popular dog breed. Twelve weeks old. Tiny, irresistible, with a red bow around his neck. The sort Gracie wanted. Golden and fluffy with floppy ears and black button eyes, this new puppy was more teddy bear than dog.

Enjoying the attention, the puppy wriggled and wagged its tail. When it started licking the boy's face, he giggled.

The mum had followed her son over.

'I'm looking for my granddaughter.' Allison began in her usual teacher's voice, then made it slower and croakier. 'It's her birthday present.'

Three more children rushed to see the puppy, squatting down, running their hands over the soft fur. Allison knelt with them, hoping she didn't appear too flexible for a grandmother.

'Please be gentle with him,' she instructed the kids. 'Pat him on the back, not around the head.'

That was just what she needed—a child's hand in the puppy's mouth. Bite marks. Screaming. When she'd imagined this moment, it had been simple. Allison took her eyes off the besotted toddlers for a moment and squinted to see beyond the slippery slide. No five-year-old girl with a bald head.

Not bald. Shaved. It must be. No chemo. Luke had kept shaving it. And his own hair.

'Where's your granddaughter?' the mum asked. 'She's going to love this puppy!'

The kindness of strangers. Or was this mum the undercover policewoman?

'She's . . . umm . . . she's . . .' Enlist the help of strangers, it was what Luke himself had done. 'She's here with my son-in-law. He won't let me talk to her. My daughter—she died—and he won't let us see our grandchild.'

The tears came suddenly, unexpectedly, trickling down her cheeks. This lie was easier than the truth. *He has been living in my house, pretending his wife died and his daughter has cancer, stealing love and money from all of us.* No-one would believe it.

'I'm so sorry.' The mum patted her shoulder, just like the children were patting the puppy. 'Are you sure she's here?'

Allison wobbled her head, yes and no. The mum pulled her up from her knees and they walked towards the climbing frame. A grandmother, a puppy, a young mum and her toddler. A family. Hopefully, Luke wouldn't take a second glance at them. When they reached the enclosed slide, Allison leant against it, the blue plastic curling up above her head. Ten metres away, towards the car park, she saw Maz with a man. Sitting on a bench, their legs touching, his arm around her. A couple in love.

At the sight of Luke, goosebumps tingled across her skin. She had to fight the urge to flee.

Next to her, kids were shooting down the enclosed slide. Like one of those big waterslides, they'd disappear into the opening at the top, whizz down the tunnel and pop out at the bottom.

Luke was looking her way, his eyes trained on the top of the slide. For a moment, Allison thought he'd recognised her. But his gaze skipped over the grandmother with the dog; a grandmother in a green cardigan and brown slacks, wire-rimmed glasses and a white bob. She was invisible to him.

Gracie must be here; Luke wouldn't choose a playground otherwise. Or had he hurt her? Was Gracie actually dead, as he'd told everyone?

'Can you see your granddaughter?' the mum was asking.

A child popped out of the bottom of the slide. Laughing. Jumping up to do it again. A girl with blonde hair. In a pink dress dotted with strawberries. Pink sandals. As she ran back around to the ladder, she saw the dog.

'Aww, puppy!'

Crouching down, the girl cuddled the dog without glancing up at the adults.

'What's his name?'

'Marma . . .' Allison had to stop and breathe. 'Marmalade.'

47

'MARMALADE,' THE GIRL REPEATED. 'I ALWAYS WANTED A PUPPY CALLED Marmalade!'

Staring at the blonde wig, Allison whispered softly, 'Gracie?'

'Daddy says I'm Macy now.' The girl sighed, world-weary. Stroking the dog without looking up. 'Macy with a M. Like Movie World. That starts with M too. We went three times.'

The girl stopped suddenly, as if realising she'd said too much. She peeked up, smiled briefly, then turned her attention back to Marmalade.

'I wish you were mine,' she said, rubbing the dog's ears.

'He is yours,' Allison murmured, squatting down next to her. 'I bought him for you. Gracie, it's me. Lally.'

Shrieking, Gracie wrapped her arms around Allison's neck. Marmalade, excited by the noise, jumped between them.

'Why're you so old?' She touched Allison's glasses. 'Why's your hair white? Daddy said you're sick. That's why we had to go.'

'I'm not sick now.' Allison squeezed her tightly, the small body familiar against her own. 'Are you sick?'

'Daddy says I'm all better and I didn't even go to America.'

So trusting. *Of course you trust your father—you grow up assuming he's telling the truth.* One day, ten years from now as a teenager, twenty years from now as a wife, thirty years from now as a mother, Gracie would fully understand what her father had done and her heart would splinter into a million pieces. Allison prayed she'd be there to help put the pieces back together.

Marmalade had crept underneath them and was licking Gracie's shin. The little girl giggled, a gorgeous tinkling that Allison had thought she'd never hear again. Gracie leant down to kiss the puppy's neck. From the corner of her eye, Allison could see the friendly mum pushing her son on the swing, watching their reunion. Was Luke watching also?

A shadow fell over Gracie's blonde head.

'Honey, what're you doing? Please don't play with other people's dogs. They may be dangerous.'

He sounded rational, caring—a proper dad who looked after his daughter. Before Gracie could speak, Allison stood up tall and faced him, creating a barrier in front of the girl and the dog.

'You're far more dangerous than any dog,' she spoke loudly.

'I beg your pardon.' Luke frowned at her. 'I have to keep my daughter safe.'

Luke grinned at the young mum nearby, a grin that said: *Crazy old lady. What can you do?*

Despite being a metre away, he didn't recognise her. Had the grandmother outfit made her non-existent in his world? Was he so cocky that he couldn't imagine Allison turning the tables on him? They all spoke at once.

'Daddy, it's—'

'I'm watching you,' warned the young mum.

'Luke.'

When Allison said his name, his eyes widened. He lunged towards Gracie.

'Daddy, it's Lally.' Gracie finished her sentence. 'She's not sick anymore!'

Luke flicked a glance at Maz, now standing at the edge of the playground with her arms crossed.

'God, Ally, it's been a nightmare. Such a bizarre story that you'll think I've gone insane. I've been set up but I don't know why. When we got to the airport, our passports had been blocked. We couldn't leave Australia. At first, I thought it was Tony, in retaliation for us living in your house. But then I worked out that it had something to do with Dr Rawson and the drug trial. No-one wanted Gracie on the trial. I think someone paid double to take her place. We've been hiding out up here while I've been trying to get Gracie on another trial. I'm so scared for her. I couldn't ring you—I thought you might be part of it . . .'

She stared at him in horror.

'Stop lying, Luke. There is no drug trial. Gracie was never sick. You have no idea how many people you've hurt with your lies. And the little person you've hurt the most.'

Gracie stroked the puppy's fur; Allison hoped she wasn't following their conversation.

Luke took a step closer to her, into the sand of the playground. His face still wore a charming smile but his voice was low. 'You needed me, Ally. You were lost and I gave your life meaning. You should be thanking me.'

Allison felt the sting of his words, blinked away the tears. She didn't want him to see her weak.

'But it wasn't just me. A whole school, a whole community. All those children, their families, your friends at the gym . . .'

'You all wanted to feel like you were doing good.' He grinned again. But now she could see through the white smiling teeth to the salesman underneath. 'I gave you all that.'

Brushing at her eyes, Allison tried and failed to stop the tears. He had no idea of the grief he'd caused. The betrayal that would make adults, and children, wary about helping others in the future. And she was furious on behalf of Gracie—he'd made a little girl believe she was sick. No, it wasn't weak to show her tears, she decided; it was human.

'Don't cry, Lally,' Gracie piped up from below. 'We got to see you.'

'Yep, you should be happy,' Luke said. 'She's all better. You weren't expecting that.'

Something was seriously wrong with him. An essential part of him—the part that made him human—was missing.

He checked his watch, then glared at Maz. She was still standing on the edge of the playground. Luke didn't shout at her for the deception, simply shook his head.

'It could've worked, Maz. You'll never know what you missed.' He turned to Gracie. 'Time to go, honey.'

'No, I'm going to Lally's.' Gracie was stroking the puppy. 'She bought me Marmalade!'

Distract, distract. That was her plan.

'Oops—Marmalade needs a poo,' she said. 'Gracie, can you help take him to the grass?'

Wrapping the dog's lead around Gracie's hand, Allison guided her to the grassed area, telling her how they had to pick up the poo in a plastic bag. Luke had taken Gracie's other hand, walking in rhythm with them. They had walked this way so many times before in Wirriga and Manly. Along the beach, at playgrounds. Together.

Would Luke pull his daughter away? What if Allison pulled her other arm? A tug-of-war with a child as the prize.

The familiar melody of 'Greensleeves' filled the air. An ice-cream van had arrived in the car park.

'Can we get one, Lally?' Gracie asked. 'Daddy says I can have sugar now.'

They looked towards the van and Luke reacted, seconds before Allison.

He snatched his daughter up into his arms and held her, despite the dog's lead still tangled around Gracie's wrist.

'I wanna ice-cream,' Gracie yelled. 'I want Marmalade.'

The dog was being jerked around, half lifted off the ground. Squealing and yelping. Allison reached out to grab the girl's flailing arm.

'Put her down, Luke!'

'I'm calling the police!' shouted the young mum with her little boy.

And then Allison realised that the police were already running towards them—a man and a woman in exercise gear. It was their rapid movement that had made Luke grab his daughter. Moments before, they'd been stretching their legs against one of the benches, their push bikes next to them. As Allison gripped Gracie's arm, the two police officers charged across the grass, closing the gap. Five seconds. Allison just had to hang on to Gracie for five seconds until they arrived.

Suddenly she found herself falling backwards, Gracie on top of her. Luke had dropped his daughter and was sprinting through the playground, across the bridge and into the trees. Maz bolted after him.

Gracie's elbow dug into her stomach and Marmalade licked her neck.

Allison tried to keep Luke in sight.

A shadow moving in the trees and then he disappeared.

48

MAZ

MAZ PUMPED HER LEGS HARDER. LUKE HAD LED THEM INTO THE DARKEST part of the forest, the high trees blocking out the sun. But she'd studied the map—if he ran straight ahead, he'd hit the river and have nowhere to go unless he decided to swim across a tidal current. His only option was to double back onto the road, otherwise he'd be caught in a series of meandering river canals blocking each direction. Did he know that too? At this rate, Maz would be able to keep up with him for five minutes, but after that, he'd win on stamina. All that training together, the beach jogs, the half marathon—he'd always been faster than her. Bigger quads, stronger calves.

Maz could hear the two others panting behind her.

'Stop! Police!'

That made Luke sprint faster.

Fear and adrenaline surged through her. She pushed herself even harder. No pain, no gain. *If you think you can do it, you can.* The distance between them was decreasing: three metres, two metres . . . Maz was almost close enough to touch him. They came to a slight rise and Luke arched away from her.

And then they were bursting through the trees and onto the shore by the river. Luke stumbled in the soft sand and Maz pitched forward, thrusting her palms against his shoulders. Off balance, he rolled to the ground.

As the police cuffed him, Maz was grateful that Allison had ignored her request. Thank God the coppers had been there. Like the whole supplements fiasco, she hadn't quite thought through all the possibilities of trying to ensnare Luke.

'Luke Branson, you're under arrest on suspicion of fraudulently obtaining money by deception and using false documents to obtain financial advantage.' The male officer puffed as he spoke. 'You have the right to—'

Before the officer could finish his warning, Luke began babbling to Maz.

'I've been set up, babe. There's a conspiracy against us. We couldn't leave Australia. Someone was trying to stop Gracie getting treatment. It was Dr Rawson—he wants money for his research. He's stolen the fundraising money and disappeared. He's taken all his records with him.'

'Luke, there is no Dr Rawson.'

'Oh, babe, you're not one of them, are you?' His sad eyes implored her. 'Dr Rawson was so good with Gracie but then something happened. I think he misdiagnosed Gracie and now he's making me the fall guy. There are no records, that's the problem. I can't work it out. Will you help me, babe? I need to get some treatment for Gracie.'

The female police officer had been listening in silence. Finally, she spoke. 'I don't think you'll be seeing Gracie for a very long time.'

That shut him up.

The Tweed Heads police station was all shiny and new—not the best place for a small child and a new puppy. Marmalade skittered along the floors and peed next to a chair. As Allison cleaned it up, the policewoman on duty at the desk waved away her apologies.

'Don't worry, he's a cutie. We've had much worse.'

Maz curled her body into the seat, happy to wait for the detectives. Her legs and stomach hurt. From sprinting. From landing on top of Luke. And from the fear. Next time she was in a police station, would they be arresting her?

The relief was written on the schoolteacher's face but Maz could see she was trying to hide it from Gracie.

'Daddy has to help the police with a few things,' Allison explained to the little girl. 'We'll go and talk to them soon too.'

The teacher couldn't take her eyes off the child. Every so often, she'd cuddle her or drop an arm around Gracie's shoulders.

'Thank you for organising the coppers,' Maz whispered.

'I was scared for your safety.'

'But you didn't think I was going off with him?'

Surely she'd earned Allison's trust by now. Hadn't Maz shown her capability?

'I trusted you, but not him. You were special to him, Maz. I think he loved you in his own strange way.'

When they'd first been talking at the park, Luke hadn't sensed the hatred inside her.

'Nope,' Maz told her. 'He's like a mirror reflecting back what you want to see. The only person Luke loves is himself.'

The afternoon stretched into evening as Allison and Maz gave their statements, and Gracie was taken to the hospital for a medical check. Apparently Luke was sticking to his story that Gracie's mother had died. But no records existed for the Bransons, only the life he'd concocted online.

'Do you think the mother's dead?' Maz asked when Gracie was out of earshot.

'I don't know what to think,' Allison said.

As Maz finished yet another coffee, a smartly dressed lawyer appeared at the front desk. Luke could pay for expensive advice. Did that mean he was more likely to get off?

Curtis called, furious that he hadn't been there for the arrest.

'Why didn't you include me in the plan, Maz?'

'You're rather recognisable.'

'I want to interview him as soon as possible. Should I fly up?'

'I think they're sending him back to Sydney.'

The detective had said that Luke would be taken before a magistrate tomorrow morning, with the request that bail be refused. If that happened, Luke would be sent to Silverwater remand centre in Sydney until he had a court date.

'Luke won't talk to you, Curtis,' she added. 'He's not saying anything to anyone.'

And Gracie couldn't remember the names of places they'd lived or other family members. Only one cousin.

'Amelia got a new bike. She's older than me.'

'And what's Mummy's name?' a friendly policewoman asked her. 'Does she have another name? Is it Sarah?'

'I called her Mummy.' Gracie scrunched up her face in confusion. 'Daddy called her Cee Cee.'

'And was her last name Branson?'

'I don't know. Daddy said we had a new one after the fire.'

Cee Cee. A nickname. Not much for the police to go on.

When Gracie returned from the hospital, she told Maz cheerfully that she'd been there before. 'It's the one that cured me.'

'How did they do that?' Maz asked.

'Daddy took me in and they gave me a green smoothie.' Gracie had Marmalade in her lap again. 'Then he said I was all better.'

The policewoman passed on the doctors' comments.

'No sign of cancer,' she reported. 'No sign of past surgery. No scars, bruising, burns. No malnutrition. They said some of the other blood tests will take a few days, but she's looking pretty healthy.'

How had Luke conned them for so long?

Presumably Luke hadn't given Gracie the Bio-Antidotes if she hadn't actually been sick. That meant the blood tests shouldn't show any banned substances. Maz put her palm up to give the girl a high-five.

'Yay, Gracie! You've got the all-clear!'

A healthy five-year-old girl. Maybe, after everything, Maz *had* saved Gracie's life by rescuing her from her crazy father.

49

ALLISON

GRACIE WAS RELEASED INTO ALLISON'S CARE ON SUNDAY NIGHT AND they took a late flight back to Sydney. Every time Allison looked at her, she had to do a mental shift. *You're here! I thought you were sick, I thought you were dead.* The detectives were liaising with the Department of Family and Community Services to try and identify any relatives.

While everyone had been mourning Gracie and worrying about Luke, the two of them were staying in a ritzy resort on the edge of the Gold Coast. Hanging out at the beach. Watching the dolphin show at Sea World. Spinning around on the Looney Tunes Carousel at Movie World. A bird show at Currumbin Wildlife Sanctuary. A wonderful holiday.

Gracie quickly tired of Allison's constant cuddles and wriggled out of her reach. Marmalade was the best distraction. But the little girl couldn't understand why Daddy had to stay somewhere else.

Early on Monday morning, Allison sat in the principal's office explaining the whole crazy mess. She had to give Declan a heads-up before the detectives came to interview him later in the day.

'That fucker.' Declan slammed his palms down on the desk. 'I can't believe he made it all up!'

Allison lurched backwards in her chair; she'd never seen the mild-mannered principal angry, never heard him swear. Thankfully, the children hadn't arrived for school yet.

'I'm sorry I didn't tell you earlier,' she said. 'I know you were organising the memorial but I wanted some facts before we announced it to the children.'

Allison focused on the pictures behind the principal's desk—portraits by the older students and photos of school events. Smiling children in a safe environment.

'Why did we believe him?' Declan held out his palms.

'He had all the evidence to back it up. And he looked like a caring dad going through a difficult time.'

She answered easily but the same question was constantly running through her own mind.

'He's a fucking sociopath.'

The swear word made her flinch again. Kind Mr Considine cursing like a footy thug in a bar fight. And he hadn't even invited the treacherous bastard into his home. Every time Allison remembered the things she'd done for Luke, her stomach knotted. The meals she'd cooked, the gifts she'd bought, her sympathy for his wife's death, her concern about Gracie. The emotions she'd shared about her marriage breakdown.

'At least Gracie doesn't have cancer and she isn't dead after all.' Allison sighed. It was the only positive.

'We need to work out how to tell the children,' Declan said. 'They're going to be so confused and the parents will be furious.'

'I know. The story's coming out in the media tomorrow,' Allison said. 'We can't lie about what's happened. That would make us as bad as Luke.'

'The scumbag has stolen the heart of our school. It'll crush everyone.'

'Maybe we can turn it around somehow,' she suggested. 'Instead of having the memorial, could we do a different community event?'

___

The children were told a simplified version of the truth. Gracie's father had made a mistake about her cancer. He'd told some bad lies and the police were interviewing him. But the best news: Gracie was alive and healthy.

A detailed explanation was being emailed to parents. As soon as it went out, the school would be bombarded by phone calls.

Allison hoped that Wirriga didn't take their anger out on her nor on Gracie. Perhaps she should read them Aesop's fable about the bee-keeper who discovers all the honey has been stolen from the hives. When the bees return, they see the bee-keeper standing there, blame him and attack. As he topples from their stings, he calls them ungrateful scoundrels who have mistaken their caring master for the thief. The moral: *Things are not always as they seem.*

At lunchtime, Allison returned to school with Gracie in the back seat. As she pulled into the staff car park, she pictured Luke the day her car wouldn't start. Had he done that? Had he been watching the house, assessing his target? Even though she'd never seen his Jeep, Allison was sure it must've been his eyes that she'd felt raking over her home. Increasing her paranoia about being alone. She'd invited in the very person who had been causing her fear.

Gracie carefully held the dog's lead. Her hair was a soft fuzz, growing back. She didn't bother with a bandana.

'Everyone's a bit confused, Gracie,' Allison explained. 'They might act a little strangely.'

'I missed them all,' Gracie said. 'Even silly Zack.'

When the children saw Gracie walking into the playground, they came running. The teachers cried, the kids whooped. And Marmalade scampered between their legs, yapping with the excitement.

Allison had hoped and prayed for this moment—Gracie returning to school, cured. She couldn't get her head around the fact that the little girl had never been sick.

'We thought you were dead.' Zack spoke for them all.

'No, I went to Movie World at the Gold Coast.'

'You're so lucky,' Selina said.

—

On Tuesday, Detective Sergeant Rejman drove Allison and Gracie to the children's hospital. After they'd walked through the main entrance doors, he asked Gracie to explain what had happened every Friday.

'We had to wait here.' Gracie sat down in a lounge in the foyer. 'Daddy got the medicine over there.'

She pointed towards the hospital pharmacy. Together, they walked into the store. Staring around at the medicines on the shelves, Allison wondered what Luke used to do here.

'Hello, Gracie.' The pharmacist came out from behind the counter to welcome the little girl. 'How're you feeling?'

'I'm all better,' she said.

'Fantastic!' He winked at Allison. 'You deserve a red frog and your special drink.'

He grabbed a pair of tongs from the counter and reached inside a huge jar of lollies to select a red frog. Then he took a kombucha from the fridge.

Gracie refused the drink. 'No, I'm all better,' she repeated. 'I don't need it.'

Luke must have told her the kombucha was her drug treatment.

'How has she been since she finished her last course?' he asked Allison. 'And how's Luke?'

Staring at the badge on his white coat, Allison didn't know how to answer. His name: *Rawson Jones. Pharmacist.*

With the red frog and a picture book distracting Gracie, the detective spoke to Rawson. Confusion and disbelief flashed across the pharmacist's face as he began to understand the extent of Luke's scam.

'It wasn't just me,' Rawson said. 'He made friends with interns, nurses. He used to talk to other patients.'

Copying their language, their emotions.

'He showed me X-rays and blood tests and emails from specialists,' Allison said. 'Could he have got those from the interns and the nurses?'

'I guess so. He was friendly with one guy in particular—a radiographer, Samir. You should talk to him.'

When the detective tracked down the radiographer, apparently the conversation was difficult. Samir refused to believe the fraud; he'd been fed yet another story.

'Luke's studying to be a radiographer,' Samir told the detective. 'With Gracie's diagnosis, he wanted to specialise in PET scanning. We discussed case studies for his assignments.'

Befriending medical professionals and patients. Gaining detailed information, reports, photos of equipment—all to fabricate Gracie's disease and the others: Jessica Moore with breast cancer, Lily Ng with head injuries, Phillip Saunders with leukaemia, Hannah Bennett with ovarian cancer.

Luke had even conned them at the hospital.

—

An email arrived from Kayleigh that night. She'd shown the photofit pictures around Hythorne. One of the younger Luxfords was up from Melbourne visiting his mother's grave and thought Luke looked similar to a guy who'd bought a horse from their stud last year. While the records were burnt in the fire, he recalled a name—Mike Carter. The reason he remembered: the guy was buying the horse as a surprise for his wife's birthday. A romantic but risky move, he'd thought at the time.

Forwarding the email to Detective Sergeant Rejman, Allison added one short line: *Luke told me this story about his wife's birthday. It must be him.*

One corroborated fact among all the lies. One tiny solid brick.

After crossing her fingers for luck, Allison put Mike Carter into the search bar on her laptop. A list of English men came up. She added a location, Victoria, Australia. When she read the top headline from October last year, Allison began to shake.

Father and toddler missing in fire

Mike Carter and his four-year-old daughter remain missing,
feared dead, after the Nicklin Creek fire. It is believed that the
father and daughter drove to an outlying farm to rescue their
horses from the path of the fire. Their burnt-out car was found
near the farm.

Six fires continue to burn across the state. Victoria is
experiencing its thirteenth driest period on record. The
predictions are for a difficult bushfire season in the hot summer
months ahead.

He'd not only faked Sarah Branson's death but his own.
Used a bushfire emergency to cover his tracks.

Who was grieving for a missing father and toddler?

—

Two days later, Allison waited in her lounge room, clenching and
unclenching her fists. That fucker—she'd borrowed Declan's
word. How dare he do this to all of them? The social worker
was in the kitchen, playing with Gracie. They'd had a number of
sessions. Detective Sergeant Rejman was supposed to be arriving
at ten o'clock but he was three minutes late. Together, Allison
and Gracie had made fairy bread and set out orange cake. The
kettle was filled with water, the teacups on their saucers.

And then the detective and a woman were coming through
the front door, down the hallway, into the lounge room. The
woman, Chelsea, bore no resemblance to the photos of Sarah
Branson. Cee Cee, as Luke had apparently called her. Long
blonde hair in a ponytail, petite body—she looked like an older,
sadder version of Maz.

But when Gracie appeared from the kitchen, the sadness dissolved in an instant.

'Oh God, it's you! Oh, Gracie. My darling girl.'

Laughing, crying, Chelsea ran towards the child. They weren't sure how Gracie would react. Mother and daughter had each been told the other had perished in a fire. Allison and the social worker watched Gracie and waited.

Gracie giggled. A little giggle that turned into a giant chuckle.

'Mummy, you came back from heaven!'

Chelsea pulled her daughter into a cuddle. Kissed her cheeks, her downy hair. Wrapped her hands around Gracie's waist.

'I missed you so much, darling.'

'Me too, Mummy. Don't go away again.'

Allison had an inkling of how the mother felt, although she'd only had four weeks of believing Gracie was dead. And Gracie wasn't even her own child. For Chelsea, it had been seven months of grieving for her husband and daughter. Even the detective had a tissue out, blotting his tears.

The mother switched between laughing and crying, pulling Gracie close and then holding her at arm's length to stare at her face.

'You're a big girl now! I hear you started school.'

'I'm in kindy. Lally is my teacher.'

For the first time, the mother looked in Allison's direction. Still crying but smiling through the tears.

Allison felt her heart might break—with happiness. Wiping at her eyes, she tried not to think about the pain that Chelsea must have been in, assuming her family was dead. The one good thing, the one amazing thing, from this whole calamity: an unexpected, unimaginable reunion.

'Guess what, Mummy?'

'What, darling?'

Which bit of the crazy story would Gracie tell first?

'I got a puppy.' Gracie pointed towards the kitchen. 'He's in the laundry. Come meet him.'

'What's his name?'

'Mummy, you know.'

'Did you call him Marmalade?'

'YES!'

Marmalade danced around them, while Gracie showed Chelsea the house and garden. The tears continued to flow. Of all of them, Gracie was the most composed, telling stories about her holiday to the Gold Coast, her friends at school. As Allison prepared sandwiches for lunch, the detective and the social worker left.

'Let's Skype Granny and Grandad,' Chelsea said. 'They'll be so surprised at how tall you are!'

'Daddy said they didn't love me anymore.'

Allison took a deep breath. Would Gracie keep stumbling over the lies she'd been told? But her mother just brushed it aside.

'Oh, silly Daddy got it wrong. They still love you.'

'I like Granny's chocolate cake.'

'I'm sure Granny will make a great big one for you when we get home.'

It was as if, upon seeing her mother, Gracie's memories had been released. Luke must have forced her not to speak of the past.

Later, when Chelsea asked about booking a hotel in Manly, Allison quashed the idea.

'Stay here for a few days,' she said. 'I've got plenty of room. And Gracie can play with Marmalade.'

Allison had said it without thinking. Done it again. Invited a complete stranger into the house.

Well, she refused to change her own kindness. If she and the community closed their hearts, then Luke would've won.

—

Over dinner, Chelsea helped Gracie with her peas and made sure she didn't spill her drink. She was a good mum, Allison could see that. Luke had executed the ultimate betrayal on her—marriage and a child. But the questions would have to wait until Gracie was in bed. Although Felix couldn't help himself as he chewed his steak.

'How did you meet him?'

'In hospital. I had a bad fall from a horse.' Chelsea didn't seem to mind answering. 'I was in there for months. He was my physiotherapist.'

Targeting another woman in a time of vulnerability. And he had a medical background, just as the detective had guessed.

'I was studying to be a vet,' Chelsea continued. 'But I postponed everything after the fall. Then my grandfather died and left me a house in Nicklin Creek. So we moved there. I got pregnant almost straight away and we married fast.'

Keen to get his hands on a free house. That sounded like Luke.

But he'd been so clever that Chelsea had had no clue she'd been scammed until the call from Detective Sergeant Rejman.

When Gracie and Felix went to feed the puppy, Chelsea opened up.

'For the past seven months, I've had nightmares of them in the fire.' Chelsea shook her head, as if to dislodge the images.

'I thought he'd drugged Gracie and shot himself. Used the fire to burn the evidence of his murder-suicide.'

'Why did you think that?'

'I had a portfolio—my family are quite wealthy.' Chelsea sipped on her glass of water. 'After Gracie was born, he started managing the funds but he lost almost a million in bad investments. He was devastated that he'd ruined our future. Apologising, desperate to make it up to me. I tried to be supportive but I was also very angry.'

'So afterwards, you blamed yourself when they died?'

'Absolutely. The horses were the only thing that kept me going.' Chelsea sighed. 'On my darkest days, I thought about following my family.'

'Thank God you didn't. He certainly knows how to manipulate people.'

They sat in silence, contemplating the horror of what Luke had done.

'I assume you've told all this to the detective,' Allison said.

'Yes, and he has the account numbers for the investments,' Chelsea said. 'He's trying to track the money trail.'

'Did Luke—Mike—ever talk about his life before he met you?'

'He said his mother died when he was younger than Gracie. The family fell apart and he was shipped off to foster homes.'

Presumably another lie.

'I wonder why he took Gracie.' Allison had been trying to understand his motives. 'Was it just to get sympathy?'

'He always called her his mini-me. Said Gracie was just like him as a kid.'

Over chocolate pudding and coffee, Chelsea started crying again. Allison understood it would take a while for her to seize hold of the truth. While Chelsea had been mourning two people she'd loved, Luke had simply finished his scam with her and moved on to a new one in Wirriga.

'We all fell for his lies,' Allison said, reaching out to hold her hand. 'He was very convincing. I can't believe you're alive and I'm talking to you. Luke and I bonded over the pain of losing our partners.'

Allison had felt his distress. The bastard should be acting in Hollywood.

'His name isn't even Mike Carter,' Chelsea sniffed. 'I married a man with a false name.'

~

Chelsea agreed to be photographed by Curtis the next morning. He turned up after breakfast and gave Gracie a big hug.

'Can I wear my purple fairy tutu?' Gracie asked.

'Sure,' Allison and Chelsea answered at the same time. They looked at each other and laughed.

The photos were taken in the backyard, with the gum trees behind. Sitting on the grass, Chelsea and Gracie cuddled and giggled. Marmalade escaped from Allison's grip and bolted over to join in the fun.

'Thanks for doing this, Chelsea,' Curtis said. 'I know it must be hard, but everyone's so angry about Luke's fraud. Your reunion with Gracie is the good news story that we all need.'

50

MAZ

THE STORY OF MAZ'S 'HEROICS' WAS ALL OVER THE NEWS, THANKS TO Curtis; he'd dramatised it as 'a sting, a pursuit and an arrest'. He made Maz into a wonder girl who'd taken down a con man 'double her size'. Mum and Dad were super impressed. At the gym, the reaction was mostly disbelief. Not about her fitness levels but about Luke. Nico spent half an hour smashing into the punching bag after he'd heard. 'I treat him like family and this is how he repays me,' he yelled.

Em-Jay whispered that one of the instructors had asked if Maz was in on it, taking a cut of the cash. Flipping hell, as if she hadn't been through enough.

Maz met Curtis for a quick lunch at Raw. He'd thought the debacle would ruin his career but it was doing the opposite. While Curtis was concentrating on the actual story now, he wanted to do a longer piece later about how Luke had managed to convince them all.

'Guess what?' He didn't wait for her to answer. 'The editor said we might do a podcast. Wouldn't that be cool! Can I interview you for it?'

She was exhausted by it all but he seemed energised.

'I guess so,' she said.

If I'm not in jail for selling illegal supplements.

'We're starting a campaign to find more of Luke's victims,' Curtis said, taking out his laptop to show her the website.

It had photos of Luke with different hairstyles and clothing. The headline shouted: *Have you been scammed by this man?*

'Have the police worked out his real identity yet?' Maz asked.

'His name's Kyle Pritchett.'

'He doesn't look like a Kyle.'

Maz tried to picture Luke with that name. It was all wrong. He had inhabited Luke Branson so well.

'His family's from Adelaide,' Curtis said. 'Just an ordinary family. His parents thought he was in Africa.'

'Why Africa?'

'He told them he was an aid worker in South Sudan, helping kids. He has a Facebook page with photos. His parents are so proud and they send him money every month. Obviously it's dangerous and he can't get home much.'

'Scamming his own parents? Seriously?'

'And his two brothers and sister. None of them knew about Chelsea or Gracie.'

'It's just plain wrong.'

When they'd been waiting in the police station at Tweed Heads, Allison had said: *Luke's the tin man. He's lacking a heart.* To betray his own parents seemed particularly cold-hearted, as bad as betraying his daughter.

'And there's more.' Curtis paused for effect. Maz could already see that he'd be great on the podcast. 'His brother's son has leukaemia. The boy is six years old and being treated at the children's hospital in Adelaide. It's all on Facebook.'

'So, he stole a cancer story from his own nephew.' Maz groaned. 'What about the physiotherapy and the swimming?'

'Those bits are true. He trained as a physio and he almost made it into the Olympics.'

Separating the truth from the lies made Maz's brain hurt. And her heart.

—

Colin—Dr Simmons—had asked to see Maz in his rooms at the hospital. Diagrams of the heart were stuck to the walls. On his desk sat a huge 3D version that came apart. A long shelf of medical textbooks filled another wall. Maz folded her hands tight against her stomach to stop the queasy feeling.

'I've got five minutes so I'll be quick,' Colin said. 'I had the results from the laboratory on the diet pills.'

'Right. Here's the letter from Border Force like you asked.' Maz passed it across the polished desk. 'It's all about liver damage.'

Colin held the letter without reading it. 'Actually, Maz, I have to apologise for jumping to conclusions. The pills didn't contain any banned substances. It's unlikely they caused your father's attack.'

'What? I don't understand.'

'I assumed the appetite suppressant would include the banned substance, Sibutramine. It was withdrawn in 2010 because it can cause cardiovascular toxicities like tachycardia, palpitations, hypertension and tachyarrhythmia.'

Maz didn't know what any of that meant but they didn't sound good.

'So the lab found no traces of this banned drug?'

Maz jiggled her legs. The queasy feeling was evaporating.

'No, it didn't contain Sibutramine. Let me look at the letter.'

As Colin scanned the piece of paper, Maz glanced at the book shelves which contained more medical knowledge than she could ever imagine. The words in the letter still hurt. *They pose a risk to your health. They show an increased risk of liver damage, hepatitis and acute liver failure causing death.*

Colin frowned and rubbed the letterhead. 'Is this the original letter, Maz?'

'Yep.'

'The chemical compound listed here isn't right for a diet pill. And it says Therapeutic Goods *Association* instead of *Administration*. It's a bit odd all round.'

Maz stared at the piece of paper in his hands. 'You mean it's not really from the government?'

'I don't know. It just doesn't seem quite right.'

She remembered Luke's reaction in Tweed Heads when she'd been talking about the letter. How he'd been encouraging her to run away with him, away from the threat of prosecution.

'Oh fuuuuuck, I bet Luke sent it.'

Implicating her in Gracie's death. Playing mind games. He couldn't have foreseen Dad's heart episode—that was a perfect coincidence to make her feel even guiltier.

'I read the articles in the paper,' Colin said. 'It sounds like something Luke could do. But, Maz, even if that's the case, please don't buy pills from overseas. You really don't know what's in them.'

Wow, she was off the hook for Dad's medical episode.

'Dad can get fit and healthy with diet and exercise alone.' She laughed, relief flooding through her.

'I'm still keen to understand what caused your father's coronary vasospasm. It may well be extreme stress from the concern about his work. I'm seeing him next week for a follow-up. By the way, I was wondering . . .' He smiled. 'That offer of a drink is still open. I'm guessing you might need a night out after these past few weeks . . . and that letter.'

Despite everything, being with Luke had made her appreciate an older man. In this office, surrounded by medical books and his framed certificates on the wall, Colin seemed especially handsome. Clean-shaven, a blue-and-white-checked shirt, chinos. The opposite of Luke's sportswear. She imagined the sort of place he'd take her—expensive, tasteful.

'You're right. The last couple of weeks have been totally insane.'

Beaming at him, Maz considered which night they could go out. Maybe Saturday week; she'd be free then. As she was about to speak, Maz caught sight of a silver photo frame on the shelf behind the doctor—a mother with a baby.

'Wait a second. Is that your . . . wife?'

It reminded her of someone. Helena. Although, she'd only glimpsed the woman for a moment that night at Allison's house. Was Colin her ex-husband, the man she'd fled from in terror?

With an embarrassed grimace, he turned and reached for the photo frame. When he brought it closer, she could see that it wasn't Helena. Oh shit, was he married with a baby and asking her for sex on the side?

'I'm single. No kids. Too much work and not enough play.' Colin let out a short laugh. 'Of course, I tell my patients that they need a work-life balance but joining your gym was the first proper exercise I've done in years.'

She gestured towards the photo. 'So who's this woman?'

'It's the picture that came with the frame.' Colin handed it to her. 'My dear mother gave it to me. She thinks that my older patients will feel more comfortable if I appear to be married.'

Maz stared at the model behind the glass. Yes, definitely a pre-printed photo.

'How funny. It must get awkward when people ask about your baby.'

'It's usually in the drawer. Mum was here yesterday so I had to put it on show for her.'

Maz's snigger became a chuckle and, suddenly, she burst into hysterical laughter. While Luke was pretending to have a dead wife and sick child so people would trust his motives, Colin's mother was pretending he had a real-life wife and baby so people would trust him in the hospital.

'This world is bat-shit crazy,' Maz said and he started laughing with her. 'I think we need to have that drink.'

At Allison's house, Gracie was out in the garden playing with Marmalade. The puppy really did distract Gracie from everything else.

'Maz, this is my Mummy,' Gracie announced proudly.

She'd been wondering about the real wife—the one who'd been deceived by Luke for years.

'Oh my God, you look like me.'

They both spoke at the same time. Curtis had shown her a photo but Maz hadn't picked up on the similarities in the flat image. It was more about the way Chelsea moved—bounced on her toes, grinned, tossed her ponytail. No wonder Gracie had accepted Maz's friendship so easily; she'd been reminded of her mother. But was Maz supposed to apologise for sleeping with Chelsea's husband?

Allison saved them from the awkwardness, coming out of the back door with a bottle of champagne and an apple juice.

'Let's celebrate.' The teacher popped the cork and sent it flying into the air. 'I want to thank Chelsea for being here with us. I want to thank Maz for her bravery. And I want to congratulate Gracie on starting school this year.'

After they'd clinked glasses, Maz told them Curtis' latest idea.

'He wants to do a photo shoot of us all together—the women scammed by Luke Branson.'

'Is he photographing himself as well?' Allison snapped. 'Along with Nico and Declan and Emmanuel. The men scammed by Luke? Or he could just film Wirriga's main street. He's scammed us all.'

51

FELIX

ON FRIDAY, THEY DID THEIR LAST LESSON ON *OTHELLO*. MRS SMYTHE asked the class for two paragraphs explaining Iago's quote when he convinces Roderigo to stab the lieutenant. A double-crossing bastard, that Iago. Getting others to do his dirty work as revenge on Othello, who never saw what was coming. Most of the main characters ended up dead thanks to Iago's machinations.

Surely Felix would get an extra mark for using Mrs Smythe's favourite word, *machination*. She also liked the word Machiavellian but that was harder to spell. Could he write about Iago's Machiavellian machinations?

Machiavellian—manipulate, deceive and exploit others to achieve your own goals.

Definitely Luke.

Although Luke would probably argue that he hadn't killed anyone in real life. Only online.

Gracie was here in the house, hanging out with that ball of fluff, Marmalade. Along with her real mother, Chelsea. When Mum had introduced Chelsea to the rest of Gracie's Gang, she said, 'We will not be Luke's victims. We will not be bitter or scared. We'll come out of this smarter and stronger.'

As Mum was talking, Felix had a lightbulb moment about that quote. *It makes or it mars us*—it was exactly what Mum was saying in modern-day words, not Shakespearian ones. He should've written Mum's quote in his assignment, hers was much better.

The socials had gone mental with Gracie's sudden reappearance. As if Luke's behaviour wasn't wacky enough, the conspiracy theories were flying around.

—*Gracie was poisoned. Luke gave her cancer.*

—*Gracie's mum was in on it.*

—*Mrs Walsh collected the money for herself.*

—*Luke started the fire in Hythorne.*

—*Gracie was in a cult and came back from the dead.*

—*Curtis, the journalist, was the mastermind.*

And Felix's favourite: *Gracie was a cyborg.*

On the bus, in the school grounds, at soccer, Felix had become a celebrity. Everyone wanted the inside story. Darcy said he should start charging for interviews. Pearl suggested he write a blog. But Felix avoided as much of it as possible by playing soccer during lunch and after school. It was harder for them to ask questions when he was running.

He couldn't believe that Luke had done the stalking, terrified them all, tried to put the blame on Mum, basically hounded Helena to New Zealand.

At home, Gracie was her usual self, apart from missing her dad.

'My mum and dad don't live together either,' Felix said, as some kind of reassurance.

Gracie liked it when Felix lay on the carpet and let her and Marmalade clamber all over him. Sometimes she sat on his knees and pretended to ride a horse.

'Giddy up, giddy up.' Gracie held the imaginary reins.

Soon, Gracie would be riding a real horse. In Victoria. With her mother. Another community which had thought Gracie was dead.

'Will you come and see me, Felix?' Gracie asked. 'Lally, will you come?'

Mum answered before Felix could. 'Oh yes. You're not disappearing on us again. We'll be coming to visit.'

<hr />

There was another beach party at Curl Curl tomorrow night—the girl who'd nearly drowned reckoned she could sneak out and get down there. She promised not to swim. Felix wouldn't go. He was working on his Bronze Cross, the level up from his Bronze Medallion. The next time someone was in trouble, Felix would be using his skills, not running away.

All that training at the gym had made him stronger too. Darcy had bought some more of the creatine supplement to bulk up, but Felix wasn't so keen. His body had been feeling better without the protein powders.

'I think they gave me the shits, you know, literally. And they made my pimples worse.'

Mum had asked for his help with this big community day—that could be his excuse for skipping the party on Saturday night.

And Mum and Dad were both coming to his soccer game tomorrow morning. They'd be standing on the sideline together. He might invite Pearl along as well.

52

LUKE

NO-ONE APPRECIATED HOW CLEVER HE'D BEEN. THE AMOUNT HE'D learnt for Gracie's cancer—chemo drugs, immunotherapy drugs, symptoms and side effects, all the terminology. Did they know how much time and effort that had taken? They should be calling him Dr Branson.

After Detective Rejman had figured out his identity and tracked down his family, the assumption was that Luke had stolen the idea from his nephew with leukaemia. Bullshit. He'd been collecting information years before, when he was still working at the hospital in Melbourne. Assessing which patients received the most sympathy, which ones people really cared about. At the time, he was dabbling in Medicare fraud but that had been boring and left too much of a paper trail. More interest and drama around sick kids.

The detective had asked him about other scams but Luke refused to answer any questions, apart from one.

'Did you harm your child?'

'No, I never hurt Gracie.'

As if he would. They couldn't paint him as an abusive father; Luke was a good dad. He'd shaved Gracie's head, that was all. And given her so much more. Made her into a special girl, the centre of a community, a life worth saving. Allison would tell them how much he cared for his daughter. Although she might be a little confused about some things. Gracie didn't have an allergy to sesame oil but he'd taken her to the hospital that night anyway. Hung out in the waiting room as a cover story. He'd played Ally's guilt perfectly; that episode had driven her into the manic fundraising and handing over cash.

The only drugs Gracie had taken were the ones given to her by Ally and Maz. Twice as far as he could tell—when Gracie had been sick with the cold. He would've stopped them if he'd been aware. Interfering women going behind his back. Particularly Maz. She didn't even know what was in her supplements. He'd never risk giving anything like that to Gracie. Was Maz still running scared about his letter? He'd asked her to visit but she hadn't yet. Luke reckoned there was a slim chance he could get her back onside.

Chelsea, though, was a different story.

She had a right to be angry, unlike the rest of them. The ones in Wirriga had only lost little bits of money—fifty dollars here, five hundred, a thousand. They could afford it. And it wasn't as though he'd hurt anyone.

His solicitor said they'd tracked Chelsea down through that horse stud at Hythorne. But he was still surprised when her request had come. He tried to get a message back to her. *I'll only allow you to visit if you bring Gracie.*

The remand centre at Silverwater wasn't the best place for his daughter but he needed to see her. She'd been his sidekick for so long. He asked his solicitor to tell Chelsea: *We can meet in the cafe. I'll buy Gracie some ice-cream. It won't feel like a jail.* Apart from the wire fences and the guards and the cameras and the security screening.

Luke had hoped and hoped, but Chelsea turned up alone. Thinner than when he'd left, dark circles under her eyes.

'You arsehole,' she hissed. 'I can't believe you did that to me. I had to see with my own eyes that you were alive.'

'I'm so ashamed,' he said. 'Please forgive me. I lost your life savings.'

'You didn't lose it. You stole it. Along with my child. And every happiness I had.'

'I was going through a terrible time, Chelsea. I'm so sorry. You know the real me. I think I had a schizophrenic episode.'

'Bullshit. I'm going to get all my money back while you rot in jail.'

Surely she wouldn't find it; he'd hidden it too well.

'How's our gorgeous Gracie?' he asked. 'I miss her so much.'

'You're never seeing her again.'

The visit lasted less than a minute.

Would his parents visit too? They must know about Gracie by now. He'd always implied that he didn't have time for long-term relationships; the aid work was too busy and too unpredictable. At the thought of his family meeting Gracie without him, Luke balled his hands into fists. She was his.

He had to talk to his solicitor, stop them from seeing Gracie and stop that detective from uncovering his other schemes. He'd erased all evidence of the bushfire fundraiser for a young couple to rebuild their home. He'd destroyed the documents related to Jack, a patient he befriended in the same hospital where he'd met Chelsea. Jack had put in thousands to help set up a physio clinic. Sadly, there were issues with the rental of the building and all the money had 'sunk into the real estate costs'.

Luke's former girlfriend and her parents had invested in a new American start-up selling gym and physio equipment. They'd consoled each other when the business went bankrupt; Luke, or Jason as he'd been known then, had lost all his own savings as well. That was ten years ago and they'd never come looking. His schemes were as watertight as possible.

He never would've imagined Allison getting on that plane to Chicago.

This was all her fault. The good teacher going too far.

Maybe he'd send a letter from Zack's parents to the Department of Education complaining that Mrs Walsh was bullying their boy because of the robbery. To do that, he'd need a computer.

Luke had been given a few options for 'working' in the remand centre. When he heard the word 'technology', he chose that. But no, he was put into a workshop to refurbish airline headsets. To rub it in that they weren't flying anywhere soon. Not a computer in sight. No chance to research his way out of here. Last year, he'd done some reading on mental health and personality disorders. Which one would help his cause? Schizophrenia? Bipolar? Severe depression? He just had to get his solicitor to present it in the right way.

53

ALLISON

ALLISON AND FELIX WERE DISCUSSING A MOVE TO A SMALLER HOUSE. Felix really wanted to be able to walk to the beach with his surfboard. Allison imagined a little place in Wirriga with a bright open study looking onto the bush; somewhere she could start creating her picture books about trees and wallabies and wombats. That would be her first series—on night-time noises and fighting a fear of the dark. Next year, she'd do a road trip with Felix to see Gracie and create a series set in a small country town recovering from bushfire. A spotlight on resilience and bouncing back.

Tony invited them for dinner to his new apartment at Freshwater.

'Have you heard from Helena?' Allison managed to ask without sounding bitter.

'Yes, she's doing well. Feeling positive about her new home.'

'And you're sure she didn't know Luke?'

It was one of Allison's many theories in her quest to understand how Luke had come to Wirriga. According to the detectives, Luke had chosen Wirriga by chance. He'd never been there before, didn't know anyone. But something must have made him enrol Gracie in Wirriga Public School.

'Helena has never heard of him.'

At the end of the evening, as they were leaving the apartment, Tony kissed her cheek.

'Thank you for coming,' he said. 'I really appreciate it. I know it's probably too late, but I'll come to marriage counselling if you still want to try . . .'

Five months ago, she'd been begging him to accompany her. Now, when she looked into the future, she could see Luke's trial coming up and, after that, some space for herself.

⸻

After Felix's soccer game on Saturday, she joined Emmanuel for lunch at a restaurant beside the Spit Bridge. Allison watched the yachts gathering until two-thirty on the dot, when the cars came to a halt and the bridge rose vertically. Luke had made it over that bridge and implanted himself in Wirriga.

'Why do you think Luke targeted Wirriga?' Allison asked, dipping a chip in her aioli. She'd ordered the fish-and-chips special; Emmanuel didn't raise an eyebrow over Allison's love of hot chips and ice-cream.

'What would've come up when Luke searched online six months ago?'

Allison cast her mind back. Not long before Christmas, Wirriga Public had held its Twelve Days of Giving to support local communities in need. The school had won that public service award from the education department and the kindness award from the mayor. The story of their goodwill made the national papers. *Wondrous Wirriga.* Feel-good articles for Christmas with some cute quotes from the kids.

—*All I want for Christmas is rain for the farmers.*

—*We need to help others.*

—*I gave my piggy bank to the family who lost their house in the bushfire.*

Had Luke identified a caring community and seized his opportunity?

—

After all the planning for Gracie's memorial assembly at school and a picnic at the gym, Declan and Nico agreed on a combined event instead. A celebration of kindness on a Sunday afternoon.

The burly olive-skinned gym owner and the pale, willowy principal stood together on a makeshift stage on the school oval.

'Thank you for coming today to join our Community of Kindness,' Declan spoke into the microphone. 'We're so pleased to welcome back our guest of honour, Gracie, and her mum. But the real heroes today are all of you. May your kindness continue to shine. Next term, in winter, we'll be collecting spare blankets for a shelter for the homeless. I'm hoping you'll help out, if you can.'

The crowd cheered.

Gracie's friends challenged her to a monkey bar competition—and for the first time, Allison watched her hanging from the bars as an ordinary girl, without the added concern of a bump or bruise. And Gracie didn't have to worry about getting tangled in her Princess Elsa outfit. This morning, she'd presented it to Allison—the dress in one hand, the wig and crown in the other.

'Can we give this to a sick girl in the hop-i-tal?'

'Of course, sweetheart.' Allison took the outfit from her. 'Did you have someone in mind?'

'Pippa. She has a sore arm with the cancer.'

'That's a great idea. We'll visit the hospital next week.'

Gracie was wearing the new clothes she'd bought with her mum—denim overalls, a purple dinosaur t-shirt and a blue cap with silver stars. She looked like every other kindy kid in the school playground.

Allison overheard a group of school parents discussing Luke's fraud.

'Where's the cash gone?' one mother asked. 'We want our money to go to the children's hospital.'

The detectives had found where he'd spent some of it. A duplex at Noosa on the Sunshine Coast, presumably Luke's next location. A black BMW waiting in the garage for his arrival. But the rest of the money was hidden.

Along with the fraud investigators, Nico was on a mission to get it back. Allison expected there were more scams—hopefully, Curtis' campaign would help uncover them.

At the far end of the oval, under the trees, Maz was teaching Zumba with her friend Em-Jay. Impossible-to-follow dance steps . . . Allison could never do that. Just like she could never do aerobics. The Wirriga Wellness Club was offering a free trial. Allison wouldn't be taking it up.

But Maz may well be coming into the school next term. On the plane back from the Gold Coast, she'd been talking about her dream of becoming a teacher.

'You can do work experience with me,' Allison had suggested. 'See if you like it.'

'Great! And I could set up a children's workout program—some strength training and cardio.'

Maz's enthusiasm was still intact; Allison would try to nudge it in the right direction.

Red and gold hearts twinkled on the walls of the school buildings, flapping in the slight breeze. The children had cut out the cardboard during the week and stuck sparkles to the finished hearts. All different shapes and sizes. Some lopsided, some symmetrical.

Felix had offered to help Allison with the lollipops and they were walking around the playground, trailed by a gaggle of children sucking on red translucent hearts.

'Thank you for your kindness,' Allison said each time she handed over a lollipop from her basket.

In the senior courtyard, Shona and another teacher had set up easels and paint. No competitions this time, so Gracie didn't have to be the judge. She'd painted a picture of a rollercoaster that she'd gone on at Movie World.

Allison had pressed Tony and Nadia into helping out on the soft-drink stall for an hour. Tony was complaining.

'I could do with a beer.'

'It's a family picnic on school grounds,' Allison reminded him. 'We can't have alcohol.'

'Perfect location for your fiftieth,' Nadia joked. 'Just need to add champagne.'

The big birthday was looming in three months and Nadia kept bringing it up. Allison had no plans so far.

'Please don't organise a surprise party. I've had enough surprises for a lifetime.'

Maybe Allison should do something completely different from what she'd planned with Tony. Two nights with her girlfriends in a five-star Sydney hotel—no planes and no men. Or a weekend on the south coast with her book club, a new place with no memories of family holidays nor Luke.

Somehow, Allison had let it slip to Emmanuel and he wanted to take her to a swanky restaurant in the city to celebrate.

'But first you have to introduce me to five of your closest friends,' she'd said.

He'd finally understood that she meant it and was organising drinks at Manly Wharf. She remembered the night they'd met—Luke encouraging her to make up a story because she didn't want to tell the sad truth about her marriage break-up. 'You can be whoever you want to be,' Luke had said. 'It's a game.'

But Luke was wrong.

There was one surprise that Allison had organised for the picnic—mostly for Gracie. Mid-afternoon, a gelato van weaved its way from the staff car park onto the basketball court. When it rang its bell, the children squealed and came running. Allison had ordered lots of flavours, including Gracie's newest favourite, cookies and cream.

'Ice-cream!' Gracie yelled and dashed towards the van, dragging Marmalade by the lead. A gaggle of kids chased after her. Bringing up the rear were Chelsea, Maz and her parents.

After they all got their cones, they stood in a huddle around the puppy.

'I'm allowed to take him to . . .' Gracie hesitated '. . . to my home.'

Home. The same word that Allison had struggled with all year. Home. Family. Community. With Gracie in her life, Allison had realised that *family* didn't have to be narrowed down to Tony and Felix; it could be expanded to include whomever she wanted.

'Marmalade will love living at your house,' Allison said. 'And don't forget Wirriga is your other home. You've touched so many hearts here, Gracie.'

Six of the Wirriga Wombats had asked if they could visit Gracie in the next school holidays. And Allison had invited Chelsea and Gracie to come back in January for a week by the beach. Even though she didn't know where she'd be living then.

Curtis wanted to take yet more photos. Really, he must have enough images by now, although Gracie didn't tire of smiling whenever her mother was around.

'Everyone in for a big group shot,' Curtis instructed.

Allison knelt down on the grass, putting her arm around the little girl. Chelsea was on Gracie's other side while Maz and her parents stood behind. The kids crowded in front of Gracie, and called for more friends to join them.

'Okay, let's say *ice-creeeeam!*'

The children screamed it back at Curtis.

'And Mrs Walsh, do you have a quote for us?'

This time, she did. She would repeat the line that the school principal had delivered earlier today. But before Allison could speak, Marmalade leapt towards her cone. The ice-cream fell to the ground in a lump and the puppy licked at it.

Gracie giggled and patted his fur. 'Marmalade likes vanilla best!'

As everyone laughed, Allison turned to Curtis who was still waiting for a quote.

'What I'd like to say is this: *May your kindness continue to shine.*'

ACKNOWLEDGEMENTS

WHEN MY FIRST NOVEL, *SIX MINUTES*, CAME OUT LAST YEAR, I WAS OVER-whelmed by the amazing responses from readers, book clubs, reviewers, bloggers, bookshops and other authors. *Six Minutes* had two launches, and I want to thank Liane Moriarty and Christina Chipman in Sydney, and Joanne Barges and Karen Hardy in Canberra, for the fabulous celebrations. Over the following months, it was a joy to meet so many readers, librarians and booksellers. Thank you all for your kind support.

It has been fantastic to work with Allen & Unwin again. The editorial team guided me on the hard decisions to shape *The Good Teacher* into a better book. I can't thank you enough for your intelligence and insight—my excellent editors, Ali Lavau and Christa Munns, and my wonderful publisher, Annette Barlow. And many, many thanks to the publicity, sales and marketing teams and all those behind the scenes for taking both *Six Minutes* and *The Good Teacher* out into the world!

Before *The Good Teacher* crossed the editorial desk, a number of family and friends gave their input. Thank you to Ingrid, Jeremy, Maddie and Caz for reading the first draft. I appreciated comments on early chapters from my fellow students and lecturers in the UTS Master of Creative Writing, with extra thanks to Zoe Downing and Theresa Miller. For feedback on the whole manuscript, much gratitude to Ber Carroll, Christina Chipman, Marisa Colonna, Nicole Davis, and my writers' group—Margaret Morgan, Katy Pike, Catherine Hanrahan and Frances Chapman.

To those who answered my research questions, thank you for sharing your knowledge: Yo, Icara, Sam, Louise and Nicky (and apologies for re-working any of your facts to fit the story). Many thanks to my lovely agent Brian Cook for his help and advice. I've also really appreciated the generosity of our brilliant writing community, especially great podcasters, the Australian Writers' Centre and Sisters in Crime.

Thank you to all of my family for their support and encouragement, especially Mum, my sisters and brother, their partners and children. All my love to Jamie, Jeremy and Tia for everything: coming along on parts of the book tour last year, making me endless cups of tea at home, answering questions on teenage slang, and so much more!

While I had the spark for this novel many years ago, I was editing it during the catastrophic bushfires at the beginning of 2020, and doing final revisions when the coronavirus pandemic swept the world. We've certainly seen the worst—and the very best—of human nature. These terrible times reinforce what a few characters say in *The Good Teacher*: we need kindness and a strong sense of community to take us into the future.

COMING IN SEPTEMBER 2022

THE LIARS

PETRONELLA McGOVERN

'One of my favourite Australian writers! Petronella McGovern consistently delivers smart, twisty page-turners guaranteed to keep her readers coming back for more!'

Liane Moriarty

The close-knit community of Kinton Bay is shocked when fifteen-year-old Siena Britton makes a grisly discovery in the national park. She believes it's a skull from the town's violent colonial past and posts a video, which hits the news headlines.

Her parents, Meri and Rollo, aren't so sure. In 1998, their classmate went missing after a party in the Killing Cave. They're horrified to discover the destructive teenage parties are still happening, and Siena was there last weekend.

While Meri is trying to keep her daughter out of trouble, she doesn't realise her son, Taj, has his own problems. And none of them foresees the danger that Siena's actions will create for the whole family.

As more secrets are exposed, the police investigate whether multiple murders have been committed. If so, by whom? And is the killer still living in Kinton Bay?

The Liars is a heart-stopping cocktail of family secrets, sinister unsolved killings and a community at war with itself.

ISBN 978 1 76087 924 2

1

MERI

THE LOCATION APP ON MERI'S PHONE PINGED AS SHE WAS SHIFTING the last cardboard box. She knew what the notification would say: *Taj has 0% battery. Ask him to recharge.* Her son was always forgetting to plug in his mobile, unlike his twin sister.

'What's in the box?' her husband asked from the other side of the garage.

'Mum's old *National Geographics*, I think.' Meri hadn't been able to throw them away in previous clean-ups.

After brushing off the dust, she slid a knife through the crusty tape. But instead of a magazine cover with the distinctive yellow border, she found a pile of exercise books. The top one had a heart-shaped label: *Meredith Carmody, Year 9 English, Kinton Bay High School, 1998.*

Year 9. The same as her twins now.

Turning her back to Rollo, she shielded the book with her body and flipped it open to a story in her neat teenage handwriting.

THE KILLING CAVE

*A furious wind shrieks through the Killing Cave, echoing
off the dark sandstone walls. It's an angry clamour of
ghosts—the ghosts of tough men, convicts and soldiers who
perished in their search for new lands.*

As she read, a shiver ran through her. What the hell were
these school books still doing in the garage? She'd meant to
throw them out years ago.

A memory came to her—searching through the big thesaurus
in the school library to find the perfect adjectives for this story.
God, such horrendously melodramatic writing. Not that Meri
would be showing anyone, especially not Rollo. They never
talked about the cave in Wreck Point National Park. No-one
did. Hopefully the whole area was inaccessible now.

Rollo was stacking crates of snorkelling equipment on the
metal shelves. If she did show him the story, would he brush
it off with some patter about the past being past? Although
the past was with them every day: they lived in her childhood
home and the twins went to their old high school. Her husband
even sported the same blond shaggy haircut as back then; Rollo
couldn't be bothered trying a new style. That was his attitude:
If it ain't broke, don't fix it.

'Do I need to fit that box of magazines back on the shelf?'
he called out to her.

She could hear the relief in his voice to be doing this job
again—moving the summer gear off the boat to make room
for a full load of whale-watching passengers. Forty *paying* customers. Maybe they could afford to get the leaks in the roof
fixed at last.

'No, it's not the *National Geographics*—just some of Mum's old papers.' After years of avoiding the topic of the Killing Cave, the lie came easily. 'I'll put them in the recycling.'

Meri lugged the box to the bins beside the garage. Out of Rollo's sight, she opened the exercise book again.

Underneath the howl of the ghostly wind is another sound— the deep drumbeat of a relentless sea smashing against the rocks thirty metres below. The mouth of the cavern opens onto the tall, majestic trees of the forest, but there must be a secret crevasse leading to a hidden pathway between the rock platform and the ocean.

The description went on for three full pages. At the end, in red pen, were Miss Wilcox's comments: *An intense, atmospheric piece, Meri. Well done on conveying the sensory details but I want you to dig deeper into this story. Tell us exactly who are the ghosts? How did they die? Why are they angry? Keep going and show me next week. Excellent work! 19/20.*

Miss Wilcox. Their enthusiastic young English teacher. Meri must have written the story in first term; later, they'd stopped talking about the cave, and their teacher had gone.

Meri ripped the exercise book in half, tugging at the old staples. Pages scattered onto the ground. Gathering them up, she scrunched them into a big ball and threw it in the bin. Then she dumped the rest of the exercise books on top.

Somewhere in those pages, adorned with pictures of Big Ben and the Union Jack, was a plan for her future career—working as a journalist on BBC television. A teenage dream, inspired by her father. Before he'd abandoned them.

Above the back fence glowed the same old view of the same old sky. A view she'd had forever. Tonight, it resembled an oil painting, feathery wisps of pink and gold clouds luminescent on a violet backdrop. Ha, she still liked descriptive words after all.

Twenty years since school and she'd never experienced a northern hemisphere sunset, never been to the BBC news studio. At least she'd made part of her dream happen: working as a reporter on the *Coastal Chronicle*. Not quite the hard-hitting journalism she'd imagined.

Staring at the clouds, Meri sighed and tried to follow Rollo's optimistic approach. *How good is life?* he'd say. She began counting out five things for which to be grateful.

1. *This beautiful sunset.*
2. *Another week of July school holidays, which means more whale-watching bookings.*
3. *Taj and Siena are happy, doing well at school, and hanging out with nice friends. Taj's strange pains from last term have disappeared.*
4. *Tonight, we'll eat the chicken casserole Rollo has cooked and watch a movie on Netflix. Ah, the excitement of a Saturday night in Kinton Bay. Oops, that isn't quite gratitude.*

She was trying to think of a fifth thing when Rollo appeared from the garage, wiping his dusty hands down his boardies. Most of the men in Kinton Bay wore shorts all winter, as if to say, *We live in a seaside town, it can't possibly get cold here.* Of course, it did. Right now, the temperature was dropping with the sun. Meri zipped her hoodie to halfway.

'I'm all done.' Rollo grinned. 'You ready for a drink?'

'Sounds good.'

Before going inside, Meri checked the location app. It listed Taj 'At Home' because his phone had died—really, he was working at the fish and chip shop on Dolphin Street. With tourists returning at last, he had more evening and weekend shifts. Siena's location was an address in Harbours End—Jasminda's house, where she was having a sleepover.

Best friends' sleepovers: they had been Meri's alibi for parties when she was a teenager. For a few seconds, Meri could smell the earthy dankness of the Killing Cave. Taste the sweetness of a Bacardi Breezer. Feel the hard rock jutting into her back, rough hands fumbling under her shirt. Fear and bewilderment paralysing her. Those first parties at the cool teenage hangout . . . Meri and her friends had been so excited. So naïve.

Swallowing hard, she focused on the sunset again. As much as she'd tried to block out that year, the fear remained. The danger of being fifteen—the age when everything had changed.

That was why Meri insisted on the location app now. So she knew her teenagers were exactly where they should be.

Safe.

2

SIENA

THE UTE HIT A DIP IN THE DIRT TRACK, BOUNCING THE PARTY OF TEEN-
agers in the tray. While the others hooted, Siena gripped the
cold metal edge with one hand and clutched the mobile with
the other. She had to take extra care 'cos it wasn't her phone—
she'd swapped with Jasminda. Mum would freak if she turned
off the location app, so she'd left it at her best friend's house
in Harbours End.

The darkness made it hard to see how far they'd driven into
Wreck Point National Park. They'd entered through the main
gate about five minutes ago. Siena had been wondering how the
party gang broke in each time, but they just opened it with a
key. From Hayley's dad.

Mottled trunks shimmered in the headlights, ghostly sen-
tries lining the track. Forest red gums. *Eucalyptus tereticornis*.
She'd had to practise saying the Latin name for her YouTube
video on the last project: protecting koala habitat. Forest red
gum leaves were their main food source. At school, almost
twenty kids had joined her new koala club. No-one from this
gang though; if they knew about it, the teasing would be brutal.

The guy on her right, Axel, had a guitar nestled between his legs, and his thigh pressed against hers. Every time they went over a bump, he slid closer. Siena inched away from his touch again. But it was impossible to maintain a gap with so many bodies crammed into the back of the ute. Twelve? Thirteen people? Arms and legs entwined.

At school last term, Hayley and her friends had been talking about Axel—an older guy who kept turning up to the summer parties. He had some kind of connection: Was he Jackson's cousin?

'Have you been out here much?' she asked him.

'Heaps.' Axel took a swig from his VB can. Gulped then grinned. His eyes raked across her chest. 'You'll enjoy your first time.'

Siena let go of the ute's side and crossed her arms over her baggy black jumper. With her dark hair in two long plaits, she knew she looked even younger than fifteen. How old was he? Hard jaw, rough stubble, brown wavy hair nearly to his shoulders—at least twenty. Sleazy with a capital S. Any other time, she would've told him straight: *You're too old to be hanging with schoolgirls.*

Not tonight. Tonight, he was her ticket to the cave—a secret party in a secret location.

Although Siena had no intention of partying with this gang.

With Axel eyeing her up like another cold beer to drink, Siena realised, too late, that she shouldn't have come alone. But Jasminda had reckoned it would be easier to cover for Siena if she stayed at home. 'And that group won't let me hang out with them anyway,' her best friend had said. 'I'll ruin your chances.'

Jasminda was probably right: she'd only arrived in KB four years ago and her parents were both tech specialists who worked at the council. Unlike Siena's dad, who was considered cool, and had been mates since forever with Hayley's father, Owen.

When the school holidays started last week, Siena had tried to find the cave with her mate, Kyle. Twice, he'd borrowed his sister's car and driven them out here on his P plates; Mum would die if she knew. Kyle understood the history of this place. He'd spent heaps of time in this national park; this was his Country. But they still hadn't been able to find the cave. Each path they followed brought them down onto the small half-moon of Wreck Beach, or back into the dense bush.

Her parents thought the trips to the national park were with Jasminda for a geography assignment. If they knew the real reason, Dad would say: *Why do you wanna dredge up the past?* And Mum would insist Siena go old school—use her news-paper records and the Kinton Bay Historical Society.

But Siena wanted to tell the real story, not repeat the same old lies. Even if only her teacher and history class heard her presentation, it might start waking up this closed-minded town.

The big bonus of this project was hanging out with Kyle. But when they hadn't been able to find the cave together, she'd come up with this plan.

The party gang always boasted about their wild nights in the cave. At six o'clock this evening, she'd tracked them down near Main Beach. The girls were from Year 9, the boys older. This was a normal Saturday night for them—quick feed from the fish and chip shop before driving into the national park for a drinking party.

Hayley had introduced her to Axel. 'This is Siena. She's a nerd. The smartest in our year.'

Her brother would have disagreed: *You're not top in maths, I am.*

Siena watched Axel strumming his guitar, his voice deep but off-key. He had all the moves: flicking his hair; tapping his foot to the beat; the slow, sexy grin. A bad boy. That was why the girls were fighting over him.

'Let me come to the cave,' she'd said. 'I'll film you singing and put it online. I've got a YouTube channel.'

Hayley had made a face and whispered to her friends, but Axel was keen. 'Cool. The acoustics are epic out there.'

At the end of the fire trail, the ute rolled to a standstill. Red gums rose around them, branches stretching high above their heads, blocking the faint moonlight. With the engine switched off, Siena could hear the forest alive in the darkness.

A harsh rasping call. The masked owl.

A warning to stay away.

And then movement and laughter as the group scrambled out—some jumping over the side, others climbing down the tailgate. Siena moved fast to get away from Axel, onto solid ground. In the mass of bodies, Hayley tripped on the rubber mat and lurched off the ute. Siena was in exactly the right spot to catch her.

'Huh, Siena the virgin,' Hayley slurred. 'You're gonna have a good time tonight and get luck-luck-lucky! But keep your hands off Axel—he's mine.'

As if Siena wanted a good time with any of this gang.

Around them, the guys heaved cases of beer onto their shoulders. Bottles clinked in backpacks.

'Let's get this party started!' Hayley shouted.

The others whooped and shone their torches crazily into the treetops. Jerks, they'd disturb the koalas in their night-time feeding.

From the fire trail, there was no sign of a path. But the gang set off between the low bushes, their torch beams creating circles of light among the ferns. Siena tried to memorise the entry point.

In the black of night, the ocean sounded close, waves crashing against rocks.

Wreck Point. Where it had all started.

'Come on, babe!' Axel grabbed her hand and pulled her along the track. Siena tried to extract her fingers, but instead of letting go, he caressed her palm with his thumb.

'Wait a minute,' she said, stalling. 'I have to do up my shoe.'

She crouched down, pretending her lace had come undone. Ahead, sneakers pounded the earth, and the smell of weed drifted in the air. Figures faded into darkness. From what she'd heard, the gang would traipse through the scrub to the cave. They'd light a campfire, drink, smoke and party. They'd frighten the nocturnal creatures. Crush plants and insects underfoot. Disrespect the animals. The land. The history.

Siena shivered.

'You cold, babe?' As she stood up, Axel draped a heavy arm over her shoulders.

Her assignment would be worth it, as long as she didn't have to put up with much more of Axel's sleazy crap. They'd lead her to the cave and she'd come back next week with Kyle. Then she would vlog it on her YouTube channel as an introduction to her history assignment.

'Let's go!' Axel nudged her and his guitar banged against her spine. Pushing it away, she noticed the skull-and-crossbones strap for the first time.

Somewhere in front of them, one of the guys let out a howl, long and low. The eerie noise curled upwards and hung in the treetops. Axel's arm had crept around her lower back. Freaking hell, she needed to get away from him.

'You know what they call this place?' he whispered, his breath hot and beery against her cheek.

Of course she knew. That was why she'd come.

'You are now walking towards'—he paused for effect, like a bad actor in an American teen slasher movie—'the Killing Cave.' Axel slapped her bum. To give her a fright. To get a quick feel.

Despite his corny performance, Siena jumped. This scumbag had no idea of the bloodshed that had happened here.

The sheer terror of the girl and her family.

A girl my age.

With legs trembling, Siena stepped forwards into the black night.

SIX MINUTES
PETRONELLA McGOVERN

'Impossible to put down and full of twists and turns you won't see coming! I loved this fabulous debut novel.'
Liane Moriarty

How can a child disappear from under the care of four play-group mums?

One Thursday morning, Lexie Parker dashes to the shop for biscuits, leaving Bella in the safe care of the other mums in the playgroup.

Six minutes later, Bella is gone.

Police and media descend on the tiny village of Merrigang on the edge of Canberra. Locals unite to search the dense bushland. But as the investigation continues, relationships start to fracture, online hate messages target Lexie, and the community is engulfed by fear.

Is Bella's disappearance connected to the angry protests at Parliament House? What secrets are the parents hiding? And why does a local teacher keep a photo of Bella in his lounge room?

What happened in those six minutes and where is Bella?

The clock is ticking . . .

This gripping novel will keep you guessing to the very last twist.

ISBN 978 1 76087 756 9